Coffee, Love and Matrix Algebra

COFFEE, LOVE AND MATRIX ALGEBRA

Gary Ernest Davis

Republic of Mathematics

Dedication

This book is for Linda.

1

⁓❦⁓

Jeffrey Albacete held the publisher's copy of the 9th edition of *Matrix Algebra*. Matrix algebra had applications to Gooogle searching, and it was clever of the designers to put graphic illustrations of that on the front cover. This looked so, so ... cool. Jeffrey surprised himself that he had thought his book looked cool. But there it was in his hands – the beautiful 9th edition of his book, a book in use by hundreds of colleges, and translated into 11 languages.

Jeffrey looked at some of the other editions of *Matrix Algebra* spread out on his desk. It was quite impressive, he thought.

"This is who I am. This defines me: the author of a highly respected text on matrix algebra, used by many college professors and their students. It's my legacy," he thought. "It's a tangible reminder of what I give to the world." And it brought in over $150,000 a year to add to his professor's salary.

He smiled, and put the copies of his book back on the bookshelf behind his desk. Sitting there together they *were* an impressive sight. One could not fail to be impressed! Not many people could lay claim to an achievement of this magnitude, he reflected.

Jeffrey was in a mood for coffee. He looked to see if any of his colleagues were around. Too bad – Kathy Riverton was not to be seen. He could rely on Kathy offering him coffee from the machine she kept in her office. The Department secretary, on the other hand, was completely unreliable with regard to coffee. Jeffrey did not like this sort of attitude. As a young man fresh from his Ph.D. he had worked in a lively department where the secretary always had a pot of coffee going. Mid-morning coffee was very important to instill a sense of camaraderie and well-being. It's how we knew the academic enterprise was on track and all was well. It's what helped us take a break to move onto the next important task of the day. He sighed. Things are not what they used to be, he thought. Not what they used to be. Jeffrey thought he would go over to The Daily Grind, the nearby campus coffee shop. He took a copy of his 9th edition with him and began the 5 minute walk across campus.

The Daily Grind was busy mid-morning. A queue of seven people stood before him. Jeffrey couldn't help counting the people in the queue. It was a habit, a sort of compulsion. He had counted things obsessively since he was a kid: windows in houses, geese flying by, even the bricks in the wall of the Daily Grind. Well, he had not strictly counted every brick, but he did count how many rows, and how many columns of bricks, and estimated the half bricks. He was confident that his estimate was not far off. Jeffrey smiled to himself. He loved numbers, and he loved counting things. It provided him a sense of control. And how often were people surprised when he gave them an unexpected numerical estimate? It's what we are, he thought, we mathematicians. We start with counting and we grow into advanced topics like matrix algebra of which, he had to admit, he was an acknowledged world expert. This was not just his opinion. The International Matrix Algebra Society held his work in high esteem. Jeffrey and others had waged something for a battle for years to extricate the teaching of matrix algebra from the International Linear Algebra Society, concerned as it was to emphasize linear algebra and vector spaces. Matrices were what was important. Everyone knew that, and Jeffrey had become frankly annoyed by the linear algebra people who wanted to start with equations and linear independence and emphasize structure. Matrices were where it was at, so cut to the chase, he believed. Get your teeth into the meat of the matter as soon as possible.

Jeffrey ordered a large mocha latte and a blueberry muffin. He looked around for an empty table, and spying one in the corner by the brick wall, he took his sustenance and his 9th edition and prepared to be content. He was flicking through his book when he heard someone call his name.

"Jeff, Jeff!".

He looked around to see Bob Fosberry waving to him from the counter area. Bob was a colleague who had worked with Jeffrey on the original grant that got the matrix algebra project under-way. They had not worked closely for several years now, but Jeffrey was glad to have company, especially that of someone who would appreciate the effort that went into getting the 9th edition into print. Bob sat down at the table with Jeffrey and took the lid from his coffee. He stopped short when he saw Jeffrey's copy of the new edition of *Matrix Algebra*.

"That's the new edition?" he asked. Jeffrey smiled and nodded. Could I take a look?"

Jeffrey was reluctant to pass the book to Bob who was drinking his coffee, toying with a doughnut, and who – let's be frank – was not the most fastidious of people. Jeffrey did not want coffee stains and doughnut crumbs on his beautiful new book.

Jeffrey hesitated then slid the book over to Bob.

"Sure," he said.

Bob admired the cover design and opened the book to the table of contents.

"You've got a lot of new material in here," he said. "Lots more applications. And up-to-date, too."

Jeffrey smiled and nodded. Bob could be relied upon to under-stand what went into producing a substantial new edition like this.

Bob regretted that he did not have Jeff's vision at the begin-ning of the matrix algebra project. They were running workshops all over the country and both had been very busy. Somehow Bob had not thought what would happen when the funding dried up and the project ran its course. Clearly Jeff had. The 9th edition of *Matrix Algebra* was tangible evidence of that.

"You've done very well with the book," Bob said. "How many colleges are using it now?"

Jeffrey thought for a moment.

"Well ... over 350, I would say. And that's not counting the translations. Though I don't always get much for those, especially from Eastern Europe and Taiwan."

Bob was impressed. He felt a pang of disappointment. If he had been clearer about what lay ahead he could perhaps have been co-author with Jeff.

"Albacete and Fosberry, *Matrix Algebra*, 9th edition," he thought. That had a very nice ring to it. The money would have been useful too.

Bob snapped out of his musings.

"Sorry Jeff, just thinking what might have been. Congratulations on the new edition. It's a very fine book."

Jeffrey smiled. He knew what Bob was thinking. He was aware of the regrets Bob suffered. He was aware too that Bob was not sufficiently focused when they had discussed the possibility of a book in the early days of the matrix algebra project. That was the past, thought Jeffrey. It's done, and there's no point dredging through those memories.

Jeffrey was focused on bigger things, and he decided to share them with Bob.

"You know, the publisher is in discussions to get the new edition into Stanford."

Jeffrey wasn't saying this to be cruel to Bob – just to show him how proud he was of his work and his book, the result of two decades of effort.

Bob look startled, and Jeffrey wondered if he had upset his colleague.

"Haven't you heard?" asked Bob.

"Heard what?"

"Stanford has adopted Gil Strang's book on linear algebra. I just read about it on an MIT blog."

Jeffrey paled. He felt dizzy. Bob jumped as Jeffrey knocked over the mocha latte. The coffee ran all over the 9th edition.

2

Focus of attention

Kathy Riverton enjoyed the 8:00 AM lectures on differential equations. Her teaching was done by 10:00 so she could talk with colleagues and undergraduates involved in her research project until noon, and then get on with writing in the afternoon. She was pleased Bert Monod, the Department Chair, had allocated her differential equations to teach several semesters ago. She had some ideas to make the course much more applied than it had previously been taught, basing the lectures around her work in the mathematics of fiber optics. It seemed so long ago that she had done her Ph.D. on this topic in Holland, and she did not imagine then that her research and teaching would become so integrated, so well-integrated in fact that a colleague had recommended her to take on the role of mentoring graduate and undergraduate research in the University. This, coupled with her large National Science Foundation grant to stimulate integration of mathematics, engineering and science applications, had given her a higher profile in the University than she had anticipated.

Her academic life would seem to be going very well indeed, except for the nagging problem with engineering students who did not, and would not, take mathematics seriously. To take her course, students were required to have passed a second course in calculus. Could they recall much, or anything at all, from that prior course? No, almost without exception. She had 32 students in her differential equations class, and 1, perhaps 2, students each semester, usually one of the female students, could recall basic techniques from calculus. What is it about students, especially the engineering students, that they cannot recall basic facts and procedures that they spent time on only a semester ago? she pondered. Kathy wished she knew more about human memory to get some idea of what mechanisms were at play – or most likely not at play – in these students' minds. She made a mental note to talk with a colleague she knew in psychology who specialized in human memory – maybe there was something not too complicated that would give her some insight into her students' thought processes, or lack of them, and help her to devise better techniques to help them recall prior material. What was worse, and particularly galling, was that a majority of these sophomore engineering students could not recall basic mathematics from high school. When they performed badly on tests the Associate Dean of Engineering had contacted the Department Chair, Bert Monod, to ask if Kathy knew what she was doing in teaching differential equations.

The Associate Dean's comments had stung and Kathy became determined to get to the bottom of her students' poor memory for mathematics. She had looked through the books on memory in the psychology section of the campus bookstore and narrowed her search down to a choice between Howard Eichenbaum's "*Cognitive Neuroscience of Memory*" and Alan Baddeley's "*Human Memory. Theory and Practice.*" She thought Eichenbaum's book was a bit theoretical and high-falutin for her at this point. Baddeley seemed to have just the right tone: a combination of practical questions, empirical work, and a theory to tie it together. She chose Baddeley's book.

Kathy was surprised how rapidly she could grasp some of the

fundamental ideas of human memory formation, and she lighted fairly quickly on the central idea of focus of attention. The more she reflected on this, the more it seemed obvious to her (even if the idea might eventually prove to be not as relevant as it now seemed) that her students' attention was rarely on the equations she wrote, or on the explanations she gave. Their eyes darted from her, to each other, to the computer screens in front of them. Once, she had been so annoyed at a student's singular lack of attention to what she was saying that she walked toward the back of the room to see what he was doing. To her utter surprise he was looking at a Website dedicated to Swedish Bikini Babes.

"Swedish Bikini Babes! You have the nerve to be surfing the web looking at Swedish Bikini Babes when I'm explaining to you the use of integrating factors in the solution of differential equations?"

The student looked at her and without an ounce of remorse said: "I'm taking a break."

Kathy was speechless. Only later, reflecting on the central role of focus of attention in the formation of memories, did she come to realize, with startling clarity, that she was going to have to do something to make her explanations of solutions of differential equations more riveting to her students, certainly more riveting than Swedish Bikini Babes!

Kathy was pondering the role of focus of attention when her student Jack Cairns appeared at her office door.

"Hi Jack, come on in."

Jack, smiling, sat at the table where he and Kathy worked on research together.

"Would you like coffee?" she asked.

"Sure," he said.

Jack got up and fixed the coffee himself, pouring water into the coffee maker and inserting a sachet of coffee. He liked extra bold coffee, calling the pumpkin and cinnamon flavored coffees "girly coffee", to Kathy's amusement.

Kathy loved Jack. She had discovered him as a freshman student majoring in psychology and minoring in mathematics. She persuaded him to join her National Science Foundation funded research-based class, and he had shone. He changed to a mathematics major and grew in maturity with great rapidity and depth. As a sophomore student he had presented at a national conference and was startled when a professor from Texas asked him to apply to graduate school.

"But I'm only a sophomore," protested Jack.

The surprised professor had replied that when he did graduate, would he bear in mind the excellent graduate program they had going at Texas, and keep them in mind as one of his choices?

Kathy checked on Jack's progress in implementing an algorithm for a numerical solution of a non-linear differential equation, and they worked together for about an hour, going over the detail of the program and the numerical results. Kathy was thinking about going home to spend the afternoon completing the paper she was writing for publication when George Prince appeared at her door. Kathy was pleased to see George. He was a short, athletic, applied mathematician who was fond of cigars and Islay whisky. His athleticism manifested in early morning long-distance bike rides, and she could never reconcile his extreme physical fitness with his prodigious consumption of cigars and whisky.

George sat at Kathy's worktable and asked how things were going. He had been a member of the Search and Screen committee that appointed Kathy and he was very pleased at her progress in research and teaching, and especially with her appointment as the Director of the Office of Undergraduate Research. They chatted for several minutes, catching up and sharing bits of gossip.

"Have you seen Jeff's new edition of *Matrix Algebra*?" he asked Kathy.

"Yes. He's so proud of it. It's like a child to him."

This was a remark that was close to the truth. Jeffrey was not married, had no children, and, so far as anyone knew, had never had a pet cat, dog, or even a hamster. Jeffrey's *Matrix Algebra* was the nearest thing to an offspring that he had, and he was as proud of his book, of its many editions and translations, as any parent was of their children.

Kathy had respect for Jeff as an elder applied mathematician, and she deferred to him on most occasions, often to George's annoyance. Lately Jeff had annoyed her with his petty attitude to some students, and his general lack of support for the applied mathematics group. His attitude betrayed a degree of selfishness she did not like.

"You know he stares at my breasts."

George was startled.

"Who?"

"Jeff: he stares at my breasts."

"What, all the time?"

"Yes. All the time. I don't think he knows he's doing it."

George was shocked.

"I guess it shows what he's really focused on," he laughed.

Kathy smiled. She could see the funny side of it, yet Jeff's – focus of attention – did disturb her. She began to ponder – just how different really was a senior professor to a sophomore engineering student?

3

Another conference

The news of Gene Golub's death had hit Jeffrey Albacete very hard. Jeffrey had worked with Gene's group at Stanford and it was there he had really learned numerical analysis, and started on the path that led to his *Matrix Algebra* book. It was several years now since Gene passed away and Jeffrey was inclined to hold a retrospective conference, re-examining Gene's influence on numerical analysis.

Jeffrey was annoyed that George Prince thought it was too soon to hold a retrospective conference.

"We had a conference on Gene's work the year he died. Don't you think we should wait a few more years before holding another?" said George.

Jeffrey didn't agree. He had been peeved at how the folks from the University of Massachusetts and MIT had taken over the earlier conference for Gene and left Jeffrey standing on the sidelines. Jeffrey saw his work, and his *Matrix Algebra* book, as standing in direct succession to Gene Golub's *Matrix Computations*. Not as seminal, of course. Not yet, but Jeffrey's book was held in high esteem by the International Matrix Algebra Society, of which he was a founding member and past President. It just felt right to Jeffrey that he should have been the one to play a major role in organizing a conference on Gene Golub's life and work.

"George Prince is welcome to his views," thought Jeffrey, "but I am plowing ahead!"

Jeffrey was good at planning. He had a singular ability to focus on one thing exclusively until it was done. It was how he had written *Matrix Algebra* and brought it as far as the 9th edition.

"The die is cast," he thought. " I will hold it in Providence at a hotel, like the Marriot. It will be a grand affair, over a couple of days, and the right people will be pleased to see how far things have come along since Gene passed away."

Jeffrey knew the earlier conference, at the time of Gene's passing, had been a moderate success – he did acknowledge that – largely due to Steve Leon's influence with MathWorks. They had put up a good sum of money that allowed the organizers to bring in some notable speakers, and put on a lavish banquet. Jeffrey didn't know yet where he could get financial support for his planned conference, but he thought he might start by sounding out the Provost. Scientific computing and numerical analysis had a much higher profile in the University these days, thanks – he must admit – to the work and energy of George Prince and Kathy Riverton. His work in matrix algebra was a cornerstone of computational mathematics, the other parts being differential equations and optimization. Despite George and Kathy's success he was somewhat peeved at how they emphasized – over-emphasized if he was honest – the role of partial differential equations in computational mathematics. It was lop-sided, he thought. In the early Stanford days there was a balance between matrices, differential equations, and optimization. Things seemed to be out of whack now, with the partial differential equations people getting all the grants, and optimization not even on the scene. Jeffrey regretted the passage of time that brought us to a state where the fundamental things seemed to be no longer valued.

Jeffrey emailed the Provost's assistant and made an appointment to go talk over his plans for the memorial conference. With planning in motion he felt energized and decided to walk over to the gym. He kept a change of clothes in his office for his regular gym sessions. He changed into shorts, a T-shirt, and sneakers and headed out for the gym.

Kathy Riverton was in the Department office as Jeffrey came by.

"Hi Jeff. Off to the gym?" she asked.

"Well ... yes. I try to go to the gym regularly," he replied.

Kathy nodded and smiled. Jeffrey looked around the office, ever hopeful that the secretary might have made coffee. His was a classic case of hope without expectation.

"You can make coffee in my office, if you want Jeff. I brought in a lot of new coffees," said Kathy.

Jeffrey declined, and said he would get a coffee at the Daily Grind, on his way to the gym.

George Prince noticed Jeffrey walking off and asked Kathy: "Off to the gym again?"

"Yes. He goes quite often these days," she replied.

"He goes a lot," laughed George, "but I'm not sure he does anything when he gets there. His belly is getting larger."

George was probably right, thought Kathy. Jeffrey did not look at all athletic, and his belly was hanging over his belt. Perhaps, she thought, stopping at the Daily Grind on the way – and probably afterwards – was not conducive to losing weight.

"Do you know he's planning a Golub retrospective conference?" George asked Kathy.

Kathy groaned. "No, surely not! It's too soon. And where ever will he get support for it?"

George and Kathy were in agreement: Jeffrey's focus on a conference was not a good idea. It was not timely, it would not have the impact of the earlier Golub conference, and it would be hard to find funding.

"You know how stubborn he is, though, once his mind's made up," said George.

Kathy hoped Jeff's stubbornness would not result in his banging his head up against a brick wall.

Jeffrey finished his mocha latte and blueberry muffin and headed to the gym. When he got there he was pleased to see it was nearly empty. He liked it better when there were fewer people around. He picked up a newspaper and went over to the cycle area, where he folded the newspaper so he could read it while cycling, and began a leisurely routine that, he imagined, would last 30 minutes or so.

Jeffrey rarely raised a sweat while in the gym. He did not go to pretend to be a sports jock, as many professors did. He liked the gym, especially, when it was nearly empty as it was now, because it was a quiet place where physical activity gave his mind a chance to idle and to mull over things. So there he sat, quietly pedaling, reading the newspaper, thinking of nothing in particular, when a thought popped into his head. He had no idea where it came from, or what prompted it. But there it was.

"My publisher," he thought. "My publisher – of course!"

Jeffrey's publisher was one of the largest academic publishers in the world. Recently they had been moving to re-invent themselves in a changing world of publishing, and had explicitly begun to position themselves as creators of learning environments. They were filthy rich, thought Jeffrey, and aggressively interested in new ventures. A bundle of thoughts jostled for attention in his mind. He could focus on education in the conference. Golub had a huge impact on numerical analysis education, and Jeffrey's book was also very influential in education. A common theme was forming in his mind: the rise and growth – the influence – of matrix algebra education could be a winning theme for the conference, and his publisher would surely love the idea. Enough, he hoped, to fund it in large measure.

Jeffrey was so excited he could not exercise any longer. He dismounted the cycle, put the newspaper back, picked up his gym bag, and hastened back to the Daily Grind, where he thought another latte and a blueberry muffin – dare he have two? – were in order.

Jeffrey was very pleased with himself.

4

George has an idea

George Prince was out the door of his house and on the road by 6:00 AM. This was late for him. Normally he would be an hour into a ride by now. Even at this hour the roads were still relatively empty and the ride from his home in Barrington, just by the University at Smith's cove, down to Little Compton would be reasonably free of traffic. He hit the County Road bridge across the strait pretty quickly, and headed on down through Main Street, Warren. The streets were virtually deserted. The view from the County Road bridges down to Wharf Tavern in Warren, and beyond were spectacular. George loved living in this part of Rhode Island. Life was good, he thought. The lovely setting of the University, the beautiful inlets, the hundreds of miles of gorgeous back roads, ideal for cycling, suited him down to the ground. There was even a store in Warren that imported Arturo Fuente Opus X Fuente Fuente cigars for him at a very good price. And the liquor store nearby always had a supply of his favorite Islay whisky. His wife Deborah Duke, was a graduate student in mathematics, and his colleagues referred to George and Deborah as "the

Royal Family". Deborah did not work in applied mathematics like George, but they could still converse about each other's work.

Soon George cycled by Roger Williams University and over the bridge with a view down to Newport. The high fences on the bridge made it hard to see much, but every so often he got a glimpse of the spectacular water views. George was amazed, yet happy for himself, that this part of Rhode Island was so relatively uninhabited. He was not surprised to learn that the State's population was declining, and there were more deaths and departures than births and arrivals.

The stretch of road along Route 24 by the coves – Old Orchard, Long Neck, Island Park and Blue Bill Coves – was always fraught with danger. Cars were not always kind to, or on the look out for, cyclists on this part of the highway, and George was always glad when he turned off onto Main Road Tiverton and began the back roads ride down to Little Compton.

The ride usually took a little over an hour and this morning he was right on target, pulling into Little Compton just after 7:20. George placed his bike against a post outside Gray's Store. This area always felt good to him. Gray's was reputedly the oldest general store in the United States, having been built in 1788 by Samuel Church. George sat for a while on a bench outside the store, sipping on the drink he had brought with him. The ride from Little Compton to the University was another 23 miles, so he took his time soaking in the ambience of Little Compton, and the increasing activity as people busied themselves at the start of day.

Just before 7:45 AM George climbed back on his bike and began the ride up to the University. The familiar roads, the rhythm of his breath, the regular motion of his legs, lulled him into a quiet contemplation. His mind turned to some problems of approximation, on which he had been working for several months. He had tried many techniques to try to get approximate solutions to the differential equations he was studying, but nothing seemed to yield positive results. The regular motion of the ride allowed his mind to step back, as it were, to see himself struggling with one mathematical technique after another. Then the flash came – who knows how it arose? Forget the mathematical techniques, the thought said, try a statistical approach. Expressed this way, it sounded obvious. We use statistics to get scientific information from experiments. He had lots of experimental results from everything he had already tried that hadn't worked. He could generate lots of data about his approximation problem. Then he could analyze it from a statistical perspective. This might – probably would – produce evidence that would satisfy a scientist, if not a mathematician. He vaguely recalled the mathematician Gregory Chaitin seemed to advocate a more experimental attitude to mathematics, and he had read something recently about the Borwein brothers who advocated experimental methods in mathematics. He felt a weight lift from him, and a wave of relief and energy soared through his body. He made the trip on to the University in near record time.

George wheeled into the University campus and paused to admire the view to the south down to Newport, and east to Fall River. It was an incredible body of water, and a beautiful setting. He cycled slowly to the Daily Grind and parked his bike, locking it in the cycle rack. He took a fresh Fuente Fuente cigar from his cycle bag, and went in to order an espresso and water. George sat outside drinking his espresso and lighting up the fine cigar. He spied Jeff Albacete sitting at a nearby table.

"Jeff!" he called out, and got up to go over to the older mathematician.

"Hi Jeff. Do you mind if I join you? I'm smoking a cigar – will it annoy you?"

Jeff smiled and shook his head.

"No, it's fine with me. I don't know how you do it," he laughed, "but it's not irritating me."

"What brings you out at this hour?" asked George. "Do you have an early class?"

"No," said Jeff. "I've just been to the gym. It's quiet this time of the morning, and I find I do some of my best thinking when I exercise."

George saw Jeff's mocha latte and blueberry muffin, and hoped that Jeff's exercise was sufficient to burn off those calories.

George mentioned his idea to tackle the approximation problem statistically. Jeff said nothing for a few moments and then spoke up:

"Well ... I'm not sure about that. The problem is that whatever you do get, you will not convince most mathematicians, because they will be looking for a proof. It's the standard in our field."

George suppressed a rising feeling of irritation.

"You're probably right, but I'm going to press ahead anyway, and see what happens."

George finished his cigar and excused himself from Jeff. He walked his bike to the gym where he took a shower and changed. He walked with the bike back to the Department and took the elevator to his office where he parked the bike in a corner. On an off-chance, George went looking for Kathy Riverton, and found her in her office.

"Hi Kathy. I wasn't sure I would find you here today."

Kathy habitually worked at home if she did not have teaching or administration to do at the University.

"Hi George. I have a computer-users committee meeting later his morning. Hence my presence at this unusual hour! Come in and sit down. Would you like coffee?"

"Thanks, no. I've just had some," said George. "I saw Jeff over at the Daily Grind. I must say I was a bit annoyed with him."

"What's he done now?" asked Kathy.

George recounted his idea of approaching the approximation problem from a statistical perspective. Kathy thought this was a great idea.

"It's sort of obvious when you say it," she said to George.

George was happy to get Kathy's support.

"What is it about Jeff that he is so negative about so many

things? Do you know how often he starts a sentence with 'The problem with that is ...'?"

Kathy laughed. That was a very good impression of Jeff.

"The thing is ... ," she said, "I've been thinking. We can either see the glass as half empty or half full. We either see the dark cloud or the silver lining. Strictly, I guess, we see both. But it's what we focus on. I've been thinking a lot about focus of attention, and I believe we should say: 'The opportunity is ...' whenever we're tempted to focus on the problem."

George was in total agreement.

"I think we should ban the phrase: 'The problem is ...' in the Department. No more negativity. Let's focus on the opportunities that problems open up for us."

5

The conference
takes shape

Jeffrey Albacete, energized by the idea that his publisher might fund an educational conference on matrix algebra – with Jeffrey as the organizer and keynote speaker – phoned his editor at the New York office. The editor listened to Jeffrey's idea and told him it was likely to be well received:

"This seems a productive idea, both for us and for you, Jeffrey. You probably know that we are reorganizing, in light of recent changes in the publishing world, and we are focusing heavily on new investments in learning environments. I feel this proposal would fit very well with our current focus."

Jeffrey was very pleased to hear this.

"However ... it's not my decision to make. I can, and I will, pass it on to the commissioning editors in the learning environments division. Of course, your proposal will have my full support."

Jeffrey felt very good. His editor was always very helpful.

"There is one thing," his editor said. "I think the learning environments folks are going to want to see a lot of technology integration. A lot. If you can do that I think they will run with it."

Jeffrey paused. He was no computer illiterate, and his book had numerous applications to technology, but it was a text, and was meant to be used as such. He could not see how he would or could provide a focus on technology integration for the conference.

"That's more up George and Kathy's alley," he thought.

Jeffrey dreaded the idea of having to bring George and Kathy in on this. They were not enthusiastic, and he did not want them appearing to make him seem less than competent. He needed some time to think. The Coffee Depot in Warren was an ideal place: away from the University, it served good coffee and had a good range of pastries and baked goods. He could be there in less than 10 minutes.

When Jeffrey arrived at the Coffee Depot he was pleased to see there was no one there he knew. He wanted some time alone to mull over the editor's phone conversation with him. The line was short, and Jeffrey ordered a Café Mocha with a pecan tart. He sat at a table by the window and idly glanced through a newspaper. No obvious answers were coming to mind. He knew what the focus of the conference should be – *From Golub's Matrix Computations to Albacete's Matrix Algebra: An Educational Journey.* His editor's insistence that technology integration play a major role was an annoyance: one he could not see how to accommodate. Jeffrey finished his coffee and pastry, and was no further along in his thinking. He flicked through the newspaper, hoping an idea might come if he distracted his mind from the task at hand. Alas, the muse did not respond. He felt as forlorn as he undoubtedly looked. He rose and walked slowly to the counter for another coffee. Nothing. This seemed to be an impenetrable problem. Jeffrey sat down at his table and sipped the coffee.

A young voice exclaimed loudly: "Oh yeah, it does matrix calculations really easily. It's way cool."

Jeffrey was all ears. He looked around and spied two young

people – possibly undergraduates – at a nearby table, hunched over a computer. Their conversation became even more intriguing to him: "Can you show them, like, in regular matrix notation? Not just as lists?" asked a young man.

"Oh sure. It's a cinch. Just use this command ... MatrixForm," said his companion, a young woman of about the same age.

```
In[15]:= A = {{1, -1, 2}, {3, 2, 0}, {1, 4, 1}}
         MatrixForm[A]

Out[15]= {{1, -1, 2}, {3, 2, 0}, {1, 4, 1}}

Out[16]//MatrixForm=
```

$$\begin{pmatrix} 1 & -1 & 2 \\ 3 & 2 & 0 \\ 1 & 4 & 1 \end{pmatrix}$$

Jeffrey was captivated. He stood up and walked over to their table. The two young people looked up.

"I'm Jeff Albacete," he said. "I couldn't help overhearing your comments about matrices. I'm something of an authority on matrix algebra. Could I ask what you are doing?"

The young woman asked him to sit down and introduced herself as Lisa De Silva.

"This is my friend Chris Perry. I'm showing Chris how easily Mathematica can do matrix calculations. It's all based on lists, but you can view the lists in regular matrix form if you want."

Jeffrey was intrigued. He knew about Mathematica but did not use it regularly, and really did not understand the syntax or the functional programming paradigm it used. Jeffrey was more familiar with MATLAB. The code for exercises in his book were written in MATLAB, but Bob Fosberry had written those in the early days of the *Matrix Algebra* project, and Jeffrey had a student update them.

"So ... do you use Mathematica a lot? Are you an expert user?" Jeffrey asked Lisa De Silva.

She laughed. "I wouldn't say 'expert', but I do know a little."

Her friend Chris chimed in: "She's being modest. She presented a paper at the Wolfram Technology conference last year. She's better than your average Mathematica user."

An idea was forming in Jeffrey's mind.

"Tell me," he asked. "Is Wolfram interested in developing new technology learning environments?"

Lisa jumped. "Oh yes, they are! It's a major focus for them right now. Especially with the development of their Computable Document Format."

Jeffrey looked puzzled, and Lisa explained that the Computable Document Format, written in Mathematica, allowed users to carry out computations within documents, such as a book.

"Could you write a whole book in C... what is it .. computing document format?" asked Jeffrey.

"Computable Document Format – CDF," corrected Lisa. "Yes, you can, and people have done."

The idea took a more definite form.

"You may know my book on matrix algebra ...?"

The students shook their heads.

"Well, it is a widely used book, into its 9th edition. My publisher is very interested in organizing a conference around the topic of my book, with a focus on technology integration. Do you think Wolfram would be interested in partnering in a venture like this?"

"Generally the Wolfram license for CDFs stipulates that they are to be freely available," said Lisa "but they do have some commercial licenses with major publishers. Is your publisher a major commercial enterprise?'

"Close to the biggest in the world," replied Jeffrey.,

"Then I reckon you'd have a good chance," said Lisa.

Jeffrey took in this information for a few minutes. He looked directly at Lisa.

"If I can arrange this, would you be interested in helping me write my Matrix Algebra book, as a ... CDF?"

"Would this be a paid position?" asked Lisa.

"Yes, I think we can swing that," said Jeffrey. "My publisher pays well for products they can promote to a market they know is there."

"Then ... yes! Absolutely!" said Lisa.

She jumped up from the table and gave Jeffrey a hug.

"We haven't done a deal yet", he said.

"Sorry to be so emotional ... it's just that I was wondering about student loans for next year, and if this comes off it could relieve a lot of pressure for me and my mom."

Jeffrey smiled.

"I understand", he said. "Then let's do our best to make this happen."

Jeffrey exchanged contact details with Lisa, and promised to be in touch within a week. He bade her and Chris goodbye and drove back to campus.

George Prince saw Jeffrey coming into his office.

"Hi Jeff. You look happy."

"Happy", repeated Jeffrey. "Yes. Happy. Very happy. Very, very happy."

"I guess we make our own luck", thought Jeffrey. "If I hadn't gone to the Coffee Depot I may never have met that young woman. But what were the chances that I would meet her anyway? Chance, serendipity, was a funny old thing", he thought.

He smiled at George.

"It's looking as though the conference is going ahead."

6

Can we torture them?

Deborah Duke was glad to see George head out on his morning bike ride. His work had not been progressing well and he had been especially moody the past few weeks. *Au contraire*, her work was doing great on all fronts. She was a graduate student in cryptography and her dissertation was almost completed. She was opening up a new line of research in computational cryptography with people at ICERM, Brown University's Institute for Computational and Experimental Research in Mathematics, and she had recently become involved with local middle school teachers in Barrington, teaching basic cryptography to students.

Deborah was planning to visit a school that morning, and when George left the house on his usual bike ride she went through all the material on cryptography she had for the teacher and students. This was the first time with this particular class, so she thought she would begin with very simple substitution ciphers. Her favorite was the dancing men cipher described in the Sherlock Holmes story "The Adventure of the Dancing Men".

The code described in this story is especially simple, and very easy to crack by counting how often each character appears in messages. It was a good example to use to get students writing coded messages and learning to decipher them by frequency analysis.

Deborah liked engaging with middle school teachers and students: it was a welcome counterpoint to her current research in computational cryptography. The kids seemed to like it, and the teachers were very grateful for a new and engaging topic that met the state and national standards for teaching mathematics. Deborah made sure to pack a copy of "The Cryptoclub. Using Mathematics to Make and Break Secret Codes." She had seen a video review of the book on the *Republic of Mathematics* website and was immediately taken by how the book provided an outstanding introduction to modern ideas of cryptography for middle school students. The students at Sea View Middle School had a very good mathematics program, and their curriculum already covered many of the topics broached in the cryptography book, so Deborah thought the teachers might warm to using it as an adjunct text for a couple of semesters. Ideally, she thought, teachers and parents could organize an after-school cryptography club around the book. Anything, she thought, to help make mathematics fun.

Mathematics had always been easy and fun for Deborah, yet she realized how many students were traumatized by their experiences in mathematics classes. She had heard from a colleague in teacher education that two-thirds of his trainee elementary teachers described themselves as math-phobic, by which they meant feeling as if they were going to vomit when they had to do a fraction sum. This mortified Deborah: how could children in elementary school not become frightened of mathematics if their teachers were literally terrified? The same colleague had told her of an experienced elementary teacher who kept a papier-maché rock labeled "The Stupid Rock" that he would throw to the child he deemed to have given the worst answer to a mathematics question. Imagine, Deborah thought, going home after school and being asked by your mother what happened today, having to reply: "Oh, I got the Stupid Rock in math." Deborah was determined to do two things in her engagement with middle school teachers and students. She would engage in real, serious mathematics, not busy work. And she would make sure to always have fun.

Deborah arrived at Sea View Middle School at 9:30 and signed in as a visitor. She met Brian Pimlico, the teacher with whom she was working, and went through the ideas for the day, and the material she had, some to leave with him, and some to hand out to the children. Mr. Pimlico was pleased and impressed. He admired Deborah's command of cryptography and her ability to translate these ideas into schemes of work for middle school students. He thought he probably should get the Principal involved in this project. He could see that it had interesting curriculum ramifications, and fitted very well with the school's mission to broaden and deepen the education of students.

Mr. Pimlico and Deborah met with the grade 7 class. He introduced her to the students and let her take over the lesson on introductory cryptography. She soon had the students working in groups, writing secret messages using the dancing men signs. Different groups assigned differing letters to the dancing men, with the aim of writing a moderately long message for the other groups to decipher. That activity, along with her introduction, was about all the class could manage that period, so Deborah planned to return the following day to work with the class again on deciphering. She reminded them of the basic idea of frequency analysis – to count how often each character occurred in a message and to match that with the frequency of letters in English. She gave them all a chart of English letter frequencies, and asked them to try to have the messages deciphered by tomorrow.

When Deborah returned the next day the students were excited to tell her how far they had got with deciphering the messages from the other groups. A couple of messages were too short to make much headway with, but the rest had been cracked competently. Deborah asked the students if they enjoyed deciphering the messages. One young boy replied:

"Yes this was fun. It's not like math, cause no one's telling you what to do, or if you're right or wrong. You just use counting and thinking to figure it out. And we did!"

Deborah smiled and thought of the writings of Jim Tanton, her favorite mathematics educator. Jim was a Princeton Ph.D. educated mathematician who worked in schools to advance the cause of mathematical thinking, and fun. One of Jim's favorite phrases was that teachers had a fear of flailing. Deborah knew about flailing from experience. How often had she flailed around, not knowing where or how to start on a problem? Yet learning to be comfortable with flailing was an essential ingredient in having fun with, and being good at, mathematics. These kids flailed until the deciphering problems were cracked. They knew what they wanted to do, they had their developed counting skills to help them, and that was it: it was all they needed.

Deborah talked to the students about what was to come next – a slight improvement on substitution ciphers, and she gave them some modular arithmetic exercises to do for homework to prepare for the next class. As she prepared to leave she said to the students:

"You know, in practice, most codes are not cracked by clever deciphering methods. In practice most codes are broken by a breach of protocol or by coercion.

A girl asked Deborah what that meant.

"Well, a breach of protocol is not following the exact procedures set down for sending a coded message. During World War II, for example, a German soldier did not reset the codes when he sent a second message and the British code breakers, including Alan Turing – have you heard of him? – were able to crack the code. So it is very important in sending codes to follow exactly the procedure laid down."

"What about coercion?" asked another student. "What does that mean?"

"Coercion is applying pressure to someone who knows how to decode the message. This person might have a code key, for example, and could be blackmailed or even tortured to give up the secret key".

A group of boys raised their hands at once.

"Please Mr. Pimlico," one boy said, "please, can we torture the other teams?"

All the students were grinning. Yes, they seemed to say, could we please torture the others?

"Alright, alright! That's enough!" said Mr. Pimlico. "Everyone quiet down."

Deborah wondered if he would want her back tomorrow.

7

The variable
quality of coffee

$$\infty$$

Jeffrey Albacete sat on a chair outside the Provost's office. He had arrived a little early for his appointment to discuss funding for the conference, but not so early as to seem overly eager. The Provost's assistant had asked Jeffrey if he would like coffee, but he declined the offer. The coffee here, he thought, resembles nothing more than dishwater. He wondered if as academics moved to higher administrative positions their taste in coffee declined. The Provost appeared and waved Jeffrey into his office.

"Good morning Jeffrey. Come on in. So we're discussing this proposed conference of yours?

Jeffrey nodded and smiled in agreement. He went over the general idea of the conference theme, from Gene Golub's seminal *Matrix Computations* to Jeffrey's *Matrix Algebra*, now in its 9th edition. He handed a copy to the Provost. Jeffrey did not mention the discussions with his editor. He could not see any possible advantage in doing so at this meeting with the Provost from whom, in all honesty, he was trying to extract as much support as he could.

Jeffrey described the proposed emphasis on educational developments in the field, and then mentioned, almost as an afterthought, that it might be a good idea to have a focus on technology, too.

The Provost was buoyant in his support.

"This is a wonderful idea, Jeffrey. I know how skilled you are in organization, and I know you can pull this off to the credit of the University. The computational mathematics group has been firing on all cylinders recently, and showing no signs of slowing down, as you, of course, know. A focus on technology, at the high level of expertise the computational mathematics people bring to the table, is just the sort of thing to bring attention and credit to the University. Every little bit helps in our recruitment efforts, eh?"

Jeffrey's nodded his head twice, apparently in slow agreement.

Technology, technology, technology, he was thinking to himself. What is it with this technology obsession? Math is math whether you use technology or not.

He smiled at the Provost and nodded again.

"So let me say", said the Provost, "I am wholeheartedly in favor of this venture. I am guessing you would like to know if the University can offer any financial support?"

"Well ... yes. That would be nice", said Jeffrey.

"I think I can say, without needing to look at all our financial forecasts, that we can, in fact, support your conference in a substantial way. Shall we say, $2,000? How does that seem to you?"

Jeffrey did not know what to say. He knew the University had budget problems. Yet this was the amount the Provost could offer for a conference that he held in high regard? A conference that would bring attention and prestige to the University and assist with recruitment? Jeffrey wanted to cry.

"Yes, that's very generous. Thank you", he said.

"Not at all Jeffrey, not at all. The University admires your work and we are pleased to assist in any way we can. Please let my assistant know if there is anything else we can do."

With that the Provost stood up and indicated the meeting was over. Jeffrey shook hands and departed the office. He hurried down the stairs, eager to get out of the building. As long as Jeffrey had worked in universities he had never understood the administrative mind-set. It seemed to Jeffrey that all the administration wanted was for the academic faculty to work harder, to add to the University's reputation, to help recruit more students, and to raise money from grants to help support the university coffers. Jeffrey, to the contrary, felt that he, and his colleagues *were* the University. It was the job of the administration to support them. The Provost couldn't even offer a decent cup of coffee. He knew the Provost had been an excellent academic in his time. What was it that transformed people when they moved into administration? Where did they get the idea that it was us who should be supporting them, and not the other way around?

"The problem with the administration", he thought, "is that they are out of touch, despite what they think. They have no real understanding of what drives the day to day work of real academics."

Jeffrey desperately needed a good coffee. He headed to the Daily Grind, whose name resonated with him this morning, to have coffee and a good think.

Jeffrey sat at an outside table with his coffee and a blueberry muffin.

"The problem is", he thought, "now I have to have the University as a sponsor for the conference, despite their parting with only a measly $2,000. I could turn down the offer, but the Provost would not view that too kindly."

Jeffrey turned to more positive thoughts. He pulled out his phone and opened the notes he took on the contact details for Lisa De Silva, the young woman he had met in the Coffee Depot in Warren. He wondered if he should call her and go over the idea for a Computable Document Format version of his book in more detail. The problem with that, Jeffrey thought, is that she needed reassurance about financial support. Jeffrey made a decision to get back to his editor and ask for a meeting with the learning environments commissioning editors. He wanted to move this project along, and financial backing was essential to a smoothly executed outcome.

Jeffrey made his way back to his office, and was reading the news on his computer when Kathy Riverton knocked at his door

"Good morning Jeff", she smiled. "Would you care for some coffee?"

Jeffrey was pleased to see Kathy. There was something about her – he couldn't put his finger on it – that always made him happy to see her.

"Sure. That would be nice", he said.

Jeffrey walked with Kathy to her office, put the water in the coffee maker and inserted a sachet of coffee. She motioned to him to sit down.

"So, what's news?" she asked.

Jeffrey took some time to answer. He pursed his lips as he thought.

"Well, I've just come back from a meeting with the Provost", said Jeffrey. "He's offered me the sum of $2,000 in support of my conference. Not enough to organize a dinner for the participants."

Kathy was thinking how she might help Jeff out of his despondent mood.

"There's a couple of things I think about that", she said. "First, he did not say no to you. It sounds like he might have actually been supportive."

Jeffrey nodded agreement.

"That's a good thing", said Kathy. "Even though the amount is small, the sentiment is strongly in your favor. The question is how to use that to your advantage."

Jeffrey couldn't quite see that, but he respected Kathy's intelligence, so he kept an open mind.

"The second thing is, and I think you'll like this a lot more, the Center for Computational Mathematics and Statistics has received a fairly large amount of support from the University. In that package there is an amount set aside for special projects.

Now, if we can inject a technology component into your conference, we can use some of the Center funds to support you."

Jeffrey told Kathy about his chance meeting with Lisa De Silva
and the possibility of a Computable Document Format version of
his book. He told her about the discussion with his publisher, and
his plan to talk with them right away about funding. Kathy had an
idea.

"Why don't we use some of the Center funding to pay Lisa for
a semester to see how far you and she can get with converting your
book? This will cost us only a little, and that way you will have
something more tangible to show people."

Jeffrey could not have been happier. He thought Kathy's coffee
was so much better than the Provost's. A lesser person might have
wondered why Kathy would offer the Center's money to help Jeffrey. Academics are notoriously self-centered, and any one would
wonder what was the motive behind Kathy's offering support for
apparently nothing in return. Yet these thoughts never entered
Jeffrey's head. He was secure in the knowledge that his work and
his book were major contributions to the field. It only made sense
to him that a younger, respectful person such as Kathy would put
what resources she could into supporting a respected senior colleague, like Jeffrey. "Not", he thought, "that there actually is any
one else like me."

8

She who pays the piper

"Please tell me I heard you wrong. You're offering to support Jeff's conference?"

George was astounded. He felt it was way too soon to be holding a retrospective conference on Gene Golub's work. He thought Kathy felt the same. Now she just told him she had offered Jeff funds from the Center for Computational Mathematics and Statistics to help run the conference!

Kathy smiled broadly at George.

"Here's the thing," she said. "This conference is going ahead whether we like it or not. Jeff has support from the Provost – admittedly not enough to host a conference dinner, as Jeff said – and he also has an idea to use Wolfram's Computable Document Format in a new edition of his book. I'm guessing his publisher is going to jump at the chance to be involved."

"I still don't get it," said George. "Why should the Center put up money to help him do this?"

Kathy's smile widened.

"Because," she said, "for a small amount of funding we essentially own the conference. I know I can get the Provost to agree to run this at the University under the banner of the Center. Jeff's publisher and Wolfram can come in as major sponsors. But essentially it will be a Center initiative."

George was astounded for a second time.

"That's, that's ..." He was about to say "devious". "That's brilliant!"

Kathy giggled.

"I think it will work," she said. "And the initial outlay is peanuts. We can pay Jeff's student, Lisa, $18 an hour for 10 hours a week for the semester. That's just over $2,500. I know that's more than the Provost offered Jeff, but it's a small amount and it should give everyone a large return."

George was, once again, impressed by Kathy's ability to see beyond the obvious. He would probably have told Jeff to stuff his conference, and left him to his own devices. Kathy's approach was a win for everyone.

"So have you met this student of Jeff's – Lisa, did you say her name was?"

"No, I haven't met her," said Kathy, "and you're right. We should ask Jeff to get her in here to a meeting as soon as possible. From what I understand about Computable Document Format, we don't need anything to get started except Mathematica, for which the University has a site license."

Jeffrey was very happy with Kathy's suggestion, and he phoned Lisa to say that an unexpected small amount of money had come through from the University and that they would like to employ her during the semester to work on converting parts of Jeffrey's book to Computable Document Format. Would she like to do that? Lisa was thrilled. She agreed to come and meet with Jeffrey the next morning.

"Lisa's agreed to come and work on the book for the semester," Jeff told Kathy.

"That's great," said Kathy. "I think this will be big a help to you Jeff. You can let your publishers know what you are doing and ask them for their support. How would you feel if you ran your conference as a Center activity?"

Jeff paused. He had not been anticipating this. He imagined a conference run by his publisher. But he could see there would be advantages in the conference being a Center initiative. He looked at Kathy. Her smile and – he could not quite put his finger on it – something about her demeanor, won him over.

"Yes, that would be a great idea," he said.

Kathy nodded and smiled. This would be good for everyone, she thought. Jeff will be even more motivated for this to succeed when it's so embedded within the University. His publisher will come on board, Wolfram was bound to agree, and the Center would have a shiny new initiative to add to its first year of operations.

♥♥♥♥♥

George was preparing a shrimp and chicken salad for Deborah and he to eat on the deck. He had chilled a bottle of Sancerre, which he thought would go well with the light meal.

"You know Kathy's putting up money to fund Jeff's conference?" he asked Deborah.

"Not her own money, surely?"

"No, no. Center for Computational Mathematics and Statistics money. Not a lot initially. But enough to get Jeff going."

"But I thought you and Kathy thought Jeff's conference was not the smartest of ideas. At this time, anyway", said Deborah.

George explained Kathy's reasoning that for a relatively modest investment the Center would essentially own the conference.

Deborah laughed. "Kathy is very cute, and that smile of hers would win over anyone. But she sure knows how to get what she wants!"

George agreed. "But everyone wins. Everyone comes out looking good. It's a way of thinking about things that Kathy has that is very positive."

George brought the meal out to the table on the deck. "Could you bring the wine, Deb?" he asked.

They sat together in the twilight, enjoying the meal and the wine. George asked about her day at Sea View Middle school.

"How's that going?" he asked. "Does it take too much time away from your dissertation?"

"No, it's fine," said Deborah. "It sort of helps clear my head to think about the elementary side of cryptography. But the funniest thing happened today."

She told George about her explanation of coercion and the children picking up on wanting to torture the other teams.

"I don't know that they really wanted to torture anyone," she said, "but they did have a gleam in their eyes!"

"How did the teacher take it?" asked George.

"Oh, he was fine. I was a bit worried that he might think I was taking his students down a dark track, but he understood. I'm getting into modular arithmetic with them now. A couple of them are very bright. There's one girl, in particular, who seems to grasp everything very rapidly."

George unwrapped a cigar and lit it. He leaned back and thought for a moment.

"You know ... ," he said. "This might be a bit far-fetched ..."

"What?" asked Deborah.

"Well, it's just the smidgeon of a beginning of a probably half-baked idea, but, what if you talked with Kathy, as Director of Undergraduate Research, to see if maybe there's a couple of undergraduates who might like to mentor these middle school students in a research project?"

Deborah thought for a moment. George poured himself another glass of wine.

"We would have to proceed very cautiously," she said. "Teachers tend to equate research with looking things up on Google or Wikipedia. They don't generally understand research as stepping into the unknown. There would be a learning curve for the teachers. And many of them have a fear of flailing, whereas research is all about flailing."

George recalled the saying, attributed to Einstein, that if we knew what we were doing it wouldn't be called research.

"Still, you could be right," she said. "There's a couple of really bright kids in the class and they might benefit from research mentoring. We would have to choose the undergraduates carefully. I think I have a topic in mind – something to do with discrete logarithms."

"Well, I think that's where Kathy could help. She has a bunch of undergraduates in her research seminar, and some of them are very personable and great communicators", said George.

"Alright. I will talk with Kathy and see what she thinks," said Deborah. "If this works it will help build bridges between the University and the school system."

"Shit!" exclaimed George. He knocked over his wine as he jumped up from the table. He brushed hard at his thigh.

'What is it?" asked Deborah, thinking a hornet might have stung him.

"F.., f...!" swore George. "The damned cigar dropped onto my lap!"

Deborah laughed. She couldn't help it. She'd been hoping for some time that George would give up, or ease back, on his cigars. Now one had bitten him he might think twice.

9

Keep plodding and smiling

Bert Monod, Department Chair, had not published an academic article in over 30 years. He did once write a letter to a Providence newspaper bemoaning the teaching of Advanced Placement Calculus in schools. "It was a waste of time", he thought, referring momentarily to AP Calculus, "we just have to try to undo what's been crammed in their heads and start over." He also thought, if pushed, that academic publishing was a waste of time. "It's not our business to write articles", he'd said when asked. "It's our job to teach students who want to major in mathematics." The facts, that very few students did seem to want to major in mathematics, that the Department did not actively help their majors find jobs, and did not keep records of their alumni, somewhat undercut his argument about teaching being the major task of the mathematics faculty. At the very least it questioned the commitment that he had to teaching and to the students, despite his professed views on the matter.

George Prince saw it differently. Basically, he said to anyone who would listen: "Bert is lazy and indifferent". George made people laugh with his imitation of Bert Monod's "Whatever" shrug. They laughed, yet felt in their hearts the sadness of being led by someone who basically didn't care.

The Department had some tensions. It was developing a strong research reputation though the work of the computational and statistics groups, but at the same time an inordinate amount of administrative work was placed on the shoulders of the junior faculty. George had begun to build a workload model for the Department, something that Bert Monod vigorously opposed. George used Lori Bailey as just one example of a junior faculty member who was overworked.

Lori had come to the Department fresh from her Ph.D. in statistics. She was keen to advance herself, and was full of energy. Lori threw herself into teaching, developing and running new courses, such as the *Introduction to Risk* course, designed for students thinking about actuarial science as a career. Because she cared, Lori had also taken on a major role in advising, including setting up a meeting once a week advising students on career options. She had written a website to help students find appropriate careers, and worked with freshman students to get them focused on jobs early in their university studies. She ran the student research group, and went with students to conferences as mentor and chaperone. Lori had instituted the beginnings of a system to track and stay in touch with alumni, using Facebook and Twitter. She was on the computer users committee with Kathy Riverton, the library liaison committee, the College curriculum committee, and the Faculty Senate. Lori had published three articles on applied statistics last year in good journals, and had a grant to work on research related to statistical analysis of obesity and diabetes with the Centers for Disease Control. George's model showed Lori as an outlier. Bert Monod was not unaware of Lori's energy and application. He had written "GOOD JOB!" on her faculty evaluation last year.

The Assistant Provost was aware of George's concerns. She

had asked him why the Department simply did not appoint a new Chair. George had no easy answer. It was a combination of individual selfishness – an unwillingness to take on the responsibilities of Department Chair, resistance from a block of older, unproductive faculty who liked the status quo, and a lack of desire to organize to focus on Department needs. Just too much inertia stemming from a focus on individual needs, he thought. The Provost had asked George and Kathy to develop a workload model for the Department, and George had begun the task, difficult though it was.

♥♥♥♥♥

Bert Monod was considering the request Jeffrey had just put to him. He couldn't see how it could be done. Nor did he understand why Jeffrey wanted to do it, except to get a free trip to Sydney. "Wouldn't we all like that?" thought Bert.

"Who will cover your teaching if you're in Sydney for two weeks prior to Easter?" Bert asked Jeffrey.

Bert should have known better than to ask Jeffrey Albacete such a silly question. Jeffrey was – even the Provost acknowledged it – a very good organizer. He moved slowly, but very surely, always with his eye on the prize.

"I've talked to Lori about it," said Jeffrey, and she's kindly agreed to cover my two classes for the time I'm gone. She's very capable."

Bert stared at Jeffrey. He seemed to give up and gave a "Whatever" shrug of his shoulders. He signed the form Jeffrey had given him and said he hoped it was all worth it. Jeffrey put the form in the mail to Human Resources and began to plan his trip to Sydney. The organizers of a conference on *Matrix Methods* had invited Jeffrey to deliver a talk, and as well known as he was in the field these invitations did not come every day. He had not been to Sydney before, in fact had not been to Australia, and he was excited at the thought of being in the antipodes for two weeks where – even on the other side of the world – his work was recognized and appreciated.

Kathy was in her office when Jeffrey knocked on her door.

"Oh, hi Jeff. Come on in. Can I offer you coffee?"

Jeffrey was grateful for the offer even if he did have to prepare the coffee himself. Kathy understood the role good coffee played in lubricating the academic machine.

He looked at Kathy for a moment, wondering how to broach the trip, then just came out with it:

"Looks like I'm going to Sydney next Easter."

"Really!" she said. "How did you manage that?"

Jeffrey explained the invitation from the conference organizers, Bert's reluctance to agree to him being away during teaching, and Lori's agreement to cover for him. Kathy kept her concerns about Lori's workload to herself. She was Lori's academic mentor, and she would talk with Lori privately about managing multiple work assignments.

"Well that's very good, Jeff. So you are as renowned in the antipodes as you are here?"

Jeffrey smiled. "It seems so," he said.

"I've been talking with the Provost," said Kathy, "about the Center, and I raised the question of new positions in the Department."

Jeffrey nodded. "Well, we've been really short changed over the past few years. The Dean seems to want to appoint full-time lecturers who are on short-term contracts and generally don't contribute anything to the academic life of the Department. I think Bert needs to stand up to the Dean on this issue."

Kathy agreed. "The thing is," she said, "Bert has no sense of direction for the Department. I doubt that he spends more than a millisecond thinking about what we really need. I decided to stop going through him, or the Dean, and just go the Provost directly. Being Director of the Center allows me to do that," she smiled.

"I hope you're right," said Jeffery. "I don't hold out too much hope that the administration is looking out for us."

Kathy understood Jeffrey's pessimistic outlook. He had been at the University a long time, and had seen severe budget cuts and layoffs of support staff and even academic faculty. His views stemmed from a desire for the sort of academic structure he saw as vital, and the realities of a university budget in times of severe constraint. Her way of working and thinking was different. She worked very hard – it did not come easily – at being optimistic. She deliberately smiled a lot, and put her case, gently, quietly, firmly and consistently to those who could make decisions. She had come to the conclusion that working with and through Bert Monod was a waste of time. She had recently decided much the same about the Dean.

Bert Monod knocked on Kathy's door.

"I thought you would want to know," he said. "The Dean has just got approval from the Provost for a new hire."

10

First you search,
then you screen

The Department was energized by the news that the Dean had given approval to conduct a search for a new faculty member. Lori Bailey asked Kathy what had prompted the Dean to make this decision.

"She didn't make the decision. The Provost did," said Kathy. "The Dean is incapable of acting on her own. She always goes cap in hand to the senior administration."

The Dean, Sara Nueberg, was a former biology professor. She might have been an accountant for the amount of attention she paid to the bottom line. That, together with her obsequiousness, and her singular lack of vision, had stifled progress in the College for almost a decade. Her saving grace was that she was personally pleasant, and knew everyone's name. George had remarked several times that she had just the right attributes to be a dental receptionist.

"Then what prompted the Provost to make the decision to go forward with a new hire?" asked Lori.

"We will probably never know", said Kathy. "The Provost moves in mysterious ways."

Lori was puzzled.

"Seriously, I will tell you in detail when we are away from the Department," said Kathy. "The walls here have too many ears."

George knocked on Kathy's door. "Great news," he said. "Looks like your talk with the Provost did the trick."

Lori looked startled and turned to Kathy, who said: "I will tell you later."

Jeffrey had to speak. "I hope we can appoint someone in matrix algebra this time. Most of our recent appointments have been in differential equations and statistics, and I think we need to address an imbalance."

George's eyebrows shot up as he looked across at Kathy. He changed the subject of discussion. "One issue we'll have," said George, "is that Irene will be away for most of the Search and Screen meetings."

Irene was the Departmental secretary. She had been diagnosed recently as needing a hysterectomy, and she was suffering considerable pain. An operation was imminent, and Bert Monod did not expect her to be functional for about 6 weeks after the operation.

"You're right. That will be a real problem," said Kathy. " I wonder if Bert can find us some temporary administrative assistance?"

Kathy went to Bert's office and asked if he thought the Department could get temporary assistance while Irene was on sick leave. Bert's infamous shrug, palms up, was equivalent to shouting "Whatever", thought Kathy.

"We're going to need someone," argued Kathy. "I don't think we can be expected to process the applications, and make travel and hotel arrangements for the prospective candidates for interview," she said to Bert.

"We have to do what we have to do," he replied.

Except, thought Kathy to herself, you don't – we do. George was right, she thought, Bert is both lazy and indifferent.

"Maybe you could talk to Human Resources," offered Bert.

"Maybe," said Kathy, but she had another idea already forming in her brain.

"Will you chair the Search and Screen Committee?" she asked Bert.

"I don't see why," replied Bert. "As Department Chair I get to interview the candidates anyway. No point doing it twice."

No, thought Kathy to herself, because then you'd actually have to do some work, like sifting through hundreds of applications and reference letters, and exercising some judgment.

"Okay," she said, "I'd better get on with it. I assume I will be the Chair of the Search and Screen Committee then?"

Bert shrugged again. "Sure," he said.

♥♥♥♥♥

Kathy walked over to the Provost's assistant's office and asked for help.

"We're in a jam," she said. "Irene will be away on sick leave for the duration of the Search and Screen Committee – well for the important part at the beginning where we process applications and make travel arrangement," she said. "Even if she does come back, she will be in no state to take on a heavy administrative load. I'm wondering if we could ask you to provide this support?"

Kathy got what she wanted: Donna Ferreira, an administrative assistant in the Academic Affairs office, would be able to provide the support the Search and Screen Committee needed. Kathy was happy. She knew Donna, and was sure with her taking on the administrative load for the committee that the search and screen process would hum. Kathy wondered what it was about Bert that he was so unmotivated even to ask? Was he frightened? Was he incurably anti-social. Did he just not care? She couldn't reconcile his indifferent approach to administrative matters with his clearly high mathematical intelligence.

"We need a new Department Chair," a little voice said in her head.

"Well, it's not going to be me!" she said out loud. "Not yet."

Kathy told George about the arrangement to have Donna Ferreira do the administrative work for the Search and Screen Committee.

"That's excellent", said George. "Donna's very efficient. She will be great!"

"George got up and closed his office door.

"The thing is," he said to Kathy, "I would like to keep Jeff off the committee."

Kathy understood. Jeff had tunnel vision. For him there was one and only one choice, irrespective of the larger concerns and needs of the Department: he had to advocate for a person in matrix algebra.

"You know," said Kathy, "he's even opposed to people in linear algebra, more broadly. He has a very narrow view of his field, and only those people doing more or less what he does are acceptable to him. I don't know, though, that we can keep him off the committee. Bert is likely to want him there. Strange that Bert does actually care about some things. The wrong things, but it shows he is not totally indifferent."

"Well, if Jeff's going to be on the committee we're going to need to ensure that he can be out-voted," said George.

" Let's draw up a list," said Kathy, and she and George spent several minutes constructing the composition of the Search and Screen Committee.

"We need to get the ad out right way" said George. "Electronically. It's how people look for jobs nowadays, despite what the Dean thinks. Can we bypass her demand for paper applications?"

Kathy agreed. "The trick is going to be to do it our way, while appearing to be doing it the Dean's way."

George rolled his eyes. "What can I say?" he asked. "I think she's not aware that we're well into a new century."

Kathy though this was a bit unfair. "She does make reference to the passage of time," she said. " I don't think she's as bad as you're making out."

"Are you aware of her technology skills? Lack of them, I mean," said George. "I'll say no more."

Kathy laughed. "Perhaps you're right", she said. "Well, let's get on with it. Do you have a copy of the last job ad we posted. We can take that and modify it. No point reinventing the wheel."

George dug up the file for the old job ad, and he and Kathy looked it over.

"Just a few tweaks will do it," said Kathy. "Do you want me to do that?"

Zaqi Yudhoyono appeared at George's door.

"Hi Zaq, come on in", said Kathy. "We're just discussing the ad for the new job."

"Yes, I heard about that', said Zaq. "That's great news, really fantastic! But here's some extra news: Bao Zhang's on the market. She's very interested in coming here."

Kathy clapped her hands in delight. George was excited. "Really? Bao's interested in moving? That would be fantastic."

Bao Zhang was a rising star in numerical linear algebra. Her work had direct application to data science and she had a couple of years experience working at MathWorks in Massachusetts.

"Jeff won't be too happy", said George. "Bao works closely with people at the University of Massachusetts Dartmouth.

George and Kathy could sense the thunder clouds forming.

11

The dog's name is Alex

Kathy Riverton and her husband Rickhart Jansen arrived for dinner at George and Deborah's house just on 6:00 p.m. Kathy had met Rickhart in Holland when she was a Ph.D. student. They had married and then returned to the United States when Kathy was offered a job at the University. Theirs was a classical two-body problem and after what seemed an interminable wait they had received the news that the University would also offer Rickhart a position, due in no small part to his expertise in computational statistics. Rickhart was not an applied statistician of any easily recognizable type: he was no bio-statistician or epidemiologist, and did not apply statistics to questions of health in any way. Rickhart's expertise lay in the theoretical and applied computational aspects of the statistics of dynamical systems. To put it in simple terms, as he had done for the Chancellor at his Inaugural Lecture, if a system – the stock exchange, for example – progresses and changes through time, how do we estimate how long it spends in any given state, and how often it returns to that state? That's what Rickhart was interested in, and it paid off handsomely for him. He had been promoted first to Associate Professor and then to Full Professor in record time. He published prolifically, had a team of colleagues and graduate students working with and for him, and currently had grants totaling $2.3 million supporting his research.

The two couples – Kathy and Rickhart, and George and Deborah – had decided that for professional reasons they would both keep their own family names upon marriage. George Prince and Deborah Duke, were, for obvious reasons, known as the Royal Family around the Department. It was not obvious to a casual academic observer that Kathy and Rickhart were connected in any familial way. Even though Rickhart's computational statistics laboratory had been amalgamated into the Center for Computational Mathematics and Statistics, of which Kathy was Director, Rickhart maintained a degree of autonomy that gave the appearance that he ran an independent entity, which to all intents and purposes, he did. The Center was pleased to count his grants in their financial reporting, but did not impose any restrictions on him.

Deborah greeted Kathy and Rick and explained that George would be back shortly. He had just taken Alex to the vet for a rabies shot.

♥♥♥♥♥

George arrived at the veterinary clinic just before 5:15. This was a new vet for him: their previous veterinary practice had changed owners and George and Deborah were not happy with the new regime. George walked into the clinic with Alex on a leash. A man in a lab coat greeted them and said: "Name?"

"Prince," said George.

"No, I mean your name," said the man. "Not the dog's name."

That is my name," said George. "Prince. George Prince. The dog's name is Alex."

"Alex!" said the vet. "Really? Your dog's name is Alex?"

Yes, it is," said George. As odd as it may seem to you, my name his Prince, and his name is Alex."

"Well now, what's wrong with Alex?" asked the vet.

"So far as I know nothing's wrong with him", said George. "We're here for an annual rabies shot." George was beginning to feel more than slightly irritated.

"I'm sorry," said the man. I didn't introduce myself. I'm Dr. Nurse. Dr. Paul Nurse. Not to be confused with the Noble Laureate of the same name."

George wondered what he and Alex had stumbled into. Was this a veterinary clinic or a halfway house for mentally disturbed individuals? He looked around to reassure himself. The diplomas on the wall looked real, and pronounced that Dr. Paul Nurse was indeed a qualified veterinary surgeon.

"Bring him through to the exam room," said Dr. Nurse, "and I'll give him a once over."

"There's no need for a physical exam," said George, fearful of a rapidly mounting bill. "He just needs a rabies shot."

"Don't worry," said Dr. Nurse. "I won't charge extra for sticking a thermometer up his rectum and looking in his mouth and ears." Dr. Nurse laughed at his own little repartee. The vet gave Alex the once over, deemed him to be in good shape, and stuck a needle in his backside.

"There you go, Alex old man. All set for another year. And what do you do Mr. Prince?"

"Dr. Prince," replied George, not to be outdone by a vet. "I'm a mathematics professor at the University."

"Indeed! Are you?" asked Dr. Nurse. "You know, I think my wife, Deirdre, would like to talk with you."

"She would? How's that?" asked George.

"She home-schools our son, Timothy." Said Dr. Nurse. He's four and he's gifted mathematically."

"Is he now?" said George. "Excuse me for seeming skeptical, but do you have evidence for that?"

"Oh yes. She has him enrolled in a Math Circle at MIT," said

Dr. Nurse. "He counts like the dickens, and can do sums that kids years older can't do. Don't know where he gets it from. I suspect it's the time Deirdre – my wife – spends with him. She's very keen to see Timothy get an education consistent with his abilities."

"I'm sure," said George.

"Would you, or someone you know, be interested in talking with Deirdre and Timothy? I know she'd be appreciative of any help or advice on how to proceed with Timothy's mathematical education."

In a moment of weakness, thinking the poor man was probably driven to extremes by an obsessive spouse, George gave the vet Deborah's phone number, and suggested Deirdre Nurse contact Deborah.

Dr. Paul Nurse – not to be confused with the Nobel Laureate of the same name – was very grateful. "Thank you indeed, Dr. Prince. This is helpful. Very helpful."

Alex, who had been sitting nose down, eyes up, taking in this strange conversation, was eager to be on the leash and out of here. He did not understand the words exchanged by George and this man, but he could sense there was something very odd going on. "And," thought Alex to himself, "what a very odd name the man has!"

♥♥♥♥♥

George arrived home just on 6:30 PM.

"Here's George and Alex", said Deborah. "How was the new vet?"

Alex looked up at her and wagged his tail very slightly, as if to say "You aren't going to believe this!"

"He was – unusual," said George. "He and wife – Deirdre, as I recall – imagine they have a mathematically gifted son. Timothy I think."

"Not another one!" laughed Deborah. "How many times have I heard that story!"

"My feelings exactly," said George. "But ... sorry about this ... I gave him your number."

"What? Why on earth would you do that?" asked Deborah.

"I know, I know. I'm sorry", said George. I sort of felt sorry for the poor chap. I imagine even he thinks his wife has gone off the rails about the kid."

Kathy and Rickhart were laughing. "What's the name of this poor vet?" asked Rickhart.

"Dr. Nurse. Dr. Paul Nurse," said George.

"Not the Nobel Laureate!" exclaimed Rickhart. "What's he doing moonlighting as a vet?" Rickhart laughed uproariously.

"I know. It is funny," said George." And here's the funniest thing: he thought Alex's name was Prince."

Now the four of them couldn't stop laughing.

"In a sense it is," laughed Deborah" He's Alex Prince. Perhaps if we can enroll him in a program at MIT for gifted dogs he can get his Ph.D. and become Dr. Prince like his daddy."

George checked on the wine he had chilling. "What's for dinner?" he asked.

Now, thought Alex, someone is talking sense at last!

12

Alexandre the Great

"Why did you name your dog Alex?" Kathy asked George.

"He's named for Alexandre Grothendieck, the French mathematician", said George.

"Didn't he win the Fields Medal then drop out of mathematics?" asked Kathy.

"That's the one," said George. "I admire Grothendicek for the way he thought about solving mathematical problems. A common approach is to think of cracking a hard nut. When we think this way the usual idea is to bring out a tough enough instrument to crack the nut open. Grothendieck imagined, instead, putting the nut in water, rubbing it from time to time until the shell opens. Another time Grothendieck thought of a problem as a marlstone – a lime-rich mudstone – that is slowly and imperceptibly surrounded by a rising tide. He didn't advocate using only strength or heavy intellectual tools to solve problems, but used a more organic approach to surrounding the problem with understanding."

"That's almost poetic," said Kathy. "But you aren't expecting Alex to solve mathematical problems?"

"No," George laughed. "No, I don't think Alex is going to crack any mathematical problems. But what I do hope for him in his doggy world is that, to the best of his ability, he will approach life's problems through seeking understanding, and being patient enough to wait until that understanding comes."

Alex looked up at George and wagged his tail.

"That's asking a lot of a dog," said Rickhart.

"It's asking a lot of anyone," said George. "How many people do you know who could do that? But I feel if we living beings do not attempt to engage understanding to the best of our ability then we are simply skirting across the surface of what it means to be alive."

"Very well put," Rickhart said to George. "I like the way you expressed that."

"Speaking of problems," said Kathy to Deborah, "did you hear that Bao Zhang will apply for the open position we have?"

"Bao Zhang? Isn't she the one who worked at MathWorks? A numerical linear algebra person as I recall George saying. Why is that a problem?"

"She's a good friend of folk at the University of Massachusetts Dartmouth,", said Kathy. "And Jeff had a falling out with some of them over the International Linear Algebra Society. They were strong advocates for general linear algebra education, whereas Jeff is strongly focused simply on matrix methods."

"Seems like a distinction without a difference to me," said Deborah. "Of course I use matrices a lot in my coding work, and I'm glad to have learned about them in the context of general linear algebra. Why does Jeff want to make such a fuss?"

"On such small difference are reputations made. Or lost," replied Kathy.

Deborah was glad to be working in a field where huge strides were being made regularly. There was simply too much to work on, to figure out, to worry about petty intellectual squabbles.

"Maybe it's a sign the field is stagnating?" asked Deborah.

"Don't tell Jeff that!" Rickhart laughed.

"Is Jeff on the Search and Screen Committee?" asked Deborah.

"Not if George has his way!" said Kathy.

"I think it might be hard to keep him off," said George. "Bert has the ultimate say as to who's on the committee, and Jeff is bound to bend his ear until Bert agrees. So I think we can assume Jeff will, in fact, be on the committee."

"Then can't you outvote him?" asked Deborah.

"Oh sure, and we will," said George. "So far the Committee is looking like Kathy as Chair, me, Jeff, Zaq and Lori. It's not a question of outvoting him: it's more a matter of the fuss he will make at every step of the process. And we will all be made to feel guilty because we are not supporting matrix algebra as Jeff conceives it to be."

"But what if there is no one in Jeff's exact field?" asked Rickhart. "Surely then he would see Bao Zhang as a good compromise?"

"We can hope," said Jeff.

"I've been thinking," said Kathy. " At the first meeting of the Search and Screen committee I think I will beg off being Chair due to other commitments, and suggest Zaq chair the committee."

Deborah looked puzzled.

"The thing is, Zaq needs the experience for his promotion, and Jeff is very fond of Zaq, so less likely to argue openly with him, as he would do with me."

"I think that's a great idea," said George. "And on that note, let's eat!"

Alex let out two loud barks. He understood what that meant.

♥♥♥♥♥

Kathy asked Deborah about her dissertation.

"It's all but done," said Kathy. "In fact I'm working on a new project now with the computational and experimental mathematics people at Brown."

"ICERM?" asked Kathy.

"Yes, ICERM. They have heaps of grant money, which means a lot of visitors. I began collaborating with a visiting Belgian guy who is interested, as am I, in constructing certain genus 2 curves that are very useful in cryptography. I'm hoping I might get a post-doctoral position there."

"That would be really great," said Kathy. "It would be good for us too for you to forge stronger links with ICERM. George tells me you've been teaching a middle school cryptography class."

"I have. And it's great! I never thought I would enjoy it this much. Partly it's the response of the teacher and the kids – they've lapped up everything I've thrown at them. But it's also this one girl, Alicia Brown, who is just phenomenal. She is going great guns on a project I set her on discrete logarithms. I actually have meant to talk with you about this, Kathy. I was hoping you might know some undergraduates who could act as mentors for her. There's a couple of other kids in that class who are also very talented, but no one as naturally gifted as Alicia at the moment."

"Sure. I think Kojo Agbeko would be excellent. He's an outstanding mathematics junior and very patient. He has been working on cryptography on and off for a couple of semesters. Would you like me to ask him?" said Kathy

"Yes, thanks. That would be great," said Deborah.

"What do you think about this vet's wife – Deirdre Nurse, wasn't it – who thinks her five year old is mathematically gifted? Do you think there could be anything to it?" asked Kathy.

"Hard to say," said Deborah, "but on balance I think it's unlikely. People often mistake fluency and talent for giftedness. The basic rule in my book is that gifted individuals take your breath away. Alicia does that for me. She can think of things in ways that are very unusual, and it always makes me wonder how she does it. I suppose that's it – if you can more or less see how someone does something then they don't seem gifted, possibly just very talented. But if they keep surprising you over with their amazing insights and abilities – out of the ordinary – then you begin to think of them as gifted. The thing is, it's very hard to educate a gifted kid. You have to proceed cautiously or they might become precociously unbalanced. If this boy really is gifted then the Nurse's will not have an easy time of it."

"Will you talk with them if they ask you?" asked Kathy.

"I guess so," said Deborah. "I think I would start with some basic counting levels that I learned about from the people in teacher education, and try to assess where the Nurse boy is in terms of simple arithmetic. For example, I might show him 8 plastic chips, tell him there are 9 more under a bowl that he can't see and ask him how many there are in total. If he's relatively advanced for a 5 year old he will be able to tell me 17, and also do it by counting on from 8: 9, 10, 11 and so on up to 17."

"What if he can't?" asked Kathy.

"If he can't, if he has to lift the bowl, and count the hidden chips one by one, then he's definitely not gifted mathematically," said Deborah.

Alex barked loudly and looked up at Deborah. "I understand," he seemed to say.

13

The right attitude to coffee

Jeffrey was sitting behind his computer and motioned to Lisa to take a seat at the end of his desk, with a view along the length of his computer to a whiteboard. Kathy Riverton knocked at Jeff's door. Jeffrey introduced Kathy to Lisa who expressed her gratitude to Kathy for the opportunity to work on Professor Albacete's project.

"Not at all," said Kathy. "I think this is a great project and we're hoping for a good outcome. Jeff, would you like coffee? Lisa?"

Jeffrey smiled and stood up from his seat. Lisa said: "Yes, thank you."

Kathy showed Lisa the coffee maker in her office and the drawers full of coffee sachets.

"That's cool," said Lisa. "Professor Albacete. I'll make your coffee if that's okay with you. What would you like?"

Jeffrey smiled and indicated dark bold roast. This could work really well, he thought. An assistant who appreciated coffee might be exactly what he needed.

With the coffee brewing Jeffrey handed Lisa a copy of the 9th edition of his book *Matrix Algebra*.

"This is for you," he said. "It's into its 9th edition, as you can see. Just came out. It's been translated into 11 languages too."

"May I look through it?" Lisa asked.

"Sure. Take your time. I'll go get the coffee," said Jeffrey.

Lisa was impressed by the careful organization of the book. It was aimed at sophomore students, yet had enough content to go way beyond that. The explanations seemed clear, there were a lot of exercises, and the highlighted applications seemed appropriate. "Am I just being too picky?" she thought. "The writing is incredibly ... well, dull! The book looks complete, but it's so boring."

"How are you finding it?" asked Jeffrey.

"Very interesting," said Lisa. "It's certainly not like anything I've read before.

Jeffrey asked if she had taken a course on matrix algebra.

"Not as such," she said. "We did a course on linear algebra in the Computer Science Department. We used Professor Leon's book."

Jeffrey stiffened.

"Oh! And how did you find that?" asked Jeffrey.

Lisa caught Jeffrey's inflection and answered cautiously.

"It was, well ... okay, I guess. It took quite a different approach to your book. You have a lot of things here that we didn't cover."

Jeffrey was pleased.

"A lot of people find that," he said. "So do you think we can make computable document formats for parts of the book? It has some MATLAB exercises, as you can see."

"I think, if I may say so Professor Albacete, the aim would be to produce a CDF version of the entire book. We may not complete that this semester, but we should have enough to show your publishers, and potentially convince them this is a viable project."

Jeffrey nodded as he sipped his coffee. He could not say more because he still didn't know just what a CDF document was. What did it do, he wondered, that my book doesn't already do?

"The logical thing would be to start with chapter one," said Lisa. "But that may not be the best showcase for what a CDF can do, just because the first chapter usually contains so many preliminaries. Would you like me to start with chapter one to show you what I think might be possible?"

Jeffrey, still unsure what a CDF would even look like, nodded slowly.

"Yes, that sounds good." he said. "How long do you think that would take? Should we meet again in a couple of weeks?"

"I was thinking," said Lisa, "if it's okay with you I would like to meet every morning, like this, for a short time. That way I could get instant feedback from you on a couple of things: whether you like how the work is progressing, and whether I'm translating your ideas faithfully into CDF. Would that be okay?"

Jeffrey was surprised and flattered.

"That seems fine," he said. "I would like to see how things look in this new format. Yes, let's meet then every day at this time."

Lisa asked Jeffrey about a few technical points in chapter one, preparatory to beginning work on a CDF of that chapter.

"Would it be forward of me to make a suggestion?" she asked.

"By all means," said Jeffrey.

"I noticed how much you like coffee. My friend Chris Perry – you met him at the Coffee Depot in Warren – and I are both coffee fans. I notice you don't have your own coffee maker. I was thinking that if you bought a larger one that held several cups of coffee, I could bring in some of the good coffee Chris and I have found when I come to meet with you each day."

Jeffrey was astounded. "Could this be true?" he thought. "A young woman, who appreciates my book, who is technologically literate – a lot more so than me – *and* who appreciates coffee."

Jeffrey thought there might be hope yet for the younger generation.

He smiled at Lisa and said: "Well, yes. I would be happy for you to do that. I'll look into buying a coffee maker this afternoon."

They shook hands and she said: "I think this will be fun!"

"It might be," thought Jeffrey. "It just might be."

♥♥♥♥♥

Jeffrey looked through his email and saw a message from SIAM, the Society of Industrial and Applied Mathematics, inviting him to a meeting in Washington DC at the National Science Foundation on modeling across the first two years of the college science curriculum. He couldn't see that this held much interest, or opportunity, for him. Matrix methods were, of course, very common in applied mathematical modeling, but he suspected the meeting would include the usual suspects involved in differential equations. He could not see accepting the invitation would be of much use to him, and he suspected nothing much would come of such a short one-day meeting. He was about to delete the email when Bob Fosberry knocked at his office door.

"Hi Jeff. How's it going?" asked Bob.

Jeff motioned to Bob to come in and sit down.

"I've just been meeting with a young woman who's working on turning the 9th edition into computable document format," he told Bob. He hoped Bob would not ask him what that really meant. Until Jeffrey saw what Lisa was going to produce he was somewhat in the dark as to what "computable document format" actually meant.

"I heard about this," said Bob. "I think it's a good idea. It will increase the readership quite a lot, I think."

"Well we have to keep up with the times," said Jeffrey. "Technology is everything these days. By the way, I received an invitation to a SIAM meeting in DC. It looks pretty interesting, but I don't think I'm going to be able to go. I guess they asked me because of my standing in the matrix algebra field."

Bob wasn't annoyed at Jeffrey. He figured Jeffrey deserved being recognized for his consistent work over many years. Bob just wished that he had such consistency. If only I could keep plodding, he thought.

"Could you forward me the email?" Bob asked Jeffrey. "I'd be interested to know what comes out of the meeting. Pity you can't go."

"Sure. I'll send you the details," said Jeffrey.

With that he stood up and told Bob he was off to the mall buy a new coffee maker.

14

It's the terroir that makes the difference

❧

Jeffrey did not want a single cup coffee maker like Kathy's Keurig. That he was sure about. He liked Kathy, she was energetic and capable, and her appearance was very pleasing, but she had taken the low road in terms of academic coffee making in his view – missed the point, he thought. Coffee for Jeffrey should be a slow, reflective process, preferably carried out in the company of colleagues. Single cup coffee makers didn't cut it.

He walked into a specialist coffee store and browsed the stock. A 4-cup seemed on the face of it to be about right. He held the carafe up to see it better and changed his mind.

"They're awfully small cups," he thought. "It's really a 2-cup machine in my opinion."

The next size was a 12-cup coffee-maker. Jeffrey wondered why the manufacturers jumped from 4 to 12 cups, without apparently a thought for 6, 8 or 10 cups. The 12-cup machines seemed to hold at least 6 decent cups, and that, he thought, was just what he wanted. Jeffrey's vision was to have coffee on whenever colleagues dropped by. That was how it had been in the days after his Ph.D. and he had yearned for regular department coffee for decades. Lisa, it seemed, was the catalyst to bring this about.

He liked the look of the Cuisinart 12-Cup coffeemaker. It was fully automatic with 24-hour programming capability and high, medium and low temperature controls. How much, he wondered. The tag revealed the price to be $99.95, before tax. Jeffrey frowned. That was way too much, he thought. He was looking for something more in the $40 range. He could not find anything suitable in the specialist store so he decided to go over the road to Target.

At Target he found a range of coffee-makers much more to his liking. One especially caught his eye: the Mr. Coffee 12-cup coffeemaker. It had brew pause and you could customize the brew strength to your taste. He liked that. The price was reasonable too – just on $45. Jeffrey wondered if that price was competitive. He took out his phone and checked the price on Amazon – $39.99 with free postage. Jeffrey thought about saving the $5, but decided against it because of the delay. He wanted the coffee-maker set up for Lisa when she came tomorrow. On the Amazon site he saw a Black and Decker programmable 12-cup coffee maker for $24.99. It did not qualify for free shipping. He wondered if Target had that model. He found the Black and Decker but it was $39.99.

"This is quite a balancing act," thought Jeffrey. "Target has the machines right here, and I can take them with me, but I have to pay tax. Amazon has them cheaper, with no tax, and sometimes – if they are over $25 – with free delivery, but I have to wait."

Jeffrey walked up and down the aisle for a few minutes, thinking this through. Eventually the thrill of the moment seized him and he decided on the Mr. Coffee 12-cup coffee-maker with brew pause and customizable brew strength. Lisa will be impressed, he thought.

♥♥♥♥♥

Lisa De Silva knocked on Jeffrey's door right at the appointed time.

"Come in," smiled Jeffrey. He was keen to show Lisa his new coffee-maker.

"That looks ... fine," said Lisa. "It should do the job."

"It holds 12 cups, and it brews according to your taste. You can interrupt the brewing, too."

Jeffrey's joy was palpable. Lisa added to it by extracting a bag of coffee from her backpack.

"It's Terroir Coffee from Guatemala," she said. It's a medium to light coffee. I know you prefer a darker, bolder coffee, but I thought it might be an idea to start with a lighter coffee that's very high in flavor."

"I do generally prefer a darker brew," said Jeffrey.

"I think, if I may be allowed to say so, Professor Albacete, drinking those darker, bolder brews may have dulled your coffee taste buds a little."

Jeffrey was surprised at this. Not at all insulted, though he did think of himself as somewhat knowledgeable about coffee, if not a connoisseur.

"This Terroir coffee, though light, has a remarkable flavor," said Lisa. "It's incredibly clean, with an almost juicy finish. It has overtones of eucalyptus and dark chocolate. It has a black currant flavor in the background, and it's tart yet smooth. It really is a delightful coffee. I hope you'll like it."

Jeffrey was amazed. "If coffee tasted of eucalyptus, chocolate and black currant," he thought, "then how did we describe chocolate or black currant? In terms of coffee?"

He knew wine connoisseurs used florid terms to describe wine and George Prince was fond of similar terminology to describe his FF – whatever they were – cigars, but what Jeffrey could not understand was how it helped to describe one thing in terms of another, especially when that other was quite different.

"Did he really want his coffee to taste like eucalyptus?" he wondered. "Chocolate maybe, black currant at a pinch, but eucalyptus?" He shuddered involuntarily.

"Is everything alright?" asked Lisa.

"What? Oh, yes," said Jeffrey. "I was just anticipating tasting this most interesting coffee."

Lisa took the coffee carafe to fill with water and came back to put on the coffee. As the hot water dripped through the coffee the aromas began to fill the room. Jeffrey was in heaven. The smell was beautiful, he thought.

"That's quite an aroma," he said to Lisa. "There's a very pleasant, perhaps slightly sharp, yet very clean aroma. Is that .... eucalyptus?" he asked.

"Yes. That's the eucalyptus scent you can smell," she said.

"Do they ...," Jeffrey did not want to display too much ignorance here but he had to ask. "Do they add eucalyptus to the coffee?"

Lisa laughed. "No, the coffee is freshly ground this morning from the beans. The aromas come from the beans themselves, and reflect the soil in which the coffee was grown."

"Like wine?" asked Jeffrey.

"Yes, like wine," said Lisa.

Jeffrey was amazed once again. To think that all these years he had forgone both the pleasure of a pot of coffee ready for any colleague or student who happened by, and the awareness and knowledge of the exquisite aromas of different coffees.

Lisa poured them each a cup of the coffee.

"I got some blueberry muffins too," she said. "I hope you like them."

Jeffrey was silent for a minute, not knowing what to say.

"This is very good, Very good. Well, I guess we can't sit around all day discussing coffee and muffins", he said. "Do you have anything to show me?"

"Yes, I do." said Lisa. "It's just a small start, but it might give you an idea of what's possible in a CDF document. Could I show you on your computer?"

Jeffrey offered her his seat, and pulled up a chair alongside. Jeffrey's monitor was huge, It was attached to a very fast machine – in recent times the best and fastest in the Department. The previous computer coordinator had bought the machine for him under the impression that Jeffery, a self-described computational mathematician, would need a machine with some grunt. It did, as Jeffrey noticed, load web pages and email quite fast.

Lisa opened up a Web browser and went to DropBox. She logged into her DropBox account and opened the Mathematica notebook from the folder she had set up.

"I sent an email to you to share this folder," she said. "Do you have a DropBox account?"

Jeffrey did not. He had been puzzled when the computer had first arrived that there was no port for floppy disks. He had wondered how he was going to get data into and out of the computer. George Prince had shown him how to use a USB stick, which worked well except that he kept leaving them in his shirt pockets and collected them, sometimes weekly, from the laundry that cleaned and pressed his shirts. He was puzzled how Lisa seemed to have accessed her Mathematica notebook on his computer.

"DropBox stores your data or programs – whatever – on their servers," she said. "You can access it either by a browser, as I'm doing now, or by a program that you install on your computer."

"Is that safe?" asked Jeffrey.

"Seems to be," said Lisa "and reliable. What's more you can share folders, and updates to documents or programs synchronize across all computers on which you have DropBox installed. My computer science professors subtract points from our grades if we don't use DropBox – no more excuses of 'the dog ate my USB stick'," she laughed.

Jeffrey was, to use a phrase he had learned in England, gobsmacked. First this incredible coffee – it really was delicious – now this simple way of transferring files from person to person, and Lisa was about to show him what she had done with chapter one. He could barely contain his excitement.

Kathy Riverton knocked at Jeffrey's door.

"Kathy, come in" he said. "You've got to try some coffee!"

15

Endless possibilities

A wonderful aroma of coffee pervaded Jeffrey's office. The smell was slightly sharp, very fresh, yet rich. Kathy was impressed.

"You've got quite the set up here Jeff. It suits you."

"Well, it's mainly due to Lisa", said Jeffrey. "She got me to buy the coffee maker and she brought some amazing coffee to try."

Kathy was impressed again. "Jeff will love you forever if you can supply him with good coffee", laughed Kathy. "I think his book – all 9 editions – is a testament to coffee. Paul Erdös said mathematicians are machines for turning coffee into theorems. In Jeff's case it's turning coffee into books. How are you doing with the CDF version of the book?"

Lisa explained that they had just started.

"I've only done a few things with chapter one: just the bare introduction to matrices. I can show you now if you like."

"I'm going to get myself a cup of this coffee first", said Kathy. "It smells just delicious."

Lisa angled Jeffrey's large monitor so that all three of them could see. She opened up the Mathematica notebook she had created for chapter one. Jeffrey was astonished.

"It looks just like the 9th edition", he said.

Lisa explained that she had set up style sheets in Mathematica to imitate the layout and coloring of the first chapter as best she could.

"I didn't know you could do that in Mathematica", Jeffrey said.

Lisa smiled and thought how common it was that casual Mathematica users saw the software as just a calculating device. She loved the integrated typesetting and computational features, and had her eyes opened to its possibilities when she saw an entire calculus book written in Mathematica.

"Now this is actually pretty simple stuff", she said, as she showed them how, with just a click, the expressions on the page became active and carried out a matrix calculation. Jeffrey was surprised.

"That's impressive", he said. "So the calculation's being carried out in the book?"

"Yes", said Lisa. "That's because the book is a computational document. It's running Mathematica in the background, and that's what's doing the calculations."

Jeffrey frowned.

"But that seems quite a limitation", he said. "Mathematica is not cheap – much more expensive than my book, for instance – and I can't see people running out to buy Mathematica just for my book, as excellent as it is."

Lisa explained to Jeffrey that Wolfram distributed a CDF player as a free browser plugin. Once that was installed in a Web browser you could read CDFs interactively in the browser.

"You don't need Mathematica", she said. "The plugin does the work. And it's free and easy to install."

Jeffrey got up and poured himself another cup of coffee. He had to think about the ramifications of what he had just seen, as simple as the application had been. Multiplying two matrices is pretty straightforward, he thought, but if the software could do it, from within a book viewed in the browser, with no need for expensive software, then there were amazing possibilities for future editions of his book. Jeffrey thought he may have been exaggerating a little, but the thought crossed his mind that this was as momentous an event as Johannes Gutenberg's invention of moveable type.

"I think this has great possibilities", said Kathy. "You know SIAM has a meeting coming up in DC on the mathematics and science curriculum in the first two years of college. The CDF as it is might be a little premature to show at that meeting, but I'm thinking there's an opportunity here to get in on the ground floor of new developments in mathematics education. Have you seen the announcement of that meeting Jeff?"

Jeffrey grimaced.

"Well ... yes. I was invited actually". He managed a smile. "I thought it didn't really seem to be something I would have an interest in, so I told them no."

"Oh, that's too bad", said Kathy. " Well there'll be another opportunity soon, I'm sure. This is an idea that's not going away."

Jeffrey wondered if he had been too hasty in saying no to the SIAM invitation. Perhaps he should have discussed it first with Kathy. It was the thought of all those differential equations people – an area in which Kathy was expert – that had turned him off accepting the invitation. Kathy was right, he thought: there will be other opportunities. Besides, the main focus for him was to get a CDF version, or a good part of one, to show his publishers. If this went well – and he had a feeling it would – then he would be the star presenter at a major conference of his own making, funded by his publisher and Wolfram, and supported by the University. Jeffrey thought he did not need SIAM's penny ante one-day conference.

"I think this is very good", Jeffrey said to Lisa. "What I would like you to do is work on the section dealing with linear equations. If you can get the software to set up the matrices from the equations, and carry out the solution of the equations, all in the book itself, I think that would really impress people."

Lisa thought that would be a fairly straightforward thing to do. She asked Jeffrey if he would like her to write the code while he watched how she did it. She thought that seeing the mechanics of the code might give Jeffrey added insight into what was going on.

"No, that's fine", said Jeffrey. "You go ahead and do it, and we can meet tomorrow. This is very good, and I think we will make great progress. Thank you for the excellent coffee", he said.

Sensing their time was up, Lisa thanked Jeffrey and said good-bye to Kathy.

When Lisa left, Kathy said to Jeffrey: "You're on a winner there."

Jeff agreed.

"She knows a lot about coffee," he said.

Kathy laughed. "That too! I meant the book: the CDF version of it. I think this will really work. It means a new avenue for you." Kathy was thinking of the educational ramifications and the kudos that might flow to the University and he Center if CDF publishing were to really take off.

"You're right," said Jeffrey. "I could probably double my income from the book with a CDF version."

"And that too!" said Kathy. "That's enough to make anyone happy. I'm glad Lisa seems to be working out."

Jeffrey nodded in agreement.

"She is very good in many ways. I'm glad I can pay her to do this work."

Kathy resisted. "*You* can pay her," she thought to herself. "*You* can pay her? *I'm* paying her."

"Jeff, could you excuse me? I think a student is waiting for me." Kathy left Jeff's office quickly.

♥♥♥♥♥

Bob Fosberry had looked over the email sent to him by Jeffrey. Bob thought this might be an excellent opportunity to get back into educational development. SIAM had a lot of clout as a mathematics organization, and their educational ventures were always well thought out. He had hesitated only slightly before sending an email offering himself as a participant in place of Jeffrey. He didn't know that they would want him, but as he recalled an Israeli visitor once saying in a different context, "A 'no' we already got." The worst that could happen, thought Bob, was they could ignore him.

His email pinged and Bob saw it was from SIAM: "Bob, thanks for getting in touch. We're delighted that you can attend the meeting. We look forward to seeing and hearing about your recent work."

So there it was, thought Bob. That easy: I just had to ask.

Bob decided he would not tell Jeffrey about the invitation, not just yet.

16

You can count on it

Kathy bumped into Deborah Duke after coming out of Jeffrey Albacete's office.

"Ooh, ooh ... that ... that man!" said Kathy.

"Who?" asked Deborah.

"Jeff."

"What's he done now?" asked Deborah.

"What he's always done. What he's always doing. Being selfish and self-centered, that's what," said Kathy. She told Deborah about Jeff claiming credit for supporting his assistant Lisa, when the money had come, via Kathy at her initiative, from the Center.

"He does have a habit of behaving like that," said Deborah. "I think in his mind the whole world revolves around him. Look at how he parades that book of his around. It's not a bad book. All the information is there, but it's so darn boring."

"You're right, of course," said Kathy, "but the fact is that Jeff is well known because of it and to many people we are well known because of him."

"Surely not," said Deborah. "Not with all the changes that have been going on around here over the past few years. Look at all the changes you've made, and George, and Rickhart's work, not to mention our younger faculty like Zaq."

"Perceptions change slowly," said Kathy. "Not until some people die will we lose the reputation as a home of matrix algebra. I don't mind that. I like to see the faculty have an influence and impact. It's just that Jeff seems to see nothing else. It's as if the world were one giant matrix."

Deborah laughed at that thought, and Kathy began to smile.

"I shouldn't let him get to me," said Kathy, "and normally I don't. I think that sometimes he goes too far. Did you know, by the way, that he's bought a coffeemaker?"

"What, Jeff? Like yours?" asked Deborah.

"No, not at all. Much fancier: an actual coffee maker. And his assistant Lisa is a coffee aficionada, so Jeff is now set up with first-rate coffee and a real coffee maker, not to mention a smart and attractive assistant. I think he's finally got what he's always wanted."

"Then why didn't he go and get it before?" asked Deborah. "The coffee, I mean."

"I think he's lazy," said Kathy. "And he wants someone else to fuss over him. It's part of his sad sense of self-importance."

Deborah shook her head. It takes all sorts, she thought.

"I need to shoot off," she said. "I'm meeting with Deirdre Nurse and her son Timothy."

"The mathematically gifted little boy? The son of your new vet?" asked Kathy.

"That's the one," said Deborah.

"Lots of luck", said Kathy, "something tells me you'll need it."

♥♥♥♥♥

Deirdre Nurse knocked on the open door of the office Deborah shared. Deborah, alone in the office, got up from her chair and walked over to welcome the woman and little boy.

"Hello, I'm Deborah. You must be Deirdre, and this, I'll bet, is Timothy." She smiled at the little boy who just clung to his mother's hand and looked away.

"Yes, hello. Pleased to meet you Dr. Duke."

Deborah laughed. "Please call me Deborah. I'm not a doctor. Not yet anyway. Maybe in a couple of months."

A slight frown crossed Deirdre Nurse's brow. "I see," she said, "well thank you for seeing us anyway. This is Timothy. Say hello Timothy."

Timothy looked at Deborah but did not speak. Deborah, in assessment mode, was beginning to entertain Asperger's as a possibility. She motioned to Deirdre Nurse to sit down, and said she would like to talk with her for a moment in the hallway. Could Timothy play with Assembler on the computer for a few minutes?

Deborah showed Timothy how Assembler worked. He was instantly captivated, and began moving the blocks on the screen into place.

"He seems to like that," said Deborah. "Let's talk for just a minute."

Deborah led Deirdre Nurse into the hallway, away from Timothy's hearing, and explained that she wanted to ask Timothy some questions. Some of the questions, Deborah explained, might seem very simple for a child as talented as Timothy, but she needed to ask them to get an accurate assessment of where he was in his mathematical development.

"The main thing is that you don't try to answer for him," said Deborah. "I'm trying to assess him, not you, so you need to let him answer on his own. I know this might seem hard, because you naturally want to help him do his best. But if you could just stay silent while I'm asking him questions it would help a great deal."

"Yes, of course," said Deirdre Nurse. "We're in your hands."

"Timothy darling," said Deirdre Nurse, "Dr. ... uh, Miss Duke wants to ask you some questions. Is that OK?"

Timothy wandered around the office without speaking. Deborah pulled out four containers of brightly colored plastic chips.

"Look darling, Miss Duke has some counters for you to play with."

Timothy sat down at the table and tipped out the plastic chips, container by container.

Deborah looked at Deirdre Nurse. "It's OK," she said, "we're just having fun."

"Now pay attention to Miss Duke. She wants to ask you some questions."

Deborah picked up some orange chips. Counted them and put them down on the table.

"Timothy, can you tell me how many chips are there?"

Timothy began to play with the green chips.

"Timothy, Miss Duke asked you a question," said Deirdre Nurse. "Can you count the orange chips for her?"

Timothy glanced at the chips and said: "Nine."

"Good," said Deborah, relieved that Timothy could at least count. He was, she thought, immensely distractible.

Now here's some more orange chips," Deborah said to Timothy, who tried to take them from her hand.

"Timothy, pay attention to Miss Duke," said Deirdre Nurse.

Deborah asked how many chips she had. He counted them one by one and said: "Eight."

Deborah then placed eight orange chips under a black plastic bowl, so Timothy couldn't see them.

"How many chips are under the bowl?" she asked.

"Eight," answered Timothy.

"Good! There's eight under the bowl, and there's nine here in front of you. Is that right?"

Timothy nodded.

"I want you to tell me how many there are in all: eight under the bowl, and nine here in front of you. How many all together?"

Timothy tried to lift the bowl, but Deborah stopped him.

"I want you to tell me without looking under the bowl," she said.

Timothy began to play with the green chips again.

"Timothy darling, can you tell Miss Duke how many orange chips there are altogether?"

Again Timothy tried to lift the bowl. Feeling he was not up to this task, Deborah let him do what he wanted. His eyes darted very quickly and he said: "Seventeen."

Deborah tested Timothy on a few more counting skills, noting that he did not seem to listen to her words, only to those from his mother. She finally asked him if he could count by two's. He nodded.

"Timothy, can you show Miss Duke how you can count by two's?" asked Deirdre Nurse.

Timothy counted: "Two, four, six, eight, ten, twelve, fourteen, sixteen, eighteen, twenty, twenty two, twenty four, twenty six ..." before Deborah stopped him, saying "Very good!"

"Now", said Deborah, "the other day I was counting by two's and I counted to twenty four. Can you tell me how many times I counted?"

Timothy thought, about half as long as a lighting flash, and said: "Twelve."

"Twelve!" repeated Deborah. "That's great! How did you figure that?"

Timothy looked away and began to play with the green chips again.

Deborah turned to Deirdre Nurse and began to discuss with her what she thought about Timothy's mathematical development.

"He has considerable strengths in some areas," she said. "And is average for his age in some others."

As Deborah talked Deirdre Nurse pulled a handful of change from her pocket.

"Timothy, can you tell mommy how much this is?"

Timothy obliged by counting the change. "Ninety eight cents," he said.

Deborah began to suspect shades of an organ-grinder's monkey. She wrapped up the conversation and said she hoped to see Timothy again very soon.

Sensing the meeting was over Timothy looked up at his mother and asked: "Did I do excellent, Mommy?"

"Yes, you did excellent darling."

Deborah saw them out, went back to her office and put her head in her hands. Kathy walked into the office.

"Are you okay, Deb?" she asked.

"Sure, I'm okay", said Deborah, "but I'm not sure about that little boy."

17

The fifth candidate

The Search and Screen committee met with the Assistant Dean to be charged with the Equal Opportunity regulations.

"The main thing," said the Assistant Dean, "is that you treat everyone equally. The questions you can ask candidates have to be approved by the Equal Opportunity Office, and those are the only things you can ask."

"But if a candidate raises an issue we can follow that with a question," said George.

"Yes, exactly," said the Assistant Dean. "However you cannot ask about a candidate's family or country origins, their religion, or even their gender. If the candidates themselves raise an issue about their religion, for example, then you can follow that up, or not, as you wish."

Some of the committee members chuckled at the thought of not asking about gender, but Zaqi cut in.

"This is actually important. When I was a post-doc there were two lecturers in the Department who were transitioning gender. They both started as men. One looked already like a glamorous woman and the other was beginning to wear dresses and had just begun hormone replacement therapy. They were both called Nicole and even lived together. It would be cruel to ask them: '*Are you a man or are you a woman?*'"

The Assistant Dean agreed.

"That's exactly the sort of scenario for which the regulations were designed. These regulations are not State or Federal law. You will not be fined or have to face court if you ask someone their gender or religion, or where they come from," he smiled. "But the simple fact is the candidate search will be cancelled if it is discovered that happened. The University simply cannot afford to even be seen to be acting improperly or unfairly."

The Assistant Dean asked who would be the Committee Chair. Kathy responded that she had the Department Chair's approval to serve as Chair but she would like to hand that responsibility off to Zaqi if the other committee members agreed. Everyone was in agreement so the Assistant Dean said that as soon as he got approval for their list of interview questions the committee could meet to consider applicants.

♥♥♥♥♥

The Search and Screen Committee met the next week. Zaqi reported that there were over 300 applications. The vast majority had come through Math Jobs but there were a handful who submitted hard copy applications. Zaqi and Kathy had spent a couple of days, rating all applications 0, 1, or 2 on the selection criteria, and sorting the applications by rank.

"I think we have about ten really outstanding candidates," said Zaqi as he handed around a printout of his and Kathy's efforts. "We need to look over the entire pool carefully to see if there are some of the top 10 we do not want there, or if there are others we would want in the top 10."

Kathy expressed a view that they should look to interview four, at most five, candidates.

Jeffrey agreed. "Keep the number down," said Jeffrey. "It looks like we have some really strong candidates, several of whom are likely to accept the job if offered it. Search and Screen lunches and dinners are okay but too many of them becomes very tiring."

Kathy proposed they each write down their top four candidates to interview and see if there was general agreement. As Zaqi collected the papers with candidate choices he could see there was remarkable agreement, except for Jeffrey's choice.

"Jeff, would you like to say something about Heinrich Zimmer?" asked Zaqi. "No one else has him on their short list."

"Well, he's very strong in matrix algebra," said Jeffrey. "As you know, I've been trying to get an appointment in matrix algebra for over a decade, but every time I recommend someone, even an outstanding candidate, I get voted down. I just think we have to have a strong matrix algebra candidate on the short list."

A short silence was broken by Kathy's saying that a short list of five would be manageable. She explained to Jeffrey that she too thought Heinrich Zimmer was a strong candidate, she would have placed him fifth on the list.

With Jeffrey mollified and everyone in agreement, Zaqi took the list to the Assistant Dean for him to forward to the Equal Opportunity Office for approval. He also took the list to Donna Ferreira in the Academic Affairs office so she could get a head start on bringing in these candidates for interview as soon as they were approved.

When Zaqi returned, the committee meeting broke up and Jeffrey announced he was going to the gym. Kathy quietly asked the others if they could meet in her office.

"You agreed pretty readily to Heinrich Zimmer," said George. "I'm not sure I want him on the short list at all. I don't think I would want to work with him."

Kathy agreed. "However," she said. "Having Heinrich on the short list will pacify Jeff." George grimaced. "And," said Kathy, "I don't think he will interview as well as the other four, and I'm not sure he really would want to come here. I've heard he's already been interviewing elsewhere and may have a job offer soon. The thing I want to discuss is who we really want."

After some discussion the committee, sans Jeffrey, agreed that Bao Zhang was the outstanding applicant.

"She is very strong in numerical linear algebra," said Zaqi, "and her work has applications to data science. She's got very strong references, including one from Steve Leon at the University of Massachusetts Dartmouth."

George smiled at the thought. "Jeff won't like that. Anyone Steve Leon approves of Jeff is likely to want to nix. You know he and Steve don't get along."

"Why is that?" asked Zaqi.

"It goes back to squabbles on the International Linear Algebra Society", said Kathy. "Jeff didn't like – still doesn't like – how that group focused on vector spaces and structure. Jeff eventually broke away and formed his own society."

"But the International Linear Algebra Society expressly focused on matrix formulations, over abstract vector space notions," said Zaqi.

"They didn't go far enough for Jeff," said Kathy. "He's a purist so far as matrices are concerned. Just start with matrices and operations on them and forget about vector spaces, he says."

"That might have some advantages for a beginner," said Zaqi, "who wants to begin calculations in the most straightforward way, but it's not going to pay off in the long run."

"Whatever the merits or otherwise of Jeff's approach, he's not likely to support Bao Zhang," said Kathy.

"Do we know whether Bao would come if we offered her the job?" asked George. "If she's as hot as she seems, she's bound to have other interviews."

"I think she will come," said Kathy. "She has family here and I know from colleagues at the University of Massachusetts that she's keen to move back to this area."

"Too bad Jeff's not here," said Kathy. "We could have some of his fancy coffee. All I've got is my one-cup Keurig coffee. Anyone for coffee?" she asked.

Zaqi got up to make himself a cup of coffee. At that moment

Jeff arrived, back from the gym. The others were surprised he was back so soon.

"The gym was closed for maintenance," he said. "You can use my coffee maker. It holds at least six good cups, and Lisa brought in some wonderful coffee. Just help yourselves," he said, noticing Zaqi preparing to make coffee.

"By the way, I was on the phone to Heinrich Zimmer and he is very interested in coming here to work with me, so I'm really hoping we can offer him the job."

18

The power of action

⁓∞⁓

The SIAM meeting in DC had gone very well. The first afternoon was devoted to plenary talks, and the following day to working groups to look at different proposals. The theme of the meeting was increasing the mathematical skills of science students through modeling, especially in the first two years of the college curriculum. Bob Fosberry came back energized. The meeting had given him the courage and the platform to talk about his own ideas on modeling in science using matrices. For many years Bob had thought about a freshman course that would introduce students to Markov chains – random models, with memory only of the immediate last phase, that are described by matrices. Markov chains had many applications in science and the DC meeting had clarified and solidified Bob's thoughts on how to construct such a course.

"What's more," he thought, "there will be a lot of grant money for this, resulting from the recent Report to the President by the

President's Council of Advisors on Science and Technology. I can get in on the ground floor here."

Bob bumped into Kathy Riverton and told her about the meeting.

"That sounds great," said Kathy. "Why don't you involve Lori in the project? She could bring in a statistical perspective, and you two could really work well together on a grant."

The thought had not occurred to Bob, but he agreed that Lori had the energy and expertise to help. He liked Lori and thought he could easily work with her.

"I'll do it," he told Kathy. "I don't know what it is, maybe something in the DC air, but I feel so much more ... energized!"

Kathy laughed. "It's making a decision and acting on it, Bob. You're being decisive. That's what's energizing."

"You may be right," said Bob. "Whatever it is I want to keep this feeling. I think I might join the gym and try to lose a few pounds. That can't hurt. Maybe I could go with Jeff?"

Kathy laughed again. "Not a good idea – to go with Jeff, I mean. By all means go to the gym, it will help keep up your energy, but you might steer clear of Jeff. He's a little too fond of lattes and blueberry muffins. You have noticed that his belly seems to be getting bigger?"

Bob smiled and thought Kathy was right. "Okay I'm off to talk with Lori, and then on to joining the gym", said Bob. "Thanks for the advice, Kathy."

♥♥♥♥♥

Lori was surprised to see Bob knock at her office door. He usually kept to himself. "Hi Bob. Come in. What's up?"

Bob explained his enthusiasm for the SIAM meeting and his idea for a novel new course, hopefully one that would be transformative for science students and serve as a model for course development elsewhere. He explained his idea of applying for an upcoming National Science Foundation grant. "These are not going to be big grants – $500,000 over 5 years", said Bob. "But enough to get this project going. I think your expertise in statistics and modeling could be very helpful for the project and I was wondering what you thought about our collaborating?"

Lori was intrigued and flattered. "It's a good idea. Pulling together all the science students in an applied modeling course like this is an attractive notion. I think you will get support across all the science disciplines. And I think it's something the Provost will support."

Lori's thoughts reinforced what Bob was already feeling.

"So ... you'd be willing to work on this with me?" asked Bob.

"More than willing. It's a terrific proposal. I can see it really going places and making a positive impact. But can I ask why me and not Jeff?"

Bob was momentarily stymied. He did not know what Lori knew abut his involvement with Jeff on the matrix algebra project – the project that led directly to Jeff's book, now into it's 9th edition. Bob had put energy back then into working with Jeff, but there were still emotional scars from that time. Bob had not moved forward for quite some time. He did not know how much of this he wanted to share with Lori. Least of all did he want her to see him as bitter and twisted.

"Jeff's busy with his project on developing a CDF version of his book", said Bob. "I think he wouldn't have the time to devote to this project. And he's planning for the Golub memorial conference. Besides, it's not clear how long it will be before Jeff retires. I see this project going a full five years, and beyond."

It was clear to Lori that Bob had made a major life commitment, and she was flattered he had asked her to be part of the project. She agreed to come on board.

"That's great!" said Bob. "That's really great." He felt a rush of endorphins. "I will write out my current plan in detail and email it to you."

"Bob, do you use DropBox?" asked Lori. Bob said he didn't know what it was.

"Here, let me show you", she said. "I will get you started and you can set up a folder for this project that you share with me."

Bob felt better by the minute. Things were moving along. He could feel it.

"Thanks, Lori. Thanks so much", he said. " I'll get that plan to you ASAP."

Bob headed off to the gym first to renew his membership. "It's been a while," he thought. "Too long, really."

♥♥♥♥♥

Lori did some background digging on Markov chains. It was not a field in which she was expert, but she remembered the basics from graduate school. A system could be in a number of states: she remembered the first baby example of rain or no-rain. And from any of those states the system could move to another state with a certain probability. It could be raining today and rain tomorrow with a probability of 0.3, she recalled. Those probabilities came from historical data. A major issue in Markov chains was to determine the long-term behavior of a system.

"This could really work," she thought. "The background knowledge required was minimal, and the concepts could be developed through applications, where they would likely have much more meaning for science students."

George knocked on Lori's office door.

"Oh hi George," she said. "How are you?"

"Fine," said George. "I just dropped by to see if I could pick your brains a bit about my workload model."

"It's funny you should say that," said Lori, "because I think I'm just about to take on another major project."

Lori explained Bob's idea and her likely involvement in it.

"I think this could really work," she said. "And anything that enhances the mathematical skills of science students is going to be a winner. Not to mention the interdisciplinary nature of the course."

"I agree, it's a great idea," said George. "I'm glad for Bob, and for you. He's needed a new direction for some time now."

Lori opened DropBox and extracted the document she had been working on for George.

"I've written down pretty much everything I'm doing," she said. "It surprised me how much it was when I put it all together like that."

"I'm not surprised," said George. "It's why I'm trying to build this workload model, despite Bert's opposition to it. It's clear to me that some people, including most of the junior faculty, are taking on too much. Can you share that document with me now?"

Lori agreed and put the document in the folder she shared with George.

"I will read it later today," said George, "and get back to you. I think I'm close to a first version of a workload mode that actually works!."

"Great!" said Lori. "We're all looking forward to seeing it. Well ... all except Bert!"

George shook his head. "Lazy specimen," he laughed. "He knows he'll show up badly in any rational workload model." George frowned. "You know," he said, "Jeff's not gong to like this project Bob and you have hatched. I will warrant that you have to develop vector space ideas as you progress through this course. Don't get me wrong: I think that's great. Students should learn about these mathematical ideas in context. It helps them anchor their memories. But Jeff won't like it: he wants to see matrices and only matrices all the way down the line."

"Well," Lori laughed. "Perhaps he's going to have to learn to be a bit more flexible."

19

Just like magic

Lisa De Silva was walking Jeffrey Albacete through the CDF version of chapter two of his book. Jeffrey was impressed. His smile widened as she showed him page after page of his book, now written in Computable Document Format, beautifully laid out, and on every page was at least one interactive computational exercise. Jeffrey was delighted to see the computations being carried out, apparently in the book itself, but in reality by the Mathematica engine underlying it.

Lisa cautioned him: cautiously on her part, for he was the professor and she the student. "I think it's a false distinction," she said. "We're so used to thinking of texts as 'books' that we find it hard to come to terms with the idea that text can be computational, and can carry out computations in real time activated within the text."

Jeffrey agreed. "It is hard to come to terms with," he said. "It's truly amazing. I feel like I'm seeing a spot of wizardry from Harry Potter!"

Lisa agreed. "It does feel a bit like Harry Potter," she said. "Some people think that Stephen Wolfram and his brother Conrad, who has really pushed the generic computational aspect of this project, *are* wizards in their own way."

Lisa asked Jeffrey if she should make some coffee. He agreed that would be a good idea. Jeffrey leaned back in his chair, hands behind his head.

"I've been thinking," he said. "We planned to work on producing as much of my *Matrix Algebra* book in CDF as we could by the end of this semester. My aim was to show my publisher and get them excited about this project, and so get them to fund the Golub Retrospective Conference."

Lisa wondered where this was going.

"In my view," said Jeffrey, "and I think I do know a thing or two about this topic ..." He laughed. "I think we have enough with chapters one and two to already knock their socks off."

Lisa wondered if this meant Jeffrey would have no further need for her. She underestimated his need for someone who appreciated his work and his book, a person with excellent technical skills, someone who was a coffee aficionado and appreciated his sensitivity to good coffee, and was pretty to boot. Jeffrey, she could not know, was in pig heaven. "This," he thought, "is how academia should be. At last," he smiled, "at last!"

"I think once my publisher sees this they are going to want to proceed full steam ahead. I am going to get them to see that they should employ you as my technical assistant to complete this project," he said.

Lisa was excited, grateful and apprehensive. "I've never worked for a big publisher – any publisher – before," she said, " I'm not sure I'd know what to do."

Jeffrey reassured her. "They are amazing," he said. "They have so many resources you cannot imagine. They will hire assistants to assist you!"

If anything Lisa was now even more apprehensive. She was seeing a side of Jeffrey that had not been obvious to her. Of course she knew he was an author of a book, one into its 9th edition. But she never thought for a moment what goes on behind the scenes in producing a book like that. If pressed she would have said that the author wrote the book, submitted it to the publisher, it was edited, then printed and distributed somehow to bookstores and to colleges, where students bought it. Someone, she thought, got it up on Amazon as well. But now she was glimpsing there was a much more extensive and detailed process going on to get Jeffrey's book into print. Feeling she might be part of that, even in a small way, was both strange and exciting.

"Do publishers – does your publisher – hire many computer science students," she asked Jeffrey.

"Oh yes, you'd be surprised," he said. "Book publishing is a highly technical and rapidly changing field. I can't keep up with it ... as you are aware," he smiled.

Jeffrey took the coffee that Lisa offered him and thought for a moment. There was no doubt in his mind that his publisher would be thrilled to see what *he* had accomplished so far. He thought he would like to take Lisa with him to a meeting because of her contacts with Wolfram Research. His editor who had suggested – insisted – on a strong technology component to the conference had been right. "Who would have thought?" Jeffrey mused.

"You know," he said to Lisa, " I think we should give a Department seminar on what we've done so far. I would like everyone to know how this project is proceeding."

Lisa was happy to go along with his idea. "Do you want me to put together a short presentation?" she asked.

❤❤❤❤❤

The seminar attracted most of the Department. There were a few graduate students present, and some undergraduates. Jeffrey did not recognize some people who Lisa pointed out, from Computer Science. Jeffrey thought the man at the side of the room, toward the back, was a professor of English. Bert Monod shuffled in and sat at the back of the room.

Jeffrey introduced the topic of the seminar – *Books that Compute* – and handed over the presentation to Lisa. She spoke for about 35 minutes, explaining Computable Document Format and illustrating the ideas with parts of Jeffrey's book.

Kathy Riverton congratulated Jeffrey and Lisa on their work. "This could have a profound effect on how we present all our course material," she said. "Not only that – I would like to get students thinking more computationally from the get-go through writing their own CDF documents."

Lori Bailey raised her hand and said she felt CDF would have a wide application, and potential impact, across campus. "A lot of people use mathematics in their work," she said. "Psychologists, business people, nurses. Even engineers have been known to use mathematics!"

George Prince chimed in: " I can see very wide applications for this. Imagine presenting a report, say, on the effects of rising interest rates on a construction company project. You can imagine a computational model, embedded in a document, changing the printout, so to speak, as different interest rates are entered. "

"Sort of like a spreadsheet on steroids?" said Zaqi.

"Exactly," said George, "except that to a manger the report looks just like a regular report would look, with text and diagrams and charts. The difference being that these diagrams, tables and charts change in real time as new parameters are entered."

"Sounds like Harry Potter to me," muttered Bert Monod from the back of the room.

Zaqi responded: " I think you're right Bert. It is like Harry Potter. It is magic. Documents can come alive computationally speaking. That's magic alright."

Bert shrugged. He hadn't meant it as a compliment.

The English professor raised his hand. "The English Department has a strong program in technical writing," he said. "Probably most of you know that. We, I, would be very interested in partnering with the Department of Mathematics in a project that helped disseminate this remarkable innovation across campus and beyond. I envisage a component in our Masters program. We would need some resources to get this going. I can speak for the

English Department and say I know that we would be more than willing to commit time and money to this." He turned to Bert Monod. "Bert, do you think the Mathematics Department would be able to contribute."

Bert's eyes opened wide and he shook his head from side to side.

"We'll need to ask Harry Potter for his wand if we're going to magically conjure money from our limited budget," he said. "Let's see what Jeffrey's publisher makes of this. Maybe they can come up with some money. For all we know, despite everyone's enthusiasm, this idea might fizzle."

A little voice in Kathy's head said: "We need a new Department Chair."

20

Make mine tea

The Equal Opportunity Office had approved the five candidates on the short list for the new position. Donna Ferreira, the administrative assistant handling the interviewing of the candidates in the Department secretary's absence, had made arrangements for travel, accommodation, meetings with the Department Chair and Dean, lunches and dinners with the candidates, picking them up from the airport and hotels, interview schedules, and numerous other details that went into a smooth hiring process. One of the candidates had emailed to say they had taken another job offer, so the short list shrank to four. Kathy was relieved because it made everyone's work much easier. The immensely talented Bao Zhang and Jeffrey's favorite Heinrich Zimmer were still on the list.

The first of the candidates arrived for interview. John Braithwaite had flown in the night before and caught the shuttle to the Marriott near the University. Zaqi met him for breakfast at the hotel and drove him to meet first with Bert Monod and then with the Dean. John Braithwaite chatted about his work in computational biostatistics and charmed the Department with his understanding of their work and his desire to be a productive member of the Department. His seminar presentation was, rather sadly, a boring affair. There were very few questions from the audience. Dinner was pleasant enough, and Lori drove the candidate back to the airport that night.

"One down," said George the next morning

"It was awful," said Kathy. "He totally bombed. I expected much better from his conversations throughout the day. But that presentation was really terrible. Even Lori said she would find it hard to work with him, despite his working in her area. Seemingly. Oh well, it's good to get the ones who aren't going to fit out of the way. Thank goodness Bao is coming in today."

Rickhart had agreed to pick up Bao from the hotel. He talked with her over breakfast and was so engrossed he almost forgot to get her to Bert Monod and the Dean on time.

"She is one out of the box," Rickhart said to the others. "I can see her working collaboratively with almost everyone in the Department."

"Except Bert," said George. "You mean she will probably work with everyone who actually works."

"Exactly!" Rickhart laughed.

"Rick, do you think you could really work with her?" asked Kathy.

"Sure," said Rickhart. " We could really use a computational linear algebra person. I've got a few projects on hold because we don't have enough expertise in that area."

"That's fantastic," said Kathy, "and of course she will be great for the data science program."

The Department met with Bao over lunch with people coming in and out as their schedules allowed. Bao demonstrated a remarkable personality. At first glance quiet and polite, she had a mercurial wit and an ability to process information rapidly and to bring a wide and deep expertise to numerous topics. Bob Fosberry was charmed.

"I don't know what the other two candidates will be like," he said. "but my money's on Bao. I would love to get her involved with the project Lori and I are planning."

Kathy asked Jeffrey what he thought of Bao.

"She's okay, I guess," said Jeffrey. "I would like it better if her work were more directly in my field. She seems quite personable and energetic. But I think Heinrich will be a better fit for the Department."

Kathy's hands had an almost independent desire to wrap themselves around Jeffrey's neck and choke the life out of him. Kathy folded her arms. "But you did think she was quite talented?"

"Oh yes," said Jeffrey, "but so is Heinrich."

After lunch Bao Zhang met with faculty members who were available and then at 3:00 PM she gave her seminar talk to the Department. Her topic dealt with new ways to overcome ill-conditioning, a property of matrices that makes numerical computations difficult and unstable. She mentioned applications to many areas and impressed the audience with her deep powers of analysis, and broad knowledge of many fields.

"She's dynamite!" Kathy whispered to Zaqi.

George had a question for Bao. "You know we're developing and strengthening our undergraduate and Master's course in data science," he said. " How do you think your work could impact that?"

"Yes, of course," she replied. "My work presented here has mainly to do with numerical analysis whereas data science in most people's view has to do with algorithms for obtaining and statistically analyzing and visualizing data." George nodded agreement.

"Yet in fact, data relationships are most often presented through very large matrices. Very large." She looked at George, who agreed. "The numerical behavior of these large matrices, their numerical stability, is critical to the integrity of the data and its analysis. Not too much attention has been paid to this fact, and it is why some data science applications have been less successful."

"Thank you," said George. "Thank you very much."

Jeffrey, sitting at the back of the room, was noncommittal.

Kathy asked Bert Monod what he thought of Bao's presentation.

"She's very lively," said Bert. "Very attractive. As good as anyone, I guess"

"Whatever," Kathy thought to herself.

Dinner that evening was a lively affair with much laughter, stimulated in good measure by the excellent wines that George had chosen. Lori drove Bao to the airport and Kathy bade her farewell, telling her they would be in touch within a week.

♥♥♥♥♥

Two days later Heinrich Zimmer flew in for interview. Lori met him at the hotel for breakfast and drove him to the University for the obligatory meetings with the Department Chair and Dean.

"How was he?" asked Kathy.

"Well, he was ... interesting", said Lori.

"Interesting?" asked George. "Interesting? Can't you do better than that?"

"I didn't mean it in a derogatory way," said Lori. "He really is interesting. He talked a lot about his different interests. He's actually quite charming. He's a little more formal than I expected, but not at all stuffy. He's ... well, he's interesting!" she said.

"Can't wait to meet him," said George. "By the way, he's been with the Dean for over an hour. That's a good sign for him. She keeps the 'interesting' ones longer," he laughed.

The Dean brought Heinrich to Kathy's office for his interview with the Search and Screen committee.

"Here is the candidate," she said. "A most interesting candidate. I must say. Your in good hands now Dr. Zimmer."

"Thank you so much Dean Nueberg," said Heinrich Zimmer. "It was a pleasure meeting you."

"And likewise," said the Dean. "Most interesting ..." she muttered as she walked off.

Kathy showed Heinrich to the room where they would conduct the interview. Not everyone was present yet, so she chatted to Heinrich about procedure, explaining that they could ask only set questions and they would ask them in exactly the same order for all candidates. He, on the other hand, could ask them anything he wanted, and if he felt there was a question he would like the committee to ask him, he simply had to raise the topic. They were then free to respond accordingly. It was a question of equity, Kathy explained. We have to treat all candidates fairly and equally.

"I understand," said Heinrich, thinking of past interviews. "If I am guessing correctly, you cannot even ask if I am a man or a woman!"

They all laughed. "You got it in one," said George.

Jeffrey came into the room and shook hands with Heinrich. "It's a pleasure to have you here for interview," he said. "Would you like some coffee? I have some excellent coffee brewing, thanks to my new assistant."

"Thank you very much, but no, I prefer tea," said Heinrich. "If you do not have any it's okay: I always carry some with me," he said reaching into his briefcase. "I'm something of a tea aficionado."

Jeffrey was taken by surprise. "How ... how interesting," he thought.

21

What does the
Dean think?

Heinrich Zimmer interviewed very well. He was, as Lori had described him, slightly formal but not at all stuffy, and very interesting.

"Are there any questions you want to put to us?" asked Zaqi as Chair of the committee.

"Yes, thank you," said Heinrich. "I would like to ask how you see the role of matrix algebra developing in the Department. How it fits in with other activities."

All eyes turned to Jeffrey.

"Well, that's a very good question," said Jeffrey, "because to a very large degree I *am* matrix algebra."

Heinrich smiled, and waited. Jeffrey explained about his time at Stanford: how he was influenced by Gene Golub and his book on matrix computations, how he had obtained a grant that allowed him and Bob Fosberry to develop a new curriculum, and how that led to Jeffrey's matrix algebra book. "Now in its 9th edition," added Jeffrey.

"Yes, thank you Professor Albacete. I am, of course, aware of your book and the developments that led to its success. I was thinking more of future directions."

Jeffrey was momentarily stumped. There would be a 10th edition in due course. Then he remembered. "There are some very exciting technological developments," he said. "I'm working on a computable document format edition of *Matrix Algebra*. It's early days, but what we have already is very promising."

"That is indeed very interesting, Professor Albacete," said Heinrich. "I very much look forward to seeing this version of your influential book. I was thinking more, however, of how matrix algebra fits in, or does not, with the research of the Department."

Jeffrey turned to the other committee members. Rickhart was first to speak. He explained that while much of his current research was analytical, there were a number of difficult matrix algebra problems that were holding up aspects of his research program. Heinrich thanked Rickhart for this information. "That is excellent," he said. "It is what I was hoping for. Matrix algebra has its own fascinating problems." He turned to Jeffrey and smiled, with a nod of his head. "My interests lie more in the intersection of matrix algebra with significant applied mathematical problems."

"I do have a lot of applications in my book," Jeffrey chimed in.

"Just so, Professor Albacete," said Heinrich. "And it is those applications that I am most keen to hear about and to pursue, should the committee be so kind as to recommend my appointment."

"Very interesting," said George.

There were no further questions from Heinrich and time was pressing, so Zaqi called the interview to a close.

"The next item on the agenda is your seminar," said Zaqi to Heinrich. "That will be in 30 minutes time if you would like to freshen up beforehand."

The committee meeting adjourned and left Heinrich to prepare for his talk.

An hour and a half later, Heinrich's seminar talk was judged to be a resounding success. Everyone said so.

"I was blown away," said Kathy, "and I don't say that too often."

That seemed to be the consensus of those at Heinrich's talk. He had displayed a very deep understanding of how matrix algebra impacted numerous significant applied problems.

"I feel," said Rickhart, "that in his own way he is as talented as Bao Zhang."

The other Search and Screen committee members agreed.

"One more to interview and then decision time," said George.

Zaqi, who had left immediately following Heinrich's talk to see Donna Ferreira came back to tell them of a new development: the fourth candidate had pulled out, as a result of another job offer.

"And then there were three!" said George.

"Let's meet tomorrow morning, first thing," said Kathy. "Zaq, do you think it's possible we can meet with the Dean around 10:00 AM?"

"I can try," said Zaqi who went immediately to the Dean's office.

Heinrich had a meeting with some of the graduate and undergraduate students. Following that, the Search and Screen committee went to dinner with him where Rickhart volunteered to drive Heinrich to the airport.

❤❤❤❤❤

The Search and Screen committee was due to meet at 8:00AM the next morning.

Kathy, George, Rickhart and Zaqi met a few minutes earlier to discuss the situation. They agreed Bao was their unanimous choice.

"She's further along in her development," said Kathy. "She has a very mature research program. That's not to say Heinrich was anything other than tremendously impressive. I just think on balance Bao would slot better immediately into the Department."

Rickhart agreed. "Heinrich is a very strong candidate and he is developing very deep and broad research interests that impact all of us. But I also think Bao is just that extra bit ahead."

The meeting began promptly when Jeffrey arrived at 8 sharp. He was a little out of breath and hung his coat behind the door.

'Would you like coffee, Jeff," asked Kathy.

"Yes, thanks, that would be good," said Jeffrey.

Zaqi volunteered to make the coffee. The committee discussed in an informal way the merits of the three candidates they had interviewed. John Braithwaite, they all agreed, would not be on the list forwarded to the Dean.

Zaqi asked each person in turn to indicate how they ranked the candidates. He reminded everyone of the instructions from the Assistant Dean: while the committee was charged to provide the Dean with an unranked pool from which she could choose who to appoint, the Dean wanted the committee's frank opinion as to who they saw as the best applicant for the job.

Kathy indicated Bao Zhang first, Heinrich Zimmer second, and John Braithwaite not on the list to go to the Dean. George and Rickhart agreed. Jeffrey was visibly disturbed.

"I feel Heinrich is an outstanding candidate," he said. "And I've waited more than fifteen years to get someone appointed in matrix algebra. Every time a candidate in my area comes up they get voted down by the committee."

Zaqi thought Jeffrey was about to cry.

Kathy spoke up. "It's not that we don't think Heinrich is an outstanding candidate, Jeff. We do. We appreciate he is in your area and could work immediately with you. He gave an outstanding seminar talk, in which it was clear he could work with many others in the Department. However, Bao Zhang is a slightly better fit, and is slightly more advanced in her research. On balance she is a better fit, but only by a small margin."

Jeffrey was very upset. "I intend to make my views clear to the Dean," he said. "I will not be around here forever and we need someone in the Department, other than me, who is expert in matrix algebra."

Kathy hoped this would not turn into an open fight in front of the Dean. Zaqi announced that the Dean could meet with them at 10:00 AM for one hour. Jeffrey went to his office and the others stayed talking for a few minutes before heading back to their own offices preparatory to meeting with the Dean.

At the appointed time the Search and Screen committee filed into the Dean's meeting room. She appeared from her office and bade them all good morning. Dean Nueberg asked if they had a list of recommended candidates. Zaqi presented her with the names of Bao Zhang and Heinrich Zimmer.

"Only two?" asked the Dean. "You are aware that if neither of these two accept an offer the search will fail? I am not allowed go back to the larger pool and look for other suitable candidates."

Zaqi said they understood. These two were the only candidates the committee felt were appointable. He told the Dean that the committee ranked Bao Zhang first and Heinrich Zimmer second. The Dean asked if that decision was unanimous.

"No it was not," said Zaqi.

"And I want to say something about that," said Jeffrey. "I want to register my deep opposition to the ranking of Heinrich Zimmer as second choice. He is not my second choice. He is an exceptional candidate and he works in my area, an area that has needed someone like him for a very long time."

"I see," said the Dean. "Well here are my thoughts. I have interviewed many, many candidates for academic positions in this School over the years I have been Dean. In my view Heinrich Zimmer is an exceptional candidate. One of the most interesting I have had the pleasure to talk with."

Jeffrey looked at the other members of the Search and Screen committee as if to say: "I told you so!"

22

Get the Department moving

Dean Susan Nueberg again asked the committee if Bao Zhang was their first choice, ahead of Heinrich Zimmer. They all agreed, except for Jeffrey who again made his views on the matter known to the Dean.

"I respect your decision," said Dean Nueberg, "so I will set the wheels in motion to contact Dr. Zhang to discuss an offer."

Jeffrey was visibly upset. The rest of the committee was relieved. Dean Nueberg then said something they could not have anticipated but were in fact prepared to raise: the possibility of two appointments.

"I think you have two exceptionally well qualified candidates here," she said, "and I will do my best to argue to the Provost for two positions."

The committee, except for Jeffrey, was delighted. Jeffrey could see a faint ray of hope that Heinrich Zimmer might be offered the position – *a* position – but he could see nothing more than a faint possibility yet.

"This University has plenty of money," said the Dean. "I don't know that I should be saying this, but ... well, it's true that so much money, many millions of dollars, is spent on activities that have no direct bearing on the education of our students. I believe there is money to support this extra appointment. I know the Board of Trustees, as well as the Board of Higher Education, is keen to develop computational science. They see it as a corner-stone of growth in science and engineering. I cannot promise any-thing, but I will talk to the Provost today."

This was better than any of the committee, except Jeffrey, could have hoped for. They felt euphoric as they left the meeting with the Dean. George thought he might have to revise his opin-ion of her. Jeffrey went back to his office and shut the door, a sure sign that he did not want to discuss anything.

News of the Dean's decision spread rapidly throughout the Department. Bob Fosberry met up with Lori and asked if she had heard.

"I have. It's great news," she said. "It will mean a lot to have those two energetic and talented young people on board."

Bob was thinking. "I wonder if either, or both, of them would be interested in our curriculum project?"

"Hard to say," said Lori. "They will have their own projects going when they arrive. What are you thinking?"

"I'm thinking if we can get them on board now – a commit-ment from them – it will strengthen our application for funding tremendously. And it will mean the project is owned more by the Department."

Bob's hopes were rising. The past fears and discontent that came from working with Jeffrey on the matrix algebra project were being replaced by strong little shoots of hope and possibilities. He could see now that this might work and turn into something of which he could be proud.

♥♥♥♥♥

Bert Monod was surprised to get the phone call from Carlisle Caruthers, Head of the Equal Opportunity Office, asking Bert to come for a meeting. What could Carlisle Caruthers want from him? Bert wondered. Must have been one of the part-time instructors saying something to upset the students, again, he imagined. Carlisle waved Bert into his office.

"Thanks for coming Bert. Sit down. I guess you're wondering why I asked you here?"

Bert nodded. "I'm guessing something to do with instructors saying inappropriate things to students."

Carlisle smiled. "We always have those complaints. Usually, thank goodness, they're dealt with by Department Chairs, such as yourself, or by the Deans. No, this has to do with a couple of comments you made in relation to a recent applicant for a job."

Bert was puzzled. There was only the job search just concluded and there were only three candidates interviewed. He could not recall saying anything to any of them that could be taken as offensive. "I'm at a loss", he said. "I don't know what you mean."

"What I mean," said Carlisle Caruthers, "is that you apparently said that even if one of the candidates would come, she was likely to get pregnant and so be not much use to the Department. You then went on to comment unfavorably on her ethnicity."

Bert was surprised. "But that is almost certainly what would happen," he said, " She's young and married. What do you expect?"

"The thing is Bert, that is totally out of line. It is irrelevant to her job prospects and job functioning whether or not she is or becomes pregnant. She has certain rights, and in saying what you did you are coming perilously close to denying her those rights."

Bert shrugged as if to say: "Whatever." He couldn't see why Carlisle was making such a fuss. He probably has to, thought Bert. What else has he got to do?

"Then there is the matter of reference to the candidate's ethnicity. While that does not impact her rights, it is counter to University policy. Had I heard about this earlier the search might have been cancelled. Fortunately for the Department, the outcome will stand."

Bert thought Carlisle had lost his marbles, but seeing the look on Carlisle's face Bert began to sense he might be in hot water.

"This matter was raised with me by someone who overheard these comments, and not by the candidate herself. So there is no official complaint, as such." Bert nodded, sensing things might not be as bad as he thought. "However," said Carlisle, "I take these comments very seriously, and I am going to ask that you undergo a short course of training. It is unacceptable that representatives of this University even think this way, let alone utter such comments."

"You're asking me or telling me?" asked Bert.

Carlisle's face was thunderous. "I am asking," he said. "But if you would like me to initiate proceedings so that you are ordered to do this then I will gladly do just that."

"No, no need," said Bert. "Let me know where and when. Is that all?"

The meeting terminated and Bert made his way back to the Department. Damned place is getting too politically correct, he thought. There was a day when we could express what we felt. When he began working here, decades earlier, he reflected there weren't even any women in the Department.

♥♥♥♥♥

"What's up with Bert?" George asked Kathy. "He seems out of sorts."

"I don't know this for sure," said Kathy, "but I've heard that he got dressed down by Carlisle Caruthers over some remarks he made. Rumor is, he has to go to sensitivity training."

George laughed. "The universe is not old enough for Bert to learn how to be sensitive. Isn't it about time he retired?"

"I've been thinking that with increasing frequency," said Kathy. "He's still got a few years to go as Department Chair. We have the numbers to push him out, but I'm reluctant to start an open fight. I doubt he would go just because we ask."

George was more combative. Perhaps it was due to his daily bike rides fending off aggressive motorists, or his regular consumption of Islay whisky, or his cigar smoking, or, more likely, just his nature. "I think we should give him the heave-ho," said George. "I for one will be glad to see the back of him."

"He does serve one purpose," said Kathy. "He does at least do the administrative work that needs to be done. Who else among us is willing to do that?"

"Ha!" said George. "But he has no vision for the Department. None. And he does not take our case to the Dean. In my view he's a waste of space."

As they pondered a potential Department Chair, Rickhart came by Kathy's office.

"So I heard about Bert's little run in with Carlisle Caruthers", he laughed. "About time for a new Department Chair, eh? That's a job I think I could do for a few years. Get the Department moving along. What do you think?"

23

The origin of words

Kathy's eyes opened wide and she was momentarily speechless. She thought she must have misheard Rickhart. He had a very busy teaching and research schedule, with several graduate students working in his lab. His research administration was already high. How, she thought, did he imagine he could take on the extra responsibilities of Department Chair?

George, somewhat surprised by Rickhart's announcement, was thinking that Bert managed to get by as Department Chair without apparently doing anything. On the other hand, Rickhart seemed to be suggesting he wanted to put some energy and vision into the job.

"Don't you think I could do it?" asked Rickhart. "The Department needs to focus on a strategic plan, with a vision for how it's going to grow and develop."

Kathy and George reassured Rickhart that they thought he had the right attributes for the job. "Who could be worse than Bert?" asked George. However they didn't see how Rickhart could find the time to devote to the job, without giving up some of his other activities.

"I have a plan," said Rickhart. "I intend to streamline much of what we do. Cut away the silly tedious chores that are irrelevant to our core functioning. Then I intend to work on developing a clear vision for the short and long term development of the Department. And then I intend to delegate. Heavily!"

"In other words," said George, "you want to share the administrative workload around the Department?"

Rickhart agreed. "And I want us to understand clearly where it is that we are headed and why," he said.

Kathy conceded Rickhart had a point, yet she was concerned his decision meant there could be open fighting in the Department. "Rick, you know there are people in the Department who support Bert. It's convenient for them. They are cozy with his lazy hands-off style of administration. They won't want to see change."

"But we have the numbers to defeat them," said Rickhart.

"True," said Kathy, "but to get rid of Bert we have to petition the Dean and get the Chancellor involved. It's an inherently messy process."

George was thinking. "Unless," he said, "we can convince Bert to step down."

"That would be ideal," said Kathy. "But I don't see how. He's got a cozy job, from his point of view: a stipend for being Department Chair, a reduction in his teaching load, he doesn't do research, his teaching is laissez-faire, he doesn't do what Rick says needs to be done in developing a vision for the Department, and he has a thick hide to boot. Nothing seems to get to him."

"Well there is this recent trouble he got himself into," said George.

"Like I said," Kathy iterated, "he has a thick hide. He will go to sensitivity training classes – what a joke! – shrug it off, and carry on as before. We would need a serious scandal for Bert to step down as Chair, and then we're talking about him possibly resigning from the University."

"Not before time," said George.

♥♥♥♥♥

Bert Monod made his way to the offices of the psychological counseling service in Providence. He couldn't help but reflect what a total waste of time this was. How did the world come to be so politically correct? All he did was speak the truth. He knew he was correct. It wasn't as if he had prejudices, or an axe to grind. He was just telling it as it was. Bert sighed. Maybe I'm just getting too old for all of this, he thought.

He found the building located in the center of Providence, not far from the Providence Place Mall, and scanned the notice board for the floor of the offices to which he had to go. He found the elevator and made his way to the third floor. The elevator doors opened to reveal the offices of PSI Cognitive Counseling Services. He opened the door to the office and walked up to the reception desk.

"Can I help you?" asked the receptionist.

"I have an appointment for counseling," said Bert.

"And your name is?" asked the receptionist. "Bert Monod" he replied. "Ah, yes. Mr. Monod you can take a seat. Ms. Robinson will be with you shortly. There are a few others yet to arrive."

Bert guessed that the reference to "a few others" meant he would be in some sort of group session. Great, just great, he thought. In futre I need to keep my mouth shut.

"Do I have to fill out any forms?" he asked the receptionist.

"No, that's all been taken care of by the University," she said.

Bert was feeling more and more out of his comfort zone. He sat in one of the chairs lined in rows, and picked up a magazine. He was just chuckling at a joke in the magazine when a woman called his name. He stood up and walked toward her.

"Mr. Monod," she said. "And how are you today?"

Bert was stumped for an answer.

"Come through," she said, "I'm Wendy Robinson. I will be your counselor."

Bert followed her into a room where two other people were seated. Wendy Robinson introduced the three and said there were two more to join them. A man and a woman arrived as she was making introductions.

"Good! We're all here," said the counselor. "Let's begin. You are all here not because you chose to be, but because someone in your workplace suggested – perhaps strongly so – that you should be here. Is that more or less correct?" she asked. Everyone in the group nodded agreement.

"This short counseling session will last for four half-days: two of them back to back today, and two on separate half days later this week. I appreciate your taking time from your busy schedules for this," she said. "But then I guess you had little choice."

Bert thought that for a sensitivity counselor she could be a bit more sensitive.

"The aim of our time together is to raise awareness of the issues that see you here today, and to heighten awareness of sensitivity to others. The format, as you have probably already guessed, is a group session. Our experience is that after the initial shyness wears off, the group setting is very conducive to bringing awareness to the forefront of your minds."

Wendy Robinson had the group talk a little about themselves, one by one. Bert was surprised to learn that the others were either senior executives in industry or academic administrators like himself. Political correctness insinuates itself everywhere, he thought, like a spreading fractal.

"So now we get down to why we think we are here," said Wendy Robinson. "Bert, would you like to start?"

"No I wouldn't!" thought Bert to himself. He sighed.

"I appreciate this can be difficult," said Wendy Robinson. "However you will find it helps to get it out. It rarely seems so bad when you do."

Bert shrugged and his mouth tightened. "I made a remark – an honest one – about a candidate for a job being likely to get pregnant", he said. "And I might have mentioned that her appointment would mean another person of her ethnicity in the department. All true!" he said.

"Thank you for your candor Bert," said Wendy Robinson. "I know that wasn't easy. What do the rest of you think about what Bert said?"

The others agreed that Bert simply seemed to be telling it like it was. "What's wrong with honesty?" one man asked. "We didn't get where we are in life without being candid." Others nodded.

"What do you think, Bert?" Wendy Robinson asked him. "Do you think it was okay to think the things you did?"

Bert was surprised. "To think them?" he asked.

"Yes. To think them," she repeated.

Bert was astonished. Now this counselor was getting at his thoughts. Political correctness was bad enough, he thought. It maybe even ran counter to the constitution. But my thoughts? Now we have the thought police?

"I don't see what my thoughts have to do with it," he said. "I'm here because of what I *said*, that someone took offense to. Not because of what I thought."

"Bert," she responded, "where do you imagine your words come from?"

24

You can't argue with the Etteretningsbataljonen

❧

Bert Monod decided to take advantage of the lunch break between sensitivity counseling sessions and walk up and over the road to lunch at P.F. Chang's, just inside the Mall. Some Asian dumplings and a glass of wine will put me in a better mood, he thought. Bert had a desperate need to feel in a better mood: the morning session had unnerved him with a focus on thought processes. As he crossed the road it dawned on him why the word 'cognitive' was in the title of the counseling service: *PSI Cognitive Counseling Service*. It's brainwashing! he thought. That thought was pushed aside by a sudden inexplicable feeling of disorientation. Bert felt as if he were walking into a brick wall. He was confused. The noise was awful.

Bert was awakened by someone asking if he could hear them. He nodded assent. "What ... what's going on?" he asked.

"You've been in an accident", the voice said. "You're okay, but we need to get you to hospital."

The paramedics put Bert in the ambulance and stabilized him.

"What happened to me?" asked Bert.

"You were hit by a Providence trolley", one of the paramedics said. "One of those red tourist trolleys. You must not have been looking as you crossed the road."

"Am I okay?" asked Bert.

"Yep, you'll survive", said the paramedic. "It's looking to us like a fractured pelvis. We'll know more when we get you to the hospital for X-rays."

Bert began to reflect on his situation, under the influence of pain medication. "No dumplings and wine for lunch", he thought, "but at least I get out of this afternoon's counseling session!" He relaxed into sleep.

♥♥♥♥♥

News of Bert's hospitalization spread rapidly around the Department.

"We need to send flowers," said Kathy. "I will order them and everyone can contribute directly to me. I'll drop by the hospital this afternoon on the way home."

George agreed. "I'll come with you," he said. "The saving grace, I guess, is that he's in very good hands in Rhode Island Hospital. I'm feeling sort of bad about the thoughts I've been having about him recently."

"Don't be silly," said Kathy. "Just because he's been banged up with what seems to be a broken pelvis doesn't suddenly make him a good Department Chair. Sympathy is one thing, sound judgment is another."

"Rick might have to step up as Department Chair now," said George. "If it is a broken pelvis Bert will be laid up for several months. He's not going to be back at work any time soon."

Kathy phoned the florist to have flowers and a card sent to Bert from the Department. Then she went looking for Rickhart.

"Have you hard the news about Bert?" she asked.

"Yes, I have. That's too bad. The poor fellow gets sent to a humiliating sensitivity training and then this. I can't imagine how poorly he feels. He's a lousy Chairperson, but I would never wish this on him."

"Will you put your name forward as Chairperson?" asked Kathy.

"You know, I will. Nothing's changed so far as my thoughts on the Department's future are concerned. We still need vision and direction, and this unfortunate accident might give us the opportunity to focus on that."

Kathy reminded Rickhart that not everyone in the Department would want to see him as Chairperson. Even with Bert out of action because of a fractured pelvis, if that was in fact what it was, some of the more senior faculty were happy with Bert's hands-off attitude to administration. They would not be happy with the activist program Rickhart was proposing. "Inger Hansen will be very vocal about your running for Chairperson," said Kathy.

"I will go and talk with her," said Rickhart, knowing full well that one did not talk to, or with, Inger. Rather one spoke and then waited for the torrential onslaught of words that constituted her version of dialog.

Rickhart remembered the time he met Inger when he arrived in the Department. She had buttonholed him about economic problems in Scandinavia, issues related to the European Economic Union, and how she could solve all those problems herself. "But I am too tired," she had said. Years later Rickhart still laughed at this conversation with Inger. Her tough attitude, he discovered, was a result of her work in the Norwegian Army. She was an intelligence officer in the Etteretningsbataljonen, stationed at Setermoen in Troms county. Rickhart had respect for Inger and her past, but he thought she was an obstacle to moving the Department forward. She had made noises recently about retiring, but Rickhart could not see what incentive there was for her to do so. So long as Bert put no pressure on her to perform, so long as his evaluations of her were always high, she could coast along doing very little and still drawing her Full Professor's salary. "I know why many people outside of universities think that tenure should be abolished," he thought.

Rickhart knocked on Inger's door. "Hi Inger," he said. "Do you have a minute?"

Inger motioned to him to come in and sit down. "It's about Bert, yes?" she asked.

"Indirectly," replied Rickhart.

"Such a terrible thing to happen to such a nice man. He is always so nice to everyone and now this awful thing happens to him just because he had to go to this ridiculous counseling. For what? Is he not allowed any more to speak his mind? He has many years of experience and knows from that experience how people will behave. Of course a young married woman is likely to become pregnant. And why he should not say that? I think the world has gone mad. And now who is going to be Chairperson, since he will have to rest for many months?"

Rickhart was about to speak when Inger went on: "Will you be running for Chairperson? I am not very happy about that as you probably know. We have to put up with much in this University. The administration is always trying to take away from us. When I came here things were different. We were expected only to teach and that was it. It was in our contract. Now everyone has always to be doing research and getting grants. Writing papers, for what? Who reads these papers? Only other academics who are also writing papers and getting grants. So what will you do about that?"

Rickhart had to admit defeat. He was stumped in trying to answer her. "Yes Inger, I will be running for Department Chair. I have some ideas I would like to see put in place. I would like to develop a vision for where we are going and why," he said.

"Well we all like to know where we are going," she said to him. "I was in the intelligence brigade of the Norwegian Army, you know, and it was important to know where we were headed and why. But already people here are working too much for too little and always the administration is asking people to do more. We are hiring young people who are hungry for tenure and who are writing seven or eight papers a year, and getting grants. I am not so young anymore. I am tired. It is not fair of the administration to be asking more and more of me. And if you are Chairperson that is what will be happening."

Rickhart explained, very gently, his vision for the Department. He explained how a workload model was very important so each person in the Department was doing what he or she did best, for the betterment of the Department and the students. "You have a very important role to play in this Department," he reassured her. You are not active in research and do not want to be, yet your scholarship is profound. You have much to offer students. We need to be re-thinking our course offerings so that you and others in the Department are utilizing your talents to better educate our students."

Inger thanked Rickhart for his words. "Okay, I support you if we can do like you say," she said. Relieved, Rickhart thanked Inger for her time and left her office. He bumped into George on the way back to his office.

"I've just been talking with Inger," said Rickhart.

"Oh yes. And how did that go?", asked George.

"She said she would agree to supporting me as Department Chair. I had to listen to a torrent from her, but I think in the end she knows change is inevitable. She's scared is all. Well, that and a little tired."

Deborah came around the corner and saw George and Rickhart. "It's official," she said. "Broken pelvis. Out for six moths minimum."

George extended his hand to Rickhart. "Congratulations Mr. Chairperson."

25

Dreaming of Alex and Ani

Lisa De Silva loved living in Wayland Square, Providence. The village feel of the Square outweighed the distance from the University: a 20 minute drive, or an hour bike ride. There was a coffee shop, three restaurants and an Irish pub, McBride's, as well as specialty stores and a second hand bookstore.

That morning Lisa was drinking a coffee and eating a pastry in L'Artisan Bakery. The coffee was good – Illy – but not outstanding, like her favorite Terroir. Illy was also an understated coffee, and one needed to be careful with sugar and cream that could dominate the subtle flavor. L'Artisan had wireless and she was working on CDF versions of Professor Albacete's book chapters before meeting friends later at McBride's pub. The work was going well, she thought, despite the turgid nature of his prose. The coffee shop was getting crowded and she was finding it hard to think and work so she packed up her laptop and wandered across the road to Alex and Ani to browse the jewelry. In a flight of fancy, she thought that if the job with Professor

Albacete's publisher came off she would come back to Alex and Ani and spend – let's see, she thought, ten times $58 for the Swarovski crystal bracelets, plus tax – about $600 on jewelry for herself. Lisa spent a good forty minutes browsing the jewelry before heading over the road to Wayland Square Fine Wine and Spirits. She was especially keen to browse their selection of Grüner Veltliner. Her friend Chris had introduced her to Grüner, saying he thought she might like it better than the New Zealand Sauvignon Blanc she was drinking regularly, and a lot cheaper to boot. She found the Grüner toward the back of the store and browsed what they had in stock. She liked the look of the Laurenz V Charming 2010 at $29.99 a bottle but, restricted by her budget, chose the Markus Huber Hugo 2010 at $10.79 a bottle.

"One day," she thought, "one day, I will visit Prague and cycle and train down to Vienna through the vineyards in the north of Austria and drink Grüner until it comes out my ears!"

She looked at the time, paid for the wine and hurried over to McBride's pub where her friends would be waiting. Chris was there with two other friends, Megan and Danny, who were mathematics students at Brown. They waved to her as she came into the pub.

"Hi guys," she said. "I'll just order a Guiness."

"We already ordered it", laughed Megan. "We saw you coming across the road from the wine store. What did you get?"

"What else?" she said. "Grüner. Chris won't let me go back to Sauvignon Blanc."

"As if I could stop you!" said Chris. "But seriously, you do like the Grüner don't you?"

"I'm only *dreaming* of going to Austria!" she said.

"How's the work going for Professor Albacete?" asked Danny.

"It's good. I'm making great progress. I have to revise a lot because after I write a version of a CDF and show it to him so many more ideas come to mind. It's sort of a cyclical process of improvement."

"Do you think the job with his publisher might come off?" asked Megan.

"I think it might," said Lisa. "We've sent them a couple of chapters and they seem quite excited. It's a matter of doing a commercial deal with Wolfram."

"Wow! You'll soon be the big-time corporate executive," laughed Megan. "Remember us when you're making a million a year."

"It's a textbook," said Lisa. "And I'm just a technical assistant. Or will be, I hope. The thing is, his prose is pretty dreadful – quite boring in fact. I wish I could jazz it up a bit. You know, write more like the kids he's trying to teach would understand and appreciate."

At that point Lisa became aware that George Prince was sitting a couple of tables away and could hear her. He waved and came over.

"Hi Lisa," he said. "Didn't expect to bump into you here, but no surprise really – you live around here, don't you?"

Lisa indicated she did, and felt embarrassed that George had heard her comments about Jeffrey's book.

"I have to say I agree with you completely," said George. "It is an intensely boring book, and somewhat pretentious in tone, to my way of thinking."

Lisa was relieved. "Do you think so?" she said.

"I do," said George, "and so do his students. He has been teaching a course from that book for over twenty-five years, and so far as any one can tell, hasn't changed a thing in all that time. Semester after semester students vote his course as the most boring they have taken or ever expect to take."

"It doesn't have to be that way, though," said Lisa. "It could be quite interesting really."

"I agree," said George, "but Jeff's not the man to make it interesting. And I doubt he'll let you tinker with his prose."

"That he will not," said Lisa. "He's very protective of his

words. He's open to suggestions about how the CDF looks, but not the structure and wording of the text. It's his baby actually."

Lisa's cell phone rang. She answered it and said "Okay. Yes, I see. Yes, of course. Okay, I'll meet you then."

"That was Professor Albacete", she said. "His publishers are finalizing a deal with Wolfram. He wants me to go down to New York with him for a meeting. It looks like I might have a job!"

"Holy mackerel," said Chris. "This calls for a celebration. How does a Guinness and champagne sound?"

The four friends and George sat around chatting for a half hour or so, happy to be celebrating Lisa's good fortune. Eventually George bade them goodbye and said he would probably see Lisa during the week in the Department. "Unless you'll be in New York then," he said.

"I could be," she replied. "Professor Albacete didn't have a firm date yet, but it sounded like they are keen to move ahead as quickly as possible."

"Okay," said George. "Well good luck, and I will see you when I see you."

The four friends paid their bill, picked up their bags and walked out into the Square.

"Do you guys feel like eating at La Laiterie," asked Chris.

"Sure," said Megan and Danny, "that sounds great. We love their food."

"Lisa, how about you?" asked Chris.

"What? Oh, yeah, sure," said Lisa. "That sounds good. But, you know what ... you guys go ahead and get a table. I'm just going to go and look in Alex and Ani for a few minutes."

26

Rest and rehabilitation

George and Kathy made their way through Rhode Island Hospital to Bert Monod's ward, and found his room. Bert was lying back, apparently asleep. His face was severely bruised. "I don't want to wake him," said Kathy. Bert opened his eyes and looked up at them. "I wasn't asleep," he said, "just thinking. Thanks for the flowers," indicating the large bouquet beside the bed.

"How are you feeling?" asked Kathy. "It looks like you took quite a hit."

"I'm okay, all things considered," said Bert. "It could have been a lot worse. The biggest problem right now, apart from the broken pelvis, is whether there's any internal bleeding. So far, so good."

Kathy asked about the treatment for a broken pelvis and Bert replied that if surgery wasn't necessary then rest and rehabilitation was all that was needed.

"When I say "all", I mean several months, both bed rest and rehabilitation," said Bert. "I think it's going to take a long time for me to recover properly from this. The best part of a year I would think. There's no way I can continue as Department Chair. You're going to have to look for someone else."

George marveled at Bert's clarity, then realized from the drip attached to his arm that he was on serious pain medication.

"Not to worry Bert," said Kathy. "It's in hand. Rick has agreed to take on the job as Chair."

"He's a good man," said Bert. "Very capable and very steady. He'll keep things going and won't rock the boat."

George turned away to examine the flowers in detail.

"You're right", said Kathy. "Rick is very capable. We will be in good hands."

At that moment Bert's physician walked in. "Hello old fellow!" he said. "Look's like the pain meds have perked you up. Let's take a look." He asked George and Kathy if he could have a few minutes with Bert, and pulled the curtain round them both. After examining Bert he pulled the curtain back and pronounced Bert as right as rain.

"Considering what he's been through," he said. "Mr. Monod's very lucky. Any more pressure on his pelvic area and we could have had severe internal damage. Not to mention major reconstructive surgery. He got off relatively lightly."

Kathy asked about treatment and the doctor confirmed what Bert had said: bed rest, a lot of it, and several months of rehabilitation. "That won't be easy for someone of your age and general physique," he said to Bert. "But absolutely necessary. The alternative is to be more or less crippled."

Bert looked glum. His nephew had rehabilitation recently for a torn anterior cruciate ligament – a football injury – and his treatment was long and arduous, even for a 20 year old. Bert groaned at the thought of months of treatment, being pushed, pulled, poked, stretched, and generally worked over.

"Are you okay, Bert?" asked Kathy.

"Yes. Just thinking about being laid up for so long," said Bert.

"Take it easy, Bert," said Kathy, as if he had a choice. "We'll come back to see you again soon."

"Thanks for coming to see me," said Bert. "Thank you George. And thanks for the flowers, they brighten the palace."

George and Kathy made their way back through the hospital labyrinth to the car park.

"I think the bed rest will actually be more painful for him than the rehabilitation," said George. "He doesn't have any interests that I'm aware of. What's he going to do for several months but lay in bed and vegetate." George laughed. "Will we be able to tell the difference?"

"George! That's not nice," said Kathy. "True, but not nice."

"You're right," said George. "If we denigrated the interest-challenged we'd never have a nice thing to say about many of our students."

Kathy, realizing George was in danger of being engulfed by a rising tide of negativity, took him off to a nearby coffee shop. "Let's have a talk," she said, "about how we think life's going to be with Rick at the helm."

♥♥♥♥♥

Rickhart filled in Dean Nueberg on Bert's condition and the necessity for a new Department Chair. "I'm willing to take on the responsibility," he said. "I have the support of the Department – a majority of them, anyway – and I don't think anyone else is likely to put their name forward."

Dean Nueberg was pleased to hear that. Strictly speaking, Department Chairs were not elected, but appointed by the Dean from a pool voted on by the Department. Having one candidate – a very capable one – made everything so much easier.

"Well thanks for filling me in," she said to Rickhart. The Assistant Dean will arrange for the ballot procedure right way. If there's only you standing then it's a foregone conclusion and nothing needs to be done further. I will talk with the Provost. Thank you for coming to see me. I appreciate it."

Rickhart left the Dean's office pleased. It was important to the smooth running of the Department that he had her support. Like most of the Department he regarded her as a nincompoop out of her depth. He thought she was typical of many mid-level academic administrators, who were generally never much good as academics and came to the job as Dean to get out of the responsibility of teaching and research, or to add to their retirement fund, or both. There was the occasional Dean who used the position to propel themselves up and on to Provost, but they were relatively rare. More common were the plodders like Dean Nueberg who occupied the position of Dean with a singular lack of vision or sense of growth and development. "But," he reflected, "she's *our* nincompoop, *our* plodder, and we have to work with her."

Rickhart decided to call a Department meeting. He didn't have authority to do that yet, not being Chair. But, doing what leaders do, he led. He sent an email to all faculty asking if they could meet the coming Friday at 11:00 AM in the Dean's conference room.

♥♥♥♥♥

The Department meeting was not, as Inger Hansen pointed out, actually a Department meeting, since Bert had not called it. It was, just a meeting of the faculty of the Department.

"What's the difference?" asked George. "We're all here to discuss recent events, and future plans. Sounds like a Department meeting to me."

"No, you are wrong, George," said Inger. "Only Department Chair can call a Department meeting, and since Bert is in hospital and did not yet send us email about meeting, we are not having a Department meeting. Rickhart has called this meeting, but only so he can act as if he is Department Chair already, and to tell us how he will be Chair. But he is not. Bert is still Chair."

Rickhart spoke. "Inger is correct," he said. "This is not a Department meeting in the formal sense of the term. Nevertheless, we do have to meet in Bert's absence. You all know about Bert's accident. His treatment will be long and drawn out, lasting for many months, up to a year. Bert has asked me to tell you that he is stepping down as Chair and that we should decide who the next Chair should be."

"When did he say this?" asked Inger. "I never heard him say this."

"He told me verbally, when I went to see him in hospital," said Rickhart.

"How we know you are telling the truth? Maybe you made up this story," said Inger.

"Inger!" said Kathy. "That is a terrible thing to say. Bert also told George and me that he cannot continue as Department Chair. I think we all know he cannot, and I think you know that. I think you are simply trying to give Rick a hard time about calling this meeting. A meeting, by the way, that we don't have to have, but *should* have in the interests of transparency."

"Ha! You say this because he is you husband," said Inger. "I have been thinking about what Rick has been saying to me about change in the Department, and I am not for it. So I have decided: I am going to nominate myself as Department Chair."

27

The workload model saves the day

$$\infty$$

"What?" George couldn't process Inger's statement that she was nominating herself for Department Chair. "Are you crazy?"

"No, I am not crazy. I have right to nominate just as much as anyone. And because I have nominated it is not correct for Rick to continue with this meeting. He is not the only person nominating for Chair, so we have to have an election and then we see who wins."

Kathy grasped Ingers' strategy of nominating to disrupt the meeting, and gain time to nominate someone other than Rickhart. His previous meeting with Inger, discussing vision and change, must have upset her. Being married to Rickhart, Kathy did not want to speak up to get the meeting back on track. She looked across the table at Zaqi. For a young and relatively new member of the Department he showed great commonsense and maturity in dealing with Department matters. Zaqi caught Kathy's concern and spoke up.

"I am wondering if we could take a few minutes break," he

said, "to let Inger and Rickhart prepare a short statement to let us know what they see as the main issues facing the Department and how they intend to deal with them."

The consensus of the voices was that this was a good idea, and the meeting should reconvene in twenty minutes. George, Kathy, Jeff and Zaqi went off to Kathy's office.

"That was well handled Zaq," said George. "I think you calmed things temporarily. What can Inger be thinking? Who is going to vote for her as Department Chair?"

"I'll tell you who," said Kathy, and she counted on her fingers the faculty who would have supported Bert in a vote and who would, most likely, now support Inger.

"But *Inger? Inger?*" asked George. "Bert was one thing, but Inger would be impossible. I sometimes think she's crazy. And she always '*too tired*'."

"Her actions only seem crazy if you imagine they have no rational basis," said Kathy. "From her perspective, change and uncertainty is the last thing she needs. She's not that far from retirement and she just wants to coast along doing what she's been doing for the next few years."

"I think that describes many of us older faculty," said Jeffrey. "Me anyway!" he laughed.

"Jeff, please! You've just had the 9th edition of your book come out and already you're working on a new CDF edition. You're not simply coasting along to retirement," said George.

"Jeff was pleased. "Thank you George," he said.

"I mean it, Jeff," said George. "We each make contributions to teaching, research, scholarship, service to the University, to the community, in our own way. In the long run, no one contribution is greater than any other." Kathy raised her eyebrows. "The main thing," continued George, "is that we are actively engaged in furthering the growth, development, and reputation of the Department and the University, even if that comes from our own self-interest."

"George is right, in my opinion," said Zaqi, "and I feel Inger has wrongly assumed that Rick means to demand that all faculty apply harder and harder for grants, and work to write six or seven research articles a year, as well as contribute to the various University committees. Inger would be frightened of a vision such as this, because she has based most of her academic life around teaching."

Jeffrey smiled. "That's true," he said, "but she's not even a good teacher. I'm not the greatest teacher in the world, but I am at least organized, unlike Inger."

Kathy wondered how Rickhart would be able to mollify Inger's concerns. "Time to go back," she said. Let's hope the meeting stays calm. Zaq, you did a great job suggesting this break. Can you pick up running the meeting when we get back?"

"Sure, I can do that. Though it might be above my pay grade," he laughed.

Faculty drifted back to the Dean's conference room. Zaqi called the meeting to order. "Now Inger and Rickhart will tell us their version of what issues they see as important, and where they think the Department should be headed, and why," he said.

Inger went first and spoke to the meeting about her many years in the Department, how the administration had tried to cut their salaries and increase their workload many times. "Bert has always been a fair Department Chair," she said. "He listens to what we want, and tries his best to accommodate us. I know we cannot have Bert back, at least not for a whole year, but I do not want us to have to suddenly be doing things we cannot do. I will try to run the Department much as Bert would." Inger stopped and looked at Rickhart. "Over to you," she said.

"Thank you, Inger," said Rickhart. "We do have, as Inger said, problems with an administration that wants us to work harder with less resources, and lower salary increases. That is a given that we address through our academic bargaining structure. Somewhat independently of that the Department is at a tipping point. We have had several new appointments over the years and two new highly talented faculty will begin next semester. The focus of the Department has changed because of this, and our reputation and impact outside the University is growing rapidly. I think we need a strategy for how the Department will grow not only over the next few years, but over the next couple of decades, after many of us will no longer be here. We need to have a strategy as a Department that tells us clearly what we are doing and why."

"But not everyone is so good as you at research," said Inger. "What are we supposed to do?"

"That's a very good point," said Rickhart. "You all know that George has been working for some time now on a workload model. In that model he has tired to incorporate a very flexible structure that accommodates everyone's unique talents, interests and abilities. George?"

George spoke briefly to the workload model. "First I just tried to model the hours people spent on different tasks," he said, "tasks that are essential to the running of the Department, but for which we get little or no official credit."

"That is what I am talking about," said Inger.

"But as the model began to take shape," continued George. "It became clear that much of our work structure is inefficient. A lot of our time is being wasted because our talents are not being fully utilized. Inger, if I may so, your own situation illustrates this very well. You spend a great deal of your time counseling female students, mentoring them advising them about careers, and generally inspiring them. Yet you get no official, or actual, recognition for that time and effort."

"I do it because I love it," said Inger. "And the students need it."

"And you are good at it, and it benefits the Department and the University," said George. "What you do in this regard is valuable and should be recognized as such."

"So how do you propose to do this?" asked Inger.

George deferred to Rickhart. "My plan," said Rickhart, "is to set up Department structures that recognize core work such as this: work that supports the Department's core values and vision.

Then within those structures George's workload model comes into play to audit people's time spent on work now officially recognized as central to the Department. The Provost is on board with this. In fact he first suggested the idea to George."

Inger was abashed. "I am sorry Rick," she said. "I was only scared that you were going to make us all work harder to do things we cannot do. If this is how it is, as you have described, then of course I am all for it. If I can be Director of Women's Mathematical Careers in the Department, then I will be happy!"

"Right," said Rickhart. "That's great. Let's get down to business. We have a lot to discuss."

28

A new author?

❧

Jeffrey Albacete and Lisa De Silva traveled from Providence to Penn Station, New York City, by Amtrak's Acela train. The trip took just over four hours and at Jeffrey's suggestion they sat in a quiet car. This suited Lisa who spent the time working on the CDF for the next chapter of Jeffrey's book. They arrived at Penn Station and caught a cab to the New York office of Jeffrey's publisher. Jeffrey went directly to the office of his editor, the person in the organization with whom he was most comfortable, due in no small measure to the continued success of Jeffrey's book. Jeffrey introduced Lisa and together they went to the technical division that was dealing with the conversion of Jeffrey's book to a commercial CDF version. This aspect of the publishing house was new to Jeffrey and he was excited to connect with a different, and highly technical, aspect of publishing.

"You know," he said to Lisa, "they think of themselves now as more of a learning company than as a publisher. The old meaning of '*publish*' was to make known, to broadcast, but that's done better by Amazon now. Textbook and educational publishers have re-conceptualized themselves as builders of learning environments. It's due mainly to their increasing use of sophisticated technology," he said, without even a hint of a thought that he might be teaching grandma how to suck eggs. Lisa nodded, and followed Jeffrey dutifully.

The meeting with the technical team went very well. They were particularly impressed with the coding for the CDF version of the chapters they hade seen. "We're only beginning our involvement with Wolfram and CDF," said one of the team, "but so far we are really impressed at the interactivity of this medium. It has real possibilities, we believe."

"And the implementation you have here is really great," said another.

"Thank you," Jeffrey replied, "we've been working hard at it."

"We're impressed by how you've used the *Manipulate* commands so creatively," said a team member. "How did you do that?"

"We .. ah .. let me pass you over to Lisa," Jeffrey said.

Lisa explained the technical aspects of her code, to the rapt attention of the technical team. "This is great!" one of them said. "We could do with you here. Has anyone discussed your working with us? Are you still a student? Are you looking for a job?"

The flood of questions took Lisa by surprise. She was flattered, but not sure what to answer. "I don't know much about the publishing business," she said. "I'm not sure what's involved. My training is in computer science and mathematics." Her questioner laughed. "Jurg over there is a theoretical physicist, and Bernadette was a computational finance major! The technical team's job is ... well, technicalities," he said. "You seem a perfect fit to me."

Lisa didn't know what to think. The technical team seemed like a group she could work with. They were fun and the job seemed cool. No one had discussed salary or working conditions, or even said outright that there might be a job for her, and suddenly here were these guys practically assuming she was coming to work with them. Lisa couldn't get her head around how, if she were offered a job, she could combine that with completing her degree. And she had been thinking about graduate school. How would that work? These questions were running around in her head when Jeffrey's editor asked if they could talk about a few possible editorial changes for a planned translation of the 9th edition into Hungarian. Jeffrey and his editor excused themselves, saying they would be back in about half an hour.

Jurg, the theoretical physicist transformed as technical support for a book publisher, said to Lisa that he very much liked what she had done in coding the CDF. "But there is one thing," he said. "The text is very boring in my opinion. Is there anything you can do to lift it and make it, uhm ... more interesting?"

Lisa shook her head. "No, that's Professor Albacete's baby," she said. "He's had that style through nine editions, and I don't see him changing it now."

"That's too bad," said Jurg, "because I think the boring prose, if I may say so in Professor Albacete's absence, will detract from the high quality of the CDF version of this work. I studied matrix algebra in my graduate degree. We did not use Professor Albacete's book, but one written by Professor Steven Leon. It was an excellent book – very interesting and very well written. It's a pity you are not working turning his book into a CDF version. Though that would be with a different publisher, of course!" he laughed.

Lisa didn't know what to say. She agreed Jeffrey's book was dry to the point of being boring – she had read the text in finer detail than most people – but she did not want to be disloyal to him. He had been kind enough to bring her to New York to meet with his publisher.

"But of course, we should not discuss this with you in Professor Albacete's absence," said Jurg. "It is only embarrassing you. I apologize. If it's okay with you there are some points we would like to go over. Bernadette can take you back to Professor Albacete while we do that if that's okay with you. Bernadette, would you mind?" Lisa agreed that would be a good idea, and followed Bernadette back to the elevator and up to Jeffrey's editor. When she had left, Jurg turned to the rest of the technical team.

"I have an idea," he said. "It's only half formed as yet so hear me out. I think that Lisa is doing a fantastic job here. She has a very innovative vision for this CDF book and her implementation is first rate. The quality of the text is holding this back from being a truly outstanding product. Not just a good-selling text, but also an award-winning product, relevant to twenty-first century students. My idea is to find another author to work with Lisa to write a text that fits her talents as a programmer."

"You mean abandon the Albacete text. Create an entirely new book?" asked one of the team. "Exactly!" replied Jurg.

"But Jurg, that would take a long time, a very long time. The Albacete text is already there, and the way Lisa is going we can have this CDF version out in less than six months. Besides, that decision is not ours to take."

"I agree with that," said Jurg. "But hear me out. What if we can get Albacete to agree that Lisa owns the copyright to the CDFs? That should be straightforward, since technically she already does have the copyright. I think he will agree not to oppose that in any way."

The others agreed. "Now then," said Jurg, "suppose we can find another author who will work with Lisa, simultaneously, on a different book, based around Lisa's CDFs, which she owns?"

The technical team pondered his and agreed it might work. "But how do we find this other author?" one of them asked Jurg.

"That," said Jurg, "should be relatively easy. The university at which Lisa is a student has just appointed a brilliant new faculty member – Heinrich Zimmer – who is an expert in matrix algebra. I heard about him from the German-American Association. I think if we approach him carefully he might just be interested in being the author we envisage."

"Sehr hinterhältig, Jurg", said one of the team.

Jeffrey, his editor and Lisa returned to the technical team's division.

"Professor Albacete," said Jurg, "I understand you have just appointed a brilliant young colleague in your area."

"Indeed we have," said Jeffrey. "Would you like to meet him? I think he could be a potential author for you."

29

Just a hunch

Lisa was both excited and concerned. She rode the train back to Providence without mentioning a word of the conversation with Jurg and the other members of the technical team. She would like to have, but Jeffrey again wanted to sit in a quiet car. Lisa tried to read, but her thoughts kept returning to the team's questions about a job, and Jurg's comments that Jeffrey's prose was boring. She had to agree that was the case, but the publisher had stuck with Jeffrey through nine editions of the book and, presumably, made a packet of money from sales to students of what, after all, is quite an expensive book. She wondered how they would market and distribute the CDF version of the book. Would they do it through their website, or though Amazon, or some other route entirely, she wondered.

When they arrived in Providence Jeffrey offered to drive her to Wayland Square. Lisa readily accepted. She was not keen to take the half hour walk after dark. As he drove Jeffrey thought about his chance meeting with Lisa at the Coffee Depot in Warren. He recalled Pasteur's saying that chance favors only the prepared mind. Jeffrey prided himself on being prepared, and he reflected hat he had indeed turned a chance meeting into an exciting new possibility.

"Thanks for your presence and support today," he said to Lisa. "I couldn't have done it without you. You and I are becoming something of a team."

Lisa thanked Jeffrey for the opportunity to meet with the publisher and went up to her apartment where she fell asleep almost as soon as her head met the pillow.

Next morning Lisa phoned her friend Chris and asked if he could meet her at L'Artisan Bakery.

"Sure," he said. "Are you on track to becoming a publishing mogul yet?" he joked.

"I will tell you when I see you," said Lisa.

They met twenty minutes later and after ordering coffee and pastries Lisa told Chris how the technical team and Jurg in particular, thought Jeffrey's book was boring. "I thought you said it was," said Chris. "I did," said Lisa, "but that's just me saying it. It's another thing to have the people at his publisher saying it. Jurg asked me to leave the room while they discussed something. I'm guessing they were thinking about how to replace Professor Albacete as author."

"How do you reach that conclusion?" asked Chris. He thought Lisa was reaching a bit far.

"It's because they are well aware that no one is going to get Jeffrey to change his prose. He can't: I think 'boring' is part of his nature. They liked what I'd done with the CDFs, but to their minds it didn't fit with the text. When I say 'they', I mean the technical team. Jurg, in particular."

"I see," said Chris, "so you think they want your technical product but they don't want Albacete as author" said Jeffrey.

"Yes, in a nutshell. I could be wrong, and I hope I am, but Jurg gave me a funny feeling when he asked me to leave the room."

Chris pondered what this might mean for Lisa. "Did they offer you a job?" he asked.

"Not yet," she replied. "But the technical team seemed

impressed with what I had done, and were talking about my working there. They asked a lot of questions along those lines. I found it rather sudden and confusing, to be honest."

"How would that work with your senior year?" Chris asked. "And what about grad school?"

Lisa sighed. "I don't know. I need to think this through. Do you have some time?"

"Sure," said Chris, "let's just sit here and chew it over."

♥♥♥♥♥

When Jeffrey arrived back at the University he bumped into Heinrich Zimmer. "Heinrich!" he exclaimed. "What brings you here? You're not due to start for a couple of months."

Heinrich explained that he and his wife were looking for housing and they were hoping to find something close to the University.

"Is she here?" asked Jeffrey.

"Not at this moment," said Heinrich. "She has gone shopping in the Mall while I came here to sort out a few things."

"Well this is fortuitous," said Jeffrey. "Come in and sit down. Would you like coffee?" Heinrich reminded Jeffrey that he drank tea. "Of course," said Jeffrey, and temporarily put aside thoughts of a much-desired cup of Lisa's excellent Terroir coffee.

"This is really fortuitous," repeated Jeffrey. "I was just talking about you with my publisher."

"Indeed?" said Heinrich.

"Well, not a commissioning editor, as such," said Jeffrey. "We were discussing the CDF version of my book with the technical team. Quite interesting it was, too. One of the team had heard about your appointment here through the German-American Association, and asked after you. I think, if you play your cards right, they might be interested in you as an author."

"I see," said Heinrich. "That is indeed interesting."

"I think so," said Jeffrey. "If you and I both had books on matrix algebra it would give the differential equations people something to think about."

"Quite so," said Heinrich. "That would be very interesting indeed. Please keep me informed, Jeffrey. I would be very interested in such a project." He thanked Jeffrey for his hospitality and for the information from the publisher. "I need to sort out a few administrative details now and then go and meet my wife. I hope to see you again soon."

Jeffrey thought how lucky he was to have Heinrich coming to work in the department. "There's that chance and the prepared mind, again," he thought. If Jeffrey had not prepared the ground in establishing matrix algebra as a field of study at the University Heinrich may never have applied to come. But just that preparation had tipped the odds in Jeffrey's favor. Kathy Riverton saw Jeffrey and commented on his happy demeanor.

"Yes, I am happy," said Jeffrey. "Things seem to be going my way for a change. My publisher is very happy with progress on the CDF version of Matrix algebra – they may offer Lisa some sort of technical job – and I just talked with Heinrich about a possible book from him."

"I saw Heinrich leaving," said Kathy. "I'm really pleased things are going well for you. We're all looking forward to a 10th edition of your book."

Jeffrey thanked Kathy for her good wishes and went back to his office to make coffee. As he thought about the last few weeks he felt satisfied. His life, he thought, wasn't too bad. Just as his 9th edition had come out in print a new, and more technical, 10th edition was in the works and progressing far faster than he could have imagined. And Heinrich would start work in the Department in a couple of months. Lisa was a boon to his life, he thought. Not only was she smart and technically skilled, she had excellent taste in coffee – outstanding, actually. Jeffrey thought he and Lisa could work on Heinrich to convert him from tea to coffee. Then all would be perfect. The aroma of the fine Terroir coffee pervaded Jeffrey's office. He poured himself a cup and looked over the nine editions of his book on his desk. "It does define who I am," he thought. "And there's more to come."

Just as he was sipping his coffee his phone rang. It was Lisa.

"Hi, Lisa," he said, "how can I help you?"

"Hello Professor Albacete," she replied. "I wonder if we can meet. I'd like to have a word with you about our meeting with the technical team at your publisher in New York."

30

Who else?

Bob Fosberry and Lori Bailey met at the Daily Grind to discuss writing a grant application to the National Science Foundation which, like everyone else funded by this agency, they referred to as the NSF. Their idea of basing an applied modeling course for the science and engineering students around Markov Chains was taking shape. They had pulled together a team of faculty from biology, physics and mechanical and electrical engineering, and the Deans of Science and of Engineering had given in-principle agreement to consider modules on Markov Chain applications in the freshman and sophomore mathematics courses for their students. Bob was of the opinion that utilizing cutting edge technology to enhance the applications they had in mind would be a major selling point to the funding body. Lori agreed.

"I don't think it's enough to just sit the students in front of computers and utilize standard technology," she said. "We've been doing that in their calculus courses. It has an effect, a positive one in general, but it's not going to have the wow factor that we need to differentiate this project." Bob agreed. "This might be far-fetched, in so far as I don't really know what I'm talking about," said Bob, "but what about the computable document format that Lisa De Silva's producing for Jeff's new book. Could we use that in some way?"

Lori thought Bob was onto something. "The NSF has been pushing more interactive teaching. What if we can get the students to produce CDFs as part of their coursework? That would be more of a practically oriented studio course that should go down well with everyone. In fact, as I think about it, I can't see why we didn't think of this before."

Bob wondered if Lisa would think about working on the grant if it came through. "We'd have to steal her from Jeff," he said, "unless she could do both jobs together. Do you think we should talk with her? It's all a bit tentative yet, but if she's agreeable, or knows someone else who could do the job, it would add a significant element to our grant application." Lori agreed. "Let's talk with her," she said "and see what her thoughts and feelings are."

Lisa was surprised to get a call from Bob Fosberry whom she had met only a couple of times before. She was even more surprised when Bob explained he wanted her to come and talk with him and Lori Bailey about computable document format applications they had in mind for a grant application. The three met in Bob's office where he and Lori explained the broad terms of their proposal and how they saw CDFs fitting into the curriculum development. Lisa thought CDF versions of their proposed curriculum materials would really make the course come alive, and be fairly straightforward to program.

"We're also interested in teaching the students to make their own CDFs," said Lori. "Our aim is to build understanding of and competence with the concepts through practical applications. So a central aspect of our approach to learning is student doing."

Lisa liked that. "It's how I learn," she said. "I think when I need to, and at other times I just do something. But mightn't this be a little hard for freshman students coming straight out of high school? They've spent several years just listening to teachers and completing set exercises. Being thrown into suddenly relying on their own resources might prove difficult for many of them."

Lori agreed. "That's why Bob and I envisage this project as a series of modules that fit into a course on applications of Markov Chains in science and engineering. If an entire semester course were based around constructing CDFs it probably would prove too much for beginning students. We're imagining a couple of two-week modules in a semester that integrate with the existing course material."

Lisa liked the idea and said she would be happy to work on the project if the funding came through. "How much work do you foresee," she asked, "and for how long?"

Bob explained that the grant would last for up to five years. The amount of effort required would depend on how central the CDFs became to the project. "It could be a couple of days a week ", he said, "or it could become fulltime."

"I see," said Lisa. "I'm definitely interested. I don't know yet where the work with Professor Albacete will lead, but I would really like you to consider me for this project. If it turns out I cannot do it, I promise to find someone for you who would be a good fit."

"Fair enough," said Bob. "Then that settles it. The only favor I would ask of you is if you could assist us with the technical aspects of CDFs as we write the grant."

Lisa agreed and they shook hands on the deal. "Now I need to go and talk with Professor Albacete about another matter," she said.

♥♥♥♥♥

Jeffrey was pleased to see Lisa. "Come in, come in," he said. " I have coffee on – your coffee."

Lisa took a cup and sat on the chair at the side of the desk.

"So, what is it that you wanted to talk about?" he asked.

Lisa explained, as best she could without using the word 'boring', that Jurg had mentioned the writing style of Jeffrey's book and whether it would fit with the new CDF version. Jeffrey said to Lisa that he understood that. "Every new venture like this requires re-thinking," he said. "I've written the previous versions of my book for a standard – some would say now, old-fashioned – book format. Now we are doing something quite different it's only reasonable they would want to revisit the text."

Lisa felt she had not made her point clearly enough. "I think they might want a new author," she blurted out.

Jeffrey didn't know what to make of Lisa's words, or her sad expression. "A new author? What do you mean, and why would you say that?"

Lisa told Jeffrey that Jurg was blunt about the writing style. He had called it dull, she said.

"Well it may be dull to him," said Jeffrey, "but even if it is, that hasn't seemed to hurt sales!" Jeffrey was quite buoyant. "Tell me why you think they want to replace me as author?"

Lisa explained the feeling she had, being led away from the meeting when Jurg realized she was embarrasses to listen to such criticisms of the book. "I feel he wants to keep me as technical programmer for the CDFs and replace you as author."

Jeffrey listened. "I see," he said. "But don't you think this would be rather preposterous? There's an awful lot of planning and work that goes into producing a book like *Matrix Algebra*. I began this project decades ago, and getting the first edition into print was a lot of work. Succeeding editions have been easier, but they all take a lot of planning and background research. Who, apart from me, would be able to write a coherent text to this level? Who, as well, would be able to work with you and integrate it with the CDFs you are producing?"

Lisa guessed Jeffrey was right. She was anxious about meeting the technical group and she had probably been a little paranoid about Jurg wanting her out of the room when he wanted to discuss something. "Professor Albacete is right," she thought. "His text might be boring, but who else could do what he had done and write in a more exciting way?"

"Oh!" she said as the thought came to her mind.

"What is it?" asked Jeffrey.

"I just thought of the answer to your question?"

"Which question is that?" he asked.

"Who could take over as author of the new version of your book," she replied.

Jeffrey smiled. "And who might that be?" he asked, thinking there couldn't be another possible author for *Matrix Algebra*.

"Professor Heinrich Muller."

Jeffrey's legs went weak and he involuntarily sat down.

31

It pays to do homework

Heinrich Muller and his wife Anna had just signed an agreement to buy a house. Prior to coming to Rhode Island they had looked at what seemed like hundreds of houses online and had narrowed their search down to just a few. The second house they saw was ideal for them: it had an outstanding view of the ocean, four bed-rooms, a deck overlooking a large garden, and a greenhouse. Anna thought the price was high, especially compared to where they were currently living in Illinois, but reasonable for New England.

After leaving the realtors office they drove to Thayer Street in Providence to try the Tealuxe tea bar. Apart from their first store in Harvard Square, which he had frequented as a graduate student, Heinrich didn't know anywhere outside of South Africa that served such a wide variety of Rooibos teas.

"Ah!" he said, "savoring the aroma of the freshly brewed tea. "This is heaven."

"Does Jeffrey Albacete like tea?" asked Anna. "Perhaps you will have someone to share your love of fine tea."

"Alas, he is a coffee man, through and through," said Heinrich. "I must say it seemed very good coffee when I visited him. He seems to be something of a connoisseur."

"Jedem das seine," said Anna.

"Indeed," said Heinrich, "we all have our own tastes, and no one is better than, or inferior to, any other. I respect a reflective intelligence, that is all."

Anna looked at the time and reminded Heinrich that it was getting close to when they would meet Kathy, Rickhart, George and Deborah for dinner. They planned to eat at Siena on Federal Hill. Anna was looking forward to meeting Heinrich's future colleagues as well as trying the Tuscan style food at Siena.

"Let's go back to the hotel and freshen up," said Anna. "I hope your colleagues will like me."

"And why would they not?" asked Heinrich. "You are very attractive and likable. I like you."

"Well that's what matters," she said, kissing him on the cheek.

The others were already at the restaurant when Heinrich and Anna arrived. Rickhart welcomed Heinrich and introduced Deborah, the others having met Heinrich at his job interview. Heinrich introduced Anna to them all and they sat down. Anna remarked that the restaurant looked very attractive.

"We haven't eaten here yet," said Kathy, "but I hear the food is excellent."

"I am looking forward to it," said Anna," Heinrich and I lived for two years in Tuscany, so I am very interested to see how American-style Tuscan compares."

"It *should* be good," said George. "The owners – Anthony and Chris Tarro – were raised in an Italian family here in Warwick, Rhode Island, but they've spent time in Tuscany, learning and visiting their family roots. I think it's going to be authentically Tuscan as a home grown American restaurant can be."

"So what have you two been doing today?" asked Rickhart.

"We bought a house," exclaimed Anna. "It's beautiful. I am

so excited." She passed around her phone with pictures of their soon-to-be home.

"Heinrich, I'm impressed," said Kathy, "you're wasting no time in getting settled."

"Heinrich loves to do his homework," said Anna. "We spent weeks on the internet searching for houses in this area."

"Looks like your homework paid off," said Deborah. "It's a really beautiful house."

"And that deck looks great for barbecues," said George.

"Yes, I need to learn how to barbecue. I wonder if I could get lessons from you, George."

"Are you taking the mickey?" asked George.

"Pardon?" asked Heinrich. "What is the mickey?"

Everyone laughed. "I thought you were playing with me," said George. "What is there to learn about barbecue? You put the meat, or whatever, on the pre-heated barbecue stand around with a beer in your hand, and when everything's burned to a crisp, serve up!"

"Now, I think it is the mickey you are now taking from me," said Heinrich. "I have seen on TV the BBQ University. I would like to learn how to barbecue properly. I do not want to become a professor of barbecue", he smiled, " but I would like to do it well."

Rickhart laughed. "I suspect, Heinrich, that everything you do, you do well,"

"I try," said Heinrich.

"Well Heinrich," said Kathy. "Since you have lived in Tuscany, how about you tell us what you think we would like?"

Heinrich was now getting the subtler overtones of 'taking the mickey' but smiled and said: "It would be my great pleasure, Kathy."

Over dinner, talk naturally gravitated to issues related to the Department. Even a side conversation on Anna's job as a biostatistician led to a discussion on how the Department had not developed in that area. "Maybe we should," said Rickhart. There's no doubt that's where a lot of activity is happening, and where jobs are for our students. We've just taken a different tack, focusing more on broader science and engineering."

Heinrich nodded, as if in agreement with Rickhart, or perhaps just indicating he was listening. However, his mind seemed to be elsewhere. "So," he said to the company in general. "I have heard some things about Bert Monod. Tell me what does this mean for the Department. Will there be a new Chairperson?"

George smiled. "Yes there has to be a new Chairperson, and," he said pointing at Rickhart, "you're looking right at him."

"Congratulations, Rickhart," said Heinrich. "This is very good news, indeed. Do you have some new plans for the Department?"

Rickhart discussed in broad terms some of the ideas he had in mind. "Especially important," he emphasized, "is getting a strategic plan in place, where we describe our vision for the Department, and the steps needed to bring that vision to fruition."

Heinrich liked what Rickhart said. "I agree, a well-articulated vision is very important," he said. "Also it is necessary to have a schedule, even a tentative one, for new developments, to know who is responsible for various aspects of a program, and to know what resources are required."

Kathy laughed. "Very well said, Heinrich. It sounds like you are running for the job of Department Chair."

"Well, of course, I am only an untenured Assistant Professor, so I cannot be," he said. "I do like to be organized." Anna agreed, "He does!" she said. "That's how we came to buy just the second house we looked at today."

Rickhart had a thought. There was nothing in their contract about a Deputy Chair of Department, but equally nothing to stop them creating such a position. Would it, he wondered, add too much to Heinrich's first year at the University if he were to fulfill that role? His organizational skills and his procedural and conceptual grasp of productive administration seemed excellent. Rickhart said nothing, but thought he would talk this over later with Kathy and George to get their feelings.

The meal exceeded expectations and, after dessert, the group broke up around 10:30 PM.

"Will you be in Providence for a few more days?" asked Kathy.

"No," said Anna. " We fly back to Chicago tomorrow morning. Unless there is an issue with the house – let's hope not! – we will probably be back just before the start of semester."

The group said goodnight and went their separate ways.

Rickhart told Kathy about his thoughts on Heinrich as a possible Deputy Chair. Kathy thought for a minute and then said she thought this was a good idea, if the main tactic was to get Heinrich an easy introduction to administration. "It will count, of course, as service to the Department in his annual evaluation," she said.

"Yes, it will," said Rickhart. "I can ease him into the role. What interests me most is picking his brains for creative administrative ideas. I would do that anyway, and he may as well get credit for his advice."

Rickhart instinctively slowed when he saw the flashing police lights ahead.

Kathy turned to look as they passed and shouted "Stop, stop, Rick. That's Bert's son."

"What?" asked Rickhart. "Bert Monod's son?"

"Yes, it is!" said Kathy. "It looks like he's being arrested."

32

Doing deals

Rickhart stopped the car a short way beyond the flashing lights of the police car. Kathy got out and walked toward Andrew Monod who was handcuffed and being spoken to by a policeman.

"Ma'am?" queried the police officer as Kathy approached.

"I know this young man, officer. He's Andrew Monod, the son of a colleague. Is he okay? Has he done something?"

"Yes, he has ma'am. He is presently under arrest and we will be taking him to the station for processing. Unless he can post bail, or someone can do it for him, he will spend the night in the cells and appear in court in the morning."

"I can post bail for him," said Kathy, reaching for her purse, then realizing it was in the car.

"You will have to do that at the station, ma'am" said the police officer. "You can follow me there now if you want."

Kathy ran back to the car and explained the situation to Rickhart. They followed the police car to the station and after Andrew was taken in for processing, sat on a bench inside. Kathy phoned Bert Monod's house and talked briefly with him. She told him she didn't know why Andrew had been arrested, but not to worry: she would post bail and bring him home.

About half an hour later another police officer spoke to Kathy about bail. She paid the bail in cash after getting pooling what she and Rickhart had on them, and asked how long it might be before she could take Andrew home.

"I couldn't say exactly", he said. "Most likely a couple of hours yet."

"Can you tell me why he's been arrested?" she asked.

The officer looked at the charge sheet and told Kathy that Andrew Stephen Monod had been arrested for trafficking in a prohibited substance, prescription narcotics.

"He tried to sell prescription narcotic painkillers to an under-cover agent," the officer said.

Kathy was horrified. "Those must have been his father's. His dad was in an accident and has a broken pelvis. What will Bert do if Andy has taken all his painkillers?"

The officer had no idea but he could tell Kathy that Andrew had only tried to sell two tablets that night. "So perhaps that's all he took from his dad?" he said. "This looks like a first offence so far as we can tell, and in the bigger scheme of things it's not that serious. Not yet, anyway. In court he should get a warning and a fine is all."

Kathy and Rickhart waited until Andrew was released at almost 2:00 AM. He looks so embarrassed, thought Kathy. "Are you okay, Andy?" she asked.

He shrugged. "Yeah, I guess. Pretty dumb, huh?"

"What were you thinking, Andy?" asked Rickhart.

"I dunno. I guess I wasn't. I saw how many tablets dad had and I thought he wouldn't miss a couple. I knew it was supposed to be easy to sell them on the street."

"Let's get you home," said Kathy. "And promise me – promise me, Andy – that you will not do anything like this again."

Andrew looked at her. "I promise," he said.

"Good! Your dad's hurt and laid up and he doesn't need this kind of stress," she said. "But, he *does* need those pain meds."

Kathy and Rickhart took Andrew home and spoke briefly with Bert. "Thanks so much," Bert said. "I couldn't have done this myself. Not in my state. And with Andy and me being here on our own, there's no one else to look out for him."

As they drove off Rickhart said to Kathy: "That's very sad. Bert can probably least handle this right now. I hope this is as far as it goes with Andrew. It seems that one unexpected mishap can lead to a chain of unfortunate events – sort of make them more likely to occur as it were."

Kathy wondered if there was anything the Department could do for Bert, but nothing came to mind. She made a promise to herself to call Bert periodically just to ask how things were. He was, after all, still her colleague. "Let's get home," she said to Rickhart. "It's very late."

♥♥♥♥♥

Next morning, Kathy was telling Lori Bailey about the night's events when Jeffrey Albacete came by. "It's lucky for Andrew you were passing by," said Jeffrey, "or he would have spent the night in the cells."

"I guess it was luck," said Kathy. "We were just going home from a dinner at Siena with with Heinrich and his wife Anna."

"You were with Heinrich?" asked Jeffrey. "Is he still in town?"

"No, they left for Chicago around 10:00 this morning," said Kathy. "They're well and truly in the air by now."

"I see," said Jeffrey. "I would have liked to have talked with him."

"You can always email or phone," said Kathy.

"No, it wouldn't be the same," said Jeffrey. "I think I need to talk to him in person."

"Cheer up Jeffrey, he'll be back soon," said Kathy, responding to Jeffrey's glum expression.

"I guess," sighed Jeffrey. "I guess," he repeated as he wandered back to his office.

"What was that about?" asked Lori. "Jeff looks down in the dumps."

"Beats me," said Kathy, "but it looks like he wants to talk to Heinrich about something important."

"I hope they haven't had a lover's tiff already," joked Lori.

"Well if they have I'll wager it's Jeff's doing. Heinrich is a charmer!" said Kathy. The aroma of fine coffee wafted from Jeffrey's office. "He'll perk up soon," she said to Lori..

Lori, feeling a smile was about to become a laugh, excused herself and made her way to Bob Fosberry's office. "Hi Bob," she said. "Do you have a minute?"

"Sure, Lori, come on in. What's up?"

"Nothing exciting," she said. "I would like to go over some of the budget figures for the grant proposal it's okay with you."

"Sure," said Bob. Let's do it." Lori logged into Dropbox on Bob's computer and opened the budget spreadsheet. "The indirect is eating up a lot of the costs, as always," she said. "The Provost raised his take this year so there's even left for us to play with. I think if we go with a CDF programmer we should be okay, though, even fulltime."

Bob nodded agreement. "That's good," he said, looking at Lori.

"I think it is," she said. "The more I've thought about the CDF idea the more I think it could be a winner. It's sort of raised another idea that might be worth thinking about."

"Which is?" asked Bob.

"It's not for the grant proposal, as such," she said. " I've been wondering if we couldn't set up a sort of focus group in the Department on developing CDFs. It seems to me this has wider ramifications than just our project."

Bob thought about what Lori was suggesting.

"I mean really something more than a focus group," she said, "I really feel that we should partner with Wolfram and get heavily into CDFs as a major part of our curriculum activity. It's the way of the future, there's no doubt about it."

"Very emphatically expressed for a statistician," laughed Bob, thinking how all the statisticians he knew, including Lori, were cautious by nature or by training.

"But it is," said Lori. "Think about it. CDF documents practically revolutionize the act of writing. It's as important a change as the printing process, in my opinion. Think about what it means – writing and computation can now be integrated into one seamless document. And the interactivity means the documents come alive, in real time. It's like Zaq said at Jeff and Lisa's presentation – it's Harry Potter made real."

Kathy poked her head into Bob's office. "You two seem to be having a spirited conversation," she said.

Bob repeated Lori's idea to Kathy, capturing Lori's enthusiasm as he did.

"I think," said Kathy, "this is a great idea. But – and hear me out on this – why not make it a Center initiative? The Center for Computational Mathematics and Statistics should easily be able to accommodate a proposal on computable document format, don't you think? And wouldn't the Center be a better unit than the Department to work with Wolfram Research?"

33

Ironing out the technicalities

Jeffrey Albacete was disturbed by Lisa's suggestion that Heinrich Zimmer might be recruited to replace him on a new book on matrix algebra. In one sense, thought Jeffrey, the idea is preposterous. He, Jeffrey, was known nationally and internationally as the author of *Matrix Algebra*, now into its 9th edition. On the other hand, if Lisa had reported accurately, his publisher's technical group was complaining about his writing style being dull. There was no question Heinrich was an engaging writer, so there was a chance the technical group's rumblings might reach the ears of senior editors who might, in turn, sound out Heinrich. That, thought Jeffrey, would be disloyal on the part of his publisher, but when it came to millions of dollars of revenue loyalty would not count for much.

Jeffrey's agitation was relieved only by the thought that he could get on an airplane and visit Heinrich in Chicago. "I could say I was visiting colleagues at the University of Chicago," he thought. But then he realized how ridiculous that would seem.

Heinrich was on a post doctoral position at the University of Illinois at Chicago and, working in the same field as Jeffrey, he would of course know any purported colleagues of Jeffrey's at the University of Chicago. He thought for a moment if there could be any reason to visit Anna Zimmer, who worked in Chicago as a biostatistician, but dropped the idea as absurd.

Jeffrey then contemplated pretending to visit relatives in Chicago, but then he would, in fact, have to visit relatives. Maybe, he thought, this is a silly idea. He began to make coffee and as he opened the container , smelling the aroma of the ground coffee, he marveled again at his good fortune in finding Lisa. It was coffee that brought that about, he recalled, because they met in Warren at the Coffee Depot.

Then it struck Jeffrey. Wolfram Research was in Champagne, Illinois, 150 miles or so south of Chicago. If he had a reason to go to Wolfram Research he would have to fly through Chicago. Under such circumstances it would be impolite not to contact Heinrich and suggest they meet up for lunch or dinner. And he did, in a sense, have a very good reason to visit Wolfram Research: he and Lisa were working on a CDF version of his book.

The aroma of the Terroir coffee pervaded the room. Jeffrey poured a cup and sat to think through his idea. He would have to take Lisa with him to Illinois. Jeffrey was acutely aware that he did not know enough about the technicalities of computable document format to be able to conduct a coherent discussion with people at Wolfram Research. And what could be his reason for going? Weren't his publishers already working with Wolfram Research on a licensing proposal for a CDF version of his book? So if Lisa had technical problems that could best be straightened out by visiting Wolfram Research, then the two of them would need to go to Illinois.

Jeffrey phoned Lisa. She was surprised when he asked if there were any technical difficulties in programing the CDFs for the book. "No more than usual," she replied. "There's always some technical difficulty or other I need to deal with, but nothing slow-ing me down significantly."

"I see," said Jeffrey. "Well … uhm … that's good, Very good. Let me know if I can help in any way."

Lisa was puzzled. "Help how?" she thought. What was Professor Albacete trying to say?

Jeffrey's frustration was rising. "An hour at the gym is what I need," he thought, so he picked up his gym bag and began the walk, past the Daily Grind, to the gym.

Forty minutes of steady pedaling on the exercise bike had brought no further clarity to Jeffrey's mind. He sighed. His idea of visiting Heinrich and talking with him in person, an idea of brilliant clarity at its inception, was now seeming somewhat silly, largely by virtue of being out of reach. Jeffrey finished exercising, showered and left the gym for his office. He arrived at the Daily Grind and thought he would sit for a few minutes with a latte and a muffin. Exercise did that to him, he found. The latte, while enjoyable, had nothing of the depth of Lisa's coffee. The muffin, at least, was fresh. Jeffrey sighed again. He couldn't simply go to his publisher and say "Look here, are you thinking of replacing me as author of *Matrix Algebra?*" They would think he had gone mad. He desperately wanted to talk first with Heinrich in person, to build the ground so that Heinrich would not dream of under-cutting him as author. Not that Jeffrey had any concrete evidence that Heinrich was planning any such thing, or would, in fact, do so if he were asked.

Jeffrey's phone rang. It was his editor relaying a message from senior management. They were having some difficulties – not seri-ous ones – in tying up the licensing arrangement with Wolfram Research, and the publishers wondered if Jeffrey and his technical assistant could fly to Illinois to meet with the folks at Wolfram. If they could discuss the proposed structure firsthand with the author and his technical person it would help considerably in moving the agreement closer to completion. "We'll pick up the tab, of course," said the editor. "Just let us know by the end of today if that will work for you Jeffrey. Thanks so much."

Jeffrey couldn't believe his luck. He phoned Lisa immediately with the request from his publisher. "I guess that would be okay," she said, "if you need me there." Jeffrey called his editor back and told him that the visit to Wolfram Research was on track. "That's excellent," said the editor. "I will arrange for the e-tickets in your name and your assistant is Lisa, as I recall from my notes. Lisa De Silva?" Jeffrey affirmed that was correct, and began to think about what he needed for the trip. He called Lisa back and explained that arrangements were set and they would leave early tomorrow morning.

Lisa had been working in L'Artisan Bakery when Jeffrey called. She closed her computer, then her eyes, and thought for a moment. "A penny for them," someone said. She opened her eyes and saw Chris. "You look deep in thought," he said. Lisa described the phone call from Jeffrey.

"That's a bit whirlwind, isn't it?" he asked. "I guess that's how big corporations do business. How will you manage with classes?"

"I only have one class tomorrow, and that involves a project I'm way ahead on. I'll email the professor and let him know. He's actually quite interested in the CDF work so I don't see it will be a problem."

"So ... is there a problem?" asked Chris. "You seem a little perturbed."

"No, probably not," said Lisa. "It's just that Professor Albacete called me just before the last phone call, asking me if I had any technical problems. It seemed strange just out of the blue like that, and then this sudden arrangement to fly to Illinois."

"Well he is a math professor," said Chris. "You do expect them to be eccentric."

"I guess," laughed Lisa. "Anyway, this should be an interesting experience. I'll keep my eyes and ears open when I'm at Wolfram Research."

"But you've been there before," said Chris. "You presented at the technology conference."

"I know," said Lisa, but this is different. The focus will be much more on me."

Back in his office Jeffrey was thinking how he could arrange to talk to Heinrich in Chicago without Lisa being present. Could he send her down to Champagne by herself while he spent time with Heinrich in Chicago? That would be ridiculous, not to mention unfair to Lisa. Better, he thought, if I stay on for a day in Chicago to confer with Heinrich. That made sense, Jeffrey thought. He phoned Heinrich to let him know of the visit and to see if they could meet up for lunch.

"Jeffrey, this is a surprise. I did not imagine you would be anywhere near Chicago. Unfortunately I cannot meet with you. Anna and I have to fly back to Providence to deal with the purchase of the house. How amusing that you are flying here while I am flying there."

34

The best laid plans

Bob Fosberry, Lori Bailey, Kathy Riverton and Rickhart Jansen met in Bob's office. Kathy wanted to discuss Lori's idea of a focused effort on promoting CDF development in the undergraduate curriculum. Kathy asked Lori to tell Rickhart what she had told Bob and Kathy earlier. Lori explained to Rickhart her point of view that students did not write enough in mathematics classes. In recent semesters she had emphasized writing in WordPress blogs where the students could use LaTeX to compose mathematical expressions, but somehow, she felt, even this did not really get to the essential core of the matter.

"Many of our students are just not getting a deep appreciation for mathematical formulas," she said. "And it seems to me that authoring CDF documents tackles this issue very directly. The formulas come alive, as it were, within the document."

"The Harry Potter effect," said Rickhart.

"Yes, the Harry Potter effect, exactly. And the computable document format allows and encourages students to be wizards," she said. "I feel this could have a really transformative effect on the teaching and learning of mathematics. Which is why Bob and I are putting it into our grant proposal. It was Bob's idea, actually."

Bob laughed. "If only," he said. "I had a sort of vague half-formed thought that it might be useful. A hunch, that's all. Lori's the one who's clarified the whole thing."

"Can you trial it in a couple of classes?" asked Rickhart. "I support your feelings but it would be nice to have some concrete experience on which to base our judgment."

Lori explained that she had already decided to use CDFs in her upper level statistics class next semester. "Even the mathematics majors have trouble understanding statistical formulas at a deep level," she said. "I'm going to devise a series of CDF projects that should help them get a much deeper appreciation of those formulas."

Kathy expressed her agreement with Lori. This seemed a no-brainer, in her view. "Look, Wolfram Research is putting a huge amount of effort into CDF development. There are already many thousands of free CDFs out there, and major publishers are translating textbooks into CDFs. Look at Jeff's publisher! We're at the beginning of a revolution in technical documentation, far bigger than applications in mathematics, but essentially based on mathematics in the underlying engine. I think this is a great opportunity and we should grab it."

"I just wanted to see how it would pan out in practice before expecting a major commitment from the Department," said Rickhart.

"I agree with that," said Kathy, "but the Department doesn't have to make any commitment, apart from faculty time and effort. The Center can take this on as a major educational development. I'm happy to do that if Lori will head it."

Lori nodded her agreement. Rickhart was still cautious. "But Kathy, faculty time and effort *are* Departmental resources. Time and effort on this project is time and effort taken from something else. This is why I want us to clarify our vision for the Department, both short and longer term, and use George's workload model to structure our work more productively. I'm happy that we see the CDF development as a major focus for the Department. I just want us to consider it in light of everything else we do."

The others agreed. "Then will you raise it with the Department, Rick, and see who else wants to be involved?" asked Kathy. "I'm assuming you will Bob," she laughed, "and if we can get a couple of others then we will have the nucleus of a team that could really do something awesome here."

"You're unstoppable", Rickhart said to Kathy. "Alright, I will send out an email to the Department asking for interest from others. Lori, can you send me a detailed description of how you see this project being structured? I only hope Inger doesn't object that I'm behaving like the Chairperson when I'm not – yet."

Rickhart had another thought. "By the way, shouldn't we involve Jeff's assistant Lisa De Silva? It seems to me that she, more than anyone else around here, has the deepest recent experience of CDF development."

♥♥♥♥♥

Jeffrey, meanwhile, scrambled on hearing Heinrich's plans. He phoned his editor and apologized profusely for an urgent development that had arisen at the University. He wouldn't, he explained, be able to travel to Illinois this week after all. Apologizing again, he asked if the visit could be postponed to the near future. It was fortunate Jeffrey could not see his editor's expression, but heard only the soothing words "Of course Jeffrey. Leave it with me."

Jeffrey then phoned Lisa. "There's been a development," he said, "Wolfram cannot meet with us after all this week. I hope you're not too disappointed."

"Disappointed, no. Perplexed, yes," thought Lisa to herself.

Next on the list was Heinrich. "Good news!' said Jeffrey. "There's been a change of plans. The publisher's messed up the arrangements with Wolfram Research and I won't be flying to Illinois this week after all. It's too bad really because I need to keep this project moving along. The upside, of course, is that I will be able to meet with you here tomorrow."

"I see," said Heinrich, silently marveling at Jeffrey's whirlwind, not to say chaotic, world. "Very good. Did you say you wanted to meet for lunch? I think Anna and I should be done with our housing arrangements by 1:00 PM. Is that too late for you Jeffrey?"

Jeffrey confirmed 1:00 PM would be ideal. "Will Anna be joining us?" he asked.

"No, I think she probably will not," said Heinrich. "Anna loves to shop and I think she is after some Alex and Ani jewelry, which she can only get in the North East. So I think that is what she will be doing. It will be just you and me, I'm afraid."

"Oh, that's good," said Jeffrey, adding quickly: "I'm glad Anna has the opportunity to shop for jewelry. I hope she finds something she wants."

Jeffrey hung up and sat down. He breathed a deep sigh. "I just want to be able to get Heinrich on side before anyone at my publisher talks to him," he thought. Jeffrey felt a little calmer and began to make coffee. As he did, the tension dropped from his body and he smiled to himself. "I'm being ridiculous," he thought. "Why would anyone imagine that Heinrich would be anything less than honorable? Even if someone approached him to write a new matrix algebra book – which they were perfectly entitled to do – why did anyone imagine Heinrich would not come to him first to discuss the matter?"

Jeffrey felt better already. The heady aroma of the coffee drew him in. He poured himself a cup and sat at his computer to read the latest reviews of the 9th edition of his book. There were reviews from the Mathematical Association of America, the American Mathematical Society, and the Society for Industrial and Applied Mathematics. The first review compared his book to previous editions and noted the presence of several substantial new applications. The reviewer also noted Jeffrey's book was in wide use in colleges and universities throughout America, and had been translated into many foreign languages. A perceptive review, thought Jeffrey. The American Mathematical Society reviewer was more critical. "This book, in wide use in the United States and beyond", it said, "contains a wealth of material but suffers from a defect in that it does not adequately connect with other works on linear algebra, in this reviewer's opinion."

"That was just it," thought Jeffrey. "In his *opinion*. And seeing the reviewer was not an acknowledged expert in matrix algebra, just what was his opinion worth?"

Jeffrey was more interested in the review from the Society for Industrial and Applied Mathematics, his target audience. This was a review by a competent professional in the field, and was much more perceptive and complementary Jeffrey noted. The review praised the breadth and depth of material in the book and the wide use of relevant applications. The reviewer expressed the expert view that Jeffrey's 9th edition had it all, and was essential reading for all students of mathematics. "The only criticism I have," the reviewer went on, and Jeffrey's eyeballs bored into the computer screen, "is that the text is excruciatingly dull. Could there be a more boring text on such an interesting subject?"

Jeffrey knocked over his coffee that ran over the papers on his desk and onto his copy of the 9th edition.

35

What's on your mind?

❧

Jeffrey was waiting for Heinrich just before 1:00 PM at Chiazza Trattoria in Barrington. Heinrich came into the restaurant a few minutes after 1:00, looked around for Jeffrey and waved. "This seems a very nice restaurant, Jeffrey. You are spoiled for good places to eat around Providence." Jeffrey agreed. His expanding waistline, despite his efforts at the gym, was testament to that. Heinrich ordered a spinach and pear salad, and Jeffrey chose the calamari as an appetizer. Jeffrey asked if everything was settled now in relation to the house.

"Yes. Everything seems now to be in order," said Heinrich. "Closing should be in thirty days."

"Thirty days?" asked Jeffrey. "That's quick."

"Yes, it is quick," said Heinrich. "That was the reason for our visit now. We were keen to arrange the closing as soon as possible. So, Jeffrey, you wanted to meet. There is something you wish to discuss?"

Jeffrey had thought carefully about where to start. "Well, as you know Heinrich, I am working with my publisher on an interesting new edition of my book. We are producing this new edition using computable document format."

"Yes, I know about this Jeffrey, and I am very much in admiration of your efforts. No sooner has the 9th edition appeared than you are starting work on a new edition with major technological changes. This is very impressive."

"Thank you," Jeffrey said. "I'm not doing it alone. I have help from a talented assistant." Jeffrey thought for a moment how lucky he was indeed to have met up with Lisa De Silva. His life had been transformed with energy since their first meeting in the Coffee Depot in Warren.

"So you must be very happy with this project, Jeffrey?" asked Heinrich.

"That's right," said Jeffrey, but Heinrich did not see an expression of happiness on Jeffrey's face. "Something is not going well?" he asked.

"Oh, no. Everything is progressing very well,", said Jeffrey. "Very well. You know, Heinrich, I would very much like to work with you on a project like this. You and I have very similar interests and I think it would be very good, certainly for me, if we could work together on a major project."

Heinrich was very grateful for Jeffrey's words. "Thank you Jeffrey. I too would very much like to work with you. I think we could form a very happy and productive team."

Jeffrey was relieved. This was going much better than he had hoped.

"You know, Heinrich, I mentioned your name to my publisher recently. Well, to the leader of the technical team, actually.

"Yes, I know," said Heinrich. "Your publisher has been in touch with me."

"They ... they have?" asked Jeffrey. The wind had well and truly left Jeffrey's sails. He slumped in his seat.

"Yes. They sounded me out about possible book projects, as

you could imagine. They are a publisher, after all," Heinrich laughed. Jeffrey could just manage a smile.

"But I told them I should talk with you first. I know how involved you have been with the 9th edition of your book, and now your new venture with CDF publishing. It is quite exciting actually. I told them I would rather work with you than think of my own publishing project just now, especially as I begin working with you as junior colleague."

Jeffrey thought someone quite muscular must have lifted the heavy weight from his shoulders. As the tension dissolved he began to relax. A warm, soothing feeling flooded his body. He wished this moment could go on forever. He seemed to recall that over twenty years ago he and ... but that was in the past. He was thrilled with Heinrich's response, and overcome with gratitude.

"Are you okay, Jeffrey?"asked Heinrich."

"Just fine, Heinrich, Just fine. Thank you."

Heinrich and Jeffrey finished their lunch, demolishing a bottle of Montellori Chianti in the process. Jeffrey thanked Heinrich for taking time to meet, and wished him a safe journey back to Chicago. Heinrich shook hands and said he looked forward to their growing working relationship, and on that note they parted.

♥♥♥♥♥

Jeffrey was sitting in his office savoring a post luncheon coffee when Lisa De Silva knocked on his door.

"Lisa! Hi, come on in," he said to her.

"Hi Professor Albacete. I wonder if you would have a minute to talk?"

"Indeed I have. Please, sit down. What's on your mind?" he asked.

Lisa told him about recent events and some of the looming decisions in her life. She told him how much she appreciated working with him on the CDF version of his book and how much she enjoyed it. "The visit to your publisher was very interesting," she said. "It opened my eyes to a lot of things. But I'm not sure it's a place I would want to work." Lisa told Jeffrey how she had been thinking of graduate school, and now Bob Fosberry and Lori Bailey had all but offered her a job on their curriculum project if funding came through.

"I'm a bit confused," she said. "And I guess I would appreciate some advice."

Jeffrey nodded as Lisa spoke. He *had* been around the block a few times, and he had known both failure and success. The thing of which he was sure was to do what you love. Let the devil take the rest, he thought. Just do what you love. He told Lisa as much.

"I appreciate that, Professor Albacete, and I'm sure you're right. The thing is it doesn't help me much. I like all aspects of what I'm doing. I want to keep working on this book with you, but I don't want a fulltime job with your publisher, or any publisher. I would like to work parttime or maybe as a consultant. Do you think that's possible?"

Jeffrey agreed that his publisher would almost certainly hire her as a technical consultant, on favorable terms. "They just want the book produced," he said.

"Professor Fosberry and Professor Bailey won't know about their grant application until about the time I graduate," Lisa said. "By that time I probably will have applications in for grad school and will be thinking seriously about that."

"What would you do in grad school?" Jeffrey asked.

"That's the thing – I'm not sure," said Lisa. "I'm very good at coming up with algorithms, with algorithm design and analysis. There are a couple of excellent graduate programs at MIT and Carnegie-Mellon. I think they would challenge me, and I would like that."

"I don't know, Lisa. Maybe one of your professors in computer science could advise you better," said Jeffrey. "The only thing I would say to you, other than doing what you love, is to ask what it is that you gossip about."

"What I gossip about?" asked Lisa, puzzled.

"Yes. What you gossip about," repeated Jeffrey. "It's the Francis Crick test. You've heard of him: the DNA biologist? He wrote once that people should choose to do what they gossip about. Presumably on the basis that gossiping is a reflection of what's continually on our mind that interests us."

"I don't really know what I gossip about," said Lisa. "Does any one know that really?" She thanked Jeffrey for his time and went away to think about his words.

In the late afternoon she sat in the Coffee Depot thinking about what Jeffrey had said. She Googled "Francis Crick gossip test" and, sure enough, Professor Albacete was right. When Chris came in she asked him what it was that she gossiped about.

"Gossip? You?" asked Chris. Lisa nodded.

"That's an easy one: Alex and Ani jewelry of course!"

36

Algorithmic design

"Chris, get real!" said Lisa. "I'm a computer scientist, not a jeweler."

"It passes the Crick gossip test," he said, and smiled at her.

"Well, yes, but that shows how stupid this is," she said. "I will admit I have a very marked interest in jewelry. I will even admit that I talk about it to the point that I might – might! – be described as 'gossiping'."

Chris smiled again. "Oh yes, you do!" he said.

"So what? I spend my time devising and coding algorithms. It's what I'm good at. Very good in fact," she said.

"I agree with that," said Chris.

"So tell me – Mr. Smarty Pants – how does a computer scientist earn a living making jewelry and still do computer science?" she asked.

"I haven't the faintest idea," said Chris. "But your original question was what do you gossip about. Now upon reflection, prompted by an astute observation of yours truly, you have a new question. Why don't you Google it, you computer scientist, you!"

Lisa thought this was becoming really silly. She had gone to

Professor Albacete for career advice, and she had come away with 'do what you love' and 'think about what you gossip about'. "Okay," she thought. "I love algorithm design, implementation and analysis. And I gossip about jewelry. And now I'm Googling that." She sipped at her coffee as the search results appeared.

"Wow! This is actually interesting," she said. Top of the search list was a link to algorithmic design of jewelry on Gizmodo. The links lead to *Nervous System*, founded in 2007 by MIT architecture and biology student Jessica Rosenkrantz and Jesse Louis-Rosenberg, an MIT mathematics major.

"Alan Turing spare us!" exclaimed Lisa. Chris laughed at Lisa's favorite exclamation. "What is it?" he asked.

Lisa read to him the details of Nervous System jewelry. "Jessica Rosenkrantz and Jesse Louis-Rosenberg use algorithms to design jewelry," she said. "They have open source and proprietary algorithms that assist in the design of unique pieces of jewelry."

"Where are they?" asked Chris. "New York?"

"No, actually they are in Somerville, Massachusetts,, said Lisa. "About an hour from here. Oh no!" she said. "What is it?" asked Chris.

"They're actually advertising for a programmer to work for them!"

Chris grinned broadly. "Well, well," he said. "Do what you love and gossip about. Who woulda thunk?"

"This is amazing", said Lisa. "I'm going to call and go to Somerville to talk with them. If this works out it sure beats working for Jeffrey's publisher."

Lisa went back and scanned the Google search results. There was another link, further down, to a site called Generative Jewelry Design 3D. This seemed to be a social networking site for jewelry designers interested in designing with generative algorithms.

"I never imagined that people were doing such things," she said. "Or that I could even think about combining computer science and jewelry." She thought that while Jeffrey Albacete's advice had seemed vague and very broad, it had effectively and rapidly steered her toward a potential new career.

"I think I know what I'm going to do,", she said.

"What's that?" asked Chris.

"I'm going to go up to Somerville to talk with the Nervous System people, Jessica and Jesse, and then I'm going to check out the Rhode Island School of Design to see if they have a graduate degree that would combine jewelry and computer science. My mind's made up," she said. "It's where I'm headed."

♥♥♥♥♥

When Lisa returned from visiting Nervous System she was even more determined. Everyone she talked to there thought the Rhode Island School of Design would be a good choice.

"You might want to take a few graduate classes in algorithm design at your University," a faculty member at the School of Design told her on the phone. "Being an algorithmic designer requires knowing a lot, technically, about algorithm design and implementation. You could do an internship and practical work to align your skills and experience." The adviser said she thought Lisa could maybe do a practicum or internship this academic year. "This is your senior year, isn't it"?" she had asked. Lisa said it was, and had agreed to talk with her academic adviser at the University about a practicum of some sort at Nervous System. She knew what she wanted to do, so she went to Bob Fosberry's office to tell him of her decision. "I can't say I'm not disappointed," said Bob. "But I'm very pleased for you. It must be exciting thinking about a career that involves design in such apparently different ways." She agreed it was.

"I will find someone who can work with you on developing CDFs", she said.

"Thanks, I appreciate it," he said.

Lisa then left to tell Jeffrey Albacete of her decision. "This is going to be tough," she thought. "He has so much riding on this project, and here I am pulling out of it." Lisa knocked on Jeffrey's office door and tried the handle. It was locked. "Some other time," she said, somewhat relieved.

♥♥♥♥♥

Jeffrey was talking with Heinrich on Skype. It had been Heinrich's suggestion and Jeffrey was surprised at how quickly he had picked it up. "Don't know why I didn't do this sooner," he said to himself. They were discussing a possible joint project and the thought had come to Jeffrey that perhaps this CDF version of *Matrix Algebra* would turn out to be so different from his previous editions that he could think of this as an entirely new venture. As a consequence, and influenced by Heinrich's kindly attitude at lunch in Barrington, Jeffrey was beginning to form an idea that he and Heinrich could co-author this CDF publication. He had put this to Heinrich and was now discussing the production of the CDFs.

"Lisa is very, very good," said Jeffrey. "I think all my luck in this venture has come from my association with her. A serendipitous meeting if ever there was one."

Heinrich agreed that this could turn out very well. He told Jeffrey that he would, as he explained in his job interview, like to focus for the time being on applications of matrix algebra in science and engineering. "So I would very much like to talk with Lisa and see what she can make of some of my ideas," he said.

"That's very good," said Jeffrey. " I will talk with Lisa as soon as possible, and get her to Skype with you about how she can implement your thoughts as CDFs."

Jeffrey signed off and walked over the to Daily Grind for a latte and a muffin. He felt so light and free of worry the past couple of days, since he and Heinrich had talked frankly about publishing. "Lisa must have taken the technical team's comments the wrong way," he thought. "I know I'm not as dynamic a writer as Heinrich, but I am very steady and very careful." He smiled at the thought of himself as a plodder. "Not many plodders have nine editions of a successful textbook to their name," he thought.

The coffee, while good, was nowhere near as refined as Lisa's scintillating Terroir brand. He thought he would give Lisa a call and tell her the news about him and Heinrich. Her phone went into voicemail. Jeffrey left a message asking her to call back, saying he had some news. Five minutes later Jeffery got a call from Lisa.

"Lisa! Hi," he said. " I have some news for you. It looks like Heinrich and I will be working together on the CDF version of *Matrix Algebra* – a new *Matrix Algebra*, really. Heinrich would like to speak with you about translating some of his ideas into the snappy CDFs you produce."

"Oh!" said Lisa. "Uhm ... Professor Albacete, I don't know what to say. I need to come and talk with you."

"By all means," said Jeffrey. "By all means, come and talk. This is probably a bit overwhelming. The project is looking much bigger and I will wager those technical people at the publisher are going to need your help. I wouldn't be surprised if they offered you a serious consultancy."

37

They are not your friends

❧

Bert Monod called Kathy and asked if she could do him a favor. He explained that his son, Andy, was due to appear in court and wondered if she might be able to be in court with him. "Even if I could get there myself," he said, "I couldn't sit in a courtroom chair for who knows how long." Kathy agreed straight away. She asked Bert if Andy had a lawyer to represent him. Bert said all they had was the family lawyer who did wills, estate planning and real estate closings. Kathy said: "Better that than nothing, I think." She phoned Bert's lawyer and agreed to meet him outside the courthouse. She picked up Andy from Bert's home and they drove together to the court. Andy was very nervous, and Kathy tried to reassure him, "It's a first offense, and a minor one," she said. "I'm guessing they will warn you and possibly give you a fine, or maybe community service. In due course you can apply to have this expunged from your record."

"What if I have to go to jail?" asked Andy. He looked terrified. Kathy responded that was unlikely in her opinion, for the reasons she just mentioned. She told Andy to do his best to relax and look calm, confident and to be alert and respectful in court. "Pay attention and speak truthfully, no matter how embarrassing it may sound in court," she said. Andy and Kathy met the lawyer who went over some points with Andy before going into the courthouse with them.

When Andy was asked *why* he had tried to sell two of his father's prescription narcotics he was momentarily stumped. "I ...," he stammered. He recalled Kathy's words, and told the judge that it wasn't for the money. "I didn't need the money," he said. "It was to try to look cool ... to be cool."

"Look cool?" asked the judge. "You mean to brag about it afterwards to impress others?"

"Yes, your Honor," replied Andy.

"I see," said the judge. "We will adjourn for ten minutes while I think about this case."

Andy turned to Kathy. "He's thinking of sending me to jail, isn't he?" Andy asked her. The lawyer answered. "No, I don't think so Andy. I think he wants you to realize the folly of trying to gain respect from people, such as drug dealers, who couldn't care less about your respect, and I think he's pondering how to do that."

The judge returned shortly after ten minutes and the courtroom rose. The clerk asked people to be seated.

"Andrew Monod," said the judge. "Please approach the bench." Andy stood up and walked to the judge's bench. He felt terrified. "Andrew, you seem to be a decent young man from a very good family. Your father is a Professor and Chair of his Department at the University. What must he think of this?" Andy replied that his father was probably ashamed and that he, Andy, felt very badly about that.

The judge nodded. "This is your first offense." He looked sternly at Andy. "And I sincerely hope it is your last. I do not want to see you before this court again. Do you understand?" Andy responded that he did.

"I have thought about appropriate punishments that are available to me." Andy was sweating profusely now. "The problem," said the judge, "is two fold. You think the drug scene, at least the minor part of it with which you were starting to engage is 'cool'. And you are having problems understanding boundaries. Seeking the approval of common drug dealers is not cool. These people are not your friends, and you need to realize they never will be."

The judge asked Andy if he belonged to any social organizations, such as sporting groups, or groups associated with a hobby. "No, your honor," replied Andy.

"I thought not,", said the judge. "Here is my order. You are fined the sum of $500. You will do community service for the next 90 days. You will do four hours each week with PSI Cognitive Counseling Services in Providence. They have a program for drug abusers and you will assist them in that program as they see fit. Do you understand?"

"Yes, your Honor," said Andy, relieved that jail was not one of orders.

"You will also do four hours each week working with Habitat for Humanity, helping build accommodation for needy families. That's all, you may step down."

Andy smiled as he walked back to Kathy and the lawyer. "Whew!" he said.

"I don't think you got off easily," said the lawyer. "The judge has given you a fairly stiff community work order. That's eight hours each week for three whole months."

Andy look concerned when he thought about what the lawyer said. "That means like more than two hours for two nights and all of Saturday or Sunday morning?"

"Something like that," said the lawyer.

"I get the drug counseling bit," said Andy, "but what is it with – what did he call it?"

"Habitat for Humanity," said Kathy.

"Yeah that," said Andy. "What's with that?"

"My guess", said Kathy, "is that you will doing something that is practical and useful every week. You will be assisting needy people in the community – helping build homes for low income families. But more to the point I think, is that after several months of doing that work you will have met some very fine people, and made some real friends – people who you will respect, and who will respect you."

"Okay, I guess that can't hurt," said Andy.

"No. I guess it can't," laughed Kathy. "Now let's get you back to your dad."

Bert was relieved to see Andy and Kathy and hear the judge's sentence.

"I'm sorry about the $500, dad," said Andy. "I've got about two hundred in savings, If you could help me out with the other three hundred I could pay you back at fifty dollars a week."

"Sure, that'll be fine," said Bert. "You know it's funny the judge wants you to do community service with PSI Cognitive Counseling Services – that's where I was when I broke my pelvis. I wouldn't have had prescription painkillers for you to sell if I hadn't been at that damned place!"

Kathy was about to say goodbye to Bert and Andy when she had a thought. "Andy, you know Habitat for Humanity is on Broad Street in Providence. How about we take a ride down there now and see if they can sign you up?"

"I guess," said Andy. "I've got to go anyway, so it may as well be now."

Kathy said goodbye to Bert. "Thanks for everything, Kathy," he said. "You've been a great help".

"No problem, Bert. Glad I could be there for you and Andy."

Kathy and Andy drove to the Habitat for Humanity headquarters in Rhode Island. Kathy parked the car, and they both went inside.

"Can I help you?" the receptionist asked Kathy and Andy.

"Yes, I have a new volunteer for you", said Kathy.

"Well, that's great! Just great," said the receptionist, surmising

Kathy meant Andy. She pulled out a form and asked Andy to fill in his details.

"You know, the biggest need for volunteers right now is at our Warwick address." She noted Andrew's address and asked if that would cause a problem for him. "You'll have to come back up 195 and then south on 95. Do you have a car?"

"Yes, I do," said Andy.

"Well, okay then, let me enter your details in the computer and the folks at Warwick will be expecting you. You've indicated Saturday morning would work best for you?"

"Yes, it would," said Andy.

"You know Andrew, I respect a young man like you volunteering to build housing for needy families. It's not every young person who gives to the community like that. I suspect you'll make a lot of good friends."

"I expect I will", said Andy. He turned to Kathy. "Thanks, Kathy."

"My pleasure," she replied.

38

How much?

Kathy Riverton told Rickhart about Andy Monod's day in court. "I think he'll be okay as long as he can grow up a bit," she said, "but it's Bert I'm worried about long-term." Rickhart asked why that was. "The problem is the painkillers he's on. They're fine for short-term use – essential even for severe acute pain – but longer-term they can create dependency. Bert is going to want more and more of them the longer he uses them for the pain."

"What's the alternative? asked Rickhart. "A broken pelvis must be very painful."

"What he's doing, physiotherapy, plus – and I wouldn't want to be the one to say this to Bert – psychological counseling."

Rickhart laughed. "I'm sorry to laugh at his misfortune," he said, "but it is funny that he should go back to the place from which he was escaping temporarily when he had his accident."

Kathy agreed. "He doesn't have to go back to the same place, even though it probably is the best, but I think he needs some help from a professional counselor."

A knock at the door interrupted them and Kathy opened it to find Lisa De Silva. "Lisa, hi. Come on in."

"I'm not interrupting anything am I?" asked Lisa.

"No, we were just gossiping," said Kathy.

"Well, it's sort of gossiping that I want to talk about," said Lisa. "My gossiping."

Lisa explained her advice from Jeffrey Albacete and her conversation with her friend Chris about gossiping. "The upshot is, I know what I want to do."

"And what is that?" asked Rickhart.

"I want to work in algorithmic design of jewelry," said Lisa. She explained her visit to Nervous System jewelry in Somerville Massachusetts and how she hoped to take a graduate course in jewelry design at the Rhode Island School of Design, coupled with graduate classes in algorithm design at the University.

"Wow! That's amazing," said Rickhart. "I never knew people did such things. And the Nervous System people are from MIT originally?" he asked.

Lisa nodded agreement. She turned to Kathy. "But I need some help. I don't know how to tell Professor Albacete that I won't be able to work for him any longer."

"Oh, I see," said Kathy. "You want to re-orient your senior year courses to fit in with your new plans."

"Exactly," said Lisa.

"Wouldn't you, whichever route you took, have allocated time to work on Jeff's project? How has that changed? Is it that you've just lost interest in the work with him?"

"No, it's not that," said Lisa. "I really like coding the CDF version of his book. I just can't see myself doing it for longer than another six months is all."

"Maybe that's all he'll need," said Kathy. "As I recall there was talk that his publisher could pay you for this work. And, as I recall, the reason you wanted to work for Jeffrey is because you could use the money for student loans." Lisa agreed that was correct. "Has anyone at the publishing house talked money?" asked Kathy. Lisa said they had not. "Then here's my advice," said Kathy. "If Jeff is agreed, go to the publisher and ask them for a large sum of money to work on this book. Here, let's figure out what that might be." Kathy did a few calculations and came up with a sum of money that made Lisa gasp.

"Do you think they would pay that much?" asked Lisa.

"I don't see why not", said Kathy. "You're talented, and you already have a score on the board as far as they are concerned. They've seen your work and they like it very much according to Jeff." Lisa agreed. "What do you have to lose?" asked Kathy. "In your mind you already had a 'no', and you were prepared to walk away to do something else, something you love. But what if you could still do that and get paid what you're really worth on the book project?"

Lisa had not imagined the scenario Kathy had described. "But why not?" she thought. "What have I got to lose?"

"It seems a lot of scales have been dropping from my eyes the past couple of days," said Lisa. "I'm seeing things I never imagined were possible."

"It's because you're thinking about work after college," said Kathy. "Most talented undergraduates have no idea of their worth, and prospective employers are happy to keep it that way. If I were you I would ask for a consultancy rather than a parttime job with Jeff's publisher. You're a student so you don't need health benefits from them, which as a parttimer they may not pay anyway. And you'll begin to establish yourself as an independent computer science consultant."

"Thank you so much," Lisa said to Kathy, "and thank you too, Professor Jansen."

When Lisa left Rickhart said to Kathy: "You know, it makes me think that we don't do enough to provide in-depth career advice to our mathematics undergraduates. I'm thinking we could run a course at the sophomore level on careers in mathematics."

"Is it part of the Department's strategic plan?" laughed Kathy.

♥♥♥♥♥

Jeffrey Albacete was very pleased to see Lisa. The CDF project was really picking up steam he thought. With Heinrich and he as co-authors and Lisa as technical expert, they had a great team.

"So what did you want to talk about?" asked Jeffrey politely. He was bursting to talk about his plans.

Lisa thought she might as well just launch into the request. As Professor Riverton had said, she already had a no for an answer. Let's see what might happen in reality.

"I was hoping we could ask your publisher to hire me as a con-sultant for the CDF book project" she said.

"I think it almost goes without saying they would agree to that," said Jeffrey. "The technical team were very impressed with your skills. Would you like me to contact them for you?" Lisa said that would be helpful. "Since it's a consultancy, the employment roles, as it were, are sort of reversed," said Jeffrey. "They have a job they want done – well, actually even that is reversed because it's a job I want done. Nevertheless ..." he was struggling to pull himself out of this tangle of thought. "The thing is, you should probably set the rate at which you want to be paid," he said, "and see if they agree. I'm sure they will agree to any reasonable sum."

"Employing an undergraduate is not that expensive," he thought to himself.

Lisa held back naming a figure. She knew Jeffrey was thinking of an hourly rate, but she had phoned Chris after talking with Kathy Riverton and he too had suggested a fee for the project. That, he explained, gave her latitude to work at her pace. If she finished sooner, good for her, and if she took longer, that was her lookout. A thoughtful client, like Professor Albacete's publisher, he said, should realize the benefit of not paying an hourly rate, which could amount to a very large amount if the project ran over. The trick, he said, is to be confident to ask for the right sum for the entire project, no matter how large that seemed at the time.

Lisa took her courage in her hands and spoke up. "You already have a no,", she heard Kathy's voice say. "I do have an amount in mind", Lisa said. "Could you tell your publisher that my fee for the project is $50,000. I can work on and deliver the project in six months for that fee."

Jeffrey gasped. His coffee cup fell to the floor.

"Are you okay, Professor Albacete?" asked Lisa.

"I … I, yes I'm fine," he said. "I don't know if they will agree to such a large sum, but I will ask."

"Thank you," said Lisa, pleased she had taken the courageous path. A feeling of strength and determination washed over her.

39

Just do it

Bob Fosberry looked over the final grant application to the National Science Foundation. He was still very unsure about sending this to the University Grants Office for forwarding tomorrow by 5:00 PM. Bob was finding it hard to believe that so many people in the University were supportive of his idea for a new applied mathematics curriculum that directly tackled the needs of freshman and sophomore science and engineering students. The Dean of Engineering had been especially supportive. His own Dean, Sara Nueberg, was happy to write a letter of support. Despite being a former biology professor, however, she did not seem to grasp the essence of the proposal. Faculty from biology, chemistry, engineering – all disciplines – and physics were very supportive. Lori Bailey was Co-Principal Investigator as were three other faculty from the science disciplines. Several others were Senior Faculty on the project. Bob had constructed an advisory board to help guide the project and an evaluation group to provide real-time evaluation. In all Bob should have been very happy to get to this point. Instead, he was anxious. He had never taken a lead role in a project of this size. When he had worked with Jeffrey on the Matrix Algebra project it was Jeffrey who had taken the lead and managed the project. In his heart of hearts Bob was not convinced he had what it took to get this project funded and then successfully executed. He remembered Kathy's favorite maxim: "A no you've already got!" and placed the final version of the application in the shared folder in DropBox. He emailed all the participants, asking for their final thoughts.

Twenty minutes later Lori responded. She said the narrative looked great. She pointed out a few typos, and made some small suggestions – just stylistic trifles, she called them – about re-wording several sentences. The Dean of Engineering responded within thirty minutes. "This is great, Bob!" he wrote. "Congratulations on taking the lead on this and pulling it together. I've attached a very strong letter of support."

Within two hours all the participants had responded, some suggesting small stylistic changes, and all congratulating Bob on getting the application to this point. Bob's anxiety level dropped. He would make the changes people had recommended and sleep on the final version before sending it to the Grants Office tomorrow. All the necessary details had been entered into the online Fastlane system, and the Grants Office had been able to view those details and the budget for the last week. Everything seemed set for them to press the submit button once he indicated that the narrative of the proposal was uploaded.

Bob walked around the hallway to Lori's office on the off chance that she might be there. Her door was open. He knocked and walked in.

"Bob! Hi!" said Lori. "Great job!"

He shrugged.

"No really, I mean it. You've done an amazing job pulling this together. I think this has a real chance of being funded. Apparently the Dean of Engineering thinks so, too."

Bob sat down. "Thanks Lori. I couldn't have done it without you and the other faculty."

"Well of course you couldn't," she laughed, "but you took the lead, you had the concept, and you pulled it all together."

"I guess so," he said. "Anyway, it's done I think. I just want to sleep on it and then send it to the Grants Office tomorrow. I'm so relieved. I was wondering if you would like to get a celebratory drink. Celebrating getting the proposal in, that is."

"Sure," she said. Can you give me about five minutes to finish up what I'm doing?"

"Take your time," he said. "I'm not going anywhere."

Lori finished her work and turned to Bob. "Do you have anywhere in mind?"

"I was thinking maybe the Wharf Tavern," he said.

"In Warren?" said Lori. "Sure that would be great. I could do with a drink overlooking the water. Let's go. Your car?"

They walked to the car park and drove the two and a half miles over the County Road bridge to Warren. The Wharf Tavern was busy that time of the afternoon. "Should we sit at the bar or get a table?" Bob asked.

"I think a table so we can see the water," said Lori.

A server arrived with menus and introduced herself. Lori said they were just here for drinks, so the server left the drinks list and said she would be back in a few minutes.

Bob asked Lori if she had ever looked at the Wharf Tavern website. She hadn't. "Well it's a laugh," he said. "They have headings for their *Menu's* and *Event's*. Or should I say *Heading's?*"

Lori laughed. "I thought only realtors and grocery stores did that."

"I feel like buying them a copy of *Eats, Shoots and Leaves*," said Bob.

"They would probably think someone misspelled the title: it should be *Eat's, Shoot's and Leave's*," she said.

Their server returned to take drink orders. Lori said she would have a *Bury Me in Bubbles*, strawberry champagne cocktail. Bob ordered a Chilean Merlot. Lori turned to Bob. "What are we going to do if we get this grant?" she asked. "It's sort of scary to think of tying ourselves up for five years. It will take a lot of effort."

"I know," said Bob, "the thought has crossed my mind about twice a day for the past month." They both laughed. "Oh well," said Lori, "it will keep us busy."

"As if you're not already busy enough," said Bob. "I think you work harder than anyone in the Department. You know you *will* get tenure. There's no need to burn yourself out."

"It's not that," she replied. "I enjoy what I do. I can't believe sometimes that I'm paid for the privilege of doing what I do."

Their drinks arrived and they sat back basking in the weather and the view down Narragansett Bay. Another drink later they both felt hungry so Bob asked their server to bring back the menus. "Of course I meant *Menu's*", he laughed.

They ordered dinner and another drink. Afternoon merged into evening, and the lights on Narragansett Bay began to sparkle.

"Congratulations again on a job very well done," said Lori. "She raised her glass to Bob.

"And very well done to you, too, Co- Principal Investigator," said Bob. "It wouldn't have happened without ya!"

"I have a feeling we're going to get this grant, Bob. Funny to think we'll be working together for five years if we do."

Bob thought about working with Lori for five years. The time spent working with Jeffrey seemed to be washing away like the shore with the incoming tide. He was beginning to feel good about himself. The pain of his divorce three years ago was receding, and sitting here in the lovely setting of the Wharf Tavern with Lori he felt happy and secure.

Lori, too, was enjoying the evening. "This is lovely Bob, We should do this more often. We should have done it before – would have if we'd been working together before this." Bob agreed. "Narragansett Bay has at night has a certain magic," he said, "Especially from this vantage point."

Lori leaned close and whispered in his ear. "You know what

would really be magic? She said. "Breakfast at 6:00 AM overlooking the Bay."

"Let's do it," said Bob.

40

Alex and Ani, and me

Jeffrey was staggered at the fee Lisa told him to ask for as a consultant on his book project. "Fifty thousand dollars for six months is a hundred thousand a year. That's more than some of our new Assistant Professors with a Ph.D. make", he thought to himself. Jeffrey called his editor and put the proposal to him, asking if he could talk to the appropriate people in the organization, who could make a decision. "Leave it with me, Jeffrey", his editor said. "I will get back to you within twenty four hours."

Jeffrey thanked him and reflected on Lisa's chances. "Five thousand seems more likely to me," he thought. " That's a couple of times more than undergraduates expect to get working on a project at the University for a semester, so ... five thousand for six months." He could see that. "Maybe ten thousand if she's lucky." Jeffrey hoped Lisa would not leave the project if she was disappointed in the sum his publisher was likely to offer her. She had brought him an amazing run of luck and he wanted that to continue.

Jeffrey's editor called him a little over four hours later. "Jeffrey, good news. It's done. We're happy to offer Lisa the fee she asked. There will be some contractual details to work through, of course. Management and the technical team are very impressed by Lisa's work and we feel she will help to bring this project to a high level of technical excellence. We're exited to be getting into this CDF business – quite a new opportunity for us."

Jeffrey would have sat down were he not already. A salty saying from his undergraduate days crossed his mind. "Unbelievable!" he thought. He shook his head, partly in admiration. "That girl was born under a lucky star." He had to admire Lisa's audacity. He would never, not even as a Distinguished Professor, have asked for so much. Yet she, just entering her senior year as an under-graduate, had not only asked for, but had been granted, fifty thousand dollars! Without much discussion it seemed. He had to call Lisa right away. Her phone rang and she answered.

"Lisa, I have good news for you. My publisher has accepted your terms for the project: fifty thousand dollars for six months. You will have to sign a contract that will detail the deliverables, among other things, but you've got what you asked for."

There was silence from Lisa's end. "Are you there Lisa?" asked Jeffrey.

"Yes. I'm here," she said.

"Did you hear what I said?" he asked.

"Yes, I heard. I just can't believe it. Thank you for asking for me. I am very grateful. Should I come and see you?"

Jeffrey smiled, happy to be the bearer of good news. "No, take it easy for a while. Go celebrate."

Lisa was feeling an odd mixture of being stunned yet empow-ered. She felt a strong need to talk to Kathy Riverton. Lisa went to Kathy's office and knocked at her door.

"Come in," said Kathy. "Lisa, hi."

"Hello Professor Riverton," said Lisa. Well, you said a 'no' I already had, so I asked, and now I have a yes."

Kathy clapped her hands in delight. "You asked for the fifty thousand? And they agreed?" she asked.

Lisa nodded, with a grin wide enough to split her face.

"Well done, girl," said Kathy. "Very well done. That must have taken some nerve."

"Oh, yes!" said Lisa. "It sure did. But I was resolved after talking to you. Either I got paid what I, and you, and now apparently the publisher, thought I was worth, or I devote myself completely to what I love. The money will be very, very useful. I'm going to have to manage my time really tightly, but I'm good at that."

Lisa thanked Kathy again and left to call Chris.

" I have some good news," she said. "I need to meet up for a drink. Can you pick me up in twenty minutes?"

♥♥♥♥♥

Lisa and Chris sat at a table at the Wharf Tavern, not far from where Bob and Lori had dinner the night before. Chris was excited for Lisa. "You're in danger of becoming a big shot," he laughed.

"Flattery will get you everywhere," she said. "What would you like to drink – it's on me. No wait, before you answer, could you drink champagne? Could we split a bottle?"

"Can't see why not," said Chris.

Lisa asked their server if the Tavern had any cold Westport Rivers sparkling wine. "If you do," said Lisa, "we'll have a bottle." The server went to check and came back with a bottle of the sparkling wine in an ice bucket. "Can I interest you in food?" she asked.

"Not just now," said Lisa. "Can we let you know later?"

"Sure," said the server. "Just let me know when you're ready."

Chris proposed a toast. "To your continued success," he said.

Lisa knew it was not polite to drink to oneself, "But, what the heck," she thought.

"So, will you have any free time?" Chris asked. "What does this mean for your new found interest in the algorithmic jewelry business?"

I will tell you one thing it means, that's for bloody sure!" she said, using a turn of phrase she had learned in England last year. "I'm buying some Alex and Ani jewelry – this afternoon, in fact. Want to come with me?"

"Sure," laughed Chris. "But don't expect me to get any for myself. It's not my style."

They finished the bottle of wine and took Chris's car for the twenty-minute drive to Wayland Square in Providence. Chris parked the car at Lisa's apartment and they walked across the road to Alex and Ani.

"Six hundred dollars is my limit," said Lisa. "I can't even really afford that right now. It's a pinch. But I feel good knowing I'm getting compensated at fifty thousand over the next six months."

Chris had a question. "Do they pay you on completion? What happens with that?"

Lisa explained the arrangement she had already received in an email. "Seventeen thousand when I sign the contract. Seventeen thousand after three months if all agreed targets are being met – or exceeded. And sixteen thousand upon successful completion."

"What about tax?" asked Chris.

"They don't take it out, because as a consultant I'm an independent contractor. I'm going to have to get an accountant," she said.

Chris held open the door to Alex and Ani for Lisa. "Thank you my good man," she said, depositing a dime tip in his hand. "Gee, thanks Ms. Bigshot!" he laughed.

Lisa was drawn to the Swarovski crystal bracelets. "Let's see," she calculated. "$58 each, plus tax. That means ten of them."

"What about some of these others here?" asked Chris. "They look like your style."

"They are pretty," said Lisa, "but I'm stuck on the Swarovski crystal for now."

She tried on all the Swarovski pieces the store had.

"They are beautiful," said the assistant. Lisa settled on 10 pieces after about twenty minutes. "I'm done," she said. "That's it. But I'll be back!"

"Glad to hear it," said the assistant as she went to wrap the bracelets.

"You know I think I'll wear them," said Lisa. She chose five for one arm and five for the other. "No, too symmetric," she said, removing one from her right arm and placing it on her left."

"Much better," said Chris laughing. "Seriously though, they do look beautiful on you."

"They do, don't they?' she said.

Lisa paid the assistant and walked out of the store with Chris. They walked toward L'Artisan Bakery as a reflex action.

"Chris," said Lisa, "how would you like to come up to my apartment and *really* celebrate?"

Chris smiled. "Will you keep the bracelets on?" he asked.

41

Let them play bocce

The thought had crossed Jeffrey Albacete's mind that if a twenty-one year old undergraduate could do so well, he, a Professor with many achievements, ought to be able to do no less. "No less," he smiled to himself. "I should be able to do a darned sight better." The only thing that had been holding him back, he reflected, was a lack of audacity. Encouraged by Lisa's example he dug into the recesses of the psyche where he imagined audacity might lie, and decided to give it a go. He dialed his editor, who answered immediately.

"Uhm, ah, ... , hi Colin," said Jeffrey. "I've, ah, been wondering if I could ask you a favor?"

"Of course," said his editor. "Anything for you Jeffrey. Fire away."

"Well the thing is ... you know I receive a good commission on the sales of my book."

"Jeffrey, let me stop you there and say it's not going to be possible to raise your commission at this point. Things are tight in the industry," said the editor.

"Oh no, no. Nothing like that," said Jeffrey. "I was just wondering, ah, if, uhm, if it would be possible to get an advance on sales," said Jeffrey.

"I see," said his editor. "On the face of it I can't see why not. Your books sell well Jeffrey and with a new semester on the horizon we should be seeing a jump in sales soon. What amount do you have in mind?"

Jeffrey's mouth was very dry, and his tongue seemed stuck to the roof of his mouth. Be audacious, he said to himself, it's what carries the day.

"Are you there Jeffrey?" asked his editor.

"Yes, yes, I'm here. Well, the thing is, I was thinking around ... uhm ... fifty thousand." There, he'd blurted it out. Now let's see where audacity takes us, he thought.

"Okay. Well, look, let me put this to executive committee – it's not my decision alone to make. I should be able to get back to you by next week."

"Next week?" asked Jeffrey.

His editor, thinking Jeffrey's remark indicated Jeffrey was surprised at the speed of the decision making progress, told Jeffrey that in a modern publishing industry timely decision making was of the essence. "We don't sit around in men's clubs, drinking whisky and smoking our pipes any more", he laughed. "Leave it with me, Jeffrey. You'll hear back from me soon."

"Well, there's one more thing," said Jeffrey. "I'm thinking of an advance on the new CDF version of my book. I understand this is projected to sell well, especially in light of the collaboration with Wolfram. That's what was on my mind. Not the previous editions, but the new version."

"I see. Very good. Leave it with me, Jeffrey," said his editor.

Jeffrey thought that didn't go too badly. He was confident that his editor would put the request strongly to his executive committee. Jeffrey reflected how strange it was that all he had to do was ask. Lisa had taught him that, as she had many other things, he thought as he made himself a cup of the excellent coffee she had recommended. Jeffrey picked up a copy of the 9th edition of his book, admiring the front cover and the binding. He flicked through the pages, pleased with the layout, and the clarity of the exposition. "Soon my little beauty you will come to life in a new form, thanks to the miracle of modern technology." He was quite excited about the new CDF edition of the book. And truly, he thought, having Heinrich on board as co-author will only make the book look even better. "As if that's really possible," he chuckled. But the new version would be different he knew that. He was pleased to be working on this project with Heinrich and Lisa, pushing the boundaries of teaching and scholarship in his chosen field. Happy with his newfound sense of audacity, married to his natural sense of achievement, he poured himself another cup of Lisa's aromatic coffee.

♥♥♥♥♥

Lisa woke a little before 6:00 AM. She stretched and turned to look at Chris. He was sound asleep. She touched the hair around the back of his neck and ran her hands down to his shoulders and massaged his back. Chris stirred and smiled. "What time is it?' he asked. "About six," she replied.

"You can keep doing that if you want," he said.

Her fingers probed the muscles in his back and then her hand moved around to his belly. "I think I'd like to celebrate a little more," she said.

Chris rolled over and held her tightly to him.

♥♥♥♥♥

Deborah Duke was the first to notice. "Do you think there's something going on between Bob and Lori?" she asked George.

"Other than their working together on the grant?" George asked.

"Duh, yes!" she replied. "Of course other than their working together on the grant. You know what I mean. Something of a romantic nature."

"I haven't noticed," said George.

"I've gathered that from the obtuse nature of your response," said Deborah. "Well I think there is."

"And why do you think that, Deborah my darling," asked George.

"Syrupy sweetness will get you nowhere," said Deborah. "Well, if it's accompanied by compliant agreeability, it might," she laughed. "I don't know. I can't be very specific. It's just the way they seem to relate to each other. There's a change in that dynamic."

I see," said George. "Maybe we should have them over for dinner."

"Oh George, don't be so damned obvious. Then they'll know we know."

"And that would be bad why?" asked George. "At least then we'd know we knew, even if they already know. Which they would, if they'd thought about it at all."

"George for someone so intelligent, you can sometimes be as subtle as a bulldozer."

"It's a guy thing," said George. "When I see Bob next I'll ask if he and Lori are doing it. Then we'll move on to important things."

"Oh, stop it George," she laughed, realizing that he was pulling her leg. "But seriously, do you think there is something going on between them?"

"I'm intrigued now to find out," he said. Then a thought struck him, as thoughts had a habit of doing. "I know, how about a Department barbecue? That way we can keep an eye on them without their realizing that's what we're doing."

"Do we have to ask everyone?" asked Deborah. "I don't really want to listen to Inger's whining."

"If we don't," said George, "it will look like an arranged dinner, but done barbecue style."

"I've got a better idea," said Deborah. "Let's have a bocce picnic. Inger doesn't play bocce. Hates it." She looked at George and raised her eyebrows.

"Well done my precious jewel," he said. "I agree entirely. How can I help arrange it?"

Deborah particularly loved George when he was agreeable.

George composed an email to a select group of people from the Department, including a couple of graduate students, and two undergraduates. "Deborah, should I invite that young woman, Lisa, who works for Jeffrey? She seems pretty sparky, and she's practically become a member of the Department since she started working for Jeffrey."

"If you want. It's your decision," said Deborah, now distracted by thinking about preparing for the class at Sea View Middle School.

"I love it when she's so agreeable," thought George. He sent the email, poured a whisky – a small one: it was still early – unwrapped a cigar, and went to sit on the deck to contemplate, as one does.

♥♥♥♥♥

Jeffrey was surprised to get the call from his editor the following day.

"Jeffrey, I put your request to my executive committee. They wanted me to reassure you that they have the greatest confidence in the sales of your book, and also in the new version, based as it is on your existing text."

Jeffrey was happy to hear that.

"But therein lies a problem," said the editor. "The fact that the text is to a very large extent based on the text of your previous editions means that the committee is not willing to provide an advance on sales for something that has already been though nine editions Their feeling, to put it simply, is that you are already being adequately compensated."

"I see," said Jeffrey. "Well thanks for trying."

"My pleasure," said the editor. "By the way, the committee thought it would make a lot of sense to pay an advance to Heinrich Zimmer, who, after all will be a new author for us. It's not an unusual situation for us to have a new co-author with an existing, more established, author. We have a policy on advances in these situations and the committee is happy to advance fifty thousand dollars to Heinrich, staggered in the usual way, of course. Will you let him know, or should I tell him?"

42

The naming of things

Lisa and Chris breakfasted at L'Artisan Bakery. "I sometimes think I could live here," said Chris. "The range of food is great, the coffee's better than average, they have wifi, ... , and sometimes the company is really great, too."

Lisa smiled and pressed his arm. "I agree. When I'm not at the University I think I do live here. Well not *here*, in this general area, because I do," she laughed, "but in L'Artisan Bakery."

"I guess it sort of helps that it's across the road from your favorite jewelry store," Chris said. Lisa thought she would have to exercise some caution in that regard. She looked at the Alex and Ani bracelets on her left arm and sighed. "I think I'll call it quits for a while. But you know, it will soon become my business."

Chris thought about what Lisa had said. "You know, if you were *now* in the jewelry business your purchases would be business expenses." Lisa looked surprised. Chris was right, of course, but the thought had not entered her head. She was still transitioning from loving and gossiping about jewelry to working in the jewelry business. "I wonder?" she thought, more to herself than to Chris.

"What's that?" asked Chris.

"I was wondering if Carolyn Rafaelian would be interested in experimenting with some algorithmically designed jewelry. We could custom design pieces for individual clients."

"Who's Carolyn Rafaelian?" asked Chris.

"She's the owner of Alex and Ani," said Lisa. "She's a jeweler through and through. Her family has been in jewelry forever."

"I don't know," said Chris. "Alex and Ani jewelry doesn't lend it itself, in my opinion, to the sort of algorithmic design you're talking about. It seems like they sort of day dream about what would look pretty and then make a bunch of those, with a few twists for good luck."

"You mean exercise refined artistic taste and experience?" asked Lisa.

"What I said!" laughed Chris. "I think you'd do better sticking with the people in Somerville, Massachusetts. Who were they again?"

You're thinking of *Nervous System.* I agree. That's what convinced me this was something I could do for a living, something I would love. But the thing is, Alex and Ani is just across the road. It's right here!"

"My suggestion," Chris said, adopting as serious an expression as he could muster, "is that you set yourself up in business. De facto you are in business because you are a consultant to the publishing industry. Which, by the way, is becoming more and more technical by the minute. Have you heard of Tim O'Reilly's *Tools of Change* conference in New York?" Lisa shook her head.

"Well, anyway, you *are* in business, and the essence of your business is applied algorithms. That's what your work is with Jeffrey, and that's what you're thinking of doing with jewelry," he said.

"*Applied Algorithms,*" mused Lisa. "I like the sound of that. I wonder if someone's snapped it up already as a domain name?"

"Let me check," said Chris. He entered the domain name in the Network Solutions search engine. "Nope, it's taken as a domain name" he said. "Just a minute." He looked for appliedalgorithms.com. "It's not being used. The message reads: *The domain name you have requested isn't available. It has been reserved on gandi.net and parked as unused.*"

"You could make a bid for the URL at gandi.net," he said.

"What about *Applied Algorithms* as a business name? Can you Google that?" Lisa asked. Chris did as she asked but found nothing obvious. "The term appears in university labs, and on personal blogs, but that's about all I can find," he said.

"I wonder if I could register *Applied Algorithms* as a trademark?" asked Lisa. "That way the owner of the applied algorithms website would have to give it up or risk trademark infringement."

Chris marveled at Lisa's apparent hard headedness. "Only if they are situated in the U.S.," he said. "Otherwise you would need a worldwide registration for your trademark, and if they are in India or China, lots of luck enforcing it. But you might be able to register the trademark and call the website something else."

Lisa scrunched her nose at that idea. "Nah! I want *Applied Algorithms* all the way down the line, or not at all. I could go sort of pseudo Latin. How does *Algorithmica Applicada* sound?"

"Other then pretentious and silly?" asked Chris.

"Or I could go Arabic", said Lisa. "The word algorithm, after all, derives from the name of Abū Abdallāh Muhammad ibn Mūsā al-Khwārizmī, the ancient Persian mathematician."

"Oh great," said Chris. "Just what we need in these politically sensitive times. An Arabic sounding name from what was Persia but is now no other than Iran. You would be on the Homeland Security watch list before you could design your first algorithm."

"I was just playing around", said Lisa. "Do you want to high tail it down to the University? I have class in an hour."

"Me too," said Chris. "Let's go."

They walked out, arms around each other.

♥♥♥♥♥

Jeffrey was surprised to get a phone call from Heinrich. "Jeffrey, I had to give you a call. I don't know what strings you pulled with your publisher, but they have offered me a $50,000 advance on our book. Subject to the contract, and payable in three installments if all is delivered in a timely and satisfactory way. But this is marvelous. You must have great influence with your publisher, Jeffrey, and I thank you for advocating on my behalf."

Jeffrey grimaced. "Oh, it was the least I could do, Heinrich. You're a new author for them, and sometimes they don't treat new authors too well. I thought I might be able to wrangle a better deal for you."

"Whatever you have said has worked," said Heinrich, "and once again I thank you for it. By the way, I have been thinking about our book. Do you think we could do with a new name, to reflect the novel aspects of this venture?"

Jeffrey winced. "You don't think *Matrix Algebra* is a good name?" he asked.

"Yes, of course. But it is the name of your previous book, Jeffrey, which is very well known and respected in our field. I was thinking that this book will be somewhat different with a focus on more applications, and with the CDFs bringing it alive."

Jeffrey was grateful for what sounded like a compliment. "What do you have in mind?" he asked.

"I have no creative thoughts on it," said Heinrich. "The best I can do at the moment is *Applied Matrix Algebra*. But I think even that sounds a bit stodgy, a bit flat. I will try to think of something more exciting."

Jeffrey couldn't see anything wrong with *Applied Matrix Algebra*. It didn't seem stodgy to him. It seemed quite appropriate, in fact. "Whatever we do, let's keep it simple and descriptive," he said. "Let's not go all modern and trendy and come up with a title like *Excite & Empower Your Life: Applications of Matrix Algebra*."

"What does that mean, Jeffrey?" asked Heinrich.

"Or, *20 ways to Increase Your Twitter Followers With Matrix Algebra*," said Jeffrey. He was on a roll now. "*How to Prevent Wrinkles:*

a 2-Month Course of Matrix Algebra. How about *Matrix Algebra and Pilates: the New Scientific Way to Lose Weight?*" he asked.

"Jeffrey, are you alright?" asked Heinrich, now concerned about Jeffrey's mental state.

"Alright?" replied Jeffrey. "Alright? Yes, never been better. Never felt so light headed." He sat down.

"Jeffrey," said Heinrich from Chicago. "Would you like me to call a doctor? Is there anyone I can call?"

Heinrich hung up and immediately called Kathy Riverton. He explained the situation and Kathy hurried to Jeffrey's office. He was sitting down, with a somewhat glazed expression. "Are you okay, Jeff?" she asked.

"Okay? Yes fine. You couldn't make some coffee, could you?" he asked.

43

Stars shine

Deborah found George and Rickhart deep in conversation in George's office. They looked up as she came into the room with a young girl. "Hi guys, this is Alicia Brown. She's in the class I'm helping teach at Sea View Middle School. Alicia, this is Professor Prince and Professor Jansen." Alicia said hello and George asked them to sit down.

"I'm taking Alicia to Kathy's research class today," said Deborah. "Alicia's become very interested in cryptography, and we thought it might be helpful for her to see what some of the undergraduates are doing."

"Very good," said Rickhart. "We hope you have a fun time in that class today. Alicia, would you and Ms. Duke like to come and talk with me after the class?"

Alicia looked puzzled. She shrugged. "Sure. I mean, if you want."

Deborah explained to Alicia that Rickhart had just become Department Chair, so he probably wanted to talk to them about something *really important*. Alicia laughed.

"It's so," said Rickhart. "I'm very interested to find how Alicia likes Professor Riverton's research class, and what she thinks of this way of teaching students. You see," he said turning to Alicia, "Ms. Duke has been telling me about how she thinks that maybe we could help introduce mathematical research, just beginning steps, into high school."

Alicia turned again to Deborah. "But I'm not even in high school," she said. "I'm only in middle school."

"Even better!" said Rickhart. "Will you come and talk with me about how you found your experience here today?" Alicia agreed she would.

"Okay then, we'd better get going," said Deborah, and they said goodbye to Rickhart and George.,

Deborah says that girl has extraordinary mathematical ability," said George.

"Ah! So she's the one?" asked Rickhart.

"She's the one," George replied. "Apparently her teachers always thought she was very good at mathematics, but Deborah's cryptography course has helped Alicia show far deeper abilities."

"Let's hope Kathy's research course is not too high powered for Alicia. We'll see when I meet with them later," said Rickhart.

George and Rickhart turned back to discussing experimental mathematics. They were both convinced it was becoming important to introduce their students to experimental methods in mathematics. Too many students saw mathematics as a cut and dried collection of facts and procedures to be rote memorized. To be fair, Rickhart had emphasized, many teachers taught mathematics that way, so one could not really put the blame entirely on the students.

"Exactly my point," said George. "Quite a few of our students go on to become mathematics teachers in schools. If we can educate them while they're here about another side of mathematics then potentially we can have some impact on what's taught in schools. At least those newer teachers will have had their eyes opened."

"I agree, I agree," said Rickhart. "So the practical question for us now is how we do that."

They looked over at the diagram on George's whiteboard. The diagram indicated a sequence of courses that, in essence, dealt with increasing understanding of experimentation as it applied to mathematics. The most common beginning form of experiment, named for Sir Francis Bacon, and described by him in his 1620 book *Novum Organum*, is essentially 'messing around' or playing.

"It's what Deborah's favorite mathematics educator Jim Tanton recommends," said George. "He's fond of getting both students and teachers to play with 'what if?' scenarios."

"I agree that's the way to begin," said Rickhart. "But what role do we see for computation in this type of course. For me, of course, it's critical."

George agreed. "We could, in principle, have students working with pencil and paper, or with concrete models, and sometimes it might be useful and important to do that. But what's driven extensive experimentation in mathematics has been the ability to perform computations that go way beyond what can be done by hand. It's the accumulation of information and the development of insights that count."

"I could not have expressed it better myself, George," beamed Rickhart. "I think getting students exposed to this way of thinking about mathematics is critical to their development. Whether we can get them to a place where they can conduct decisive experiments is another question."

"It might be a question that requires grant funding to answer," replied George.

♥♥♥♥♥

Jeffrey was surprised to hear again from his publisher. This time it was not his editor, his primary form of contact with them, but an event organizer, Carol Johnson. She wanted to get back to Jeffrey about organizing the Golub Retrospective conference. Jeffrey was pleased she had called. The conference had moved to the back of his mind with all the developments in relation to the new book. He reflected it was odd the conference idea had led directly to the book when his editor had suggested the conference would need to have a technology focus. Jeffrey wondered if he was hearing right when Carol suggested New York as the venue. "I don't think that's a good idea," he said. "I think Providence would work much better. The American Mathematical Society has headquarters here, and Providence has a number of good conference venues, and it's just the right size for this sort of event." Carol said she understood Jeffrey's thoughts on the matter, and agreed about the charms of Providence. "The thing is," she said to Jeffrey, "the company is looking to make this a major marketing event. The intention is to offer a number of substantial prizes. Your new book should feature prominently."

"I see," said Jeffrey. "Perhaps Providence is over-rated."

"Not at all," said Carol, "but I think we can better plan and execute a major event in New York."

"But what about the University?" asked Jeffrey. "They've agreed to support the conference financially and I can't see that being a possibility if it's held in New York." Carol reassured him that such matters could be ironed out in discussion. "We're in talks with Wolfram Technology to participate," she said, "so this will be good for everyone involved."

Jeffrey was concerned. This was supposed to be a conference honoring the memory of Gene Golub, a pioneer in matrix calculations. Now, it seemed, it was becoming a publisher's love-fest and showcase. He expressed his concerns to Carol Johnson.

"I understand," she said. "We will pull together a group of distinguished speakers nationally, and internationally." Jeffrey was impressed. "We want this conference to really pop. The theme, as you so rightly pulled me back to, is honoring the contributions of Gene Golub. Our management committee is dedicated to that, and sees this as an opportunity to show how we are contributing in a high-end technology manner toward just that goal."

Jeffrey was not entirely convinced. "I was hoping I could help choose the keynote speakers," he said.

"Absolutely," said Carol. "That's why I'm talking with you now. You are our main adviser on these matters, Professor Albacete." Jeffrey was mollified. "Could I ask your view on a suggestion that came to me?" Carol asked him. "How do you feel about having Dr. Heinrich Zimmer open the conference? He is an incredibly dynamic speaker, and we thought having him do that would set just the right tone for the conference."

44

The attractions of pie

Jeffrey's amygdala – that almond-shaped seat of his emotions – was working overtime. Providence seemed a natural place to hold a small, yet influential conference. The city was small and attractive, with an abundance of conference venues. On the other hand New York could offer a vastly greater range of – everything. But if the conference was too big, and – dare he say it? – too flashy, it would get away from him. He was proud and pleased that Heinrich had accepted the job offer and would soon start work at the University, but already Heinrich had become co-author on Jeffrey's book, been given $50,000, for what? For just being co-author, the junior one at that? And now Heinrich would be the keynote speaker for the conference. To cap it off Heinrich didn't even appreciate coffee. For a moment Jeffrey thought everything was changing too fast. Change at this pace is not good, he thought. It could be very stressful, and was not conducive to productive achievement. Jeffrey was a slow, methodical planner. He got things done by chewing them over carefully, and getting things moving, slowly yet surely. This hurly burly activity was not to his liking.

Jeffrey began making himself a cup of coffee. That calmed him considerably. As he listened to the coffee brewing he thought how meeting Lisa had been a stroke of good luck. He could not blame her for the rapid acceleration of mad activity associated with the book and the conference. She has been there for me, he thought. She introduced Jeffrey to excellent coffee, prompted him to become self-sufficient in that regard, and worked with him to produce a new and exciting format for the next edition of *Matrix Algebra*. She had even warned him that the technical team at his publisher saw his writing as "boring". How right she had been!

A thought entered Jeffrey's head that had never been there before. Thoughts come and go, sometimes lingering, and other times just making fleeting appearances. This one was brand new. Jeffrey began to wonder if he was getting old. Chronologically that was true, of course, but he had never felt "old". Now he wondered. "Is it because I'm just getting old? Is this just a natural reaction to a younger, more energetic generation?" Jeffrey sighed. This thought was probably going to become a regular visitor to, if not a permanent fixture of, his mind. He was going to have to face up to what was looking increasingly a fact: he was now the older generation, possibly wiser and more knowledgeable, though around Lisa and Heinrich even those potential saving graces seemed to have taken flight.

Something clicked in Jeffrey's head. Maybe it had to do with the effect of the coffee. Whatever the origin, he slowly, yet very surely, felt an increasing sense of comfort that he had talented young people such as Heinrich and Lisa by his side, in his camp, working with him. Jeffrey had never been an "elder" before. He was always the outsider, struggling to get his point of view across, fighting over the years with the International Linear Algebra Society, forming his own society with a group of like-minded people, and working hard, and steadily, on the nine editions of his book: his well-known, respected, widely used text-book, translated into many different languages. "Maybe I just need to give in and go with the flow," he thought. Heinrich and Lisa supported his work. They were helping to bring his book to a new format, to reach a younger generation. Jeffrey began to realize with clarity that he could not do this by himself, that he needed these young, talented, energetic people.

Jeffrey began to fret about the role of the University in the planned conference. He had already committed the Provost's $2,000, and Kathy had provided Center money to employ Lisa to work for him, on the understanding that the University, and the Center, would host the conference. "I had better go talk to Kathy," he thought.

♥♥♥♥♥

Bob Fosberry and Lori Bailey were at the Daily Grind for coffee and pastries. "I like this place," said Lori, "with it's funny old run-down ambiance – the brick walls and old posters. It's comforting."

Bob agreed. " I think it's why Jeff still comes here," he said, "despite having that fancy new coffee. That and the fact that it's close to the gym."

"Does he actually go to the gym?" asked Lori. "I can't believe he does anything there. His belly is getting bigger, if anything."

"Haven't you seen him?" asked Bob. "He generally rides an exercise bike, relatively slowly, and reads the news. I think it's just a way of him getting quiet thinking time."

"Well good for him," said Lori. "I could do with some of that!"

When Kathy Riverton had suggested Lori as a partner on the National Science Foundation grant application, Bob had not given too much thought to Lori's workload. In fact, the only thought that did come to mind was that she must be very efficient to successfully manage so many different projects. Now that he and Lori were close, he had begun to worry about how much she was doing. "How's the obesity-diabetes project coming along?" he asked her.

"It's funny you should ask that," she said. "We've had a sort of breakthrough. A mini one, but important." Bob understood the "we" here referred to Lori and her graduate student. "What is it?" he asked.

"The Centers for Disease Control keep statistics on the percentages of people with diabetes, who are obese, and who are physically inactive, for each U.S. county. They have done since 2004. The percentage obese, and percentage inactive, behave pretty much as you would think – as anyone would think. They are normally distributed, like height, for example, with a bell-shaped curve. But the percentage obese is nothing like that, not for any of the years for which there's data."

"So what does it look like?" asked Bob.

"It's much more peaky, with longer tails away from the average," said Lori.

"Is that significant?" asked Bob.

"I think so," said Lori. "Variables that have a normal distribution – a bell-shaped curve – we sort of understand fairly well, and know how to deal with statistically speaking. It's the odd distributions – like the percentage obese – that leave us a bit in the dark as to what's happening."

"And that's the breakthrough?" asked Bob.

Lori laughed. "No, that was obvious as soon as we looked at the data. The insight we've gained recently is that the data seems to be very well described by a normal inverse Gaussian distribution."

"I don't know what that is," said Bob.

"Well you're excused, dear Bob, because very few people do. It's one of those horribly complicated things that statisticians use to describe earthquake patterns, financial hiccups, and turbulent water flow."

"So the distribution of percentage obese people across U.S. counties fits a similar description?" asked Bob.

"Exactly," said Lori. "And what's scary is that we can now describe with great precision just how this time bomb of increasing obesity is marching across the whole of the United States. I hesitate to think what's going to happen by 2020."

"That is scary," said Bob. "Can education help reverse this trend?"

"That's part of what the grant from the Centers for Disease Control is about," said Lori. "The usual methods of informing people don't seem to work. The attractions of fast food, rich food, sweet sugary pies, seem to be too much to be counter-balanced by any normal education program. So we're working on the idea that more graphic visual displays of the science of the obesity explosion might open people's eyes."

"Long enough to take them off the pie in front of them," said Bob.

Jeffrey walked into the Daily Grind carrying his gym bag. Bob waved and he came over to sit with them. He dropped his bag. "I'm just going over to get a coffee," he said. "I think I might get a slice of pie for a change instead of a muffin. The Key Lime looks really good."

45

Keep moving and learning

The email from the University of Southern Cyprus contained one of those annoying invitations to a conference of which Jeffrey had never heard. He paid it no heed, and the memory of it had all but faded when, as he was selecting his slice of pie, the sight of the fresh baklava in the Daily Grind brought it back to the surface. He mentioned to Bob and Lori how annoying were the so-called "international" meetings organized by tin-pot universities to gain attention and supposedly help build their reputation. "As if I'm going to travel all the way to Cyprus to be lauded as the great U.S. expert so they can parade their conference around as significant," he said.

Bob was not so sure. "The University of Southern Cyprus is less than 25 years old" – Jeffrey rolled his eyes and shook his head – "but," said Bob, "it's grown rapidly and had some very well respected programs. The Department of Mathematics is quite vigorous."

"Could you send the email to me?" Bob asked Jeffrey. "If you're not planning to go I might think about it."

Jeffrey was taken aback. The last email he forwarded to Bob had resulted in Bob attending a meeting in Washington, DC and preparing a grant application to the National Science Foundation as a result. Bob may not have had the requisite get up and go on the Matrix Algebra project in the past but he seemed to be on a winning streak now. Better, thought Jeffrey, to have another look at the invitation from Cyprus, and to ask around to see if Bob might not be correct in his assessment.

"Yes, of course, I will forward it to you when I get back from the gym," Jeffrey said to Bob.

"The University of Southern Cyprus has a small but very good applied statistics group," said Lori. "If there's something on the conference program about statistics we could both go," Lori said to Bob.

Jeffrey thought he could easily fob Bob off, but now that Lori was interested it would not be so easy. She was highly focused and never seemed to forget anything.

"Well, maybe I was too hasty," said Jeffrey. "I wasn't aware that the University of Southern Cyprus had such an up and coming reputation. Perhaps I should give it a second look."

Bob shrugged. "You might enjoy it, Jeff. Take a break for a week and be feted as the international expert. Which of course you are!" he hastened to add. "Who knows, you may even be appointed their keynote speaker."

Jeffrey was thinking about what this "honor" might mean when Lori turned and waved to someone. "It's Bao Zhang," said Lori. "She's not due to start work for a few weeks yet. I wonder what she's doing here so early?" Bao came over to the table and said hello to Lori and Jeffrey, both of whom were at her Search & Screen interview. "Bao, this is Bob Fosberry," said Lori. "Bob – Bao." Bob shook hands with Bao and Lori said how pleased she was very to see her. "What brings you here so early?" asked Lori.

"I've been doing some work for MathWorks in Natick, Massachusetts," said Bao. "I've also been looking for an apartment, and I called to see if an office had been allocated to me yet. I was surprised to find that Bert was no longer Department Chair. Rickhart kindly arranged for my office, so here I am!"

"We're very glad to have you here," said Lori. "Jeff, you must be thrilled to see Bao?"

Jeff set his mouth in that peculiar expression somewhere between a smile and a grimace. "Good to see you, Bao."

"And you too, Jeff," she said. "I've been hearing about your new book venture. It sounds very exciting. I would love to hear how it's progressing."

Jeffrey was surprised that Bao would know anything at all about his book. "How did you hear about it?" he asked.

Bao laughed. "You and I have the same publisher. Despite their efforts at confidentiality, word spreads fast in-house."

"Well, it's pretty technical," said Jeffrey. "We've been working on creating CDFs – I don't know if you've heard of them – into the book."

"I heard about that," said Bao, "and it's what intrigued me. A couple of other mathematics books have been produced using computable document format – one calculus book in particular is very good – but there's nothing like this in the field of linear algebra."

Jeffrey winced. "Matrix algebra," he corrected Bao.

"Right", she said, aware of Jeffrey's sensitivity and overly fine distinctions, but not particularly concerned to respect them. "I'm a reasonably accomplished Mathematica user so I know quite a lot about CDFs."

Jeffrey was not merely surprised: he was astonished. "But you do work for MathWorks," he said. "You just came from there. I would have thought you were a committed MATLAB user."

"Oh, I am," said Bao. "But these days I find it helps to know something about everything. Technology moves fast. MATLAB is a great environment for doing simulations, as is Mathematica, but I think the MathWorks folks are green with envy about the beautiful environments one can now create in Mathematica. I would love to take a look at how your new book is coming along, if that's okay with you?"

"Sure," said Jeffrey. "I can show you later today if you'll be around."

"Yes, I will. Thanks, that's great. I understand that Heinrich will be your co-author on this new book," said Bao. "You must be excited about that. "

Jeffrey's mouth tightened. "It's certainly brought a new perspective," he said. Jeffrey excused himself, shook hands with Bao, and headed off to the gym at a quicker pace than usual.

Bao turned to Lori and asked: "So, are you two moving-in together?"

Lori's jaw dropped. "Who told you?" she asked.

"I was having dinner with George and Deborah last night. She felt sure there was something happening and George was of the view that someone should come right out and ask. I guess that someone is me," said Bao grinning.

"Well, you got it right in one," said Bob. "I admire your nerve though. Most young assistant professors would be scared to death of offending anyone who might be on their tenure committee."

Bao laughed. "I'm not worried about tenure," she said. "I'm pretty sure I will get it okay. I am talented and I do have some good achievements to my name already. But even if I didn't for some reason I could always got to work for MathWorks, or Mathematica, or half a dozen other companies."

"I admire your confidence, Bao," said Bob.

"Confidence or lack of it is irrelevant, in my view," said Bao. We take our feelings and thoughts too seriously, I think. Just focus on the job to be done, use the common sense and brains we have, and do a good job. Then what will be, will be. That's my view."

"It seems to work for you," laughed Lori.

"I think it works for anyone," said Bao. "We are creatures of movement. The trick, in my view, is to not get caught up thinking 'do we feel good?' – sometimes we just feel bad – or think this our 'nature' or not. Just be glad to be alive and use the skills we have. And keep learning."

Bob had heard from the others that Bao was an outstanding young mathematician. He had not expected someone so dynamic. "Lori and I have just submitted a grant application to the National Science Foundation," he said, hoping to interest Bao in what they were planning.

"Yes, I heard about this from George. I have some ideas," she said as she dug her fork into a baklava.

46

As long as you're happy

⌘

Lisa Googled *Applied Algorithms*, looking for any sign the name was being used in business. She found Applied Algorithm labs in universities, and courses called Applied Algorithms, but no business named *Applied Algorithms*. Her first check had arrived from Jeffery's publisher – advance payment on her work as a technical consultant for them – so she decided not to wait a moment longer and form a company, and to register the name *Applied Algorithms*. She went to the Legal Zoom website and registered as a customer with them. This had been Chris's idea. He told Lisa that Legal Zoom could do all the work in setting up a limited liability company and registering a trademark. "It's not strictly necessary to register the name of your company as a trademark," he said. "It is a legal entity after all. But it helps protect your growing brand." Lisa wondered how Chris knew so much about the details of forming a company and registering a trademark. "My dad's a business adviser," he said. "It's what he does. I guess I picked up a few things by osmosis."

Lisa went through the process of starting a company with Legal Zoom. She formed the company in Delaware as Chris advised, because of the lower reporting and taxation requirements in that state. Satisfied, she then started the process of trademark registration. The Legal Zoom website advised her that would take longer and she would get results of a search from them within a week. Then the thought struck her that she would need a business bank account. But that would require the articles of formation of the company, which would not arrive for some time yet. "Oh my!" she thought. "What have I let myself in for?" She phoned Chris and asked if she could speak with his dad. Chris laughed. "I guessed it would come to this pretty quickly. Sure thing. How about later this evening? Should I invite us both around for dinner?" Lisa agreed and then breathed a sigh of relief. "Holy crap!" she said out loud. "I'm freaking well in business!" The woman at the adjacent table in L'Artisan Bakery smiled and said "Congratulations!"

♥♥♥♥♥

Kathy Riverton was pleased to welcome Deborah and Alicia Brown to her research class. "It's a good day to come," she said. "The students are giving presentations shortly so you will be able to get a quick overview of what they're doing." Kathy introduced Deborah and Alicia to the class and asked the students to introduce themselves. As the students worked on their research projects Kathy beckoned Deborah and Alicia to come and look at what Kojo Agbeko was doing. He was a junior, working on new methods of encryption. Alicia was immediately interested. "Alicia's working on cryptography at Sea View middle School," Deborah told Kojo.

Kojo asked if they would like him to explain what he was doing. "Of course," said Deborah who, after all, had an almost completed Ph.D. in cryptography. Kojo explained he was looking for something called discrete logarithms: "For instance," he said", which powers of 3, when you keep the remainder after dividing by 17, might give you an answer of 13?"

Alicia looked at Deborah. "Four, and twenty," she said. "Actually, four plus any multiple of sixteen."

Kojo was taken aback. "Well, yes, that's right. How did you figure that so quickly?" Alicia shrugged.

"Alicia's been working on calculating discrete logarithms at Sea View," said Deborah.

"She has?" asked Kojo. "That seems pretty advanced for a middle school project!"

"Alicia seems to take to it," said Deborah.

"So what sort of things are you doing, Alicia?" asked Kojo, warming to this bright young girl. Alicia explained that she was trying to find faster ways of calculating discrete logarithms for elliptic curves over finite fields. "Really?!" said Kojo. "That's neat, that's really very neat." He looked again at this little middle school girl. "Would you like to see what I've been doing on that problem?" he asked. Alicia nodded and sat next to him. Deborah looked at Kathy and smiled. "I guess it was a good idea after all," she said. "I had my doubts at first."

Kathy and Deborah left Kojo and Alicia talking about their common interests. Ten minutes later Kathy announced it was time for presentations. She decided to take a gamble. "Alicia, would you like to take five minutes to tell the class what you've been working on?"

"Sure thing," said Alicia who wished school could always be like this.

♥♥♥♥♥

Jeffrey returned to his office from the gym. He started coffee brewing and sat at his computer to look at the email from Cyprus. If both Bob and Lori were independently interested in this conference, he thought, then there might actually be something to it. He read the email carefully and noticed the registration date was only a week away. "Typical!" he thought. "These tin-pot conference people could not organize a one-hole golf course." He was about to trash the email when he noticed the conference would have a section devoted to matrix algebra. "Maybe," he thought, "I could squeeze some travel money out of the Provost." Jeffrey filled in the registration details, pulled out his credit card and entered the information on the registration page. Feeling better that he had taken action, he pushed the submit button and went to pour himself a cup of coffee. He was thinking about his new book when he heard the ping of a new email. He walked over to his computer and saw, to his surprise, that a contact person for the Cyprus conference had responded, almost immediately.

"Dear Professor Albacete," the email read, "we are extremely honored to have you as a speaker at our conference. We would like to ask you to open the conference and to give a general talk about developments in your field. Can you please let me know at your convenience?"

Jeffrey thought they sounded very disorganized, yet he admired their common sense and taste. "Alright," he thought, " I will do it." He emailed back saying how pleased he was to be able to attend their conference and he would be delighted to open the proceedings.

"Cyprus eh?" thought Jeffrey. "They must have more common sense than I gave them credit for. Well, this might be fun."

Jeffrey now felt pleased he had not palmed the email off onto Bob. He wondered how Lori was so knowledgeable about Cyprus, but then thought she was knowledgeable about pretty much everything. "Good thing I accepted", he thought", "otherwise poor Lori would have to spend a week in Cyprus with slow as a turtle Bob. What a nightmare!" he chuckled to himself.

♥♥♥♥♥

Bob and Lori were walking back form the Daily Grind, after saying goodbye to Bao. "She's sweet," said Lori.

"And freaking smart!" said Bob.

"Smarter than me?' asked Lori.

'Well no, probably not, but, boy, she's got ..."

"Balls?" asked Lori.

"I guess that's what I wanted to say," laughed Bob. "She's sure gutsy."

"She is that," said Lori. "I wonder how she and Jeff will get on? He seemed a little cool toward her."

Bob wondered. He knew Jeffrey well, and was aware how suspicious he was of people even slightly outside his field. But Bao was a human whirlwind, who did not respect people's feelings about boundaries. Lori interrupted his thoughts. "You know, I've got all my preparation done for the semester and classes don't start for over a week. Do you fancy a few days away in New York?"

Bob smiled. "Nothing would make me happier," he said.

47

A tornado hits town

⧈

"You and I have the same publisher," Bao had said.

The memory of the words played around the edges of Jeffrey's brain until they came into full consciousness. "What book could she be writing?" Jeffrey thought. As he savored his coffee the question danced around his cortex, but no answer came. Annoyed, Jeffrey picked up his copy of Bao's job application file, still lying on his desk. He thumbed through it until he found the names and emails of her referees. He knew one of them well, another by reputation, and had not heard of the third, a professor from China. He toyed with the idea of contacting at least one of them to ask if they knew what Bao's forthcoming book was about. This seemed a little blunt, he thought. There had to be a better way to get at this. Jeffrey phoned Paul Jamieson, the referee on the list with which he was most familiar.

"Paul, Hi. Jeff Albacete here. Yes, I'm fine. And you? I'm calling about Bao Zhang. She's due to start here shortly – yes, it's great we're lucky to get her – and I was wondering if you could fill us in on her recent work? She talked about some of that, of course, at her job interview, but I was wondering if you could tell me something about the directions she's been working on with you."

Professor Paul Jamieson chatted with Jeffrey for ten minutes or so before Jeffrey came out and said: "I hear she's written a book." Paul Jamieson said he didn't know about that but the people who might were at MathWorks. "You could ask her yourself, Jeffrey. I think she's going to be in your neck of the woods about now."

"Of course, of course," Jeffrey smiled. "Well, thanks Paul. Good talking with you."

Jeffrey drummed his fingers on the desk. "Why not call my publisher?" he thought. Jeffrey phoned his editor. "Colin, hello, it's Jeffrey Albacete. Just catching up on developments for the new CDF book." Jeffrey chitchatted for several minutes before broaching the topic of Bao Zhang's book. "I don't know the details," his editor said. "Someone else is handling it. Let me check and get back to you. On the other hand, Jeffrey, you could just ask her yourself. I believe she's in Providence this week." Jeffrey thanked his editor and hung up.

George Prince knocked on Jeffrey's door. "You haven't seen Kathy have you Jeff?," he asked. Jeffrey said he hadn't.

"You look troubled," George said.

"Oh no, Just wondering about Bao Zhang's new book is all."

"You mean *Matrix Methods in Data Mining?*" asked George.

Jeffrey sat down. "You know about it?" asked Jeffrey. "How do you know?"

"We had dinner with her last night, Debbie and I. She told us about it then. It's not supposed to be a secret is it?" said George.

"No, no," said Jeffrey. "I heard from her yesterday that she'd written a book. I just didn't know what about. Didn't think to ask her at the time."

"I think you'll appreciate it, Jeff. It draws heavily on *Matrix Algebra*. Looks like she's a fan of yours," said George.

George left to look for Kathy Riverton and Jeffrey to ponder the news about Bao Zhang's book. He was naturally suspicious of anyone with strong connections to MathWorks, and was slow to warm to Bao because of her connections with the University of Massachusetts. "You can never be too careful in this field about who knows whom," he thought. Dark clouds of anxiety filled his being. He put his hands behind his head and looked out the window, thinking.

"A penny for them," said Kathy Riverton. Jeffrey startled and turned to face her.

"Oh, hi Kathy. George was just looking for you," he said.

"Thanks. He found me. You look deep in thought, Jeff."

Jeffrey sighed. "I was just thinking about Bao Zhang's new book, and Heinrich's new contract, and Lisa's new contract, and ... well, I guess things got the better of me."

Kathy sat down. "Jeff, I appreciate change such as you're going through is hard. But think of the positives. You have a fantastic assistant who is not only bright, full of energy and technical know-how, but understands good coffee." Jeffrey smiled. "And, Heinrich and Bao are going to contribute strongly to the Department and to the development of matrix algebra. You should be pleased. Just think of yourself as the godfather of a very strong research group."

While Jeffrey couldn't say it, couldn't articulate it, and couldn't spit it out even if the words came to him, that was exactly what was worrying him. Kathy had hit the nail on the head. He was no researcher: he was a scholar. He pulled together other people's ideas and thoughts and through hard work and much thought put them together in a compelling form. He was no originator of deep thoughts, or profound ideas. Heinrich and Bao were just too clever for him. They would surely push him into the shadows.

A tear formed in the corner of Jeffrey's eye. Kathy pulled her chair closer. "Jeff, cheer up. This should be the culmination of decades of work on your part. You have created the conditions under which we could attract two such brilliant young people. They respect you, as we all do." Kathy paused to think she should not gild the lily too much. "You and Heinrich have a great project going. Lisa will make this really happen. And Bao – as forceful as she is – respects your work. Relax, and be happy."

Jeffrey smiled and thanked her, just as Bao appeared at his door. "Hi Kathy. Hi Jeff," she said. "Jeff, I thought you might be interested to see the proofs of my book later. I think you'll like it"

Kathy stood up. "I'll leave you two to talk things over."

"It sounds very nice," he said. "I don't know much about data mining. I know data science is all the rage, but I'm afraid it's left me behind."

Bao told him that matrix methods were the best introduction to data mining, in her opinion. "The problem is that many computer science people do not understand numerical analysis, so their techniques cannot go so deep. I'm hoping this book will open their eyes," she laughed.

Jeffrey asked if Bao would like a cup of coffee. "Sure," she said, and he poured her a cup of the recently brewed Terroir.

"This is very good coffee," said Bao. "Very, very good. I didn't know you were such a coffee connoisseur Jeff."

"It's not me," Jeffrey smiled. "Though I do appreciate it. My technical assistant Lisa is the coffee aficionada. She bought this."

Bao looked around Jeffrey's office. "You've got quite the setup here," she observed. "You've got a great assistant who knows computer science and coffee, and Heinrich will be working with you on the new book. Things are going pretty well for you."

Jeffrey had to admit as much.

"I drew on your book quite a lot when I was writing my *Matrix Methods* book," she said. "It was a big help. There's nothing else like it. No one else has organized the field as well as you." Jeffrey thanked her.

"I think I'm going to be pretty happy here," said Bao. There's a lot going on and I like the people. Plus it's not too far from Math-Works."

Jeffrey grimaced.

"I hope we can work together, Jeff. I would like that. I have an idea for a project on matrix methods in pattern recognition. Would you be interested in working on that?"

Jeffrey didn't know what to say. He nodded and said: "That sounds good."

"Great!" said Bao. "Would you have some time tomorrow to talk about it?"

Jeffrey agreed that would work, and thought about Kathy's words to him; "Relax, and be happy."

48

Do your homework

Heinrich and Anna Muller had just moved into their new house. Heinrich was standing on the deck, admiring the views. He envisaged a large barbecue to the right of the deck, where he could entertain colleagues and students. Heinrich had been reading up on barbecue techniques and he was a fan of BBQ University. "This, I think, will be just about perfect," he said to himself. Heinrich heard the doorbell and Anna's voice welcoming someone. Anna called out to him: "Heinrich, it's Kathy and Rick. And they've brought Bao Zhang with them." Heinrich came to the front of the house to say hello.

"This is a surprise," he said. "Hello Bao, I'm very pleased to see you."

Kathy presented Anna with an orchid for the house and Bao gave Heinrich a box of Pu-erh Tea.

"Thank you very much, Bao. Where did you get this tea?" he asked.

"Where else but online?" Bao laughed.

"Well I appreciate it very much. Did you know I like fine tea?"

"Of course!" said Bao. "Who doesn't know that?"

"Come in and sit down," Anna said. "Or would you like to look around the house first?" Kathy and Bao went off with Anna to tour the house and Rickhart stayed with Heinrich.

"Can I offer you a beer, Rick?" Heinrich asked. "I have only a limited range at the moment." He opened the refrigerator. "Would Sam Smith Nut Brown Ale be okay?" he asked. Rickhart recalled the times as a student when he traveled from Hoek van Holland by ferry to England. Sam Smith Nut Brown ale had been one of his favorite drinks then. "Yes, that would be great," he smiled.

"So, Rick, do you have a barbecue grill?" asked Heinrich.

Rickhart laughed. "Yes, I do, as a matter of fact. Why do you ask?"

Heinrich explained that he was in the process of buying a new grill to put on the deck and he wanted people's views on what they thought was a high quality grill. Rickhart laughed again. "I'm just a simple Dutchman, Heinrich. If the gas ignites easily and stays on while the food cooks I am happy. Although," he added, "cleaning a barbecue grill is another matter. I would choose on the basis of which was easiest to clean." Heinrich put his finger to his lips and digested this information.

"So, Heinrich, tell me: you are going to co-author the new *Matrix Algebra* book with Jeffrey?" asked Rickhart.

"Yes. That is correct. Jeffrey has been quite amazing. He spoke to his publisher and they have given me a generous advance on projected sales. I am looking forward to working with Jeffrey and his assistant Lisa. I think Jeffrey is also quite excited by this project."

Rickhart nodded slowly, digesting what Heinrich was saying. "So you think the computable document format will really work?"

"Oh yes," said Heinrich. "I think many technical books – in mathematics, science, engineering, economics, business – will come out soon in this format. The interactivity is almost magic."

"A bit like Harry Potter?" asked Rickhart.

"Just so!" said Heinrich. "Just like Harry Potter."

Anna, Kathy and Bao retuned from their tour of the house. "This is a beautiful house, Anna" said Kathy, "and the views are gorgeous. I think you chose very well." Anna and Heinrich thanked Kathy. "We tried," he said.

"Heinrich, you make me laugh," said Kathy. "If our students would put as much time into their homework as you do into everything you do then their grades would pick up enormously."

Heinrich smiled. "I think preparation is very important."

"So Bao, George tells me your book is about to come out. Do you have a copy?" asked Rickhart.

"I do," said Bao, reaching into her backpack that she carried like a purse. She pulled out the proof copy of the book and passed it to Rickhart. Heinrich looked over at the title and contents page. "This is wonderful," he said. "Fantastic even! It is so good to see a numerical analyst produce a book like this. Data mining is becoming even more important these days."

"It looks very good," said Rickhart. "Congratulations."

Heinrich looked at Anna. "Do we have some cold wine to celebrate Bao's book?" Anna said there were a couple of bottles of Sancerre in the wine cooler in the basement. Heinrich got up to go and get them.

"Well this is a good start to your academic life here," Rickhart said to Bao. "What's the publication date? I ask only because our Provost is a stickler for only counting publications toward tenure that were published while faculty are here. If the book's published this week, for instance, it won't count toward your tenure materials."

Bao laughed. "What a silly policy. Sounds like the Provost never published anything himself. He's not a biologist or a medical person by chance, is he?"

"He is, as a matter of fact. He's a former Associate Dean of Medicine."

"Ah," laughed Bao, "that explains it. He's a career academic administrator who couldn't quite get his research going, so took the easy path of ordering people around."

Rickhart admired Bao's candor. "In any case, it is a very nice way to start your career here. You can relax this semester knowing you've got this under your belt."

Bao was puzzled. "But it's what I do. I've spoken to Jeff about a new project on matrix methods in pattern recognition and he seems quite interested."

"Really?" said Rickhart. "That surprises me."

"I would be very interested to hear more about this project," said Heinrich coming in on the tail end of the conversation. "I am very interested in applications that have to do with pattern recognition." He opened the wine and asked who would like some. Kathy and Anna indicated they would. Bao said she would prefer a beer. Heinrich poured the wine and opened another three beers. "Tell me more about this pattern recognition project," Heinrich said to Bao.

Anna told Kathy and Rickhart they would get nothing more out of Heinrich for the next hour. "We're quite close to the water," she said. "Would you like to go for a walk?"

♥♥♥♥♥

Just on an hour later Anna, Kathy and Rickhart returned to the house. "It really is quite stunning," Kathy said. "Being so close to the ocean is a joy."

Heinrich looked quite animated and Bao was smiling broadly. "What have you two been cooking up?" asked Kathy.

"We have thought up a plan for a program on pattern recognition," said Heinrich. "Bao and I think we have a good chance of getting a decent grant to support this work. I am very excited by this."

"Bao, did you say you mentioned this to Jeff?" asked Kathy.

"Yes, I did", said Bao. "He seemed to like the idea."

"Oh dear," said Kathy, thinking of the conversation with Jeffrey in which he made it clear that he thought of himself as a scholar and not an original researcher. Kathy hoped there was some place for Jeffrey in this new project that would allow him to feel valued. She was struggling with words to express this when the doorbell rang. Anna went to see who it was. "Jeffrey!" she said. "What a pleasant surprise. Come on in." Anna led Jeffrey through to the dining area where the others were seated. "Look everyone, it's Jeffrey." Jeffrey smiled at the gathering and said hello to everyone.

"Jeffrey, can I get you a drink?" asked Heinrich. A beer or glass of wine?"

Jeffrey thought for a moment. "Well, maybe I'll try some of the wine." Heinrich poured him a glass. "Sit down, Jeffrey, please," he said.

Jeffrey sat down and sipped at the Sancerre. "This is quite flinty," he remarked.

"Jeff, Heinrich and I have been talking about the pattern recognition project I mentioned to you," said Bao. "Heinrich thinks his could be quite big, and that we stand a good chance of being funded. Good news, eh?"

Jeffrey looked startled. "Oh! Uhm ... yes, that's very good news." Changing the subject he handed a package to Heinrich. "You know my assistant Lisa is an expert on fine coffee. I've learned a lot from her. Anyway, this is a Terroir coffee, a very fine brand. I thought you might like it. Just something to welcome you to the area."

Heinrich did not miss a beat. "Thank you so much Jeffrey. This will be an excellent addition to my range of fine products for our first barbecue we will soon have. By the way, do you have a barbecue grill, Jeffrey?"

49

Learn from the master

Jeffrey saw the proof copy of Bao's book and picked it up. He read through the table of contents and turned to a chapter that looked especially interesting to him. He read for a few minutes and turned to Bao. "This is really very good," he said.

"Thank you Jeff. I appreciate your compliment," she replied.

"I'm not saying it to be polite. You've done an outstanding job." Jeffrey was coming to see Bao through new eyes. Her connections with MathWorks and the International Linear Algebra Society still made him suspicious – of what exactly he was not sure, just a general feeling that this was not a good thing. But her book was quite excellent, and it was clear to anyone in the know that she had, as she said, drawn extensively on his *Matrix Algebra*. Jeffrey sighed. It's like Kathy said, he thought, I'm the godfather so to speak of a strong group.

"Are you okay, Jeffrey?" asked Heinrich.

"What? Oh, yes. I'm fine thank you Heinrich. I was just thinking how lucky I am – we are – to have you and Bao here with us. I don't know that I will be able to keep up."

"What is to keep up?" asked Heinrich. "You are already '*up*' Jeffrey". It is we who are lucky to be able to work with you." Kathy smiled at Heinrich. As much as Jeffrey could irritate her she wanted the best for him.

Bao spoke up. "You are a lot older than ether Heinrich or me, so if you were to go head to head with us on solving a difficult problem we would get there before you, for sure." Kathy wasn't sure this was meant to be reassuring. "But that is not how to think about it. This is not about competition but cooperation. Together we are stronger than any one of us. I learned long ago in Tai Chi that the aim is not to defeat an opponent but to overcome one's own contentious nature. Competitiveness that pits us one against the other and has the potential to hurt other people is childish. Like Heinrich, I feel lucky to be part of this group."

"Thank you Bao," said Jeffrey.

"Now Jeff," said Bao. "We want the *Pattern Recognition* book out by the end of the month. We will want your five chapters by two weeks." Jeffrey look stunned as Bao dissolved in creases of laughter. "See, old habits die hard," she said. "I am only joking, Jeff."

Jeffrey gave a wan smile. "I think I could do with another glass of this wine," he said to Heinrich.

Heinrich brought Jeffrey the wine and said: "Jeffrey, you didn't tell me yet if you have a barbecue grill."

"No, I don't," Jeffrey replied.

"Very well. Then as you know I am studying the art of barbecuing extensively. Although I have yet to test my hand, I have a wide theoretical knowledge." Heinrich smiled at his own characterization of his skills. "So, since you have no barbecue grill and Bao shows no interest in learning, I will declare myself the barbecue master of the Matrix Algebra group." He nodded and waited for Jeffrey and Bao's agreement. "As such I will conduct lessons on the art of barbecue There will be no tests, of course, but I expect your full cooperation." Heinrich's eyes were sparkling with mirth. Bao laughed to herself. Jeffrey didn't know what to think. Puzzled, he looked over at Kathy. She nodded her head up and down indicating "yes".

"Well, okay Heinrich. I would be happy to take barbecue lessons from the master. Even if he hasn't cooked so much as a sausage yet." Now Jeffrey smiled.

"Excellent!" said Heinrich. "I will go tomorrow and buy the barbecue grill, bearing in mind Rick's excellent advice to look for the one easiest to clean, and next weekend we can do a barbecue. Yes?"

Jeffrey smiled again. "Yes, okay Heinrich, I will be happy to assist."

Rickhart looked at the gathering and thought he couldn't be happier. This small group of colleagues was getting along very well. The younger ones clearly had respect for Jeffrey's efforts and were including him in their current plans. "I think we should eat," he said. "And since Heinrich has yet to demonstrate anything about barbecue except talk, I propose we get pizza. Heinrich, do you want to come with me to get pizza and more wine. You can pick out the beer."

Heinrich smiled and bowed. "I follow the master," he laughed.

♥♥♥♥♥

George and Deborah were sitting on their deck drinking a glass of wine. George was toying with an Opus X Fuente cigar. "I just can't seem to get things to work," he said. George had been trying to get his idea going, of applying statistical techniques to numerical analysis. He had read what he could to see if anyone else had a similar idea. The nearest he could find was work of Nick Trefethen on potential theory in the approximation of functions.

"Have you talked to Lori?" asked Deborah. George said he hadn't. Although Lori was an excellent statistician she wasn't a numerical analyst. It wasn't clear to George that there would be anything to gain by talking to her. "But it can't hurt, and you never know," said Deborah.

George nodded and cut the end from his cigar. He knew that the gloomy, slightly depressed, feeling he had was usually a precursor to an insight, as if his brain were chewing things over below consciousness, taking energy from the rest of his thoughts. But that knowledge didn't help his overall feeling of irritability. He looked at the scene form the deck and sighed. "You know we have it pretty good, Deb." She smiled at him. "We get paid to do work we like, we are pretty much masters of our own fate – but don't get me started on the senior administration! – and we live in an area of outstanding natural beauty. What's to complain about?" Deborah agreed.

"Then why do I feel so darned irritable?" he asked.

"Oh, George, it's self-inflicted, you know that," she said. "You had an idea – a good idea – and getting it to work in practice is proving harder than you thought. Have faith in the power of your mind. Relax and keep thinking. It will come."

George lit his cigar. "You're right," he said. "Of course, you're always right." George thought about the two new hires in the Department. "Things should pop with Bao and Heinrich arriving. Bao is a whirlwind. I don't think anything can slow that girl. And Heinrich is no slacker."

Deborah agreed, and was thinking about the bocce match she and George had planned. "The reason for that has evaporated," she said, "since Bao came right out and just asked Lori and Bob if they were ..."

"Doing it?" asked George.

"Planning to move in together!" said Deborah. "Anyway, we could go ahead and still have the match. What do you think?"

"What I think," said George, "is that since Heinrich is so keen to learn about barbecuing, we should have a barbecue."

"That's a great idea," said Deborah. "You know I think I will ask Lisa, Jeff's assistant, to help pick some of that great Grüner Veltliner she drinks. When do you think we should have everyone over?"

George drew on his cigar. "Strike while the iron's hot. What about this weekend?"

Deborah agree. "When it comes to barbecuing, you're the master"

George smiled and drew on his cigar. Deborah was right. She was always right.

50

Thou shalt not steal

The paper Lori had agreed to review for publication was troubling her. The journal had asked for her report within three months and she had started almost right away. It did not take long for alarm bells to begin ringing. The authors were claiming credit for a new statistical method, but when it was applicable in practice it turned out to be a well known technique. As she progressed through what was shaping up to be a poorly structured paper, the words had an increasing sense of familiarity. Then it dawned on her: the authors had lifted a couple of pages directly from one of her own papers. There was no attribution, no quotation, just her words melded into the text. Lori dug out the paper of hers from which she thought the authors had lifted her words. Sure enough, the text was identical. At first she was stunned, then somewhat understanding in that she thought the authors imagined her words could not be improved upon, but only briefly before becoming furious at this blatant example of academic cheating. She finished reading the paper. There was nothing much there except the claim for a new method that boiled down in practice to tried and true statistical technique. The authors concluded with overblown claims for their ideas, and suggestions for follow-up work. Lori wrote a quick and terse rejection report and pressed the "reject for publication" button. She got up from her desk still furious at this blatant plagiarism. As she started walking to the Department office she bumped into George Prince.

"Hey Lori," he said. "You don't look too happy. What's going on?" Lori told him about the paper and her rejection of it. "That's terrible," George said. "We all know this goes on but it's awful to see it first hand and up close. Well, at least you discovered it quickly and dealt with it."

Lori agreed. "But what's worrying me, George, is that one of the authors is a quite senior and well-known statistician. The other authors seem to be graduate students. I don't get what's going on with them. And I don't know if this is a one-off."

George agreed it was problematic that a senior academic would be involved in plagiarism. "It's possible he's running a paper production factory," he said. "I would be on the look out for similar papers from them." Lori agreed and told George she would phone the chief editor of the journal to let her know about the situation. "I'm wondering," she said. "If I shouldn't let a few other journal editors know."

"I would," said George. "Stop this rot before it goes any further."

"What's the rot?" asked Rickhart as he walked by. Lori explained the situation to him and Rickhart's face darkened. "This is very serious and very bad," he said. "Can you send me a copy of the paper?" Lori said she would. "By all means get in touch with the editor of the journal," he said. "I think this is also a matter for the statistical societies: they need to be aware of what these authors have been up to and put them on a watch list. Once I have the paper from you I will be happy to contact the American Statistical Society and the Institute of Mathematical Statistics. I think it might be best if you and I write a letter together, Lori, since you're the referee for the paper." Lori was surprised by Rickhart's decisiveness but reflected that he didn't get to be Full

Professor in record time by being indecisive. "Sure, I'd be happy to," she said.

Lori continued to the Bob's office, thinking she wanted to tell him all about this excitement.

♥♥♥♥♥

Deborah Duke phoned Lisa De Silva to ask about Grüner Veltliner. She wanted to know where Lisa bought it, and if she would go with her to help pick out some for the barbecue this weekend. "I'd be glad too," said Lisa. "I could go after my last class. How about meeting at noon?" Deborah agreed to meet her in car park three. The drive to Wayland Square took just on 20 minutes and Deborah found a parking spot just around the corner from the wine shop, by Books on the Square.

"You live around here, don't you?" Deborah asked.

"Just across the road," said Lisa.

"How nice! You've got everything here," said Deborah. "I like where George and I live, but his has a great village feel to it, so close to downtown Providence."

They waked across the road to Wayland Square Fine Wine and Spirits and Lisa led Deborah to the back of the store where the owner kept the Grüner.

"Wow, they have quite a range," said Deborah.

"It's why I like this place, apart from it being just across the road from me," Lisa laughed.

Deborah browsed the wine and picked out a dozen bottles, three each of four differ varieties. "Is this as good as its price indicates?" asked Deborah, holding a bottle of Laurenz V Charming 2010.

"Oh yes, it is," said Lisa. It's one of my favorites. I didn't used to be able to afford it for myself. I'm sure you'll like it."

Deborah thought for a minute and said "You know what? I'm going to get this as an anniversary present from me to George. Let me get some beer and some red wine and we'll be done."

The store alarm rang and a young man bolted through the front door. A store employee ran into the street shouting and waving. Two burly men outside McBride's Irish Pub grabbed the miscreant and dragged him back to the store. The employee demanded the young man hand over what he had taken. It was a bottle of Lagavulin 21 year old whisky. The store clerk shook his head "You've got taste at least," he said. "Why does a kid like you steal something like this?" The young man shook his head. "You know, I should call the police. You will probably come back here and try to steal again. Or go somewhere else and do the same." The young man said nothing. "Okay, get out, and don't come back," said the store clerk. He thanked the two men who had grabbed the thief and said he didn't know what was going on with young people these days.

Deborah and Lisa watched the event with surprise. "Let's not try to get out without paying for the Laurenz V Charming," whispered Deborah.

"No, I want to be able to come back here again," Lisa laughed.

"I don't know what drives someone like that young man to steal like that," said Deborah. "If all he wanted was whisky there are a lot cheaper ones to steal. He might secrete smaller bottles in a coat, or something like that. But he just grabbed an expensive bottle of Scotch and bolted. He didn't look like a derelict or a drunk. It's not as if he actually needed that particular expensive bottle of whisky."

"I think it might have something to do with my generation," said Lisa. "I see that sort of behavior often. It's impulsiveness coupled with a sense of entitlement."

"But you're not like that," Lisa said.

"No, I'm not," said Lisa. "But then I'm lucky. I know what I want to do. I'm good at it, and people are now willing to pay me well for my skills and knowledge. That makes me something of an outlier for people my age."

"But it didn't just happen to you," said Deborah. "You worked for it. You work hard, and you invested time and effort acquiring new skills. That's why you're in demand."

Lisa shrugged. "I guess not everyone my age wants to do that," she said.

Deborah paid for the supplies and went to get the car while Lisa waited at the store. They loaded the wine and beer into the car and began the drive back to Deborah's home.

"I think we're pretty well stocked up for the barbecue," she said. "George is looking after the food, so I think we're okay. I'd better let people know this afternoon. Heinrich will be surprised to see how George does a barbeque. He said he wanted to learn, so here's his chance."

When they got to the house they found George sipping a glass of whisky. "You'll never believe the price I paid for this Lagavulin," he said. " It was practically a steal."

Deborah and Lori laughed, and explained the incident at the wine store. Deborah showed the wine for the barbecue to George.

"Well," said George, bowing low to Deborah and Lori, "the maestro is ready and willing to give barbecue lessons to all who wish to learn. All they have to do is pay attention and learn from the master."

"George, it's a good thing you know what you're talking about because you're so darned pompous!" said Deborah.

"Moi? Pompous?" said George. He pulled an Opus X Fuente Fuente cigar from his short pocket, smiled, and went out on the deck to smoke.

51

Make mine meat

⌘

"Ach so!" said Heinrich when he read Deborah's email about the barbecue " It looks like George is one step ahead". Anna came over to read the message. "Well you have not bought the barbecue grill yet, Heinrich, so maybe you can use this opportunity to look at George's?" Heinrich agreed. "It's best," he said. "I rarely do things well when I rush."

Anna wondered what would be polite to take to Deborah and George's barbecue. "Some wine, perhaps?" she asked Heinrich.

"You know Anna, I think that is a good idea, and we should take some excellent wine with which people are unfamiliar. I think we can find some Grüner Veltliner. That's a good Austrian wine as you know, and there are some excellent varieties. I think no-one here has likely tried it before."

Anna agreed and gave Heinrich a hug. She was so happy to have made this move. She smiled at Heinrich: "I love our new home," she said.

♥♥♥♥♥

Alex was happy. The movement around the house meant something was happening, and he had a good idea what it was.

"BBQ! BBQ! BBQ!" he thought, his tail wagging hard. Alex loved barbecues There was so much meat! Deborah would shoo him away from the meat trays but George would always sneak him some, and when the guests came and the meat started cooking – HEAVEN! He raised his nose and sniffed the air. He could rely on some of the guests slipping him pieces of cooked meat. It was so easy to tell who were the softies. He would go to a likely suspect, sit on the floor, wag his tail, and look up with his eyes wide open. A soulful look worked best he found. A woman was more likely to succumb. "Oh, you're adorable!" were the words that told him meat was imminent. Oh yes! Alex was looking forward to this.

"Hi Alex, old boy," said George stopping to pat Alex's head. Would you like a little piece of meat? Don't tell Debbie." George cut a fatty piece from a steak and passed it to Alex. Alex took it very carefully from George's hand – he loved to savor the smell – and then slowly chewed it. Oh yum! It was always just a little piece, and he wagged his tail in anticipation of more. "Not now you little guts," said George. "You'll get plenty when everyone comes. Someone's always suckered by your big brown eyes." He rubbed Alex's head again.

"George, you're not giving Alex meat again?" asked Deborah. No wonder he can't learn it's not his mealtime yet. You know he pesters the guests until they give him something. He's going to get fat."

Alex was wounded. Fat?! Deborah should know how hard he chased the seagulls at the beach, and swam into the water to retrieve the sticks that George threw. "Why did George do that?" wondered Alex. "As long as it makes him happy," he thought "I'll keep bringing them back to him."

He looked up at Deborah. "Don't give me that soulful look Alex. I know what you're up to you little rascal. Now shoo out of here." Alex made an undignified exit, looking back at George. "She's your wife!" he thought to himself as he ran into the back-yard to see if any seagulls had dared invade his territory.

"This will be fun, George. Did you see the wine I got?" Deborah showed him a bottle of the Grüner she had picked up from Wayland Square with Lisa.

"Looks good," said George. "Have you tried it?"

"I might have opened a bottle," she said. "Would you like a glass?"

"Just a small one," said George as Deborah poured the wine for him. "I'm about done. Should we take a break and drink this on the deck?"

"This is very good," George said. "Different to what I expected. I thought it would be sweeter than it is being an Austrian wine, but it's not sweet at all. More like a sauvignon blanc but with different overtones. Spicy, peppery even, and no oak that I can detect. It's good. How did you get onto this?" Deborah told George about her and Lisa's trip to Wayland Square Fine Wine and Spirits. George was surprised at Lisa's knowledge of fine things. "For a kid she sure knows a lot," he said.

Deborah was thinking about the Department newcomers. "Bao is a fireball, isn't she?" Deborah asked George. He agreed. "She talks quietly but she sure is direct. If she wants to know something she comes straight out and asks," said Deborah. "She said she would bring her husband. I'm looking forward to meeting him. He's an engineer," she said in answer to George's half-formed question.

"And Heinrich is certainly interesting," said George. "Grass doesn't grow under his feet, despite his cautious approach to everything." Deborah didn't think Heinrich was cautious as much as he was thoughtful. He strikes me as someone who really likes to do his homework," she said.

The doorbell arrived and guests began to arrive. Alex's ears pricked up and he ran up the steps to the deck, and to the glass door, but Deborah had closed it. He sat there, tail wagging, nose against the glass.

Bao Zhang introduced her husband Ri. "His name means 'very intelligent'" she said. "And sometimes that's true." Both Ri and Bao laughed. Ri shook hands with Deborah and George. "Thanks for inviting us," he said. "Bao and I are staying with friends. We've been looking for an apartment, but I'm keen to see your house. It looks very beautiful."

"Thank you," said Deborah. "Are you looking around here?" she asked. "Do you work nearby, Ri?"

Ri explained he did not. "I work for Raytheon in Waltham, Massachusetts," he said. It's about an hour from here. Bao has been thinking about an apartment halfway, somewhere near Sharon, but I like this area so much. Rhode Island has so much water, and so many beautiful inlets and coves, I like it."

The doorbell rang again as Heinrich and Anna arrived. Heinrich presented Deborah with two bottles of Laurenz V Charming 2010 Grüner Veltliner. "It's an Austrian wine," he said. "I think you will like it."

"Oh, I know I will," Deborah laughed.

Heinrich wanted to see George's grill. "Oh this is very nice, George. A Blaze 5-Burner model. I am impressed. And you have the infrared burner and rotisserie. That is an excellent choice of grill."

George laughed. "I did some homework", he said. You can operate it if you want, Heinrich."

"Ja? I would like that. Thank you, George."

"As long as it lights easily, stays alight, and is easy to clean", a voice said behind them.

"Rickhart!" said Heinrich. "How are you?" They shook hands. "Actually, you know, there is another consideration," said Heinrich. "Some models of grill have been known to overheat in spots. You can develop a magnesium burning fire and that is very hard to put out. Such fires have been known to burn down an entire house."

"I can see you've done your homework," Rickhart laughed.

"I try to," said Heinrich.

More guests arrived and Deborah was serving drinks. "Ah, you already knew about Grüner. You must think I am very foolish," said Heinrich.

"Not at all," said Deborah. "I just thought you had excellent taste."

George showed Heinrich the food for the grill and they carried it out together to the deck. Alex followed dutifully. George showed Heinrich how to light the grill and adjust the temperature. Soon the food was beginning to cook and the smell pervaded the house. Alex was getting excited. Heinrich beckoned Anna to take a look at the grill. He handed her the tongs and showed her which pieces to turn. "I'm just going to the bathroom," he said. I will be back in a minute."

Anna stood by the grill and turned several pieces of meat. Alex sat by her, his tail wagging, his big brown eyes looking up at her.

"Aren't you adorable," she said. "Would you like a little piece of meat?"

Alex's tail thumped the deck, and he let out a little yelp. Anna passed him the meat after testing the heat. "Here let me just put it on the deck here for you while it cools."

Alex sniffed the hot meat and looked up at Anna. He liked this lady. He thought he would stick with her for the rest of the day.

52

To argue is human,
to cooperate divine

Lisa and Chris arrived about an hour after the party had begun. Chris wanted to bring wine, but Lisa assured him Deborah was well stocked. "It's your doing," she said to Chris. "You introduced me to Grüner and now it seems no one wants to drink anything else."

"An understandable reaction," Chris laughed.

Deborah opened the door and welcomed them. "Hi guys. Wow, Lisa, I love your dress. Where did you get it?"

Lisa blushed. "I have to confess I shopped at Nordstrom – my first time ever. My consultancy check arrived. I've never had that much money in my life. Can you believe it – seventeen thousand dollars?"

Fantastic!" said Deborah as Inger Hansen approached.

"Seventeen thousand dollars?" Inger said. "Somebody has give you seventeen thousand dollars?"

"Well not give exactly," said Lisa. "I have to work for it."

"But what work you do that somebody gives you seventeen

thousand dollars?" asked Inger. "You are just a baby. Somebody must have too much money," she laughed.

Embarrassed, Lisa turned away. Chris changed the subject and asked Deborah if Alex was around. "I've heard about him from Lisa and I'd really like to say hello."

Inger followed Deborah. "Do you know what she is doing to make such money?" Deborah explained it had to do with working for Jeffrey's publisher as a consultant.

"Ah! Publisher!" said Inger. "Well those people have more money than sense. So it's Jeffrey she has to thank for this."

"Indirectly, I suppose," said Deborah. "But I think what she makes and why is between her and Jeffrey's publisher. Apparently they value her skills, which are pretty exceptional. Either way, it's really none of our business."

"No need for you to snap at me, Deborah. She is the one bringing it up in the first place," said Inger.

Deborah walked away from Inger, furious at having this unpleasant conversation in her house.

"What's the matter?" asked Rickhart as he caught the look on Deborah's face.

"Oh, it's Inger," said Deborah, and explained the conversation to him.

"Leave her to me", said Rickhart. "I will have a word with her." Deborah thanked Rickhart and caught up with Chris. "Alex should be out on the deck," she said. "If I know him, he's caught the attention of some adoring woman and is now lapping up food from the barbecue."

Alex was seated next to Anna, wagging his tail and occasionally barking as he anticipated her giving him more meat. "Okay Alex, enough of that," said Deborah. "Come here and meet Chris." Alex turned to look at Chris, sized up the unlikelihood of getting any food from him, and turned back to Anna, with another bark.

"Here", said Anna," give him this piece of meat and he will be your friend too." Chris took the meat from Anna and patted Alex on the head. "Who's a good boy then? Would you like this?"

Alex took the offering from Chris and sat in front of him wagging his tail. Had he misjudged this young man? He was conflicted. He looked back to Anna, and then at Chris, and began barking.

"Okay, enough Alex. George is going to deal with you." Deborah signaled to George to come and deal with Alex, with the result that Alex was put on a leash further down the backyard with a bowl of his regular food. Resigned, he lay on the grass looking up at the people on the deck, savoring the delicious scent of barbecued meat.

As the afternoon turned to evening people, content and well fed, began drifting away to their homes. Heinrich thanked George for the excellent practical lesson in operating the barbecue grill and he and Anna said goodbye. With all the guests gone George unleashed a chastened Alex and came into the kitchen to talk to Deborah. "I'm glad Rickhart spoke to Inger about her behavior toward Lisa. She seemed unrepentant and couldn't see she had said anything unpleasant. You know the line she always uses when she behaves like this: *I only tell the truth!*"

"I'm hoping," he said, "that Rickhart puts it to her that it might be time for her to consider her position in the Department."

"You mean ask her to resign?" said Deborah.

"Not as such," said George. "But she's becoming more and more personally difficult, as we all know, and her productivity is very low, almost as bad as Bert's. Students don't like her, they complain about her accent, which seems to be more difficult to understand with each semester, and about her harsh words toward them. It's not clear to me that she serves any useful function any more, if she ever did. She and Bert got their jobs at the University at the same time and neither of them have been exactly ornaments to the Department."

"It's probably a good thing for the Department if both Inger and Bert take their leave, said Deborah. "As a grad student I can't say they contributed much to my education, or to any of the grad students for that matter. How about we leave this mess and go to bed? We can clean up in the morning?"

"I'll just make sure there's nothing out that Alex can get to, and then we can call it a night," said George.

♥♥♥♥♥

Jeffrey was preparing for his trip to Cyprus. His talk on the history of orthogonal polynomials was almost complete. He fussed as usual over the details, changing the format of the slides a little here and there. He was very pleased with the look and feel of his slide presentation. Lisa had shown him how to use LaTeX Beamer for his presentation and had pointed him to ShareLateX on the Web so he didn't even have to download a LaTeX installation. The result, he thought, was very professional looking indeed. Jeffrey thought how a lot of his academic life had been hampered by not having an assistant, like Lisa, to help him with technical matters. "Don't forget the coffee," said a little voice in his head. Jeffrey smiled. Life has its ups and downs, he thought. At first he was opposed to appointing Bao Zhang over Heinrich, but now he had gotten to know Bao better he was happy to have them both as colleagues. Heinrich was a little more odd than Jeffrey had hoped for – what was the obsession with barbecues about? – but a most interesting and useful colleague. Their energy and drive had unnerved him at first, but now he could see that they respected him and wanted him to be part of a team. Then there was this Cyprus thing. At first he was dismissive of their "International Conference", seeing it, as he recalled: "another tin-pot university trying to promote itself." But Bob and Lori had been right. The mathematics department was of a much higher quality than he had imagined: they had been very kind and supportive in asking Jeffrey to open the conference. And they seemed to be unusually friendly. Jeffrey had been asked if he would like to lead a small group of students at the conference. It was their custom, he was told, to try to engage students fully in the conference activities, so each participant was asked if they would mentor a group of students, meet with them over breakfast, and take them to lunch one day of the conference. Jeffrey had not heard of this idea before but it sounded an excellent practice to him. He wondered if he should send his assigned group of students a copy of the latest edition of his *Matrix Algebra* so they would get a better idea of his prominence in the field.

Kathy knocked at Jeffrey's door and walked in. "You're looking pleased with yourself Jeff."

Jeffrey smiled. "I guess I am," he said. "You know I'm glad after all that we appointed Bao. I wanted Heinrich over her, and I still would stick to that point of view. But Bao is a very strong colleague and I think we can all work together well. I think the main thing is getting along together, despite any slight differences we might have."

Kathy was pleased. She wondered though if Lisa might not be adding something to Jeffrey's coffee.

53

The unexpected pleasure of Greek coffee

Jeffrey Albacete was renowned as an entertaining speaker. Contrary to the widely acknowledged soporific nature of his writing, Jeffrey's talks were models of wit and engagement. Rickhart Jansen had once remarked that Jeffrey was the only academic he knew that he wanted to continue talking over the allotted time. The average academic, given some time in the spotlight, will drone on and often go over their allotted speaking time unless stopped by a conscientious and unintimidated moderator; assuming said moderator has not already nodded off. Other academic scoundrels will put the blame for their boring presentations on the allotted time, saying "I could explain this in more detail if I had more time." These reprobates know full well the time allotted to them and have had months to prepare their moment in the sun, knowing that they themselves have had to suffer similar mind-numbing presentations from others. Jeffrey did not fall into either of these categories. He was that rare bird who would be asked to continue speaking if his listeners did not have to go elsewhere, and the room in which he was speaking was not otherwise occupied at the end of his talk.

So it was that the attendees at Jeffrey's opening talk at the University of Southern Cyprus International Mathematics Conference buzzed with undisguised glee at the end of his talk. "I wish you could talk for another hour. That was really enjoyable Professor Albacete," said Ivan Medvedev from Moscow. Jeffrey thanked him and was enchanted when Agape Galanis pressed his arm and said: "Professor Albacete – may I call you Jeffrey? – I loved your talk. It was so factually interesting and romantic. Yes, you brought a wonderfully romantic story of intellectual development to life. I have never experienced anything like it." Jeffrey smiled and thanked her. "Would you, I wonder, be free for coffee later?" she asked.

"Well there is a break at 4:00 after the workshops. Perhaps we could meet then?" said Jeffrey.

"At the registration desk?" asked Agape.

"Yes, at the information desk. That would be easiest," said Jeffrey bidding her αντίο.

"Oh," she shivered, "and you speak Greek, too. Αντίο μέχρι να συναντηθούμε και πάλι." Jeffrey had no idea what this meant, having exhausted his stock of Greek with one word, learned the day before, but gathered Agape was pleased. Her took his leave and headed to the next talk on the agenda.

As Jeffrey made his way to the lecture rooms two students called out to him. They were two of his mentor group with whom he breakfasted earlier that morning. "Γεια σας και πάλι ο καθηγητής", they said. "We were at your talk. It was very excellent, most enjoyable." Jeffrey thanked them, and reminded them that he was to lunch with them and the rest of their group tomorrow.

"We do not forget, Professor," they said. "We will see you tomorrow at breakfast."

Jeffrey basked in the warmth of his reception in Cyprus. "What wonderful people". He thought. "So welcoming and generous, and so cultured as well," Greece, he reflected, was the home of mathematics, even though there had, of course, been arithmetic calculations and some geometric reckonings long before Pythagoras of Samos had started mathematics as it is now known, no more than 500 miles to the northeast of Cyprus.

Jeffrey went to a talk on models of fish populations in which the speaker used matrix methods extensively. Then there was a half hour break for refreshments and two more short talks before lunch. The head of the matrix algebra group had asked Jeffrey to lunch with several Department members and some other international visitors, and at the lunch hour Jeffrey wandered the dining room feeling a little confused and disoriented. Someone caught him by the elbow. "Jeffrey," said his host, "this way. We have a table waiting." Jeffrey followed and joined the group. "Very nice talk this morning, Jeffrey. Very, very enjoyable," said one. A strikingly beautiful middle-aged woman, next to whom he was seated, leaned into him and said, with a soft french accent: "I was enchanted. Orthogonal polynomials are my specialty and I thought I knew everything about them. Yet you opened up new vistas for me." Jeffrey was about to thank her when he felt her hand resting on his thigh. "I, I, ... I am glad you enjoyed it," he said.

"Forgive me, I did not introduce myself. I am Colette Lefevre from Paris. I suspect, Professor Albacete – may I call you Jeffrey? – there is a lot more you could tell me perhpas – in a private conversation?"

Jeffrey looked around and loosened his collar. "Well, yes, I, ah ... there is, of course, a lot more to this topic than one can discuss in an hour. It's important I think, not to go overtime and to keep the audience interested."

Colette squeezed his thigh. "You certainly interested me," she smiled.

Jeffrey had heard abut conference romances, but this was the first time he thought one was imminent. Someone was keen to discuss the new edition of Jeffrey's book and his mind drifted away from Colette's attention. At the end of the meal Jeffrey was feeling a certain tingling excitement, like champagne bubbles rising in a glass. As everyone rose to go to the next talks Collette shook hands with him and pressed a note into his hand. "It's been a pleasure meeting with you Jeffrey, and I hope we can continue later," she said.

Jeffrey left for the next talk, unfolding and glancing down at the note. It had just a room number at the Grand Resort, the hotel where he was staying, and a phone number. Jeffrey put the note in his pocket and his mind on other matters. "This is silly," he said to himself. " She probably does want to talk about orthogonal polynomials."

The afternoon session went very well. Jeffrey led a group working on advances in applications of matrix algebra. He wished that Heinrich could have been here. Never mind, he thought, this will give us a lot of new ideas for the *Applied Matrix Algebra* book.

Jeffrey ended the workshop and walked toward the book display. As he walked past the registration desk, Agape Galanis slipped her arm into his and said: "I'm glad you came. Let's get some coffee."

"I could do with that," said Jeffrey, who liked the dark Greek coffee, which to him seemed identical to Turkish coffee. "Where's the best place to get some?"

"I have some excellent coffee in my room," she said. "I think you will enjoy it more than anything you find here."

Jeffrey hesitated for a millisecond. Best to go with the good coffee, a little voice in his head said. "I would like to try that," said Jeffrey.

Agape squeezed his arm. "I know you will like it. I have a feeing you are enjoying the charms of Greece."

Jeffrey had a rising feeling that he was about to enjoy them even more.

♥♥♥♥♥

That evening Jeffrey was taken to dinner by three of the

Department faculty. He enjoyed trying new dishes and was over-whelmed by the level of hospitality. Around nine o'clock he began to feel quite tired. "I think I need to sleep," he apologized. "I've done quite a lot today."

His hosts told him not to worry, to go to the hotel and get a good night's sleep: he would wake rested for tomorrow's events. Jeffrey thanked them and made his way back to the Grand Resort. He took the elevator to his floor and put the key in his door. He took off his shoes and flopped on the bed. The phone rang. Not expecting anyone, he picked it up and said: "Hello?"

"Hello Jeffrey, this is Collette. I wonder if you would like a nightcap? You could show me what else you know about orthogonal polynomials."

54

Speed can be dangerous

Jeffrey was surprised that the Department had supplied wine and beer for the student lunch. "The legal drinking age in Cyprus is 17," said Stavros Koumas. "We do not have hang-ups about alcohol, like you Americans," he laughed. "Children here are often served wine with meals. As a result, students are less likely to think it is cool to be drunk in Cyprus." Jeffrey was relieved. He did not want to be seen to be contributing to the delinquency of underage students. If this policy worked in Cyprus – and he had seen no evidence from the students so far that it did not – then so much the better for them. "It's not as if the drinking age of 21 prevents American students from holding booze parties," he reflected.

His mentor group arrived at the small seminar room where the lunch had been set up for them. "Γεια σας καθηγητής" they greeted him as they came into the room. Jeffrey was very pleased to see this small group of students with whom he had breakfasted the past two days. They had all come to his talk and seemed keenly interested in his book and his work. Jeffrey was surprised to learn that the students earned course credit for attending the conference, and thought this was an excellent way to introduce them to research and scholarship. In many ways, he thought, people back home could learn a thing or two from academic practices in Cyprus. The students began to eat and drink as they chatted to Jeffrey about his impressions of the conference, of the University, and of Cyprus in general.

"I haven't actually seen much of Cyprus," he said, "apart from the University and the hotel." An image came to him of the previous night after Collette Lefevre had come to his room with wine. He smiled at the recollection.

"It seems you are happy to be here," said one of the students, picking up on Jeffrey's demeanor.

"Happy? Yes. I would say I am quite happy about my experiences in Cyprus," he said.

A student knocked on the seminar room door as she opened it to come in. Jeffrey was surprised to see this student. She was quite a large girl, even by American standards. Relatively short, she was dressed in a purple top, a very short black skirt, which did not do justice to her substantial thighs, and very high heels. Jeffrey was about to ask who she was when one of the students introduced her.

"This is our friend Angeliki," he said. "She is a student here and was supposed to meet with her mentor group, but she slept in this morning and has lost them. Is it okay if she sits with us Professor?"

Jeffrey could see no reason why not, and invited Angeliki to join them. Angeliki thanked Jeffrey and poured herself a glass of diet cola, but did not eat, as she chatted with the other students.

Just then Jeffrey's cell-phone rang. He excused himself and answered the call. It was from his publisher, with a request that had to do with the new book. "Will you excuse me for a minute?" he asked. "I just need to take this call." Jeffrey stepped outside the room and spoke to his editor. The conversation was very positive with Wolfram agreeing to a licensing arrangement for the CDF version. Jeffrey spoke for several minutes and had almost finished the conversation when a student rushed out of the room and said to him: "Professor, come quickly. There's something wrong with Angeliki."

Jeffrey apologized to his editor, hung up, and went back into the seminar room. Angeliki was lying on the floor, apparently unconscious.

"We tried to wake her, but we could not," said a student. "She is breathing okay, but I don't know what's wrong with her." At that moment Angeliki opened her eyes, raised her head and vomited on the floor.

"Oh!" said the students, as if one voice, and jumped back without thinking.

"I will help clean it up," said a student who went looking for a mop and a bucket.

"I think we should call someone," said Jeffery, feeling increasingly nervous that Angeliki had collapsed while in his charge. "Is there a doctor on campus we can call?"

"Yes, there is a health service. I have the number. I will call them," said one of the students. He spoke briefly to a nurse and then to Jeffrey. "They asked if she is breathing okay or if vomit is obstructing her breathing. If she seems okay then just let her sleep. They said they could not do anything else themselves. They said to call back immediately if she worsens."

The seminar room was now not a pleasant place to continue eating or meeting, so Jeffery suggested the students leave and he would catch up with them later. He turned to one of the students, Nicholas Panas, and asked if he would stay.

"Sure, I can do that Professor," he said, and the two of them sat and watched Angeliki for vital signs. Her breathing was deep and sound, so Jeffrey thought, following the advice of the health service nurse, to let her be and to keep watching her.

"Do you know what happened?" he asked Nicholas.

"Oh yes. She exchanged her diet cola for a glass of wine and it seemed only a minute later – you were outside on the phone – she collapsed."

Jeffrey was surprised, for the fourth time that day, that something as simple as a glass of wine would cause such a strong reaction.

"She is dieting," said Nicholas.

This again surprised Jeffrey because he imagined that someone on a diet would not be able to produce such copious amounts of vomit.

"And she has been taking amphetamines to suppress her appetite. I think that is maybe what reacted with the alcohol," said Nicholas.

"I see," said Jeffrey. He looked at the time, and figured he could probably miss a couple of short talks before he himself was missed.

A half-hour later Jeffrey suggested to Nicholas that they try to call Angeliki's parents. "I think we should look through her purse to see if there's a home number we can call". Jeffrey lifted Angeliki's purse from her side and opened it to look for a home number. Seeing it was all Greek he handed it to Nicholas.

"Yes, I think this is the home number," said Nicholas. "Should I call it?"

"Yes, go ahead," said Jeffrey, "then maybe I should speak with her parents. Do you know if they speak English?"

"I think so," said Nicholas. "Let me try." He dialed the number and began speaking with Angeliki's mother. He nodded to Jeffrey and handed the phone to him.

"Hello. This is Professor Albacete. I am an American professor visiting the University. Yes, Angeliki is okay – she is sleeping. Yes, it's an unfortunate mishap. I think it would be best if you could come and collect her. Okay. Good. We will see you shortly then."

"They are coming," he said to Nicholas. Jeffrey was relieved to pass this problem off to the girl's parents. But then a feeling of apprehension took over. "What if they blame me?" he thought.

Jeffrey told Nicholas that it was okay for him to leave. "I can look after her," he said. "Her parents will be here shortly."

Jeffrey sat alone with Angeliki, feeling sorry for this chubby girl, trying to lose weight, who now lay sprawled on the floor with vomit in her hair and her legs and thighs exposed. There was no point, thought Jeffrey, in trying to cover her with the tiny three-inch skirt she was wearing, as embarrassing as it was for him , and would be for her if she were awake. Besides, he did not want someone to come into the room as he was tugging at her skirt. They might get the wrong idea. Twenty minutes passed when a man and woman entered the room.

"Oh, Angeliki," said the woman. The man frowned, and looked at Jeffrey. "How did this happen?" he asked.

"I, ... I don't know," said Jeffrey. "I was out of the room on a phone call – my publisher back in America – when I was told what happened. Apparently ... according to the other students ... she has been taking amphetamines," he said.

Angeiki's father still frowned. Her mother tried to wake Angeliki. Upon waking, Angeliki looked up at her mother, then her father, and said: "Σκατά!", which Jeffrey gathered was not polite because of the effect the words had on her parents.

At that point, Jeffrey was horrified to see that Angeliki had wrapped her arms around his leg.

"Θα μείνω μαζί του," she said, and Jeffrey gathered this was also not terribly politic because her father's frown deepened.

"Would you like me to leave?" asked Jeffrey, doing his level best to extricate himself from Angeliki's vice-like grip.

"I think that might be best," said her father. "I cannot imagine why she said she wants to stay with you."

Jeffrey apologized again and left the room. He was mortified. He phoned his airline to see about changing his flight back to America. "Yes, this afternoon, As soon as possible, really," he said. "Yes, I'll pay the difference."

Jeffrey went looking for the Department Chair. "I'm sorry," he said, upon finding him. "I have to leave. Yes, right away. A family emergency, yes. Of course I have thoroughly enjoyed the confer-ence. It's been wonderful."

Jeffrey collected his belongings from the hotel and took a taxi to the airport. Not even when the doors of the plane were locked did his anxiety subside. It was only when the plane was in the air that he could breathe a sigh of relief. "There's a very good reason why in America we have laws about students not drinking until they're twenty one," he thought.

55

Guard your energy

Bao Zhang settled into her new office. She liked the outlook, over the trees and pathways from the car park, with a view the other way over the center of the campus. When Zaqi came by she was wearing a painter's mask, and was busy spray painting a wall lilac.

"Are you allowed to do that?" asked Zaqi.

Bao stopped and took off the mask. "I asked central administration and they said they couldn't see why not", she said.

"I hope you got it in writing," said Zaqi. Bao replied she had the response in an email and legally that was as good as pen on paper.

"Would you like me to paint your room too?" she asked Zaqi.

"No thanks. Not lilac anyway. It's a very girly color."

"Well in case you hadn't noticed, Zaq ... " she said.

Zaqi looked around the room. He liked Bao's furniture. A chrome and glass desk sat in the corner, with a new computer on it, a plastic sheet covering both. The desk was very different from the standard catalog desks that most faculty were issued. "Did you buy that desk yourself?' asked Zaqi.

"No, the Department bought it. I just had to ask. It was cheaper than the standard issue," she laughed.

Zaqi marveled at Bao's ability to get what she wanted by just asking. He thought he could learn a thing or two from her.

"You don't think like most people," he said. Bao took this as a compliment.

"You can help if you want," she said, pulling a mask out of the packet, and handing him a fresh can of lilac spray paint.

Zaqi laughed. "Might as well. If you're going to get caught doing this I may as well go down with you."

Together they painted the section of wall directly opposite the door. Bao had chosen this color to have an immediate mood effect on anyone entering the office.

She removed her mask and said: "We'll pull the tape off the edges when it dries a bit. Good job don't you think?"

Zaqi stood back to admire their effort. "It looks very good actually. I'm surprised," he said.

Bao was surprised that he was surprised. "I chose this color very carefully. It has both a calming and enlivening effect on people, if that doesn't sound contradictory. It calms the nerves and lifts the spirits. Ideal for a workspace."

Bao took some beautiful blue and white flowers from a packet, and unwrapped a vase. She placed the flowers in the vase and arranged them, placing the arrangement on a ledge by the newly painted wall. "What do you think?" she asked Zaqi.

"Spectacular," he said. "You really have an eye for this. Would it be too much to ask you to help me decorate my office?"

Bao agreed but said Zaqi had to suspend judgment about certain colors and arrangements being too 'girly'. "It's all about the energy," she said.

Zaqi laughed. "Okay, I'm in your hands." He was thinking that if color and flower arrangements were what gave Bao her energy then she could paint his room pink if it would help. "Where did you learn this stuff?" he asked.

Bao explained that she was taught energy training since she

was a little girl. "I first learned simple Qigong," she said, "and then Tai Chi. As part of that training we learned about energy in our environment. I still have a lot to learn." She looked very serious for a moment, as if focusing on some deeper vision. Then she burst out laughing. "But don't worry Zaqi, you don't have to learn Tai Chi just to decorate your office! Let's go and see what sort of mess we have to fix."

As they headed to Zaqi's office they bumped into Jeffrey.

"Hello Jeff," said Zaqi. "I thought you were in Cyprus until the end of the week."

"Well, ... yes. I was supposed to be. But something came up," he said.

"Oh? Nothing serious I hope," said Zaqi.

Jeffrey, too, hoped it was nothing serious. "Oh, no, no, just a case of suspected food poisoning. Something I ate. And I wanted to get back to the doctor here. It seems to have settled down okay now that I'm home."

Zaqi asked how Jeffrey's keynote talk had been received. "Oh very well," said Jeffrey. "I got a lot of compliments. People seemed very happy." He was remembering Agape Galanis and Colette Lefevre. "Very happy," he said. "I would have liked to have stayed the week, but these things happen."

Zaqi and Bao continued on to Zaqi's office.

"That's not the story I heard," said Bao.

'What do you mean?" asked Zaqi.

"A friend of mine was at that conference. She said Jeffrey got a girl drunk and her parents are thinking about suing the University."

Zaqi's jaw dropped. "Jeffrey? Got a girl drunk? I don't believe it."

Bao shrugged. "I'm only going on what my friend wrote in her email. I don't know the whole story."

Zaqi was smiling and shaking his head. "Oh my goodness," he said. "Poor Jeffrey. He was probably just getting a bit lively at the conference and things got out of hand."

"There are ways of getting lively at a conference," said Bao, "but one of them isn't supplying undergraduates with alcohol."

Zaqi knew Bao was right, but he couldn't dare ask Jeffrey his side of the story. He knew that these rumors had a habit of growing monstrous appendages and that in all likelihood Jeffrey had not been doing anything with any bad intentions. "It's not like him," said Zaqi.

Bao shrugged. "You know him better than I do," she said. "Let's take a look at your office."

Zaqi opened the door for Bao. Old computers and computer parts were strewn all over the office. Bao looked around, taking in the feel of the space. She sensed Zaqi's love of all things technical.

"I would paint that wall gray," she said, pointing to the wall to the right of the door, opposite Zaqi's desk.

"Gray?" asked Zaqi. "I thought you said the color was supposed to be energizing."

"It will be when we're done," said Bao. "And I would replace your desk with something like mine – chrome and steel. This room needs to assert that you are a techno-freak. Preferably a little less subtly than having computer parts laying around the floor."

Abashed, Zaqi explained that he just liked collecting old computers. "There's something about them that makes me feel good," he said.

Bao explained the nature of addiction. "Have you noticed that cigarette smokers say how good smoking makes them feel? Yet look at the harm it does them. And people who drink too much, or over eat? They all do it because it makes them feel good. You need balance, a little of what you like, to keep you happy. But you also need discipline to enhance your energy flow. I think we could take one or two of these old computers and make a display out of them."

"But I'm not interested in art work," said Zaqi. "I want the computers to be working."

"Then that's the sort of display we will make," said Bao. "But let's not overdo it. If you have computers lying around like this it just makes you feel tired when you enter the room. There's so much to look at, too much distraction. It upsets your mind rather than calming it. You need to ask: am I gaining energy or am I losing it?"

Zaqi agreed. "I'm in your hands," he said.

As they moved old computers outside the office, Jeffrey appeared at the door. He seemed upset, sad and almost about to cry.

"I'd like to tell you what really happened", he said to Zaqi.

Bao asked if Jeffrey would like her to leave.

"No, you should hear this too, Bao. You probably will hear rumors anyway, and I'd like to set the record straight. It's been bothering me all the way home."

Jeffrey explained the circumstances of his sudden departure from the conference in Cyprus. Zaqi said he thought he would have left just as Jeffrey did.

Bao put both hands on the back of Jeffrey's shoulders. He looked like he was about to cry. Her touch was calming and soothing. A calm energizing feeling, like warm water, flowed through his body.

"It's not your fault, Jeff," said Bao, "and you've been very disturbed. You need to feel calm and relaxed and get your energy back."

Jeffrey looked at her and thought, once again, how fortunate they were to have hired this talented young woman. He began to feel safe.

56

Go with the flow

Jeffrey was relieved to have told his conference story to Bao and Zaqi. Sitting chatting with them helped him feel calm, safe and relaxed. Bao asked if she could get Jeffrey a cup of his excellent coffee. He agreed and when she came back with enough for the three of them they sat drinking the flavorsome brew, thinking about Bao's decorating ideas for Zaqi's office.

"Do you think my office could do with being decorated?" asked Jeffrey.

Bao laughed out loud. "Forgive me, Jeff. I don't mean to be rude. But the short answer is: Yes! Definitely, absolutely, a must! Are you kidding?"

Jeffrey smiled. He was becoming fond of Bao's straightforward answers. In a way he didn't yet understand, her approach seemed to clear the air of mental fog. Things seemed so straightforward and clear when she spoke.

"I guess I do let things pile up a bit," he said.

"And collect dust and give you allergies," said Bao.

"So we should just clean it all out?" said Jeffrey. "The trouble with that is I will probably go back to stockpiling things I can't bring myself to throw out."

Bao thought that, among other things, Jeffrey was probably a bibliomaniac. The evidence, she thought, was more or less clear from the multiple copies of books, stored to overflowing on his office shelves. Simply mentioning this to him, she thought, was probably not going to provide enough insight to help him.

"Here's what I think, Jeff. You will probably never stop stockpiling. The trick, in my view, is to face up to this tendency you have, admit it openly, and manage your piles. Bring some order into the chaos. Surround the growing piles with boundaries and limits. That way you might begin to feel more in control of the urge to collect and keep things that most of us wouldn't find necessary."

Jeffrey's mouth formed into a thin smile. "I guess you're right Bao. I could do with some order. Sort of corrals for the different collections?"

Bao agreed and told Jeffrey that he might need some help from her. Otherwise, she said, he was likely to get distracted by his collections rather than manage them.

Heinrich Zimmer knocked on Zaqi's door. "Hello. Kathy said I might find you here."

Bao laughed. "Just the man to bring some order to chaos."

Heinrich looked puzzled and Zaqi explained they were trying to help Jeffrey organize his office.

"Ja, that would be very good. You do have something of a mess there Jeffrey. I am glad to help organize if that is something you want."

Heinrich explained he had arranged a meeting with Lisa De Silva to discuss the next steps for the new book. "I was wondering if we could meet with you Jeff, in about an hour."

Jeffrey agreed. "But I guess not in my messy office."

"I was hoping that is indeed where we could meet," said Heinrich. "But I need to get a cup of tea, and answer some emails, so I will see you in an hour?"

As Heinrich left, Bao asked Jeffrey how the book was coming along. Jeffrey was happy with the progress, very happy. Things were moving along fast. Lisa was an excellent Mathematica programmer and Heinrich's applications added breadth and depth to the existing text.

"I feel as if I'm just the director of an ensemble," he said, "and the others are doing the work."

"And is that a bad thing, do you feel?" asked Bao.

Jeffrey thought for a moment and said that it wasn't. It was just not something he was used to feeling. "I've done things on my own for quite some time," he said. "No one helped me write *Matrix Algebra*. I did that by myself, and steered it through nine editions. It feels strange not doing the writing."

"But Heinrich and Lisa are doing a good job, no?" asked Bao.

"Oh, they're doing a great job. I couldn't be happier. I guess I just wonder ..."

"What is your contribution?" asked Bao.

"Exactly!" said Jeffrey. "I don't feel like I'm contributing to this new book."

Bao laughed. "And Lisa's writing CDFs from which text? And Heinrich's writing applications based on which text?" Bao asked.

Jeffrey got the point. "I guess you're saying I should go with the flow?"

Bao looked at Jeffrey with a gaze that held him. "Let the energy flow," she said. "Relax completely. Feel the energy and go with it."

Jeffrey again felt as if warm water had pervaded his body. He felt calm and relaxed.

"Thank you Bao," he smiled.

♥♥♥♥♥

Jeffrey was looking through his collection of books. So many of them he thought. How to begin to organize them?

A knock at the door brought him out of his thoughts and he turned to find Heinrich and Lisa arriving for their meeting. They sat at the small table in Jeffrey's office and Heinrich began the discussion by bringing Jeffrey and Lisa up to speed with his thoughts about new applications. Jeffrey was reminded of the conference talk on applications of matrix algebra and mentioned it to Heinrich. "A very nice idea," said Heinrich. "Do you have an email address so we can get more details? We will have to acknowledge the author," he said, making a note in his cell-phone.

Heinrich explained where Lisa was in coding his applications. "She is doing a fantastic job. This book comes to life because of her coding. That brings me to mentioning something to you Jeffrey. How do you feel if we include Lisa as a co-author on the book? She has done more than enough to deserve that in my opinion."

Jeffrey stiffened. He had never thought of Lisa as a co-author, and the thought was disconcerting. She's an undergraduate, he thought. Reasons why she should not, could not, be a co-author were jostling in his brain to be expressed. Then, for a reason he couldn't fathom, Bao's image appeared in his awareness. A steady warm flow of water began to move through his body. Slowly and very surely he began to relax. Completely.

Jeffrey turned to Lisa and smiled. "I think having Lisa as co-author is an excellent idea," he said. "We wouldn't be here if it weren't for her."

Lisa thanked Jeffrey for his kindness. Heinrich said this was very good, and they could now move forward with further implementation. "I think we are not only on target with the proposed publication date, but we are actually ahead of schedule. This feeling I like very much." Heinrich smiled and leaned back in his chair.

Jeffrey did not understand what just happened. He knew only that a warm feeling pervaded his body – he was reminded of his time with Agape and Collette – and he felt relaxed and calm.

"This is very good Jeffrey. I think we're going to produce a book that will – how do you say it? – knock their socks off!"

Lisa laughed and – to her and Heinrich's amazement – so did Jeffrey. Lisa had not heard Jeffrey ever laugh like that. He smiled often, but she could not recall an outright belly laugh. She could not know of course that in the course of some decades no one had ever heard Jeffrey laugh out loud.

Heinrich stood up. "Do you mind, Jeffrey, if I make myself a cup of tea? Your coffee smells very nice indeed, but I prefer tea."

Jeffrey laughed again. "Whatever you fancy, Heinrich. Each to their own."

Lisa excused herself to go to the restroom. As she walked down the hallway she bumped into Kathy Riverton.

"Hi Lisa. How are you doing?" asked Kathy.

Lisa looked at Kathy and wondered if she dared ask a question.

"What is it?' asked Kathy, seeing Lisa's expression.

"I was wondering if – forgive me for asking – is Professor Albacete on medication?"

57

Retreat, to advance

The one-day retreat was Rickhart's idea. With the arrival of the two new faculty members, Bao and Heinrich, and his taking on the job of Department Chair, Rick wanted to stimulate thinking about the Department's future. Inger, in what she thought of as a completely supportive statement, declared the planned retreat a total waste of time. "We know what is the future: just look at the past," she declared.

Undeterred, Rickhart contemplated a rural retreat such as the Stone House in Little Compton or a venue in downtown Providence such as the Courtyard Marriott. The Stone House, he thought had the advantage of getting everyone away from the usual day-to-day distractions. It had a large reception room, a bar, beautiful lawns, and was close to the beach. The Courtyard Marriott on the other hand was centrally located, close to good restaurants, and gave everyone the opportunity to take a break in the middle of the day to eat or shop. Bao gave her opinion that Rickhart should flip a coin and choose whatever came face up: Heads for the Stone House and tails for the Marriott. That way, she said, if you are disappointed in what comes face up then you know the other choice is best for you. Rickhart tried tossing a coin but was still undecided. Bao laughed. "I was only kidding," she said. "I would choose the Marriot. It has excellent meeting facilities and at lunch time we can all walk up to P.F. Chang's in the Mall!" Rickhart admired Bao's audacity and decided she was right. "The Marriot it is!" he declared.

So it was the Department members found themselves at breakfast at 8:00 AM in the Courtyard Marriott in Providence. Inger seemed especially pleased. "For something which is total waste of time the food is very good!" she said. She helped herself to a second serving of fruit cup with Greek yoghurt.

Jeffrey had fretted about the quality of hotel coffee and the previous day had phoned the hotel to enquire if he might provide his own coffee. The management, at first wary of the legal implications of bringing in outside food, despite Jeffrey's protestations that coffee was a drink and then losing the argument through having to admit that coffee beans were indeed not yet liquid, relented when Jeffrey assured them he would supply the coffee beans in hermetically sealed containers. He had Lisa deliver the coffee beans to the hotel so that at breakfast that morning the delicious aroma of Terroir coffee pervaded the room.

"I'm sorry we didn't arrange any tea for you Heinrich," Jeffrey said, indicating to anyone who was paying attention that he was far from sorry and viewed Heinrich's tea drinking as a precious habit to be discouraged.

Heinrich was not fazed. "Thank you Jeffrey, but I have my own supply of tea, as you can see". He pulled a small wooden box from his bag and opened it to reveal an array of teas, all arranged by type. "I like to come prepared", smiled Heinrich who then asked a waiter for some just boiled water.

George arrived slightly after everyone had started. He rode his bike from Little Compton, reflecting that the Stone House would have been a better choice for him. He changed his clothes in a hotel restroom, slightly peeved that the hotel could not provide him with a shower unless he paid for a room. He found Deborah and picked up a fruit cup and some muesli. Deborah sensed George's irritability and put it down to his not having smoked his morning cigar. "You can have your cigar after the mid-morning break," she said. "They have a little courtyard next to the meeting room." George gave her a "whatever" look. Deborah said to him that his early morning rides were supposed to put him in a good mood – they usually did – and he should stop doing a Bert Monod impression. Abashed, George ate his breakfast in silence.

Zaqi sat at a table with Bao, Lori and Bob. Unbeknown to the others, Lori and Bob had spent the night at the hotel, which explained the feeling Zaqi had that they seemed especially happy and refreshed. Bao smiled.

Kathy, sitting with Rickhart, was delighted to see the whole Department assembled at breakfast. "We haven't done anything like this in my memory," she said. "Everyone looks pleased to be here." She noticed George eating in silence and spied Inger. "Well, almost everyone. I'm going to get some of Jeff's excellent coffee. Can I bring you some?" Rickhart said that would be nice, and turned his thoughts back to the arrangements for the day. He knew that, left to their own devices, the faculty would wander from one topic to another, seemingly passionately engaged, but in fact doing a more or less random walk through a field of vague associations. He had an agenda and wanted to stick to it and deliver an outcome. How to do that without having to herd cats was what occupying his mind at that moment.

Kathy returned with the coffee. "You know, it's a pity Bert couldn't be here," she said. "I think he had good intentions despite his general ineptitude to lead." Rickhart raised his eyebrows but said nothing. Kathy said she was going to cheer up George and went over to where he and Deborah were eating breakfast. Bao noticed Kathy's leaving Rickhart to sit by himself, and went over to sit with him.

"I think there is good energy here this morning," she said. "It is a little stuck in places, but I think it will flow well."

Rickhart, not used to Bao's way of thinking, said he hoped so.

"I think I will make an announcement in a few minutes," he said, "to get everyone on the same page for the first activity today."

Bao laid a hand on Rickhart's arm. "If I may make a suggestion, Rick, I think that may not be the most productive approach." He frowned. "Your aim, surely, is to get people energized, but without shocking or disturbing them."

Rickhart agreed that was indeed his aim. "That's why I want to clarify the purpose of the first activity," he said.

Bao explained that, to her mind, the energy flow in the room was currently good. All that need to be done, she said, was to direct that energy. Not disturb it, or break it up, just guide it.

"All right, then what would you do?" asked Rickhart.

Bao asked him what was the purpose of the first activity. He explained it was to focus on the new possibilities for the Department: to describe what they thought these might be for each person from their own perspective, but for them to stay grounded in reality, and not to construct fanciful wish lists.

Bao closed her eyes and thought about what Rickhart had said. Rickhart observed her for a few minutes, and then concerned she seemed to have fallen asleep – he knew how hard she worked – asked if she was awake. Bao's eyes opened immediately, she smiled, and nodded to indicate that indeed she was. Rickhart let her be and drank his coffee, thinking how he could move people on to the morning's agenda. Bao opened her eyes, looked at Rickhart and said: "Clear the field."

Rickhart was confused. "What field?" he asked.

"The field of obstructions," Bao said. She explained to Rickhart her idea. "What you want is for people to focus on positive development opportunities."

Rickhart agreed.

"When their energy is high and flowing freely they will do this without thinking," she said. "It is in their nature. It is why they chose this line of work."

Rickhart was skeptical. He had seen too many arguments and too much negativity about planning to be convinced that the faculty were all naturally disposed to thinking positively about the future.

"But that is because they have too many mental obstructions," she said. "Clear those away and their pure intentions will shine through."

Rickhart was listening. "How do you propose we do that?" he asked.

Bao explained to him a technique used by Bruce Lee to rid himself of unwanted but intrusive thoughts.

"You write the thought on a piece of paper," she said. "Take great care to form the words correctly, Write slowly and accurately. Then fold the paper and crumple it. Place it in an urn and set fire to it. Watch as the paper burns and turns to ash. Watch the smoke send the thoughts on the paper into the sky. Say goodbye to those thoughts."

Rickhart thought about what Bao had said. This might work, he thought. If we could ask everyone present to take turns in writing their worst fears for the Department and themselves on pieces of paper and set fire to them as Bao had described, what should be left is only their positive feelings. "Clear the field," he thought. "Clear away the negativity and what's left is what we want to hear." Rickhart smiled at Bao. "Okay, let's do it!" he said. "Can you see if the hotel can find something in which we can burn paper, and set it up in the courtyard?"

Bao went off to consult with the hotel management and Rickhart rose to speak to the gathering. "Good morning folks. I'm glad to see you all here. I wonder if you would follow me to the courtyard. We're going to do some clearing of fields."

58

And so to lunch

Inger took to the task with gusto. "I think we don't have enough paper to record all my complaints," she laughed.

Her comments were abbreviated: "More money!" "Tell administration to support us, not put obstacles in our way!" "Students need to do homework." She put the crumpled notes into the urn and set fire to them. She laughed as the flames burned and the paper turned to ashes. "I think this is the best idea anyone have," she declared. "We should do this a long time ago!"

George deliberated longer over writing his fears and concerns. "I worry that my current research might be a lot harder than I first thought," he wrote. "Perhaps I plunged into a difficult area too fast, without thinking it through well enough. Now I'm not sure if it's wise to commit to an area of research that might take me a long time to master." Satisfied he turned to Kathy: "Now we're supposed to set fire to it?" he asked. Kathy nodded agreement.

"But I sort of want to hang onto this piece of paper. It's an explicit statement of what I think I've been feeling for quite a while."

"And probably what's been making you grumpy," said Deborah. "I think Bao's idea is that we take care to write these thoughts so they do represent our worries, and then we destroy the written thoughts by fire," she said. "That's supposed to help us let go of the thought. To be free from worrying about it."

George shrugged. He crumpled the paper, placed it in the urn, and set fire to it. He watched as the flames grew and the paper burned. He watched the smoke rise from the flames. "There goes my thoughts," he said. Oddly, as he contemplated the ashes in the urn, he felt lighter. He turned to Deborah. "It does feel better," he smiled. "Let me do another one."

Rickhart was surprised to see both Bao and Heinrich participating in this activity. Neither of them, he thought, has been here long enough to have fears and worries about the Department. Bao was writing: "I worry that people here might not like me. I know I can be very forthright, and that can upset some people. I am worried that I will not be respectful enough of other people's feelings." She thought about the written words for some time. Heinrich thought she had fallen asleep. He was about to touch her arm to check, when Bao opened her eyes, smiled, crumpled the paper, put it in the urn and set it alight. She watched the wisps of smoke rising from the urn. When the paper was only ash she clapped loudly and laughed.

Heinrich decided to try this activity. He stroked his chin for several minutes as he thought what to write. "My biggest concern is that I do not upset Jeffrey in the writing of the new book. He has been very kind to me, asking his publisher for money for me, and I worry that he might feel the book is no longer his." Heinrich followed Bao's example in setting fire to the paper and he watched it burn with interest. "Ja, there it goes," he said. Bao asked if he felt better. "I don't know," he said, "but a little freer I think is how I feel!"

Jeffrey was slow to take to the activity. He couldn't think of what fears he had. There was that nonsense with the student in Cyprus, but that was her fault. He was not to blame in any way. He just felt embarrassed, not fearful. He watched as the others put their concerns on paper and set fire to them. Not wanting to appear difficult he wrote: "I worry that I might not be able to get any more Terroir coffee!" He smiled and set fire to the paper. "There's an end to that silly thought," he said to no one in particular.

The burning of written fears and apprehensions went on for the better part of an hour. As the activity wound down people were smiling and laughing.

"This was a good idea Rick," said Bob, whose only real concern was whether he could pull of the curriculum project with Lori. "We should do it more often."

Rickhart had been thinking about what to do next. "Let's take a 10 minute break for refreshments," he said, "and meet back in the conference room to think about our future plans."

George came up to Rickhart with an idea. "What if I tried to link up my ideas of statistical numerical analysis with your work on statistics of dynamical systems? I think we could find some common ground there." Rickhart agreed. "Sure thing, George. It's a good idea. Let's talk about it." An image appeared in Rickhart's mind of a field in which the weeds had been pulled and the flowers were now pushing though. "Son of a gun!" he thought, "Bao was right."

The thing most noticeable about the resumed meeting in the conference room was the relaxed feelings of the participants. People were smiling and laughing, and generally positive. "The energy is very good," said Bao. "Very high, and flowing well."

"Perhaps I should focus them now on getting some future development ideas written down," said Rickhart. Bao touched his arm. "I think that would block the flow of energy," she said. "Just let them do what is natural. Stay relaxed, with open minds."

Rickhart and Bao walked around the room talking to people.

"I have an idea about the CDFs that we talked about before," Lori told Rickhart. "I'd really like to pursue that." Rickhart asked if she would like to write it down. Lori agreed that was a good idea and went looking for Bob.

The conference room buzzed with activity and the faculty chatted about other ideas and put them down on paper. Rickhart was delighted and amazed. "I wouldn't have believed this approach would work if you'd described it to me yesterday," he said. "It runs counter to every instructional idea I've had. We get productive activity by doing nothing."

"Yes," said Bao, "Clear away the obstructions, relax, and let the energy flow. That is all."

"And is that how you do your own research?" asked Rickhart.

"Of course!" said Bao. "I do not always have free flowing energy, and I am not always as relaxed as I would like, so I do Qigong and Tai Chi exercises. They help."

Rickhart said he wished he had learned Qigong when he was younger. "I wonder if I could learn how to relax better now?" he asked.

Bao laughed. "You can learn relaxation techniques at any time. Qigong – it just means energy work – is very easy to learn, easy to practice, but powerful in releasing blocked energy. You could try it."

Rickhart thought that maybe after lunch Bao could lead the group in a short Qigong session. "Would that be possible?" he asked. Bao agreed. "So long as it is short," she said. "Ten minutes is plenty to start. Just enough to help people relax."

Rickhart thought it was about time to wrap up this session. They had been discussing and writing plans for over an hour and a half. He was thinking about what time they had for another activity to pull things together when Bao looked at him. "Time for lunch?" she asked beaming. "P.F. Chang's?"

59

The Creative Capital

❧

As Jeffrey looked out the window of P.F. Chang's over lunch he thought Providence was the ideal place for the conference he had in mind. The problem is, he thought, the publisher wants to turn this solely into a money making exercise. He shuddered at the thought the conference might be held in a hotel in Times Square. Jeffrey was determined to get his publisher to hold the Gene Golub Retrospective Conference in Providence. New York, he thought, was too busy and dirty, and way too noisy.

"You look very thoughtful, Jeffrey," said Heinrich.

Jeffrey explained his concerns about the conference being planned for New York. The advantages of Providence were obvious to him. "Good accommodation," he said, "T. F. Green airport only 15 minutes away. Compare that to getting to New York by plane, train, or bus! Providence is clean and peaceful, with the river separating downtown from Brown University, and the American Mathematical Society headquarters is just a few minutes away in Charles Street."

Heinrich agreed that Providence was a most attractive city, and a perfect place to hold the conference. "Is the publisher immovable on New York?" he asked.

Jeffrey said he was afraid so. Heinrich thought about what might get the conference organizers to change their minds. Nothing seemed obvious. "I like Manhattan," he said, "but the crowds can be overwhelming, and it is not so straightforward to get to, I agree. Even from here it's a four-hour train ride to Penn Station, which is very crowded, and then one has to wheel luggage, fighting through the crowds to a taxi stand to take an ugly taxi ride to the hotel. This, I agree, would be much more convenient for us and for travelers coming in from elsewhere."

Jeffrey's mouth formed into a thin, tight grimace. The thought of the conference in New York made him glum.

Lori, walking back from the washroom, noticed Jeffrey's countenance. "Is something troubling you, Jeff?" she asked.

Jeffrey explained his concern about the Golub retrospective being held in Manhattan and his apparently futile desire that it should be held here in Providence.

"And there's nothing you can do to get them to change their mind?" she asked.

"Apparently not," he said. Lori said she was sorry about that and went back to her table. She mentioned the problem to Bao, who was sitting with her, Bob, and Zaqi.

"Hmm," said Bao. Maybe there IS a way." Lori was intrigued.

"What would be the biggest lever we could use?" Bao asked.

Lori thought, but could not imagine what pressure anyone from the University could exert on Jeffrey's publisher. "Maybe Wolfram?" she said.

"I think maybe Wolfram," echoed Bao.

Lori suggested that if Wolfram Research were in discussions with the University about a broad program of CDF development, maybe they could put it to Jeffrey's publisher that it would be good publicity for them and the University if the conference were held in Providence.

"It's worth a try," said Bao.

"As Kathy would say: *a no we already have*," laughed Lori.

♥♥♥♥♥

After lunch, when the stragglers had made the five-minute walk back to the Courtyard Marriott, Rickhart announced that Bao would lead them through a short Qigong exercise.

Inger was unhappy. "So now we are to become physical jerks?" she asked, crossing her arms.

George smiled and thought that Inger didn't need to get physical to show she was a jerk.

"It's only for ten minutes," said Rickhart. "I think it will get us into the right mood after lunch."

"Okay, okay," said Inger. "I just hope we don't have to sit on the floor. And I hope she realize I am not flexible as I was."

Bao laughed. "No sitting on the floor," she said, "and no flexibility required."

"Then what sort of exercise this is?" Inger was puzzled.

Bao asked everyone to stand and to relax, with their feet approximately under their shoulders and knees slightly bent and over their toes. "Now imagine you are holding a big, and somewhat heavy, ball, about the width of your shoulders," she said. "Just hold that ball in front of your face. If your body feels like it wants to move by itself, let it. Don't force the movement, and don't fight it. Just feel what your body wants to do, and let it do it. Keep holding the ball."

Zaqi hoped no one was going to walk into that room and see a bunch of people knees slightly bent, holding their arms in front of them apparently staring into space.

Suddenly Deborah turned to the left and her body dipped down. Kathy moved to help her, thinking she was about to fall. Bao stopped everyone for a moment.

"What happened to Deborah is natural," she said. "Deborah's energy is moving and the body follows. Just do like she does. Don't force it, and don't fight it. Just go with the flow."

Five minutes later people were bending and turning in strange but spontaneous movements. Except for Jeffrey. He was still standing with knees bent and arms open as if supporting a ball, but was otherwise very still. What was not obvious to a casual observer was that Jeffrey's mind was thinking very hard about the problem of moving the conference to Providence. Bao came by and placed one hand on Jeffrey's back and another on his front, just below his sternum. She left her hands there for a moment, to Jeffrey's evident surprise, and then said: "Jeffrey, you are thinking too hard about something." Jeffrey looked abashed. "Well, yes. I'm thinking about the Golub conference," he said. Bao asked him to try again and this time to think of nothing. "Just stand quietly holding the ball, and leave the mind empty. If a thought comes," she said, "let it go, don't dwell on it. Just jeep holding the ball." Jeffrey said he would give it another try.

Bao walked around the room, watching the exercises, encouraging people with smiles, as their bodies turned and dipped.

Suddenly, Jeffrey fell down with a crash. Zaqi bent down to help him up. "Are you okay, Jeff? Are you hurt?" he asked. Jeffrey laughed out loud, to everyone's relief and surprise. "I'm fine," he said. "I don't know what happened. It was like a giant hand just grabbed me and threw me to the floor. I didn't feel anything. I'm not hurt. I'm okay," he laughed again.

Bao stopped the group and asked everyone to stand as before but now to shake their hands vigorously as if flicking water from their fingers.

"Well done, everyone," she said. "How do you feel?"

Inger was first to speak. "I feel very relaxed," she said. "Not irritable at all." The room burst out laughing, Inger included. Several others said how relaxed they felt.

Bao explained that if they could do this for twenty minutes each day they would, in a couple of months, relax much more deeply than they ever had before. "You will cope with stress better," she said, "and you will feel more relaxed and happier. Less irritable, as Inger said, and you will be generally more creative."

"Very apt," concluded Rickhart, "for Providence - the Creative Capital."

"Aha!" said Jeffrey. Everyone turned, waiting for him to speak. "I think I might have an answer to my problem," he said, somewhat embarrassed to have spoken so loudly. He didn't know why he had shouted: it just came out of him spontaneously. "I think we might be able to get my publisher to rethink Providence as the place to hold the Golub conference if we can get Wolfram Research to exert some influence," he smiled.

Lori and Bao looked at each other, smiled, and said nothing.

60

It's only fair

Bert Monod phoned Rickhart to say he was ready to come back to work. The phone call surprised Rickhart, who asked if Bert was up to standing in front of class for an hour at a time. Bert explained that he might have to sit in a chair at the front of the room. It depended, he said, on how much pain was involved in standing for a length of time. Rickhart was not happy. Another semester of rest might be best, he told Bert. But Bert was immovable. "No, my doctor said I'm fit enough to return to work, and that's what I'm going to do."

Rickhart agreed to give Bert as light a teaching load as he could, thinking how unfair that was to the other faculty since Bert did not do any research, or carry out any form of scholarly activity. Rickhart was not about to give Bert administrative work to do in light of the Department's experience of him as chairperson.

"I will come in later today to talk about classes," Bert said.

Rickhart, amazed at Bert's audacity, said only: "I will see you when you get here, Bert."

Rickhart sat at his desk, his hands together in front of his face, his fingers drumming.

"Uh oh! That looks serious", said George, coming into Rickhart's office.

Rickhart explained the conversation with Bert.

"Good grief!" said George. "In all honesty, I thought he would announce his retirement."

"I hadn't thought about it," said Rickhart. "Too much else to do, I guess. But now you mention it, I wonder why he wouldn't retire? Does he need the money, do you think?" George didn't know.

"What will you give him to teach?" asked George.

"That," said Rickhart, "is the 64 million dollar question."

George wished Rickhart good luck and said he didn't envy him having to deal with Bert.

Later that morning Bert Monod knocked on Rickhart's door. Rickhart asked him to come in and was shocked at Bert's appearance. He used a walking stick that he leaned heavily on, and looked 10 years older.

"Are you doing okay, Bert," Rickhart asked.

"I'm getting by," said Bert. "I had to use a walker for a while there. I've been going to physiotherapy regularly, but other than that it's been hard to exercise."

Rickhart pulled up a chair for Bert, who came right to the point. "I want to teach two courses of first year calculus," he told Rickhart. "Preferably on Tuesdays and Thursdays."

Rickhart decided there had to be a clean break with the habits of the past. He explained the calculus courses were already allocated. "What I can offer you is finite mathematics, and the introductory course on quantitative reasoning."

Bert said nothing for a minute and then gave a shrug. "Whatever. You're in charge, I guess."

Rickhart said he knew how hard it might be for Bert to accept, but, yes, he was now in charge and he had the overall interests of the Department and the students to think about.

"Bert, I'm sorry to say this to you, because I know how difficult this accident has been for you, but I'm going to have to give you an extra course."

Bert was not happy and made his anger plain to Rickhart.

"The thing is Bert, we're introducing a work load model – the one George has been working on – and if you are coming back to work, as you seem keen to do, you, like everyone else, has to fit in with this model. Perhaps taking another semester for recovery would ensure you're up to teaching a full load in the Fall?"

Bert was not happy. He explained to Rickhart that when he was Department Chair, until Rickhart took over, he would make allowance for circumstances and give people lighter teaching loads if necessary.

"That may be so, Bert," said Rickhart, "but the other side of the coin is that you never lightened the teaching load of faculty who were publishing eight papers a year, bringing in multiple grants, and working hard on University committees. You focused on teaching as the be all and end all of our academic existence and frankly you played fast and loose with that."

Bert leaned on his cane and rose from his chair. "I don't have to stand here and take this," he said.

"No you don't," said Rickhart. "You can leave if you want. But I *will* be allocating you three courses to teach. Given your conspicuous lack of scholarship I wish I could give you more teaching. That, however, would not fit the workload model and might appear to be unfair. I hope you can realize that all faculty, and that includes you, need to be treated fairly. The old days are over, Bert."

Bert stomped out of Rickhart's office, muttering: "We'll see about this."

Rickhart sat down and put his head in his hands. Kathy came into his office and asked if he had been talking with Bert. "I saw him walking down the hallway talking to himself. He didn't look happy. And he looks so old and frail."

"Yes, I've been talking with Bert," said Rickhart. "And yes, you're right: he is old and frail. The accident has knocked him about badly. He wants to come back to work. I told him he would have to teach three courses. I followed the workload model. He was, let's say, less than happy."

"Change is hard," said Kathy. "He's getting older, and then there's the accident. He's used to getting his way. I'm sure he doesn't like it now that you're in charge."

Apparently not," said Rickhart. "But I'm not cutting him any special deals. Not with his record."

Kathy wanted Rickhart to go with her to the Daily Grind for coffee. "You need a break," she said. "Let's see if we can find George."

The three of them walked to the Daily Grind and ordered coffee. George had his usual espresso and a glass of water. "Do you mind if we sit outside?" he asked. "I wouldn't mind a cigar." "Those damned things will kill you," said Rickhart. George agreed. "That's what Deborah says. However, I have a resting pulse of 43 beats a minute, my blood pressure is 90 over 60, I ride a bike hard every day, and I have check ups twice a year. No sign of anything bad yet," he said.

"Yet!" emphasized Rickhart.

George was keen to hear about the meeting with Bert, and Rickhart filled him in on the details. "Seems to me," said George, "that the workload model is working."

"Look, I have compassion for Bert," said Rickhart, "but what I can't do is give him an easy ride at the expense of the rest of the Department."

"Especially given his dismal record as Department Chair," said Kathy. "We've had to work around him, not with him."

"The Department has to move forward," said Rickhart. "We had a great retreat. Some wonderful ideas came out of it, and now we have to work at implementing them. Dreams and ideas are fine, and we have some very good ones, but executing them takes hard work – from everyone. And I just don't see Bert contributing in that way."

Rickhart's phone rang. "Excuse me," he said, taking the call. "Yes, yes. I see. Alright, I will come and see you right away."

Kathy and George looked at Rickhart, waiting for an explanation.

"It was the Dean," he said. "She wants to see me. Bert has submitted his resignation."

61

What do we need?

﹏﹏

Dean Nueberg's door was open and she waved Rickhart in. "Thanks for coming to see me right away," she said. "As I told you on the phone, Bert has submitted his resignation. All I need you to do is read his letter and sign this form acknowledging that you've done so."

Rickhart read through the letter that, as he expected, was vitriolic in tone. He signed the form Dean Nueberg had given him.

"He seems pretty upset," said the Dean.

Rickhart agreed, and explained the conversation he had with Bert about teaching.

The Dean nodded, indicated her understanding, and said she thought Bert was of an age where adjusting to change is difficult.

"For some people, maybe," said Rickhart. "I know professors in this University, and elsewhere, who are into their eighties and who are as mentally fresh as twenty year olds. They have no difficulty accepting change."

"Yes, some people, I agree," said the Dean, "but Bert is not one of those people."

She told Rickhart she would discuss replacing Bert with a

new, younger, faculty member. "The Provost may not agree to this request," she said, "since we got both Bao and Heinrich in the last search. However, he did not make Heinrich's appointment conditional upon not replacing the next person to resign, so I think I have a case for a new faculty member. The thing is," she said looking looking over her glasses at Rickhart, "the Provost and Chancellor are now insisting all new hires fit the Department, College, and University strategic plans. There's no automatic right of replacement of retiring faculty. So I am going to have to ask you to make a case based on your strategic plan, mine for the College, and for you to make it consistent with the University's strategy." She smiled at Rickhart. " Since the computational aspects of mathematics your Department has focused on are very much in favor with the senior university administration, I believe you can probably do this fairly easily."

Rickhart was grateful and thanked the Dean. As he walked back to his office he thought about what area would be best served by a new appointment. "The faculty can sort this out," he thought. "I'll email them with the information that the Dean is asking the Provost for a new line and get their input on which area the prefer. And why."

The email doubly surprised everyone, except Kathy and George who were surprised only that the Dean was proposing a new line.

"I thought she'd say Heinrich filled that spot," said George, and Kathy agreed. "It's good news for us," she said. "It means she supports the growth of our Department - not what one might expect from a biology professor."

A casual observer would think that Jeffrey barely registered the news in Rickhart's email. He was drinking coffee at the time, and he seemed to read the email as if it were of no particular interest. However, a more careful observer would notice Jeffrey's free hand drumming on the desk top. The email set his thoughts in the direction of a new hire, specifically a new hire in matrix algebra.

Jeffrey had never been accused of empire building. That would be unfair, especially since he was so patently inept at building anything. However all who knew him would affirm that he promoted his own field of matrix algebra wherever and whenever he could. And with Lisa's arrival on the scene, and Heinrich and then Bao taking up their positions, some scales had dropped from Jeffrey's eyes. Contrary to what he imagined might be the case, Bao had turned out to be an ally. Jeffrey could see the nucleus of a strong matrix algebra group. A new appointment in matrix algebra would cement the strength of this embryonic group. "This," he thought, "could really be a major part of my legacy."

Inger was adamant the Department needed someone to teach the calculus courses regularly taught by Bert. "He was such a good teacher," she said. "All the students love him. He was very popular." George knew why Bert was popular: he rarely gave a grade below a B and then only when a student failed to turn in homework and didn't sit the final exam.

Lori thought she would love to have another applied statistician in the Department. There were so many openings for students to get well paying and satisfying jobs if they had a strong statistics background. But she felt too junior to push her specialty and decided to wait and see what others said.

Kathy, unlike Jeffrey, *was* an empire builder and was widely acknowledged throughout the university to be good at it. She built the Center for Computational Mathematics and Statistics from a tiny group of faculty and students to a major research and education center impacting many people across the University. Kathy had very definite ideas on new appointments. Bao Zhang had her full support and Kathy was pleased for Jeffrey, and the Department, that Heinrich was offered a job. But Kathy's focus was on numerical analysis and statistics and now she wanted someone in the hot area of multi-scale methods. That's where the excitement was currently, and an appointment in that area could push the Center's profile along very nicely.

George was conflicted. Like Kathy he wanted to build strength in numerical analysis. On the other hand, his thoughts were turning more to statistical analysis of numerical methods, and he could see the advantage of appointing the right type of statistician.

Zaqi had no strong views. "I really don't care who we appoint," he said, "as long as I can work with them, you know, have some point of contact with them. I would only prefer someone who is very technologically competent."

Rickhart tried to steer the conversation back to the needs of the Department. "I know we are in the middle of building a vision and strategic plan for the Department," he said, "but this opportunity came upon us without warning. We didn't plan for it. If we do get this extra position we are unlikely to get another for a few years. So we need to think carefully."

In the past, Jeffrey would have taken Rickhart's words as a sign that matrix algebra was to be sidelined yet again. But that was the past. Jeffrey now saw a glimmer of light toward which he was moving. He decided to send out feelers to his colleagues worldwide, asking them for news of up and coming experts in matrix algebra, particularly those who had recently completed their doctorate.

Rickhart meanwhile had plotted a chart of the faculty, their expertise, and their professional interactions. Lori and Bob's interaction had become intensely personal, he reflected, but they were now solidly connected professionally. With a large drawing of this network taped to the wall of his office, it was becoming clearer to Rickhart that there was one area in which the Department was remarkably deficient, an area that was critical to their mission. He asked Kathy and George to come and look at his diagram.

"What's missing," he said, "what's glaringly obviously not there, is someone expert in employment. Someone who can educate our students on how to get jobs."

Kathy was puzzled. "But isn't this supposed to be an academic appointment, Rick? It sounds like you're talking about a career counselor."

George agreed with Kathy. "Sure, we do need to pay attention to where our students are going to get jobs," he said, "but I think that's the function of career services. Although, I agree we do need to pay more attention to this."

Rickhart elaborated his reasons. "Career counseling can never be specific enough for our students," he said. "Career services cannot understand the finer details of employment as a mathematician. Only we understand that. For some years now I have been feeling disturbed that we educate students then send them out in the world to hope for the best in terms of jobs. In this difficult economic climate, I don't think that's good enough, if it ever was. We cannot continue to bury our head in the sand in relation to student careers. And if career services cannot do it, we have to."

"So you're suggesting we hire someone – a mathematician – with expertise in job placement, or career counseling?" asked Kathy.

"Something like that," said Rickhart. "Or possibly someone a bit older who's had a career as an entrepreneur."

"And would this person have to have a Ph.D. in mathematics or statistics?" asked George.

"Of course," replied Rickhart.

"And where do you expect to find this person?" asked George.

Rickhart replied that he had no idea. Not yet.

62

Who loves you?

Jeffrey was buzzing around like a bee. There was, he thought, simply too much going on. Jeffrey didn't like to work at speed like Bao Zhiang and, to some extent, Heinrich. Jeffrey wasn't exactly a Slowsky, but he did tread steadily and cautiously. Now he was deep into the production of the new book, *Applied Matrix Algebra*, a potential position was opening up with a real possibility he could enhance the matrix algebra group. And his publisher had called to say that, after all, they wanted the Gene Golub Retrospective Conference to be held in Providence. Jeffrey thought for half a second that maybe he should go easy on the coffee but rejected that idea out of hand. The thought of the gym popped into his head and he decided that, since exercise was such a well-known stress reliever, he would spend an hour there. He picked up his gym bag and headed out of his office. Heinrich saw him and said hello. "You look in a particularly cheery mood, Jeffrey," he said. Jeffrey acknowledged he was and explained he was off to the campus gym for some exercise. Heinrich thought this was an admirable thing to do, and asked if he could accompany Jeffrey.

"But you don't have any gym gear," said Jeffrey. Heinrich

explained that he wanted to join the gym, had been meaning to since he arrived, but had not got around to joining yet. This, he said, was a perfect opportunity to take a walk with Jeffrey and at the same time sign up. Jeffrey shrugged. "Okay then, follow me."

As they walked along the path from the Mathematics Department building toward the Daily Grind, beyond which lay the gym, Jeffrey mentioned to Heinrich that the Gene Golub Retrospective Conference was, after all, to be held in Providence.

"But that's excellent, Jeffrey. However did you manage that?" asked Heinrich.

"I didn't," said Jeffrey. "They called me and told me that was the arrangement. Something to do with the University, I guess, and possibly Wolfram Research. I don't know."

As they walked Jeffrey asked Heinrich what he thought about adding another person to the matrix algebra group.

"You are thinking of the possible new position, since Bert resigned?" asked Heinrich.

Jeffrey said that was indeed his thinking. Heinrich reflected on what Jeffrey said, and did not speak as they passed the Daily Grind on the way to the gym.

"So what do you think, Heinrich? Should we make plans to look for another young expert in matrix algebra?"

Heinrich thought this was a very good question. "Of course," he said, "I would be very glad to have someone else join our little group."

"But?" asked Jeffrey.

"Yes, you are right: there is a *but*. I do not know enough about the politics of the Department, and people's sensitivities. I know that Rickhart is doing an excellent job articulating the Department mission, and developing a strategic plan. I would not want to step on his toes in that regard."

"I think he wears steel capped shoes," joked Jeffrey.

Heinrich was puzzled. "I am sorry Jeffrey, I do not understand."

"Just a joke, Heinrich. You can't hurt his toes if he wears steel capped shoes."

"Oh, I see!" said Heinrich. "Very apt. Yes, quite funny. But I think he would notice I was still standing on his toes, or his shoes."

Jeffrey decided not to go further down that road. "Of course everyone will have their own thoughts about who we should appoint, and in what area," he said, "That's the way it's always been." And until now, he thought, without saying it out loud, I've always lost out.

"Now that you're here Heinrich I think we have a good case to make for building a nationally prominent group in matrix algebra."

Heinrich thought about this as they came to the gym entrance. He was not sure.

"Here we are," said Jeffrey. "I could sign you in as a guest, if you like, and you can fill out the application as we leave. It's very simple really. Nothing to it."

Heinrich was pleased to have Jeffrey show him around, but didn't think he would stay as long as Jeffrey would be exercising.

"Perhaps if I just look around for a few minutes and then fill out the application. I can see you back in the Department," he said.

They signed in and Jeffrey showed Heinrich the weights area, the racquetball courts, and the pool before heading to the exercise bikes and treadmills.

"This is where I spend most of my time," said Jeffrey. "I find it relaxes me."

Heinrich thanked Jeffrey and said he would head back to the Department.

"You haven't told me if you think it would really be a good idea to look for a new faculty member in matrix algebra," Jeffrey said.

"Ja, I think so. I think we could put this to Rickhart and the others. It would be good for us. Okay, well I will see you later," said Heinrich as he left the gym.

Jeffrey looked around for a newspaper and picked up a copy of the Providence Journal that had been left in a disheveled state. He straightened out the paper, laid it out on the exercise bike he had chosen, and began to read and pedal.

After 40 minutes Jeffrey was feeling relaxed. The paper held no further interest. He folded it and stretched, bringing the bike to a halt.

"Enough for today," he thought. "Don't want to overdo it." He wiped down the exercise bike, put the newspaper on a table, and went to shower and change. Feeling as relaxed as he had been in some time, Jeffrey left the gym and walked back up toward the Daily Grind. "A coffee," he thought, "is most definitely in order."

The coffee shop had the usual bunch of mid-morning customers and he absent-mindedly counted the number of people in the queue before him. Someone behind him called his name.

"Jeffrey. Hi, how're you doing?" It was Ernest Billingham from mechanical engineering. Jeffrey greeted him and said it was a while since they'd seen each other. Ernest asked Jeffrey what was new. Jeffrey didn't know where to start.

"Well, there's a lot going on," he said, "Looks like we might be getting another new position."

"I heard about this," said Ernest. "Bert's retiring I hear. You've just made two new appointments, haven't you? The Department will be unrecognizable."

Jeffrey shared with Ernest his thoughts about getting someone else with expertise in matrix algebra.

"Well, you know," said Ernest, "that would suit us right down to the ground. Your new fellow, Heinrich is very good with applications and he's already set up collaborations with a couple of people in my department, so, yes, to get another one like him would be great. And it would fit very well with the University's strategic plan"

Jeffrey was gratified to hear this. For many years he had that felt he and his work were better appreciated by the engineering college than by his own department. A vague notion was forming in Jeffrey's brain. It was too early to share it yet with Ernest. Jeffrey ruminated as they neared the counter. He ordered a latte and a blueberry muffin. Ernest ordered and they found a table.

"So you think there's more of a need for matrix algebra in mechanical engineering?" he asked Ernest.

"Oh, most definitely," said Ernest. "And civil engineering too. I sometimes wish we had our own matrix algebra group in the College of Engineering."

A half-formed idea in Jeffrey's brain began to take shape. "Would the Dean of Engineering be wiling to think about ... a more formal collaboration?" Jeffrey asked.

"I don't see why not," said Ernest. "It would be in all our best interests. Why? What do you have in mind?"

63

Code and conquer

On the walk back to the Department from the gym Heinrich bumped into Lisa De Silva. He asked her to his office to discuss the chapter they were modifying for the *Applied Matrix Algebra* book.

"I know you are a coffee aficionada," he said, "but I only have tea. Can I interest you in some?" Lisa nodded agreement.

As he made the tea, Heinrich asked Lisa about her plans beyond the book. "It seems to me," he said, "that you have an opportunity to make good money working for book publishers. They need your technical know-how."

Lisa explained her thinking about that, and her desire to merge her interests of algorithms and jewelry. "I even have a possible name for my business," she said. "*Applied Algorithms*."

Heinrich interest was piqued. "I did not know one could apply computer science to jewelry making," he said. "This is very interesting indeed. Is anyone else doing this?"

Lisa told Heinrich about *Nervous Systems* in Somerville, Massachusetts, not far from the University.

"Interesting!" he said. "I would very much like to visit these people and see how they work. I have a very strong interest in applications of mathematics, and what is computer science but another branch of mathematics? Do you agree?"

"I'm not so sure," said Lisa, taking her tea from Heinrich. "Some parts of computer science are very mathematical, others seem, well ... more like computer science!"

They both laughed. "You are right," said Heinrich, "nonetheless there is a very large overlap. Have you read the book by Christopher Steiner – *Automate This: How Algorithms Came to Rule Our World?*" Lisa hadn't. "It gives a sense of how algorithms have changed the world, especially finance," he said. "It's somewhat short on details, as many popular books are, and I feel it lacks a little focus, but is worth reading nevertheless." Lisa wondered where Heinrich was headed.

"Reading this book," he said, "helped me focus on how algorithms can disrupt entire industries, and create new ones often making people rich in the process."

"Like Google?" asked Lisa.

"Ja, like Google," said Heinrich. 'So I have been thinking how I would like to develop what I am calling *disruptive algorithmics.*"

"As an academic discipline?" Lisa asked, puzzled.

"At first, maybe." Heinrich said. " But I am also thinking as a possible business venture. I feel that a proper marriage of mathematics and applied algorithms can provide new ways of operating in many areas of business. Many people are already doing it. If we think carefully we develop a competitive advantage."

"Like Google?" Lisa asked again.

Heinrich laughed. "I guess a discussion like this will always come back to Google because it is something with which everyone is very familiar, even if they do not know the basic mathematics behind it. So ... I am thinking of starting with a seminar, or perhaps better described as a workshop, on disruptive algorithmics. Would you be interested to participate?"

Lisa was hesitant to answer. She liked the idea very much and she also liked Heinrich. He seemed to always be very straightforward, and to tell people exactly what he was thinking. It would be good working with him, but she felt she already had too much on her plate. "I would very much like to," she said, "but I have so many things going on right now. I have to finish my senior year, I'm working with you and Professor Albacete, and I am thinking very seriously about a graduate degree combining jewelry making and applications of algorithms. I don't know that I could really contribute."

Heinrich understood. "You don't need to contribute, not as such, not unless you want to. But would you consider at least coming along to listen to what I have in mind?"

Lisa agreed she could do that.

"So, now," said Heinrich, "let me show you my revisions of the chapter I am working in, and let's see how you can turn this into a magical CDF."

♥♥♥♥♥

Bob Fosberry was trying to get his old MATLAB codes rewritten in Mathematica. He would have been happy enough to stick with MATLAB, a language he knew well, but the lure of producing CDFs was too strong. He thought Mathematica had got the drop on MATLAB in this respect and that the folks at Math-Works must be sweating bullets. He was scratching his head when Bao came by his office.

"You look puzzled, Bob," she said.

Bob asked her to look at the code, knowing that she was a professional level MATLAB programmer. Bao looked over the code, in deep concentration, occasionally saying only "Hmm."

"This is quite good code," she said. "Did you write this?"

Bob said he had indeed written the code.

"So what's the problem?" she asked.

Bob explained that a piece of his code was hard for him to translate easily and efficiently into Mathematica.

"I can do it in an ugly, forced, way," he said. "But there surely must be a simpler, more elegant and efficient way to do it."

Bao thought for a moment and said: "Sure, sure. I think this is not too hard."

Bob was amazed. "You think you can do it? I didn't know you were an accomplished Mathematica programmer too."

Bao laughed. "I would not say *accomplished*. No, not at all. But I do know a few things. Here, let me try."

Bao opened Mathematica and worked for twenty minutes on recoding part of Bob's algorithm. "There, I think that does it," she said. "And I saved it as a CDF, so you can see how it runs."

Bob looked at Bao's Mathematica code. "So simple," he said. "And incredibly efficient. Damn, you're good!" He ran the CDF and it worked perfectly. "This is great," he said, "because now I can embed this into a web page on the site I've set up. As much as I love MATLAB this is something I couldn't do before."

"Horses for courses," said Bao. "Sometimes MATLAB does things better, sometimes Mathematica. Sometimes – more often than you might imagine – Python beats them both."

Bob was thinking that he needed to expand his repertoire of programming skills. "Problem is," he thought, "every year that passes seems to make it that much harder to learn a new programming language, let alone new programming techniques." He thought maybe he should sit in on Zaqi's scientific programming course. The new faculty members were incredibly versatile in programming, whereas he always had to work hard at it. It had taken him several years to feel he was fluent with MATLAB programming. As if reading his mind, Bao said: "I think it's good to learn a new programming language every few years. Things change so much. Look at the new statistical language Julia that's in development. That might suit you Bob, because it looks very much like MATLAB, so you're learning curve would be shallower. It's set to replace R as the major open source data analysis package I think."

Bob wondered if there was anything Bao didn't know something about. "A replacement for R?" he thought. "Now there's something Lori would be really interested in. We could learn it together." He imagined cozy evenings, as winter came on, drinking hot chocolate and coding in front of an open fire. That, he thought, could really work. That was something he could definitely set his mind to.

'I think," he said to Bao, "I might look into learning Julia."

Bao smiled. "I think you will enjoy it," she said, "and I have a strong feeling you will be successful."

64

Good karma, bad karma

Jeffrey was sanguine about his publisher agreeing to hold the Gene Golub Retrospective conference in Providence. He recalled that he had told everyone at the Department retreat that he thought he might be able to get the conference moved, but he hadn't actually done anything about it. Maybe it was Bao's mysterious energy that did it? What a load of rubbish, he thought, ridiculous Eastern mysticism. Bao was a smart woman – anyone could see that – but her ventures into Tai Chi and what-not seemed more than a trifle suspect to Jeffrey. And this burning of written thoughts – did anyone take that seriously? What on earth was Rickhart thinking when he got Bao to hold that session? At least, Jeffrey thought, I got rid of my anxiety about not having excellent coffee.

The thought playing on Jeffrey's mind was the suggestion from his publisher that Heinrich open the conference. Jeffrey was not ungenerous. He could see the obvious attraction of a young dynamic speaker such as Heinrich. But weighed against this was the long experience Jeffrey had in the field, and the influence and impact of his seminal work on *Matrix Algebra*. The scales tip heavily toward me, he thought. "The question is how to say that without appearing to big-note myself?" He was pondering that question when Lisa knocked at his door.

"Hello Professor Albacete", she said, "I have something interesting to show you. May I use your computer?"

She sat at Jeffrey's computer and opened DropBox. Jeffrey was getting used to storing files in Dropbox but thought for a moment that it seemed only yesterday that storing data on floppy disks was the big new thing. What on earth, he wondered, is around the corner?

Lisa opened the CDF she had stored and showed Jeffrey the new chapter she had been working on with Heinrich. Jeffrey was impressed. "Pretty neat, huh?" she asked.

"Pretty neat indeed", said Jeffrey, "and this was Heinrich's idea?"

Lisa nodded yes.

"I see", he said. "This is impressive." The scales tipped slightly back to Heinrich.

Jeffrey wondered. "Do you think", he asked Lisa, "that Heinrich would be a good choice to open the Gene Golub Retrospective conference?" The instant the question had been formed Jeffrey recalled a phrase that a lawyer should never ask a question to which they don't already know the answer.

"Yes, I think he would be very good", said Lisa.

Jeffrey looked at her as if waiting for elaboration.

"He's very clear, and very energized", she said. "Quite exciting, really."

Jeffrey recalled earlier concerns of Lisa's that the technical group at his publisher found his text boring.

"I see", he said again, "then perhaps I should step aside for him?"

Lisa was shocked. "Oh no! I didn't mean that. I think both of you should speak. You're the father figure, so to speak. You wrote the definitive text. Professor Muller is much younger ... less experienced. He is he future ... well, so are you. I'm not expressing this well", she stammered. "I think you should do it together."

"I see", said Jeffrey yet again. Together. That's something I hadn't considered."

"I know. I mean, maybe not", said Lisa, "but I think it would work." She was about to say: "The old and the new; tradition and innovation; interesting and ..." but she held her tongue.

"You really think that could work?" Jeffrey asked.

Lisa indicated she did.

"I see", said Jeffrey, hopefully for the last time that day.

Lisa pulled something out of her backpack. "I found an exciting new Terroir coffee for you", she said.

Jeffrey took the packet from her, opened it and savored the delicious aroma. "What", he thought, "have I done to deserve this? It must be my – what did Bao call it? – karma."

♥♥♥♥♥

Bao Zhang alternated between moments of silence when she appeared to be asleep, and rapid fire typing. To a casual observer her periods of quiet followed by energetic behavior might be faintly reminiscent of a bipolar disposition. However, Bao was supremely balanced. She was at the beginning of writing a grant application to the National Science Foundation. Sally Grenzel in the grants office had sent around a very interesting request for proposals that stimulated Bao's imagination. This was a training grant focused on research-based quantitative exploration of data by undergraduates. Everything seemed to line up. She envisaged Lori and Rickhart being on the project, as well as George and Kathy. There were several people in biology, physics and engineering who had ongoing research projects involving both graduate and undergraduate students, so she could see a strong interdisciplinary focus to the proposal. Then there was the infrastructure grant the Physics Department had received to buy a super computer. Everything lined up. This was a perfect grant opportunity.

Lori came by Bao's office and saw Bao apparently asleep at her desk. She stopped and began to tiptoe way. "Lori", said Bao. "Come in."

"I thought you were asleep", said Lori.

"No, not asleep. Just thinking", said Bao, who explained the grant proposal.

"Are you interested?" she asked Lori. "You are a key person because of your statistical work."

"I don't know," said Lori. "I like the idea very much. The stars seem to be lined up on this one. But I already have several projects going and I've got a National Science Foundation grant application in with Bob. You remember that one?"

Bao understood. "But bear in mind that many grant proposals do not get funded", she said. "Best to write the ones that we are passionate about and see what happens. I have a new saying: you cannot be too rich, too thin, too hot, or have too many grant proposals."

Lori agreed it was worth listening to more details.

" I tell you what", said Bao, "let me see who I can round up and we can go to the Daily Grind and discuss this proposal."

So it was that Rickhart, Kathy, Lori, George and Bao sat at a table outside the Daily Grind discussing Bao's grant proposal: outside, to accommodate George smoking a Fuente cigar.

"George", said Bao, "I don't know how you smoke those cigars and still ride your bike so hard. Don't you get out of breath? They can't be doing you any good."

"That's what we all tell him", said Kathy.

George shrugged. "So far I seem to be in perfect health."

Bao thought George was generating bad karma. "It will catch up with you George", she warned.

"So tell us about this proposal", said George, changing the subject.

Bao explained the grant parameters.

"They call the emerging field computational and data-enabled science and engineering", she said. "Even the acronym's a mouthful: CDS&E."

"Is there an explanation in words of one syllable?" asked George. "Something simple enough the Chancellor might understand?"

"Yes", said Bao. "Using computers to carry out mathematical and statistical research into modeling, simulation and visualization."

"Hmm", said George, "not exactly words of one syllable, But I think the idea is clear enough. This seems perfect for us: it's what we already do. The grant could have been written for us."

The others agreed. "If this is a wave coming our way then we should get out our surf boards and ride the wave", said Rickhart. "It fits in perfectly with our developments in data science. It's ..." He was stuck for a phrase.

"Good karma?" asked Bao.

65

Team players

Jeffrey arranged a meeting with the Dean of Engineering and Ernest Billingham from mechanical engineering. He wanted to discuss an as yet vague proposal that he, Heinrich, and perhaps anther as yet to be appointed person, move from the Department of Mathematics to the College of Engineering. The Dean asked if Jeffrey envisaged this group in a department, such as mechanical engineering, or as a small independent group within the college, servicing all engineering departments. Jeffrey had not thought through his ideas to that degree.

"I was just thinking that engineering seems a better home for us because that's where we find more people applying matrix methods," he said.

The Dean smiled. He was used to academics putting forward proposals to improve their own lot. Rarely, in his experience, did they think about the larger good. "Have you discussed this with Rickhart Jansen?" the Dean asked.

Jeffrey said he had not. "I would like to get the feeling about the idea from engineering before I talk to Rickhart about it," said Jeffrey. "It's early days yet."

The Dean said nothing for a minute and looked at Jeffrey. The thought "Loyalty would be nice," entered his head. "The idea has some attractive points to it," he said. "I'm delighted you're thinking about our needs in this regard. There are some issues I need to think through. Can you leave it with me Jeffrey?"

The meeting over, Jeffrey made his way back to the Department of Mathematics, feeling satisfied he had raised his idea with the Dean. He made his way to Heinrich's office and knocked on the door. "Do you have a minute?" he asked.

Jeffrey explained his idea of moving to engineering to Heinrich.

"I think this is a good idea for us," said Jeffrey. "It would give us more support and many more opportunities."

"No, I don't like this idea," Heinrich said.

Jeffrey could not believe his ears. Surely anyone with half a brain could see that matrix algebra would be far more supported in engineering. It would find a natural home there, unlike the Department of Mathematics where Jeffrey had struggled for decades to get support. And Heinrich certainly had more than half a brain. He surely must see the sense in this proposal?

"I don't like it because I would not be comfortable in engineering," he said. "I have only limited experience at this University but I have been talking with people, and there is general agreement that engineering has very bad attitudes to students."

"Well they have a lot of students," said Jeffrey. "They're bound to have a few that don't come up to the expected standard and they have to let them go."

Heinrich explained that was part of what he meant. "They recruit vigorously, but entirely without discrimination," he said. "They recruit students into engineering who cannot pass basic high school algebra, and who need remedial courses. Would you want to drive over a bridge constructed by such student? I wouldn't. Having recruited such weak students they put them into demanding course and are not unhappy to fail 40% or more of them."

Jeffrey said he thought those students had been given a chance but were just not up to snuff.

"And you think this is okay, Jeffrey, to fail so many students, to crush the dreams of so many students and their parents? This is an educational institution: our job is to educate. Everyone."

Jeffrey thought Heinrich was beginning to sound like a starry-eyed romantic. He never expected this from Heinrich whose own standards were so high. Thoughts of pig's ears and silk purses were forming in Jeffrey's brain.

"And then there is the matter of crowding more and more students into classes," said Heinrich. "Even in our mathematics classes the Associate Dean of Engineering keeps enrolling more and more students, even though enrolment is closed. I have seen 40 and 50 students enrolled in differential equations in a classroom designed for 32 students. How are instructors expected to grade the homework and examinations of almost double the number of students? The standards are falling, Jeffrey, and this is not the way I want to see university teaching. No, I am not happy with how engineers are treating students. I would not want to be part of that."

Jeffrey was deflated. He was sure that Heinrich, an excellent researcher, would see the idea of moving to engineering as a golden opportunity. "If he'd been here as long as I have he would think differently," thought Jeffrey.

"Okay, well I'm sorry you feel that way, Heinrich. I think this would be a good opportunity for us."

"I am sorry, too, Jeffrey," said Heinrich, "because I can see this is important to you. Perhaps we can figure a way to work more closely in research with the engineering faculty?"

Rickhart knocked on Heinrich's door. "Jeff," he said. "I was looking for you. I just had the Dean of Engineering on the phone. Could I have a word?"

♥♥♥♥♥

"What were you thinking, discussing this with the Dean of Engineering without talking to me first?" Rickhart asked Jeffrey.

Jeffrey wasn't sure what to say. "Well, when Bert was Chair ..."

Rickhart interrupted him. "Bert is not Chair," he said. "Bert has left the University. Both you and I know that he had a totally indifferent attitude to leading this Department. You were at the retreat Jeff. You know the things we discussed – the plans for the next five years, the formulation of our mission. We hire Heinrich and you want to take him with you to engineering? What were you thinking?"

"Well, it just that there are more applications of matrix algebra in engineering," he said. "And it's not exactly as if I've had total support for matrix algebra over the years in this Department."

Rickhart was thinking, but said nothing. Jeffrey had to be the most isolated, self-centered, self-promoting, but essentially low achieving, academic of his experience. His book, after all, was a textbook, not a research monograph. "Now he gets a talented person in his field and he wants to leave?" thought Rickhart.

"Look Jeff, for us to survive as a Department, let alone grow and prosper, we need to pull together. If there's something you think that you need to develop your field that you're not getting presently, let me know. You and Heinrich get together and figure out if there's something I can do for you and I will, of course, consider it seriously. And please – no more thoughts of moving to engineering."

Jeffrey agreed. " I didn't mean to upset anyone, , he said. "I was just thinking about opportunities." He and Rickhart shook hands and Jeffrey went to his office.

Rickhart went back to talk with Heinrich. "Are you aware of Jeff's proposal to move him and you to engineering?" he asked.

Heinrich explained he was now, and that he was totally opposed to it. "Both Jeffrey and I have strong connections in research with several engineering faculty," he said, "but I am totally opposed to their teaching practices. I think it is a poisonous atmosphere in that College. I would not want to be part of it."

Rickhart laughed. "I'm glad you were able to express it so diplomatically," he said.

Heinrich was confused. He didn't think he was especially diplomatic. To the contrary he thought he had been rather strong in his views. He caught Rickhart's expression and said: "Oh! I see. This is a joke."

"Tell me," said Rickhart. "Did you think the retreat helped us bring our mission and strategic plan into focus?"

"Oh yes, it was very good indeed," said Heinrich. "I am all in favor of such activities, and I thought we got a very clear result from it."

Rickhart was reassured. "That's good," he said. "Heinrich, if you need anything to help you in your research or teaching you will let me know, won't you?"

"Of course," said Heinrich. "Why would I not?"

66

How are we doing?

Deborah Duke was very happy with the experience her middle school protégé, Alicia Brown, had in Kathy Riverton's research class. It was not clear to anyone that this experience would be productive for Alicia. An undergraduate research workshop is not the sort of atmosphere in which a middle school student would normally thrive. Alicia's love of cryptography, and her breathtaking talent for it, had been a decisive factor in her partnering with an equally talented mathematics undergraduate, Kojo Agbeko. Deborah was concerned for Alicia that now her experience at the University was becoming disjointed from her school life. Alicia seemed to be living, mathematically speaking, in two different worlds. Part of Deborah's aim in introducing cryptography into Brian Pimlico's class at Sea View Middle School was to increase the connections between the University and the school. That had happened by virtue of Deborah teaching in Mr. Pimlico's class, and Alicia attending Kathy's research class. But Deborah was hoping for more, and she could not quite pin down her dissatisfaction.

"It's not that the experience at Sea View is not good – it is," she explained to Kathy. "It's just that … I don't know. Something is missing."

"Perhaps it's the teacher?" said Kathy.

Deborah was puzzled. "What do you mean? Brian's been very, very supportive. He's taken on board most of what I've suggested and has come up with projects in cryptography himself. I'm really happy to be able to work with a teacher who is so committed."

Kathy laughed. "I'm not asking you to defend him," she said. "I'm thinking that *he* – and you of course – may be the essential link between Sea View and the University."

Deborah was puzzled again. "I'm not understanding what you're getting at," she said.

"You play a significant role now in his world," Kathy said. "How much of a role does he play in yours? Has he visited my research class? If he has I must have been absent that day!"

"Oh!" Deborah saw Kathy's point. "He's the essential link, isn't he? More essential than me. But what do you see him doing in your class? He's a great teacher but he's nowhere near as accomplished a mathematician as Alicia in his class. He might not fit in very well. And even if he were able to fit in, how could he do it, teaching as he does every day?"

Kathy agreed these were difficulties, but in her experience every desire came with its attendant difficulties, and most often there was a way to work around them.

"Being here is the easiest issue to deal with," she said to Deborah. "It's simple really: he can't be here. At least not during school hours."

Deborah wondered where this apparently defeatist line of thought was leading.

"And we can't be at Sea View. There's no way we can, even occasionally, hold our research class at Sea View. And even if we could, he's not participating. He's merely a spectator", said Kathy.

Deborah was about ready to throw in the towel.

"So he's stuck there and we're stuck here," said Kathy. "That means we need to establish a communication line. Sea View is near enough that we could, with a large injection of cash, build a dedicated line. We could possibly find the money. But there's a simpler solution in my opinion. Let's try Skype."

Deborah hadn't thought of that. It could work, she thought. Often enough guest speakers had talked in her classes from various parts of the world. It seemed possible. "Okay, but what about his participation in your research class?' asked Deborah. 'How do you envisage that happening?"

"I think," said Deborah, "the critical issue is that we want him to see what takes place in this class – and for him to invite any students of his to similarly participate – so that he can interact with us on how we are achieving our teaching goals."

Deborah thought about this for a minute. "So you're saying that he would act as a sort of critical teaching friend? He could give us a critique, from his perspective, on how well we are doing, pedagogically speaking, in the research class?"

"Exactly," said Deborah. "And don't you think the National Science Foundation will be over the moon at our innovative form of assessment?" she laughed.

Deborah's admiration for Kathy, already high, took a step up. "Thanks Kathy for working through this with me. I really appreciate it."

"No problem," said Kathy. "Let's just hope Mr. Pimlico doesn't judge us too harshly!"

♥♥♥♥♥

Rickhart received the Dean's email that the Department of Mathematics was due for external review. He had participated in am external review before, but never managed one. This, he thought, is a very big deal. In this, his thinking was in a different realm to that of the former Department Chair, the recently retired Bert Monod. Rickhart recalled vividly the last external review. George had taken on the job of responding to the reviewer's comments and suggestions. He addressed all their concerns and set up action items, with responsible faculty, due dates, and required resources. Bert argued that we shouldn't tie people down by naming them and giving due dates, and then forgot to forward the document to the Dean's office. Rickhart recalled Bert's statement at the time: "Don't worry too much about this sort of thing. No-one takes it seriously."

Rickhart intended to take the forthcoming external review very seriously. In his mind it was a way to push forward the articulation of the Department's mission, and the strategic plan, still in development. Rickhart, actually, couldn't be happier. He phoned George and Kathy and asked them to meet him in the Daily Grind.

The three of them met and sat at an outside table to accommodate George's ongoing love affair with his Opus X Fuente Fuente cigars.

Rickhart explained the forthcoming review and his hopes for it and the Department.

"That's a lot of work," said George. "I hope it's all going to prove worthwhile this time."

"Bert's not in charge any more," said Rickhart. "We're taking this seriously. The thing is, I'd really like you two to help me coordinate the review. The first and most critical thing is to find suitable reviewers."

"Not sycophants or control freaks," said George.

"Exactly," said Rickhart. "I want reviewers who are well respected, and who will give us honest and constructive assessments of our efforts. So I wonder if you would give some thought to that."

George and Kathy agreed. Kathy thought it would be helpful to start an initial internal assessment to prepare. "I'm thinking that we know some things work and others don't," she said. "I would like to do a first rough pass at the excellent, the indifferent, and the ugly."

Rickhart agreed. "Anything that helps us to take an honest look at ourselves is helpful." He was well aware that academics, like most people, were fond of gilding the lily. A conference poster here, a presentation there, could easily be blown up into a fantasy world-class reputation. "We don't want to dismiss anyone's contribution," he said. "That's very important. But we do need to get everything into perspective. And I agree it helps to do that before the reviewers come to do their job."

George said he though the recent retreat would be viewed favorably by the reviews. 'I know it was only one day, but you did get the Department mission focused, and we got a good start on the strategic plan," he said to Rickhart.

As they were discussing planning for the external review, Jeffrey came into the Daily Grind, fresh from the gym. He got a latte and a muffin and came outside to the table where the others were sitting.

"Hi Jeff," said Rickhart. "We're just discussing our forthcoming eternal review."

"Oh those things," said Jeffrey. "What a waste of time. Who takes that sort of thing seriously?"

67

That wasn't part of the plan

⚮

"*We* do!" said Rickhart in reply to Jeffrey. "We must if the Department is to have any sense as an entity."

Jeffrey explained he was basing his view on past experience. Nothing, he explained, had ever happened as a result of previous reviews, nothing at all. Why would this time be different? Rickhart wanted to say because Bert was no longer running things, that it was no longer his prerogative to dismiss an external review as if it were a mere annoyance like a buzzing mosquito. Instead, he said that as Department Chair he was making the review a priority and he expected everyone to pitch in and help.

"I'll help, of course," said Jeffrey. "Just tell me what you'd like me to do."

"I need some assistance with data," Rickhart replied. "We need to get everyone's up-to-date CV and extract information from them: number of publications over the last six years, grants, quality of journals in which people have published, quality of book publishers – you probably lead in that regard, Jeff – citations to publications, and anything else you can think of that amounts to quantity and quality of work and impact. We need to build a strong and accurate case for our productivity." Jeffrey agreed he could do that.

"Meanwhile I will work on strengthening and fleshing out the strategic plan," said Rickhart. "We've got a few months before the review to get it in shape and present ourselves as a Department that knows where it's headed and how."

Jeffrey was about to ask where his subject, matrix algebra, figured in the strategic plan when Bao Zhang arrived at the Daily Grind. "Hello all," she said. "I was told I might find you here."

"Just in time Bao to help with planning for the external review," said Kathy. "I'll bet you didn't plan on being thrown into this your first semester here."

"No, it was quite unexpected," she said, "but quite exciting". She looked at Rickhart and giggled.

Rickhart laughed. "I'm glad you find it funny Bao. We're going to need a sense of humor as this progresses."

"It presents some very interesting possibilities," said Bao. "Which is why I wanted to talk with you." Bao had already talked about her grant proposal to the National Science Foundation, focusing on science and engineering research training for mathematics and statistics students. Rickhart had said at the time he agreed everything seemed to line up for this grant. "The thing is," said Bao, "I've been digesting the request for proposals a little more: it's clear – very clear – that the National Science Foundation expects participating departments to be transformed as a result of this grant. If we get the grant, our entire department would be expected to become more computational in nature. All students, even those intending to be teachers, would be expected to take scientific computing, at the very least."

Rickhart was thinking about the implications.

"That's a change I would like to see, I think," said George. "But I doubt everyone would. I think there will be a push back to allow mathematics majors a choice to pursue different options."

"That's why I raised it," said Bao. "The National Science Foundation is very clear about their intentions, and I feel – as George said – it would be a big change for the Department. I'm in no position to influence that change, but it's what will be expected if we get the grant."

Rickhart thanked Bao for raising the issue. "It's something we are going to have to think about seriously and urgently," he said. "Bao needs to move forward with her application and the rest of the Department needs to come to grips with the implications of getting this grant. Even if Bao doesn't get the grant, the door has opened to our thinking about the possibility of a fairly radical and imminent modification of our undergraduate curriculum. We need a Department meeting."

So it was that at 10:00 AM the next morning Rickhart convened a meeting in the Dean's conference room. Item number one on the agenda was the forthcoming external review.

"Ah, those things are such a waste of time," said Inger. "Nothing ever happens and we spend our time scurrying around like mice looking for the bits of cheese. It's a cruel joke of the administration to do this to us so it looks like they are doing something." She gave a nod and a broad smile.

"What may have happened in the past – or more to the point, not happened – is the past," said Rickhart. "We're concerned with what's happening now and how it impacts our future. I am taking this review very seriously, and I expect you all to do the same."

"That's all very well to have such nice words," said Inger, "but if the administration give us no resources to do what the reviewers ask, then are we expected to contribute more of our time or even our own money?"

"Resource issues are part of the equation," said Rickhart, "and on the principle that she who complains gets the job, I'm putting you in charge, Inger, of analyzing the resource implications of our plans, and to revise that in light of the external reviewers report." Everyone laughed, Inger included. "I can do that and I am happy to tell the administration where to put up or shut up," she said to more laughter.

Rickhart passed around copies of a two-sided sheet of paper. "As a first pass I've allocated tasks to you. Let me know if you are happy – or unhappy – to do what I've put you down for. We all need to pull together, and getting these tasks done is important to taking this review seriously."

He then moved to the second item on the agenda. "Some of you will know that Bao has been working on a grant application to the National Science Foundation. It seems to fit us like a glove – we have everything in place and even though there will be stiff competition I feel we have a decent chance of getting this grant. That's for information. What we need to discuss are the implications if we do get the grant. And even if we don't, the discussion will still open new avenues for us." Rickhart asked Bao to explain her understanding of the National Science Foundation expectations if the grant is awarded.

"They expect significant changes in the undergraduate mathematics and science curriculum," she said. "Especially to focus on computational mathematics and statistics in relation to computation and data processing in science and engineering."

Alex Bell, a mathematical logician, was worried. "Are you saying that we would put more emphasis on those areas, as we have been doing the past few years, or that essentially the whole Department should focus on computational teaching, if not research?"

Bao looked to Rickhart for help. "The latter, I feel," said Rickhart. "We are not a large Department and we cannot do everything. The issue for me is how we can best use our resources and talent."

Jeffrey raised his hand. "What would be the role of matrix algebra if we had a heavy – even compulsory – computational focus?"

Rickhart sighed. "It's a good question, Jeff. There are several of you who will feel this way and will ask similar questions. Bao has laid out what she thinks is a minimal change to the Department's undergraduate curriculum that would satisfy the National Science Foundation should we get this grant. Could you all please look it over carefully, think about any issues you have, and let's meet again the same time next week?"

Inger raised her hand. "Inger?" said Rickhart, expecting the worst. "I think this is excellent idea," she said. "I congratulate Bao. She is new to the Department but she has already brought the breaths of fresh air. If the National Science Foundation will supply the money, I say: do it!"

68

A lazy Saturday

Lori and Bob decided it would be a lazy Saturday. So when the alarm went off at 6:00 AM Bob was jolted awake and confused. "I thought we were taking it easy today?" he said. "We are," Lori replied. "And that means not cooking breakfast. If we want to eat at Nick's on Broadway this morning without a wait, we'd better get a move on." Bob's feet hit the floor and he stood up. His legs, getting the idea, steered him clopping toward the bathroom. He turned on the shower, undressed and savored the hot, steamy water waking him. Lori appeared, undressed, and asked him to make room. She took the Jean Paul Gaultier shower gel and massaged his neck, shoulders and back. "This," he thought, "is better than whatever it was I was dreaming about." He smiled broadly as her hands slipped around to his front and she massaged his belly and legs.

"Your turn," he said, as he squeezed some of the shower gel into the palm of his hand. He gently washed her, feeling he exquisite curve of her breasts. The gentle massaging caress grew and exploded into a full sexual union.

"That was lovely," said Lori, kissing Bob and turning off the water. "Let's get dressed and scoot, so we'll get something to eat. I'm starved!"

They arrived at Nick's just after 7:00 AM. Already the restaurant was filling up. "This place is so darn popular," said Bob. "It's a good thing you got us up early."

Their server brought coffee and Bob ordered black beans with two eggs, grilled tortilla, tomato salsa and avocado-cilantro crème. Lori decided on the sautéed local vegetables with two poached eggs and grilled bread.

'Do you think I could get a Mimosa?" Lori asked their server.

"Could you make that two?" Bob smiled.

Their coffee came, followed in rapid order by their drinks.

"Chin-chin," said Lori, holding up her glass to Bob. She lent across and kissed him on the lips. "I'm so happy," she said. "Let's just have a fun day chilling out. What do you want to do?"

Bob laughed. "Nothing! Just chilling."

"We should do something," said Lori. "We don't want to just wander around, do we?"

"No, I guess not," said Bob. "How about we go to the Hope Street Farmers Market? They'll be setting up soon – I think it opens at 9:00."

"Great idea," said Lori, "and then how about we go down to the School of Design Museum? There's an exhibition there I'd like to see."

Their morning plans in place, and intimate happiness fully on the rise, they savored their breakfast.

"I think I might have another Mimosa," Lori said to their server.

"Make that two," said Bob.

♥♥♥♥♥

Rickhart had not seen this coming. He was delighted, of course, but the thought had been pushed to the back of his mind until Kathy announced at 6:30 that morning that she wanted to get pregnant. "I'm 38 she said. It's now or never. And I think I want it to be now."

Rickhart was even more surprised when she meant *right now!*

They lay back, exhausted. "If that doesn't do it, nothing will!' she laughed. "I think after that I'll probably have twins!"

Rickhart kissed her, slid out of bed and put on his robe. "I will make us some breakfast," he said.

"That would be nice. What do you have in mind for today?" she asked.

"Well the external review and the strategic plan are on my mind, as you might expect. I was thinking I could sort of take it easy, but just – slowly maybe – do a little work on that."

Kathy laughed. "Right! Slowly! I'll believe that when I see it. You'll be working hard all day long. You know what I wish?" she asked.

Rickhart thought she already just got what she wished, but thought it best to say nothing. He looked at her.

"I wish we were back in Holland right now. I would love to be in Amsterdam, going for breakfast at a little café, walking along the canals."

Rickhart had a sudden pang of homesickness. "That would be very nice," he said. "If we were rich we could hop on a plane now and be back by Monday noon. But how about this – we could take the ferry to Block Island."

Kathy laughed so heard she thought she would cry.

"I know it's not Amsterdam, but it's not too bad," he said.

Kathy doubled up with laughter again. "No, no. You're right," she said. "It's a good idea. It will be lovely. Let's get going. I would like two eggs over easy, one rasher of bacon, toast, and orange juice, please. Oh, and coffee. Do we have some of that good coffee of Jeff's? I'd like that, please"

"Coming up!" said Rickhart.

"You have to treat pregnant ladies nicely, you know," she said.

"We don't know you're pregnant yet!" he scoffed.

"Well after breakfast, for dessert, we'll have to make sure," she smiled.

♥♥♥♥♥

Lisa and Chris strolled, hand in hand, to L'Artisan Bakery in Wayland Square for breakfast. At a little after 10:00 AM the bakery was nearly full. Chris found a small table by the window, and someone came to clean it off for them. "Will this do?" he asked. Lisa indicated it was fine. "Two coffees please," she said to their server. "Are you hungry?" she asked Chris. "I could do with a bagel," he said. "Me too," Lori said to their server.

'What do you want to do today?" Chris asked. Lori wasn't sure. "I don't have anything specific in mind. But, you know, I wouldn't mind taking a ride up to *Nervous Systems* in Somerville, Massachusetts. Would that be okay?" Chris laughed. "Your wish is my command. But I'm surprised you don't want to spend some time across the road in Alex and Ani." "Are you kidding?" Lisa said. "That goes without saying. You know I'll probably buy something, too."

"Remember it's a business expense," said Chris. "Since you're actually in business now."

She leaned across and kissed him. "Thanks, Chris, for being so supportive."

"The pleasure," he said, "is all mine. Really! It's been such fun seeing you grow through these amazing developments. Would you have thought this time last year you'd be doing and thinking about what you're doing now?"

Lisa admitted her life had taken a roller coaster ride since the accidental meeting with Jeffrey Albacete at the Coffee Depot in Warren. And Chris was now a big part of her life. That was unexpected, but made her very happy.

"You know what," she said, "how about we have lunch at McBride's around 2:00 and then take a ride up to Somerville?"

"Okay," said Chris, "that's a plan. But it's only 10:30 now. Alex and Anni won't take you that long. What do you want to do until then?"

"We could go back up to the apartment," she said, smiling. "I'm sure you'll think of something."

♥♥♥♥♥

Jeffrey woke as usual at 6:30 AM. He rubbed his eyes, yawned, and got out of bed. He showered and made his way to the kitchen where a pile of dishes in the sink greeted him. "Should have put them in the dishwasher," he thought. He looked for a fry pan and finding the one he wanted in the sink, squirted it with washing-up liquid and washed it clean. He put two eggs on to fry and two slices of bread in the toaster. The coffee machine, on a timer, was beginning its brew. Breakfast ready, Jeffrey sat at the kitchen table with his laptop. There was a supportive email from his publisher, saying how pleased they were with developments on the new book. Heinrich emailed him a draft of the new revised chapter, and Lisa had deposited a couple of CDF files in DropBox. Jeffrey dropped some egg on himself and ketchup ran down his front. He got up to get a napkin and wiped off the food. He perused his emails again. "You know," he thought, "I'm pretty lucky to have all this. If anyone's doing better than me this fine morning I'd be very surprised."

69

We all have fantasies

⁂

Jeffrey took a walk along the Appian Way in Barrington, leading down to a beach. He liked this walk. It was not difficult and there were usually relatively few people on the track this time of a Monday morning. On the inlet he could see people kayaking. George and Deborah kayaked and had tried to interest him in joining them once, but he gave a thin smile and said he didn't think it was for him. Jeffrey had no interest in learning how to do an underwater roll if the kayaked tipped over – perfected by the Inuit peoples as he recalled from a National Geographic television program – and he was sure he *would* tip over. They had also tried to interest him in riding a bicycle along the East Bay Bike Path and Jeffrey had declined that too. The path, admittedly with beautiful views, was over 14 miles end to end, and if he were to ride with them George was bound to want to do the whole 29 miles or so. Too much, Jeffrey thought, way too much. What is it, he thought, about cycling freaks like George that they had to ride so hard and push the envelope so much? Exercise for Jeffrey was a slow, gradual affair, best done in the gym or on a quiet walk such as he was taking now.

To his surprise, someone called his name. "Hello Professor Albacete." Jeffrey looked at the young woman who had spoken to him but did not recognize her.

"I was a student in your class two semesters ago. Do you remember me?"

Jeffrey tried to nod yes and no at the same time. He did his best to smile but looked like a deranged person with his head bobbing about and an absurd expression on his face. He was trying to speak when the young woman said: "Agnes. Agnes Duchamps. I was in your matrix algebra class. I enjoyed it very much."

"Ah yes," said Jeffrey. "I do remember you now. I see so many students over the years that I can't always recall names. What are you doing now ... Agnes?",

"I'm working as an acquisitions editor ... well, training, really. For your publisher as it turns out."

Jeffrey looked more closely at this young woman. He could not recall her as one of his former students. He thought he would have because of her very alluring figure, his eyes drawn magnetically to her – let's face it, he thought – magnificent chest.

"That's ... that's very interesting," he said. "How did you get into that line of work?"

Agnes explained how she answered a job posting. The interview went well and they hired her to train in acquisitions. "It's interesting work," she said. "I get to meet a lot of authors and prospective authors. Maybe I should come and talk with you, Professor Albacete?"

Jeffrey was imagining how delightful that would be when the image of his own editor appeared in his mind. "Ah, well, yes," he said. "That would be something to look forward to." He smiled. "The thing is, I have my own editor who discusses forthcoming projects with me."

"Perhaps I could write under a nom de plume," he said out loud as he thought to himself.

Agnes laughed. "Why would a well-known author like you write under a pseudonym, Professor Albacete?"

Jeffrey was lost for words. He couldn't say: "To meet with attractive young acquisitions editors." At least he thought he couldn't say that. "I was just fantasizing," he said.

"I think it's good to fantasize," said Agnes. "It's an essential part of the creative process, I find. Do you fantasize often, Professor Albacete?"

Jeffrey was now experiencing a marked tumescence and wondered if it was becoming obvious to Agnes. "I, ... uh, probably more often than I should," he said.

Agnes told Jeffrey they should stay in touch. "You never know what opportunities might be just around he corner," she said. She gave him her business card and underlined her cell phone number. "I live quite close to the University," she said. Jeffrey was surprised. He thought she must live in New York where she surely worked. "I work from home two days a week and travel to New York for the other three days. I also travel a lot," she said. "So call me if you have one of those fantasies and you'd like to do something about it." She smiled. Jeffrey was dumbstruck. "I ... I ..." he tried to speak. Agnes held out her hand. "It was so nice bumping into you Professor Albacete. Please stay in touch."

Jeffrey watched as she walked away. To an observer he would appear to resemble nothing more closely than a fully charged Van de Graaf generator, ready to discharge.

♥♥♥♥♥

Zaqi was working on a hard numerical analysis problem and not getting very far. He thought he knew the literature well but nothing in his repertoire of known techniques was helping with this problem. He entered a search phrase in Google Scholar wondering if there was something he had missed. A lot of standard references that he already knew came up. On a whim he entered the same search in the regular Google search engine. Up came the same references at the top, with a few new links to web pages scattered around on the next pages. He checked them out and found that they linked back to work he already knew. One site, linking to the work of Colette Lefevre was something he hadn't seen before. He checked out her web site but did not find any publications. He clicked on a link to her personal web page and looked again for publications. Nothing. Idly, he clicked on the link to photographs. At first he was embarrassed and wondered if people might think he was looking at pornography. There were many photographs of Collette Lefevre, scantily clad, engaged in highly flirtatious behavior. Zaqi was about to leave the page thinking it was none of his business what some eccentric academics put on the web when one photograph looked familiar. He looked again quite closely. Puzzled, Zaqi went looking for George and asked him to look at the photograph too. "It is Jeff, isn't it?" asked Zaqi.

"George laughed. "Damn right!" he said. The caption simply said "Cyprus".

Zaqi was nervous, but George couldn't stop laughing. "So now we have some idea of what Jeff got up to at that conference."

Zaqi wondered what they should do. "I think we shouldn't mention this," he said. "I don't think Jeff would want this known to people. On the other hand he wouldn't want it left there either. What do you think we should do?"

George was still laughing. "Maybe we could *accidentally* leave a computer on at this site so he could *accidentally* see it", he said.

"No, that's terrible," said Zaqi, " we couldn't do that. My goodness! He will be upset if he sees this!"

Zaqi heard the sound of Jeffrey's voice as he walked down the hallway. Instinctively he stepped in front of the computer Jeffrey looked into Zaqi's office and said hello.

"Hi Jeff," said Zaqi, looking for something to say. "What have you been up to?"

George snorted.

"I was walking on the Appian way," he said. " Down by the beach. Actually I bumped into this ex-student, quite lovely. She asked me," he said with an air of worldly wisdom, "about my fantasies."

Both George and Zaqi burst out laughing.

"I'm not that old," protested Jeffrey. "I can still have fantasies you know."

"Oh, we know," said George. "We know."

70

Moving on

News of Jeffrey's peccadillo, if indeed one could call it that since he was single – lets' say his "predicament" – spread throughout the Department. Faculty were generally incredulous, then highly amused. No one it seemed could avoid laughing out loud, after the initial shock of seeing their colleague in all but naked episodes on the Web. Everyone was very careful not to say a word of this to Jeffrey. It's one thing to be laughed about behind one's back, quite another to one's face. The Department was nothing if not considerate of feelings. Still it was funny, and the source of much comment, not to say amusement.

Jeffrey himself contributed unwittingly to the ongoing mirth by occasionally saying such things as: "You know what I would really like right now." He was puzzled why people within earshot would burst out laughing, and he put it down to a form of stress release. He thought perhaps too many of the faculty were doing too much, always administering grants, preparing new grant applications, teaching new courses, planning new courses, writing strategies and mission statements. If they didn't ease up on themselves they would go mad, he thought. Perhaps their uncharacteristic laughter was a sign some of them already had. Jeffrey thought it best to keep to himself for a while and avoid whatever possibly contagious lunacy was making its way around the Department. His office was his sanctuary. He put coffee on to brew and admired his collected editions, including translations, of his book *Matrix Algebra*. It was a fine collection, he thought, a really solid contribution to the field, something for which both colleagues and students would remember him. Coffee poured, the delicious aroma pervading his office, Jeffrey sat back in his chair to think about the new book in preparation. Heinrich knocked on the door and came in. Jeffrey welcomed him and offered a chair.

"Jeffrey," said Heinrich", have you seen the pictures of you on the Web?" Jeffrey, his mind turning to an award or a promotion of his book, smiled and said: "No, I haven't. Something new from my publisher? Flattering I hope."

"Not exactly," said Heinrich. "I think you should see them." Heinrich sat at Jeffrey's computer and clicked to open the revealing Web page. Jeffrey looked, puzzled at first, and then gasped. He sat down, his legs having gone from under him.

"I am sorry to be embarrassing you Jeffrey," said "Heinrich. "I thought you should see these pictures."

Jeffrey looked at Heinrich without saying anything. He was confused and speechless. Gradually he came to, and told Heinrich not to worry. "It's not your fault Heinrich. Thank you for telling me. I wonder what possessed Collette to put those pictures on her Web page?" Heinrich had no answer.

"I will get in touch with her and ask her to take them down," said Jeffrey. He picked up his phone, found Collette Lefevre's number in his contact list and dialed.

"You are doing it right now?" asked Heinrich. Jeffrey nodded, his eyes wide open.

Collette answered and Jeffrey explained he had seen the pictures. They were embarrassing to him, he said, and asked if she would take them down. Collette explained these were her travel snaps, her mementos, and that she liked sharing them. She said that as an American Jeffrey worried too much. "We are more tolerant on the Continent," she said. "Relax Jeffrey, nothing bad will happen to you."

Jeffrey hung up. He shook his head. "Nothing doing," he said to Heinrich. "She wants to keep them there. I guess I'm going to look publicly foolish for the rest of my days." Curse modern technology," he thought.

Heinrich coughed to attract Jeffrey's attention. "I could perhaps help," he said. Jeffrey was puzzled. "I know some computer science students," said Heinrich. "They are excellent – let us use the word – *hackers*. I think for the right amount of money they could help you resolve this predicament. Should I contact them?" Jeffrey nodded affirmatively.

Heinrich made a phone call and explained the situation. He put his hand over the phone and asked Jeffrey: "Does $2,000 seem too much?" Jeffrey indicated the sum was fine. A small sum really, he thought, to get rid of the offending images.

The realization that Heinrich was probably not the first person to see these photographs was dawning on Jeffrey. Now it became clear to him why people had been laughing the past few days when he said certain things. They knew. Jeffrey leaned forward and put his head in his hands.

"Jeffrey, if I may say so, this is nothing to worry about. I am sorry you are embarrassed but this is your own personal business. You have done nothing wrong. I think in Europe you would not be so concerned. Americans, I think, are a little more puritanical."

Jeffrey hoped Heinrich was right.

"And I have good news for you," said Heinrich. "I am progressing much faster than I expected with the new applications. I think the book could be complete in a little over a month."

Jeffrey was surprised. "That is good news. And the CDF's? Is Lisa progressing okay?" Heinrich explained she was.

"We should all meet then, as soon as possible," said Jeffrey, "to think about how we will wrap this up. I would love to have the book out by the conference."

"I think that will be a certainty," said Heinrich. "As I under-stand it the publisher wants to make a big deal of the new CDF format at the conference. We will be done well in advance."

Jeffrey was pleased to hear this news. At least, he thought, something is going right today.

♥♥♥♥♥

Lisa De Silva wanted to talk to Kathy. "I'm a little confused," she said, "and I could do with some advice." She explained to Kathy that the book project with Professors Albacete and Zimmer was progressing faster than they had anticipated. "It's due mainly to the efficiency of Professor Zimmer," she said. "He's brilliant."

"But that's a good thing isn't it – that it's getting done sooner?" asked Kathy.

"Well I guess," said Lisa. "The only thing is I'm concerned that the publisher might want some of the money back."

Kathy asked why Lisa thought that might happen. "I don't know. No one has said anything, but I guess I'm anxious they might."

"You're feeling guilty," said Kathy. "The project is taking less time than you'd planned for, so now you're sitting around doing nothing, as it were, and still collecting money."

"Exactly!" said Lisa.

Kathy asked if Lisa had the contract from the publisher with her. Lisa took it from her backpack and gave it to Kathy. They sat together reading through the fine print.

"Nope! You're all set," said Kathy. "As far as I can make out they contracted with you to deliver a product. They specified a latest completion date, but not a penalty for an early completion. Why would they? You're home free. As soon as the book's deliv-ered they will pay you what's outstanding." Lisa was beginning to understand through experience the advantage of a fixed fee for a specified contractual product.

"If I'd be working on an hourly rate I would have been paid a tiny fraction of what I've actually got," she said. "I have you to thank for that Professor Riverton."

Kathy was pleased to be able to help. "For some reason," she said, "men, in general, seem to be able to look someone in the eye and say: *The fee is fifty thousand dollars*, whereas most women have a harder time with that."

"I can see why," laughed Lisa. "It seems so ... so macho!" They both laughed.

"I think women want to negotiate more around a relationship," said Lisa. "I know that's what I would have done if you hadn't advised me on the amount to ask for. Professor Albacete actually asked for me: I was too chicken."

Kathy smiled. "So all you have to do is think about your career from here on out. It helps to have money in the bank."

Lisa thanked Kathy again and thought she knew, from here on, exactly what she wanted to do.

71

An excellent idea

Bao and her husband Ri had settled on a town-house in Barring-ton. Although Ri worked an hour away in Waltham, Massachu-setts, he loved to live near the sea. He thought, too, that living so close to where Bao worked would make his wife happy, and a happy wife is worth a great deal.

Bao was planning dinner when Ri asked her would she mind if he asked Jeffrey over. "Something's come up at work," he said, "and Jeffrey's expertise seems just what's needed. Do you think he'd mind? Would you?" Bao could see no reason why he would, and she was happy to have him over. She phoned Jeffrey and explained that Ri would like to discuss something professionally with him. Jeffrey was happy to come over for dinner. Nothing, as it turns out, would make him happier, since he was contemplating what to eat and looking in his cupboard at cans of chili and baked beans as real possibilities. The thought of Bao's excellent cooking brightened him up right away.

Twenty minutes later Jeffrey rang the Zhang household door-bell and Ri answered the door. "Jeffrey! Thanks for coming. Come on in."

Jeffrey noticed that Ri was not wearing shoes and that inside the door was a tidy pile of men and women's shoes on a mat. "Would you like me to remove my shoes?" he asked Ri.

"If it's no trouble," said Ri.

Jeffrey thought that of course it was no trouble – one simply slipped off one's shoes – but it seemed a modern and silly affectation to him. Probably connects one's energy, or *chee*, or whatever Bao called it, to the energy of the house, he thought, and chuckled to himself.

"Sorry?" said Ri.

"Oh, nothing," said Jeffrey. "I was just thinking of something funny that happened to me today. Nothing of any consequence." He handed Ri a bottle of Spätlese Riesling he had picked up on the way over.

Ri thanked him and led Jeffrey into the kitchen where Bao was preparing the meal.

"Hello Jeffrey," she said, "thanks for coming over. Ri has some top-secret mission he wants to discus with you. I don't even know if I'm allowed to listen."

Jeffrey was startled, then relieved when Ri and Bao laughed at her joke.

Ri opened a bottle of Sancerre and offered Jeffrey a glass. Drinks in hand they sat down in the living room. The open plan of the town-house meant that Bao could see and talk to them as she cooked.

"Thanks for coming over, Jeffrey," said Ri. "There's been some developments at work that require some expertise in your field."

Jeffrey was gratified to hear that. In his experience, many engineers used matrix techniques extensively in their work, and seemed happy to collaborate with him when special expertise was required. "Anything I can do to help, of course," he smiled at Ri.

"That's great," said Ri. "I appreciate your willingness to help." Ri explained that questions of matrix techniques kept arising in recent engineering projects, and while the engineers had a general background in those techniques – "Many of them learned from your book," said Ri – they were feeling increasingly out of their depth.

"This," thought, Jeffrey to himself, "is what students need to hear when I insist they get their homework assignments correct. It's not for nothing that I set high standards."

"We've been wondering," said Ri, " if it's possible for the University to set up a consulting group to have faculty and graduate students work on some of these industrial problems – a sort of mathematical and computational consulting group. With special emphasis on matrix methods, of course."

"Of course," laughed Jeffrey. "Yes, I can't see why not. It's an idea that fits very well with our current mission. I would be very happy to raise it with our Department Chair, but you can take it that you have my complete support.

"That's wonderful," said Ri. "Can I get you another glass of wine?"

Jeffrey wished the delightful cooking aromas would soon transpire into steaming plates of food.

♥♥♥♥♥

Jeffrey raised the idea of the consulting group next day with Rickhart. "It seems a perfect opportunity to promote our expertise and to potentially bring a cash flow into the Department," Jeffrey said.

Rickhart was very taken with the idea. "I like this a lot," he said. "It has everything going for it. We can run consultancy workshops with faculty, graduate students, and even advanced undergraduates. I think we should run it by the Vice-Chancellor for Industrial Technology Transfer. I think he will be very supportive."

Jeffrey thought this was suddenly growing into an entity that went way beyond what he and Ri had discussed. "Of course our focus will be on matrix methods," he said.

"Initially, of course," said Rickhart, "but I can see this growing into something much bigger."

Digesting Rickhart's thinking, Jeffrey saw himself as Director of the Center for Mathematical and Computational Consulting. "That should be worth a course release or two," he thought.

"I will have to put it to the Department, for their consideration," Rickhart said, "but I don't see anyone objecting. It's not increasing anyone's workload – the workshop will count as a course for teaching purposes – and potentially brings us many benefits. Leave it with me, Jeff, I'll ask for feedback from the Department right away. Well done by the way. This is just the sort of initiative I've been hoping for."

Jeffrey left the meeting with Rickhart, feeling especially pleased. At long last, he thought, my work and ideas are being appreciated. As he walked back to his office he bumped into Lisa De Silva.

"Professor Albacete," she said, "would you have some time to go over the latest CDFs for the book?"

Jeffrey smiled at her. She, he thought, had been the beginning of his string of good luck. There had been one or two incidents – the student in Cyprus and that exhibitionist Collette Lefevre – but mostly his life had taken a turn for the better since he met Lisa. "Yes, of course I have time for you. Come on in."

Rickhart, as promised, put the idea of a mathematical and computational consulting group to the faculty. Support was in the main very strong. There were, as he had expected, the odd dissenting voices. Inger wanted to know how much extra work this would create and whether the administration would provide the necessary resources. Rickhart explained, by email to all, that this was essentially an entrepreneurial activity undertaken by the Department, at its own risk. "We put in a relatively small amount of our time, time we would spend teaching anyway, in order to build a reputation for mathematical consulting to industry." The potential payoff, he explained, was considerable.

With this level of support from the Department Rickhart arranged a meeting with the Vice Chancellor for Industrial Technology Transfer to discuss University support for the idea. The energetic and esteemed Vice Chancellor was all for it. "A great idea," he said, "what do you need from me to make it happen?" Rickhart explained that a small space in the Technology and Manufacturing Center would be ideal. "Just the use of a meeting room, is all," he said. "I feel it would look better to people from industry if we met in an environment with which they were familiar. Sitting in a classroom might invoke memories they'd rather forget."

The Vice Chancellor understood and said that wouldn't a problem. "From the administration's perspective it would be important to appoint a Director and a small advisory board," he said. "The usual sort of thing."

Buoyed by the Vice Chancellor's support Rickhart met with a few mathematics faculty as well as the Dean of Engineering and the Dean of Science. He sent out an email to the Department of Mathematics and to other potential stakeholders:

"*Folks,*

as a result of a very creative initiative of Jeff Albacete, and detailed discussions within the Department and the broader University, I have decided to move ahead and establish a Center for Mathematical and Computational Consulting. We will need a small advisory board, comprising some Department faculty, wider University representation, as well as industry representatives. I am very pleased to announce that, as a result of wide discussion and unanimous support, Dr. Heinrich Zimmer will be the founding Director of this new consulting center."

72

Finish and celebrate

Jeffrey had a right to be peeved: the consulting venture, so potentially lucrative for the Department, was his idea. He was the person who raised the Center for Mathematical and Computational Consulting with Rickhart. How could anyone think otherwise? He had used the exact phrase of Ri's when they discussed the idea at Ri and Bao's house. Jeffrey was feeling seriously slighted. "What's the point," he thought, "of having an original idea if someone steals it away from you and effectively gives it to someone else?"

He bumped into Bao on the way to his office. "Oh Jeff," she said, "that was so nice of you to take Ri's idea and push it the way you did. You were very decisive. And then to think of Heinrich as Director! That is so selfless. Signs of a true leader." Jeffrey was surprised and confused. He didn't know how to react. His mouth formed into a thin smile. He felt a need to sit down.

"Are you okay, Jeff?" Bao asked.

He nodded. "Yes, fine. Thank you. I just need to sit down for a moment." Bao walked with him to his office. "Perhaps if you have some coffee?" she asked. "Here, let me put it on for you."

As Jeffrey rested and Bao made coffee, Heinrich knocked on the door and peeped around at Jeffrey. "May I come in Jeffrey?" he asked.

Jeffrey nodded assent and Bao said she would leave them to talk. "You must have much to discuss!" she said.

"Jeffrey, I hope you are not upset at Rickhart giving me the job of Director of the new consulting center," he said. "I thought you should be the Director because it was your idea. However, Rickhart convinced me I was the person for the job and that you would be happy about that. But I am not so convinced."

Jeffrey could not blame Heinrich for what had happened. "It's okay, Heinrich. You're a young man with energy and ideas. You will make a fine Director. I'm probably getting a bit old in the tooth for this sort of thing anyway," he forced a laugh. Relieved, Heinrich said he wanted to discuss the book. "We are coming close to getting this finished. I have been thinking: while we have been working hard at getting this book done, no one else has any idea of how novel and beautiful is the final product. I think you should give a talk to the Department, Jeffrey, about the book. It was, after all, your idea."

"Well, I don't know about that," said Jeffrey.

Heinrich was insistent. "You should do it Jeffrey. It is only right to promote something so good in which you had a strong hand in the making."

"Well if you think so," said Jeffrey.

"I do, Jeffrey. I do," said Heinrich.

So it was that on Friday that week the faculty gathered in the Department seminar room to hear Jeffrey talk about progress on the new book. This, as Zaqi remarked was the culmination of the work that went into the book since Jeff and Lisa first gave a talk on the idea. And now Heinrich had joined them, so Zaqi was keen to hear how the book had developed.

Jeffrey began the talk and described the overall idea of the book. He then introduced Lisa who discussed the planning and execution of the computable document format applications in the book. "Actually," she said, "the whole book is one large CDF."

Heinrich then spoke about the new applications he added to the book's content, and Jeffrey spoke about the impact the book was likely to have on people working in the field of matrix algebra.

Deborah leaned to Kathy and whispered: "I don't understand how it is that Jeff is such an engaging speaker in seminars, when his students routinely describe him as boring in class." Kathy nodded and smiled. "I know. It's as if he comes to life in seminars. I think it's because he feels free to be himself. In class he's *The Great Professor Who Must Know All*." She laughed: "I think the weight of being an expert in his field bogs him down in lectures. He can't find it in him to be spontaneous because he is too busy being serious."

The assembled faculty and students gave Jeffrey, Heinrich and Lisa a round of applause. "Excellent talk guys," said George. "Really good. You must feel very pleased and proud the book is done."

Jeffrey and Lisa beamed and thanked George. Heinrich said there were a few technical issues to attend to, so strictly speaking the book was not yet finished, but would be in the very near future.

"We can rely on you to be precise, Heinrich," laughed George. Heinrich smiled at what he perceived to be a compliment.

Rickhart made an announcement: "Thanks to Jeff, Heinrich and Lisa for an outstanding presentation. To celebrate the writing of the book the Department is hosting coffee and" – he looked at Jeffrey – "muffins at the Daily Grind. See you there in 10 minutes." Another round of applause followed and the group made their way to the Daily Grind. Rickhart, walking with Kathy, George and Deborah, made an observation that Jeff was probably wasted giving undergraduate lectures. "He's not got his heart in it, and he is quite outstanding as an expositor of ideas in his field to a more mature audience. I thought his talk was very good, as always."

"Just what I was saying to Kathy," said Deborah.

"So what are you saying, Rick?" Kathy asked. "Either he snaps up his lectures somehow or he spends his time giving seminar talks? How can we do that? The Dean is never going to allow it."

"I'm not so sure," said Rickhart. "It's a question of money, isn't it? If we had the money to replace Jeff as an undergraduate instructor she wouldn't complain. She'd probably thank me!"

"You'll never convince Jeff to give up teaching his beloved matrix algebra," said George. "It's part and parcel of who he is. It's what his life has been since he was a young academic."

They continued discussing Jeffrey as they made their way to the Daily Grind. Rickhart let the cashier know he was paying for everyone.

"George, this may be one of those days you'll have to forego a cigar. I think it's too cool to sit outside."

George, to his surprise, agreed, adding: "It's not as if I'm addicted to them you know."

When coffee, tea, muffins and pastries had all arrived Rickhart stood up and raised his coffee cup. "To the book writing team – Jeff, Heinrich, and Lisa. A job very well done. You make us all proud, and bring great credit and kudos to the Department. Cheers!"

"Cheers!" echoed the group.

Jeffrey stood up to say a few words. "I couldn't have done this without a lot of help," he said. "Most of all from Lisa and from Heinrich, but also from the Department as well. Kathy provided the money to hire Lisa and without that we probably wouldn't be here today. The Dean argued for two positions and we got both Bao and Heinrich. I think both of them have been enormously instrumental in getting the book finished. Heinrich, of course has been the driving force behind the great new applications, but Bao has taught us all a thing or two about energy and focus. So thanks to everyone ... and again to Lisa for introducing me to excellent coffee!" A round of applause followed.

"See," whispered Kathy, "when he's not lecturing to students he can be quite eloquent."

"The question," said Rickhart, " is how to harness that eloquence."

73

Coffee, tea or cat poo?

Lisa took a bag from her backpack. "This is why I came to see you, Professor Albacete. I found some coffee I think you will enjoy." She produced a coffee grinder and a bag of beans.

"Oh, I don't know about that, Lisa. It's a messy process," said Jeffrey.

Lisa smiled. "It's worth it. Just wait until you taste this coffee." A gentle grind and Lisa put the coffee on to brew. The aroma was alluring and subtle. "Rich," thought Jeffrey.

Lisa poured them both a cup and they sat savoring the flavor.

"This is *very* good!" said Jeffrey. "It's rich and smooth, not a hint of bitterness." He took another sip. "Almost a chocolate flavor." He looked at Lisa. She agreed. "It has a very long aftertaste," he said, "Sort of a slightly nutty taste. Thank you, Lisa, this is very good coffee. I am indebted to you."

Lisa was pleased he enjoyed it. Sharing fine coffee had been an unexpected pleasure of their relationship. "It's an Arabica coffee from Indonesia," she said. The subtle rich aroma of the coffee pervaded the hallway.

Zaqi knocked on Jeffrey's door. "Hi Jeff. Hi Lisa. Something smells good."

"Would you like a cup?" asked Jeffrey.

Zaqi took the coffee and picked up the bag of beans. "Oh my goodness," he said. "Jeffrey I cannot believe you drink this!" He laughed.

Jeffrey smiled. "I think it's pretty good Zaq. Very interesting and rich coffee."

"Do you know what it's made from?" asked Zaqi.

Jeffrey was puzzled. It's coffee, he thought, from coffee beans. "I'm not sure what you mean," he said.

"It's made from cat poop," said Zaqi. "Civet poo, to be precise."

Jeffrey put down his cup and looked at Zaqi. "Cat poop?" he asked. "What do you mean ... they make coffee from cat poop?"

Zaqi explained that kopi luwak is made from coffee beans fed to civets, and the digested beans are harvested from the civet poo.

Jeffrey was bewildered. "Why do they do that?" he asked.

"To give it a rich flavor, I guess," said Zaqi. Now he and Lisa were laughing.

Jeffrey looked at them both. "Oh, I get it. It's a joke. Very funny. Cat poo indeed!" Now Jeffrey laughed.

"Actually, Professor Albacete, Zaqi is dead right," said Lisa. "The beans are harvested from civet poo. Kopi luwak is prized as a rich, subtle coffee by connoisseurs, and I guess you can see why."

Jeffrey looked at Lisa, then Zaqi, and back to Lisa again. They were not joking. He wasn't sure if he wanted to raise the cup to his lips again.

Zaqi laughed. "Go ahead, Jeff. I don't think anyone's got sick yet from drinking kopi luwak."

Jeffrey took a small sip. It *was* very good. Outstanding coffee, he thought. He smiled. "The things one learns. You are full of surprises, Lisa."

"And loaded," said Zaqi. "This stuff is expensive."

Jeffrey looked at Lisa. "I hope you didn't spend too much."

"It's a present," she said, "to thank you for everything you've done for me." Lisa explained the one catch was that, once roasted and ground, the coffee should be drunk fairly quickly – within a week was best.

Jeffrey chuckled. "We'll have to have a coffee party."

Heinrich poked his head around the door. "Something smells very good," he said. Jeffrey offered him a cup of the coffee. "This might even convert you from tea, Heinrich."

Heinrich took a sip, then another. "This is very good. Very good indeed. Actually Jeffrey, you are right. If I had experienced this coffee when I was younger perhaps I would not now be a tea drinker!"

As the noise from Jeffrey's office became louder, and the laughter echoed down the hallway, along with the rich aroma of the kopi luwak, person after person was drawn to see what was going on.

"I think you'd better make another brew," Jeffrey said to Lisa. "It looks like everyone wants a taste of cat poop!"

♥♥♥♥♥

George liked the idea of a coffee tasting. His own choice would have been a whisky tasting followed by a cigar appreciation, but he was alone in the Department in that respect. "What do you say, Deb? Should we hold a coffee tasting afternoon? Maybe some light food, nothing to rich to swamp the coffee flavors."

Deborah agreed. "The only thing is," she said, "I don't think we can afford the kopi luwak – it's around two hundred dollars a pound."

George whistled. "That's about seven Opus X Fuente cigars," he thought. "Let's get Lisa's advice on what coffees to get."

Deborah sighed. "We *could* afford kopi luwak, and other things, if George would halve his cigar consumption," she thought.

George made himself an espresso and went out on their deck to smoke a cigar and think about his research problem.

Lisa was keen on the idea of a coffee tasting when Deborah put it to her. She thought a variety of quality coffees from different regions would be a good choice. Deborah wasn't sure about food. "I don't want to serve anything that will override the coffee flavor," she said. "It's sort of an afternoon tea, but with coffee. I want the food to be tasty without being too filling."

"It depends on the coffee," Lisa said. "For example, with a mild Brazilian coffee, a biscotti or a buttery shortbread would be ideal. Whereas, with a heavier spicier coffee from Java you might want to serve soft cheeses, sautéed mushrooms and fresh basil." Deborah laughed. "How do you know so much about coffee and what goes with what?" she asked. Lisa said she thought it was probably long nights – sometimes very long nights – spent coding and fiddling with algorithms that got her drinking a lot of coffee. "Eventually I realized that I'd better start taking coffee seriously and drink good quality coffee. It sort of became obvious that some snacks go with some coffees but not with others. A Google search solidified my thoughts."

The coffee tasting took place at George and Deborah's house on a Friday at 4:00 PM. "I know most of you would rather be down the pub at this hour on a Friday," he said. "So thanks for coming to our 'afternoon tea'" – he laughed – "and we'll still have time for the pub later."

George was surprised to see Heinrich and Anna when he opened the front door. He felt even the thought of so much coffee would turn Heinrich away. "I am flexible," said Heinrich. "I am willing to taste what my colleagues are enjoying, especially when it is of a good quality."

Rickhart, overhearing the conversation, thought that was what characterized Heinrich: it wasn't that he was expert in this, or fancied that, but that he was devoted to high quality. "I wish," thought Rickhart, "we could bottle that and sell it to students, administrators and faculty, in that order."

Bao Zhang and her husband Ri had brought over fresh peach scones, and an apricot torte to go with a delicate Tanzanian Kilimanjara coffee she had helped Lisa choose. "This is such fun," said Bao. "Such good energy with all this lovely coffee and beautiful food."

Heinrich thought Bao's peach scones were the ideal accompaniment to the Tanzanian coffee he was sipping. "Well, I am very surprised," he said, "at how enjoyable it is to be coffee drinking." Everyone laughed. "Perhaps next time you can hold a tea tasting?" said Deborah. Heinrich agreed that would be an excellent idea.

Jeffrey noticed a rich aroma coming from the kitchen. "That smells like ... is it? Cat poo coffee!" Lisa smiled. "Just for you, Professor Albacete. I couldn't resist."

74

Scrap the strategic plan

Rickhart was thinking. The Department retreat had led to many useful ideas, and he had been working hard to incorporate them into a strategic plan. But now he was not so sure. A colleague in California had explained to him at length about the Toyota model of continuous improvement. He recommended Rickhart read Eric Ries's book "The Lean Startup" and that is what got Rickhart thinking. He liked this book very much. He especially liked the idea of basing a startup of any nature on a minimal viable product and formulating and testing a hypothesis about this product. Rickhart extended the meaning of *product* to *educational outcome*. He now felt that his ideas about a strategic plan, so appealing when he first thought about it, were outdated. He could see the problem: the Department would be very enthusiastic in formulating the strategic plan, the goals, the timeline for implementation, the responsible people, and the resources needed, and then, faced with the reality of the big task in front of them, would promptly forget it and go back to what they were doing.

The continuous improvement model of Ries's seemed a much more attractive alternative. He needed to sound out this idea with someone who was in their office now and willing to stop thinking about teaching, committee meetings, or their research, long enough top hear him out. Bob and Lori were talking in Bob's office and Rickhart asked if he could interrupt. He explained his thinking after reading Ries's book, and how he would like to use that model for continuous improvement for Department developments. Bob was not so sure. "I don't get how this would work in practice," he said.

Rickhart used Zaqi's *Introduction to Scientific Programming* as an example. "So Zaq taught this first as a small upper level elective course, just to see if it would work at all. Then, when he got feedback from the students, he modified the course and taught it again. Now it's a sophomore course and it seems to run very well. But I'm guessing," he looked at Lori, "that's it's still being improved."

"Oh yes!" Lori laughed. "He's always coming up with improvements to the course – largely as a result of student feedback."

Bob said he understood how that might work for a course, but he couldn't see – not yet anyway – how it might work for a program.

"Such as?" asked Rickhart.

"I don't know off the top of my head," said Bob. "Oh, okay, suppose we wanted to test the idea of an actuarial program. How could we use this lean startup idea to do that?"

"Very funny," said Rickhart. "You know how we would do that: we would start with Lori's *Introduction to Risk* course."

"Yeah, I'm sorry," said Bob. "I was yanking your chain a bit. Well, all right then. What about the CDF proposal that's been floating around? How would we develop a minimal viable product, or whatever it is we develop, so as to experiment and learn how it works?" Lori nodded agreement. Rickhart agreed that was a good example. "I guess we'd have to start with our target audience. In our case it would be who we want to impact and why. We're not exchanging a product for money, but we want to impact the right people, to convince them this is a development worth taking seriously."

"So let's say the engineers or the business school," said Bob.

"Let's be even more specific," said Lori. "The mechanical engineers."

"Okay, the mechanical engineers," said Rickhart. "So let's say we want to produce a CDF that is sufficiently intriguing and useful enough to them that they want to partner with us in further CDF developments – so it's in their interests and in ours. How do we do that in the simplest way so that it's still a viable product?"

Heinrich knocked on the door. "Excuse me Bob and Lori," he said. "I just wanted to talk with Rickhart for a moment, if that's okay?"

"Sure, come on in," said Bob.

"Thank you," said Heinrich. "I have an interesting suggestion," he said to Rickhart. "I have been working on a small matrix algebra problem with some of the mechanical engineers and Lisa has turned it into a very nice CDF. They are very excited about this and I am wondering if we have some mechanism to expand this project."

Rickhart, Bob and Lori burst out laughing.

Heinrich smiled. "I did not think it was so funny, what I said."

"No, no it was not funny at all. But it was very timely," said Rickhart. He explained the Lean Startup model to Heinrich.

"I see," said Heinrich, "So it is pure good chance that I come by at this exact moment with an example of the very minimal viable product about which you are talking."

"Chance," observed Bob, "favors only the prepared mind. Though I must say *we* were prepared by only about ten minutes!"

"So Heinrich," said Rickhart," is there any way we can measure how useful this CDF is to the mechanical engineers?"

"Measure it?" asked Heinrich. "That is indeed a very good question. Let me give that some thought. I think I would start by looking at how they use it, on what projects, and with how many people. That would give us some indication, no?"

"Yes, I think that would begin to assess impact," said Rickhart. "Excellent! Time, you guys, for me to buy you coffee – and tea! – at the Daily Grind."

They walked together to the coffee shop and met up with Jeffrey who was sitting just inside the door, working on his laptop. "Hi Jeff," said Rickhart, "can we join you?"

Jeffrey looked up. "Sure. I was just playing around with something. Sit down." He moved over to make room for the others and put his laptop next to him on the seat, closing it as he did so.

They chatted about Heinrich's work with the mechanical engineers and the CDF Lisa had built. Jeffrey listened with interest. It only made sense, he thought, for he and Rickhart to continue to develop their connections with the mechanical engineers. He had tried to do that and it had ended badly with Rickhart upset with him.

"Lisa did a very good job," said Heinrich. "She is excellent at streamlining the code so that she seems to get almost something for nothing. I think that was something that impressed the engineers."

"I wish Lisa weren't going to the School of Design," said Jeffrey. "We could really use her around here full time."

"Maybe we could make her an offer?" said Rickhart.

"We couldn't afford her!" said Lori. "She's doing well with her applied algorithms business. Very well for an undergraduate."

"So Jeff, what are you working at, on that laptop of yours?" asked Bob. "You seemed very busy when we came in."

Jeffrey smiled. "Oh it's nothing much. Just something I was playing around with."

"Come on, out with it," said Bob. "You're not usually shy, Jeff."

"It's nothing much," said Jeffrey. " I was just playing around with a CDF. I'm not very good at this sort of thing yet – nothing like Lisa. But I think I've learned a lot from her. I was working on this application for students. I thought we could probably get them to understand some of the programming ideas better if we did it through a CDF. I just made a little example. It's no great shakes."

"Does it work?" asked Rickhart.

"Oh sure, it works," said Jeffrey. "I don't know how useful it will be though."

'Would you like to find out?" asked Rickhart.

Bob and Lori laughed.

Jeffrey was puzzled about their laughter. He didn't think he had said anything funny.

Heinrich leaned over to him. "It is serendipity," he said. "Just good luck and a prepared mind!"

75

A dead give away

George was the first to notice that Jeffrey's demeanor seemed different. If that wasn't so, he was the first to articulate it. "There's something different about Jeff," he said to Deborah.

"Like what?" she asked.

"I don't know exactly. He seems more ... well, a bit more lively than usual. Sort of animated."

"Perhaps he has a girlfriend," said Deborah.

George snorted. "Yeah right! We're talking about Jeff here."

Deborah reminded George that Jeffrey was far from a monk. "There were those photographs of him with that French woman on the Internet. By the way, whatever happened to them? I wanted to show someone – alright, alright, I know I shouldn't have – but I couldn't find them."

"That was a fling," said George. "Nothing unexpected there – but a girlfriend? That entails a relationship. You're not serious are you?"

Deborah shrugged. "I don't know. But it's a possible explanation for his looking livelier. Look how you were when you met me."

"And still am!" said George.

"So what would be convincing evidence that he has a girl-friend?" asked George. "Apart from seeing her in the flesh."

"I don't know," said Deborah. "Maybe he's dressing differently. Taking more care of his appearance. Socks. See if he's wearing different and brightly colored socks. That's usually a dead give away."

"Socks?" asked George. "Are you serious? I bought new colored socks recently because I liked them. That doesn't mean I'm having an affair with someone else."

"But *why* did you buy them?" she asked.

George thought for a minute. "I think because I wanted to feel chirpier," he said. "As if the bright socks would brighten my mood."

"Right," said Deborah. "The buying of different style or color of socks indicates something about one's mood. That's all I'm saying."

George thought this was worth looking into. "I'll try to see what sort of socks he's wearing, hopefully without him noticing."

Jeffrey was drinking coffee when George knocked on his office door. "Come on in," Jeffrey said. "Can I get you some coffee?"

George took the cup, grateful for the delicious taste and aroma of kopi luwak. Jeffrey was very lucky, George thought, to have found someone as talented as Lisa and with such excellent taste.

"Oh no!" he thought. "He couldn't be having an affair with Lisa?" George thought for a moment. Didn't Lisa have a boyfriend? That young man – Chris. Still, he'd heard about younger students falling for older professors. That wouldn't be right. Jeffrey was not Lisa's teacher or adviser, but he was still in a much greater position of power in the University than she was. George looked and felt glum.

"Are you okay George?" Jeffrey asked.

"What? Oh, yes. Fine, thanks. Just thinking about something."

George thanked Jeffrey for the coffee and went looking for Kathy.

"Have you noticed that Jeff seems more lively these days?" he asked her.

Kathy said she hadn't noticed anything especially different. "I think he's pleased the book with Heinrich is coming out soon, and I know he's happy having Lisa for him. But no, nothing really different."

George was beginning to think he was imagining things. "Still," he thought, "there is something different about Jeff, and I can't quite put my finger on it."

George walked around to Bob's office and found him talking with Lori. "These two," he thought, "seem inseparable lately."

"Bob," George asked, "have you bought any new socks recently?"

Bob and Lori look startled for a moment and then laughed.

"What an odd thing to say," said Lori. "What made you think of that?"

Before George could answer Bob pulled up his pants leg and showed George a pair of brightly colored socks.

"Indeed I have," he said. "It started when Lori and I first … started going out together. How did you know?"

"Just a hunch," said George. "Something Deborah said about men and socks."

"Like women and handbags?" asked Lori.

George was thoroughly confused now. He asked Bob if he'd noticed anything different about Jeff.

"Can't say I have," said Bob.

"You mean," asked Lori, "like a different spring in his step. Like he's a little more lively than usual?"

"Exactly!" said George. "I thought I must have been imagining it. So you've noticed it too?"

Lori agreed. "Perhaps he's found a girlfriend. Oh, that's why you were asking about Bob's socks." George nodded.

"I see," said Bob. "So you're suggesting we need to get a look at Jeffrey's socks?" They all laughed.

"Something like that," said George. "Unless you've got a better idea."

"Other than asking him outright?" said Bob.

"Bob! Don't be so crass," said Lori. Bob wanted to know what was crass about asking someone if they had a girlfriend.

"It's indelicate and insensitive – ergo, crass," she said.

Bob shrugged. "It gets to an answer."

"Not if he doesn't answer," she replied.

"So socks it is," said George. "I'll keep my eyes open".

Bao Zhang thought MathWorks must be very worried about Wolfram's development of CDFs. MATLAB was now looking distinctly like last century software. She liked MATLAB and was a relatively expert user, but the wow factor of the CDF environment was something MATLAB could not currently match. She had engineering colleagues who thought CDFs were just a glitzy add-on to Mathematica, just froth and bubbles. She wasn't so sure. Jeffrey and Heinrich's new book was a convincing example of how powerful a CDF version could be. It really comes alive, she thought. And if MathWorks didn't do something about MATLAB it would probably be dead in ten years. Anyone could transfer the code to Mathematica, and the algorithms were by and large the same. Change, she reflected, is inevitable. What is strong and powerful today, can become toast in the not too distant future. She had an idea to use CDFs for her new course on numerical analysis next semester. Rickhart had talked to her and the others about his ideas on continuous improvement. She read Eric Reis's book and was inspired. A small, useful CDF was all she needed. She could try it out on some students in Kathy's research seminar and get feedback. Bao wanted some technical advice on localizing variables in a CDF and wondered if Lisa was around. She went to Jeffrey's office to see if Lisa was there, or if Jeffrey knew where she was.

Jeffrey asked her to come in and offered her a cup of kopi luwak.

"Thanks," she said. "This is very good. Have you seen Lisa?"

Jeffrey said Lisa was planning to come by at 2:00 PM. "Was there something you wanted to ask her?"

Bao explained her problem with defining variables in a CDF and said she thought Lisa could help. Jeffrey smiled and said he was afraid he couldn't be much help, though he agreed Lisa would know.

Bao couldn't help but notice Jeffrey's lively attitude. His energy levels were higher, and he seemed balanced and energized.

"Jeff," she asked, "do you have a girlfriend?"

Jeffrey was surprised. "How did you guess? Does it show that much? Look," he pulled up his trouser leg, "she bought me these new socks."

76

Energy and laughter

The Department members and friends, assembled at The Wharf Tavern in Warren, eagerly awaited Jeffrey's arrival with his new girlfriend. George, drinking a scotch and soda, said he couldn't imagine what she would be like.

Rickhart, holding an Argentinean Malbec, smiled and said he never imagined anything like this. Kathy, next to him, was drinking water. Deborah was surprised because she knew Kathy's taste in white wine. "Are you the designated driver?" she asked.

Kathy laughed. "No! But, actually, there *is* a reason." She looked at Rickhart, and he seemed to indicate it was okay with him. "The thing is – I'm pregnant."

Deborah gasped and jumped up to hug Kathy.

"What's going on?" asked George and Zaqi at the same time.

"Kathy's pregnant!" said Deborah. She stood up and said loudly to everyone present: "Kathy is pregnant." A small silence was followed by tremendous applause. People jumped up to congratulate Kathy and Rickhart.

"You sly dog," George said to Rickhart. "And we thought you were working hard every night on the strategic plan!"

The usual questions followed: "When are you due? Do you know if it's a boy or a girl? Do you have any names in mind? I'll bet your parents are pleased!"

The one that Rickhart had considered, but temporarily dismissed, was whether he would take family leave. Frankly, he couldn't see how to with the responsibilities of being Department Chair.

George put the question to him. "What will happen when you take family leave?" Rickhart said he wasn't thinking about it yet. "Maybe I'll ask you to fill in for me," he said to George.

"Be happy to," said George. "Maybe I could get a cigar allowance from the Dean?"

In the noise of congratulation no one noticed Jeffrey come in with his new girlfriend, until Bao turned around and saw them standing there.

"Hi Jeff," she said. Jeffrey smiled and introduced his friend, Emily. Bob shook hands with her and said she was pleased to meet Jeffrey's friend whom she had heard about.

Then Kathy noticed. She jumped up and went over to Jeffrey and Emily. Jeffrey introduced them and then Jeffrey and his girlfriend Emily became the center of attention.

"Sit down," said Deborah. "Here, take this seat," she said to Emily. She pulled up another chair for Jeffrey. Kathy waved to their server who came and took drink orders for Jeffrey and Emily.

Deborah explained to Jeffrey that they'd just been told that Kathy is pregnant. Jeffrey smiled and said congratulations.

Of course, everyone was dying to know how Jeffery and Emily met, but no one it seemed wanted to be indelicate. Except Bao, who had no such inhibitions. "How did you and Jeff meet, Emily?" she asked.

Emily smiled. "It was through Jeffrey's publisher. I'm a conference organizer, and the publisher contacted me about the conference to be held in Providence. Jeffrey and I met to discuss details, we seemed to click, and ... well, here we are!"

Bao clapped her hands. "So romantic!" she said. Bao went to talk to George about something and he seemed to nod in agreement. A few minutes later several bottles of champagne were brought to the tables.

Bao rose and announced a toast. "I know you can't drink, Kathy, but here's to your new baby – may he or she be healthy and live a long and happy life. And here's to Emily and Jeffrey's relationship – may it also be long and happy."

"Hear, hear!" said the assembled folk, followed by clapping.

"Your colleagues seem very nice," said Emily to Jeffrey. "Happy and full of energy."

Jeffrey smiled at her. "I guess they are," he said. It had never struck him that was the case, but gathered here, seeing everyone together, happy about Kathy's news, and apparently happy to see him and Emily, he guessed she was probably right. "It's not something I'd thought about before," he said, "But I *can* see it through your eyes." She squeezed his hand.

Bob and Lori came over to say hello to Emily, followed by Heinrich and Anna.

"Emily's very cute," George whispered to Deborah. "I'm surprised." Deborah knocked him on the head. "George! Stop it!" "Well, I'd never think of Jeff as a catch," he said, "but she looks like anyone would be pleased to be seen with her. So Jeff must have hidden depths that we're just not able to appreciate." Deborah wanted to put a paper bag over George's head and a sock in his mouth.

Heinrich had a thought. He discussed it with Anna, who agreed. He stood up and made an announcement. "I think some of you are now beginning to be hungry." He looked around. "We can eat here, where the food is so-so, or we can go back to our home where I am very happy to make a barbecue." He looked around again. "I have been watching BBQ University." Laughter followed.

"A barbecue it is," said George, expressing the general agreement of those gathered. Anna said she and Heinrich would leave to get things started, and everyone could meet at their house in about half an hour.

Jeffrey looked at Emily and raised his eyebrows. She squeezed his arm and said: "I think it will be fun. Should we pick up something to drink?" Jeffrey, thinking more of Heinrich's coffee deficit, said he thought that would a good idea.

The odors from a sizzling barbecue greeted the guests as they arrived at Anna and Heinrich's home. Lisa and Chris came over to meet Emily. "I didn't have a chance to talk with you at the tavern," she said. "I'm Lisa, and this is my friend Chris." They shook hands and Emily said how pleased she was to meet Lisa. "I've heard so much about you from Jeff," she said. "He sings your praises at every opportunity." Lisa, being diffident, said it was nothing. "He says meeting you at the Coffee Depot in Warren changed his life." Jeffrey, within earshot, smiled. "I had no idea that there was such a thing as cat poo coffee, before Lisa," he laughed.

"Jeff tells me you are looking at graduate school at the Rhode Island School of Design," said Emily.

Lisa explained how she waned to marry her skill in computer science with her interests in jewelry. She asked if Emily knew about *Nervous Systems* in Somerville, Massachusetts. Emily said she hadn't.

"It's pretty much what I'd like to do," said Lisa. "The algorithmic side of things allows us to come up with some pretty amazing and unique designs."

Emily took out her business card and handed it to Lisa. "Call me," she said. "It seems to me that sometime soon you might want to hold a display of your work, and maybe that of colleagues. I think it's something I'd like to organize."

Lisa excused herself and Chris, and went to find them a drink. "Boy she's attractive!" said Chris. "He scored there. I'm surprised!"

"You don't think that she would find Professor Albacete attractive?" she asked Chris.

"Can't see how," he said. "What about him would attract her? Especially a woman as lively as she seems to be."

"The same thing that attracted me to you," she said.

Now Chris was really surprised. "Which is?" he asked.

"That you make me laugh."

77

Tea, muffins and prizes

⦿⦿⦿

Jeffrey looked at the finished version of *Applied Matrix Algebra* on his computer monitor. It looked quite beautiful. Hard to imagine, he thought, that he would be the author – co-author – of such a technical book. Jeffrey's initial irritation at Lisa as co-author had long since passed. He was actually glad to see her name on the cover. Without her input at the conception, and all the way along, this book would never have come into being. Besides, it was clear from the description of the co-authors that Lisa was the author of the Mathematica codes and not of the mathematical content. No one would, or should, be confused she contributed to that.

Jeffrey looked over his many print editions and translations of *Matrix Algebra*. This new book was an unexpected change of direction for him. The entire collection warmed him. "This is indeed who I am," he thought. There was no doubt that Lisa had been a fantastic help – an inspiration, even. And Heinrich had pushed the project along with his innovative and creative applications. But when all was said and done it was Jeffrey's work upon which they built, his years of scholarship and effort.

A picture of Emily came to the forefront of his mind. He smiled. "No point dwelling on the past," he thought. The future looked rosy. He put coffee on to brew: just his by now familiar Terroir coffee, and not the very strange, but oddly delectable, kopi luwak. "Cat poop indeed!" he thought. He was amazed when he thought about it just how much his life had changed since meeting Lisa. He smiled at the thought of those times past when Kathy's Keurig sachets were the height of his daily coffee experience – that and his trips to the Daily Grind. He drank his coffee and thought about the blueberry muffins at the coffee shop. He couldn't, in all conscience, walk to the Daily Grind just for a blueberry muffin. That's not what one did: one went there for coffee and then if one was in the mood, possibly order a muffin. The thought made his tummy rumble. "Perhaps," he thought, "I could order a tea?" Heinrich's tea tasting had opened Jeffery's eyes to a wide variety of tea styles and flavors. "Not," he snorted, "that I'm a tea fan!" But he felt he could, occasionally, drink a cup of better quality tea. So there it was: the reason he had been searching for. He picked up his laptop and walked to the Daily Grind.

The coffee shop was bustling that time of morning and Jeffrey compulsively counted the people in the queue. He must have counted the bricks in the wall a hundred times. He pulled his mind away from his compulsion and looked to see if there were any blueberry muffins left. Four fresh specimens beckoned. There were seven people in the queue before him. His anxiety level rose. To his relief the two people at the head of the queue did not order muffins. He watched, anxiously, as the next person ordered two blueberry muffins. He had an urge to step forward and grab one of the muffins for himself. Years of self-control held him in check: it just wasn't polite. He fretted as, second in the queue, the person before him ordered. Thank heaven, no muffin! Jeffrey sighed and ordered a Rooibos tea and a muffin.

"Tea today, Professor Albacete?" asked the server. "Not your regular latte?"

Jeffrey smiled. He didn't want to say that he had much better coffee back in his office and the real reason he came to the Daily Grind now was for the muffins. "No, not today," he said. "I've decided to try something different."

Jeffrey placed the tea bag in the cup of hot water, balanced the muffin on his laptop and looked around for a table. He spied one just inside the door and made a beeline for it. Settled, he took a sip of the tea. Quite a strange flavor, he thought, but not at all unpleasant. He guessed it could grow on a person, as it clearly had on Heinrich. Jeffrey chuckled to himself at the things he had learned: South African tea and cat poop coffee, among others. Jeffrey opened the laptop and looked again at *Applied Matrix Algebra*, a complete book in CDF format. He knew this was not the first such venture, and would be far from the last as CDFs took hold, but to him it was extraordinarily satisfying.

A voice said: "Hi Jeff." He looked up and saw Bob Fosberry with Lori.

"Do you mind if we join you?" asked Bob. Jeffrey signaled to them to sit down as he slid over. As he reached for the laptop Bob noticed the book on the screen.

"That's it?" he asked. "That's the finished product?"

Jeffrey nodded.

"Do you mind if I take a look?" asked Bob. As Bob went through the table of contents Lori squeezed next to him to get a better look. She pointed to a section and asked Bob to go to that. She pointed to the interactive application and asked him to click on it. As it ran in real time Lori was captivated. She had the same feeling every time she ran these applications. How cool, she thought, to have this level of interactivity in a document.

"It's very good, Jeff," she said. "Really, very good."

Jeffrey thanked her and said he couldn't have done it without Heinrich and Lisa. He wondered if Bob and Lori were feeling a little jealous. He knew – everyone knew by now – that they were not waiting to hear about their National Science Foundation grant application before getting started on their project. It was common knowledge that they were working on a CDF version of a book for their proposed course on Markov Chain applications for freshman and sophomores. Jeffrey thought they might be finding it hard going without the expertise of someone like Lisa. He knew Bob was unlikely to pull off a technical book project like that on his own. His expertise was more with MATLAB. Lori, on the other hand, he wasn't so sure about. Perhaps she could do it. Still, he thought, what they produced was unlikely to be as professional as *Applied Matrix Algebra*, and that was probably making them just a whisker envious.

"There are some good things here, Jeff, really well executed," said Bob. "But I think the text could have been integrated a little better with the CFD. They're what gives the book magic."

Jeffrey bristled at Bob's suggestion. Since when, he thought, did Bob become an expert on writing textbooks?

"Oh, I think that's neither here nor there," said Lori. "No one writes a perfect book not even Nobel Laureates. It's an outstanding achievement, Jeff, and you should be proud of what you've all accomplished."

Jeffrey smiled and thanked her. He *was* proud, very proud.

Heinrich came into the Daily Grind with Lisa. He looked around and saw Jeffrey with Bob and Lori. "Ah, Jeffrey I have been looking for you. Excuse me, Lori and Bob, do you mind if we speak with Jeffrey?"

Lori and Bob shook their heads.

"Thank you," Heinrich said, sitting down next to Jeffrey. "So, I have some news. Our book has been nominated for a prize and I have just had a message – quite unofficial as yet – that we have won."

Jeffrey was almost speechless. "Our book? A prize?" he asked. Heinrich nodded.

'It's quite exciting, Professor Albacete. You deserve it," said Lisa.

Jeffrey was still taking in the news.

"The Chancellor wants to display it as her Academic Innovation of the Month," said Heinrich.

Jeffrey understood that. He also thought any one of his nine editions of *Matrix Algebra* should have been selected for the Chancellor's honor, but not once had he been recognized, not until now.

"And, here's something else," said Heinrich. "We have been invited to present at the Wolfram Technology conference."

Jeffrey appeared puzzled. "The Wolfram Technology conference?" he asked.

"Yes," said Heinrich, assuming Jeffrey didn't know about the conference. "Stephen Wolfram's conference in Champaign, Illinois. It's a conference on all things Mathematica – they are very excited about our book. We have become almost famous, Jeffrey."

Jeffrey didn't know what to say. Things were happening much too fast for him. Bob and Lori shook hands with Heinrich.

"This is fantastic news," said Lori. "Where to from here, Heinrich?"

"I don't know," he said. "Maybe a nationally televised mathematics reality show?" He laughed.

They basked happily in this wonderful news. Jeffrey, looking around at his colleagues, thought that, all things considered, life was treating him very well, at last.

19042985R00223

Made in the USA
San Bernardino, CA
09 February 2015